Kaia

Daughter of the Sea

by

H. E. Thomas

&

P. D. Garty

To Sora
for just being you
Thanks for every word
everytime every hour.
may the sea guide you
Hannah Thomas
H E Thomas

In memory of Jacob Lee Thomas, elder brother, from the sister you thought you'd never have.

For Professor Edward Francisco who lit the flame, kindled the fire, and kept it burning from first draft through the final writing. Without you, this story would never have been born.

In appreciation of our families and friends, especially other Pellissippi writers, who gave their support and provided thoughtful critiques.

Words cannot express our deep appreciation to Marty Wood for her editing and critiques. You've kept us going and helped us write a much better story.

Kaia
Daughter of the Sea

Copyright 2014
H. E. Thomas & P. D. Garty
All Rights Reserved

Chapter One - Lady of the Sea

The surf smashed and roiled. For thousands of miles waves had met no shoreline, until now. Wave after wave of white breakers burst upon the shore. Moonlight fell upon the shore, reflected off the waves as they rose and then rolled in a milky cascade. The waves tossed and struggled around black rocks, until they wasted their long pent up energy. Spray tossed high into the air by the breakers pushed against tall black cliffs that rose far back behind the shore. Spray hugged the shore like a fog. The sea and mist had long battled the black cliffs. For the moment, the cliffs held them at bay. But over eons, even the cliffs could not stand against the relentless attack of the sea.

Pieces of the cliffs lay broken and littered the shore, scattered around pieces of driftwood. The trunk of a fallen tree, driven by waves, pounded against rocks buried in the surf, battering them, smashing them – and then moving on with the current to bash other obstructions. A particularly large black boulder lay halfway between the breakers and the cliff walls. Everyone called it the black rock, and named the shoreline after it. The beach was cut and crafted by nature, but something was out of place. The moonlight shone brightly on a lone conch shell sitting on top that black boulder.

The pattern of the waves changed, scattering around something new in the water. The object grew larger and moved forward, closer to shore with each wave. First, a face with long black hair rose above the waves. The woman continued toward the shore, undeterred by the waves or wind. She was dressed in silver moonlight and was undeniably female, but of indeterminable age. Her figure appeared strong and firm, but her eyes held within them ages of sorrow. She walked out of the ocean, awkwardly at first, unsure of her legs. Rivulets of salt water ran down her skin in long sinuous streaks, and the wind wildly tossed her hair.

The Lady of the Sea came here often. Tonight, she had called out to one who would soon be here. It was her duty and obligation. A command wasn't necessary. She would come out of love. But, after tonight, would the depth of that love be understood?

When she reached the deserted shore, she began to slowly pace along the surf. As her legs became stronger, she looked up at the darkened sky. A nearly full moon crept over the cliffs. When it was full, it would begin, and where would it lead them? To look at that place was to stare into fear and darkness. She needed to sweep it away and concentrate. The future was not yet formed, yet she could no longer see it. That was dangerous. Anything could happen. There wasn't time.

She wore a small golden conch shell on a golden chain around her neck and held the shell against her chest. Six other women with long black hair followed her. They all wore small black conch shells and carried tridents.

The Lady of the Sea stopped and looked out over the churning ocean. Then, with determination, she turned away from the waves and walked toward the black rock. When she reached it, she stopped and lifted her shell to the moon. The six others walked up behind her and lifted their shells as well. Out of the mists along the black cliffs, another woman appeared and walked toward them. She wore a silver shell that reflected the moonlight. When she reached the Lady of the Sea, she knelt.

"Lady," she said.

"Child," the Lady said and laid her hands on the kneeling woman's shoulders. The woman looked up. The Lady released her and reached down to lift the conch shell from the rock. She offered it to the kneeling woman. "I place a great burden on you. I do not do this lightly. Take this and know the truth of it."

The kneeling woman held the shell in the cup of her hands and lifted it in front of her chest. The Lady once more placed her hands on the kneeling woman's head. The woman remained still while the six others swayed back and forth to the sounds of the surf. Sounds of distant drums echoed from the conch shell. The drumming sounds became insistent. Then the kneeling woman's eyes opened wide, and she stared up first at the Lady's eyes, then at the moon. "I see all the way back to the great ice. The ancient shamans speak. I hear, but do not understand."

"You alone see what I see, hear what I hear. You know our memories all the way back to the first Lady of the Sea."

"I'm afraid."

"Child, I feel death all around us. What I do is necessary. Seldom has the shell been offered to one who is not the Lady of the Sea. Time is short. I can no longer do this alone."

"I see her, the one you're thinking about. She's tumbling in

2

the waves, running on the shore, always moving, always reforming, never certain. What does it mean?"

"She's the one I've waited for."

"Will she be one of us?"

"I can only hope. It seems to me that time has stopped. Everything awaits her decision. I fear the destiny of all may be in her hands."

"You put too much faith in one person."

"Sometimes, one person can move the entire world."

Why, why in our lifetime?"

"I am but the Lady of the Sea. Who can stop the tide?"

The kneeling woman bowed her head. "I go with the current." She looked back up. The Lady of the Sea and the woman met eye to eye in silence, a silence that lingered for several minutes.

The Lady spoke. "Child, you have seen and know what you must sacrifice."

The kneeling woman removed her silver conch shell and offered it to the Lady who placed it around her own neck, beside the golden one. "One cannot rule without sacrifice," the Lady said. She turned, and one of the women with a trident handed the Lady a black conch shell on an elaborate string of black pearls. The Lady placed it around the neck of the kneeling woman and fastened it. "These are fit for a princess."

"I am honored to be in your guard."

"You held the shell tonight for one purpose. You are now my eyes and my ears. I will see what you see and hear what you hear."

"Lady..."

"Permit it. It must be so. Too much is at stake."

The Lady turned and walked toward the sea. The guard followed her. So did the woman. When they reached the shore, the woman with the black pearls knelt in the surf. Waves broke over her and washed her body in salt water. She used her hands to splash water into her face on onto her hair. The Lady and the others walked out into the waves and disappeared. Moments later seven curved, black fins moved outward into the ocean.

The kneeling woman held her arms out to the waves, then rose and walked toward the cliffs. She disappeared in the mist.

Chapter 2 - Kaia

I've been watching a nearby pod of seven orcas swimming north, not far from James' sailboat.

"Kaia," James said from the helm. "You seem distracted."

I am. It's my eighteenth birthday. Oh, I don't think differently than yesterday. I doubt I'm taller or smarter. I ate the same things for breakfast. I still wear the same shoes and the same smile. And I'm sailing with James. Yet something holds me back, and I've been uneasy about it all morning. There's a sense of foreboding, a feeling, just out of the reach of consciousness. Well, at least I'm here on the ocean and not at home. Home...I become an adult today. How soon can I leave and have a life of my own?

I'm more alert today than I ever recall being. The world is sharply in focus, filled with new colors like the change in fall leaves after a hard frost. There are twin horizons in front of me: the rocky shore and the endless ocean. I scan the ocean with anticipation, expecting something, anything unusual to happen. One of the orcas spy-hops. A bright flash of sunlight reflects off the waves and glares in my eyes. I wince and turn away. For the last thirty minutes my legs have itched and my shoes have pinched my feet. It's an uncomfortable feeling, and it's getting worse. I want to kick off my shoes and dive into the ocean. That would be easy, but foolish. James and I are about a mile off the coast of California.

I'm a strong swimmer, but not that good.

My cell phone interrupts with a familiar tune, my birthday message. I realize we must still be in range of the cell tower on shore. I reach for my phone.

"Kaia," James says sternly from the helm.

Ignoring him, I read the text message.

Go to the shore, to the black rock at full moon;
look to the sea. - LS

Whoever LS is, she hides her identity well. The text definitely can't be from my mother, Lana Stone. Those are her initials, but not her personality. But the text messages had to be from a woman. The previous messages were all too nurturing, something Mom is not. As usual, a picture is attached to the message, a conch

4

shell on top a black rock, on some nameless shore.

The text messages began on my twelfth birthday. Six years to ponder her messages, and six years for them to haunt my dreams. I suspect if I could just look around that black rock, or off to the side of the picture in the phone, I might see something special, something life-changing. In recurring dreams, I walked that shore only to find vague, shapeless things that wouldn't coalesce into something substantial – something I could name, and in naming - know. I wanted to wade in the surf, but feared it. Something was there, something that enticed me to lose myself and swim too deep.

Once again, and stronger this time, I feel the compulsion to dive off the boat and into the ocean. I glance up from the orcas to meet James' eyes. I anchor myself there. His face flashes concern.

"Are you okay?"

I can't tell him the truth. Whatever "it" is, "it" wants me in the ocean. I resist. I must resist. I try callback on my phone. I'm not surprised that it doesn't connect. It never had before.

"When's the full moon?" I ask.

"Tonight."

A chill runs up my spine like a sudden gust of winter wind. It takes me back to the picture in the phone, a black rock on the seashore. She said to go to the black rock, to go there...tonight. For a fleeting moment I consider whether I should go. No, I must go. She'll be there. I'm finally going to meet the mysterious LS.

A painting of a black rock seascape hangs in Granddad's parlor. It comes sudden and unbidden to my mind, and appears beside the picture from the phone. Automatically my mind considers the two. The picture in the phone moves. It rotates, aligns, and scales to superimpose over the painting. The black rocks and the seashore match, but there is no conch shell in Granddad's painting. Yet it must be the same place! Why hadn't I noticed that before? What had Granddad said about that painting? He'd spent an afternoon on that seashore with his mother, shortly after his father died.

The boat jerks with a gust of wind and leans leeward. I automatically adjust my balance and look over at James. Granddad bought me these sailing lessons with James Cersea. We're on James' thirty foot sloop. James, ah, who wouldn't like James? He's handsome, athletic, articulate, and charming. He's also twenty-four and a college graduate. I'll start college in the fall. We sailed out of

5

his father's marina this morning.

"Kaia, pay attention."

He's being my teacher again, and not my friend. I flash him a glare. Right! This is a lesson. Enough daydreaming, it's time to rejoin the world.

It's good sailing weather. The skies are clear except for feathery high cirrus clouds that glisten bright in the sunlight. A few gulls soar near the sailboat. The sea rolls gently, and driven by the wind, we slice through the water. The wind tosses my long black hair and, as I watch, it rustles through James' dark brown but sun-bleached hair. We're both deeply tanned from days of sailing and wear swimming suits and T-Shirts. James' shirt reads 'I'd Rather be Sailing,' while mine has a picture of an orca with a spirit orca riding above it.

"James, I need to call Granddad."

He gives me another stern glance, that of a teacher to an inattentive student. I ignore him and speed dial. For six years I've confided LS' text messages to Granddad, and, in return, he's given me good advice concerning the messages, good advice that I seldom received from my too busy parents. I'm not the daughter Mom wanted. I know that. I try to be Daddy's little girl. My parents are wealthy and so much is expected of me, more than I am willing to give. But that's not who I am. I'd rather race cars, scuba dive, or sail with James. I wish I had a responsible older brother to take the chaff. Then I could live my own life.

That's why I never told my parents of the birthday text messages from LS, even though I shared them with Granddad. He kept them a secret between the two of us. There were other reasons as well: too often the messages had warned me about Mom. I learned to listen the hard way.

Granddad answers, and I give him the latest text message and my belief the black rock in the phone is the same rock in the painting that hangs in the parlor.

"Where are you?" he asks.

"Sailing with James."

"Good. He knows the location. I'd feel better if he went with you."

"Granddad, do you really think that's wise?"

"Please don't go alone. You can trust him."

Trust him? Do I need to trust him? Why? I close the phone

6

and meet James eyes once again. "James, I need your help."

"I heard my name mentioned. Somehow I suspect I'm already involved."

Yes, he is. I don't know why I think that. I just do. I know we must go to the black rock tonight. It's too important. It's no longer a desire, it's become a need. James must go with me, but as a friend. There's no room for misinterpretation. I must choose my words wisely.

"James, Granddad wants me to ask you to go with me to the black rock, tonight."

"You're kidding. It's haunted, you know."

"It's that well known?"

He nods. "My grandfather died in a shipwreck there, long before I was born. I went there once with my father to lay a wreath for him on the black rock."

James' face changes while he speaks. There is a visible flash of pain. It makes my need for him to go with me even more awkward. Need, yes, I need for him to go... just like I can't ignore the need to go there myself.

"I can go alone."

"I won't allow it. It's no place to be alone after dark. I'll go, but first today's lesson, bring us into dock under sail."

"Why can't we just motor in as usual?"

"What would you do if the motor failed, call the Coast Guard?"

"I would if I were in a power boat."

"You're not helpless because you're in a sailboat."

"Yes, sir!" I say and flip him a quick salute.

James raises his eyebrow and then relaxes into a smile. He invites me to take the wheel, and I move to replace him.

I steered us toward the harbor but remained distracted by today's text message. I played the possibilities over and over again, trying to imagine what I would see tonight. Forty-five minutes later we were on final approach. The wind blew inward toward the dock at a slight angle. I steered the boat slightly upwind from the dock and had James drop the mainsail. The boat slowed. James had already dropped the foresail, a Genoa, on the deck and secured it. Both sails were down and we coasted downwind. I hoped I'd gauged our momentum correctly and eyeballed the dock. Grant Gregson,

James' tall Norwegian friend, stood at the end of the dock and waved to me.

I smiled back but inwardly cringed. If I messed up, I didn't want a witness. James was at the motor. If I was too fast he'd use it as a brake and I will have failed.

During my sailing lessons, James told me that Grant used to hang around the marina when they were both kids. James invited Grant to crew for him when they were teens. Together they raced his sixteen foot sailboat. They became close friends and now Grant worked at the marina as a mechanic. One day, when he had the chance, Grant told me that James accepted him his close friend even though his family was poor.

I hope I can be that generous with my friends.

"Whoa, a bit too fast," James said. He dropped a line over a stern cleat and tossed the other end to Grant on the dock. Grant caught the line and quickly wrapped it several times around a pole at the end of the dock and pulled. The boat slowed and swung in toward the dock bumpers and hit them with a jolt. James anticipated it and jumped to the dock to secure the bow line.

"Good for a first attempt," James shouted back to me.

"I'm sorry, James."

"I didn't expect you to be perfect the first time."

"I failed." I knew why, I was distracted by the text message and all it implied. It was not something I could tell James. One does not become distracted when one is steering a boat.

"Kaia, I know you too well. You're far too competitive."

"I'll practice," I promised.

Grant finished mooring the stern line and jumped aboard. He helped James drape the mainsail back and forth over the boom in preparation for furling it.

"Is it okay if I freshen up before we leave?" I asked.

Grant glanced at me and raised an eyebrow. I knew what he was thinking, and he was wrong, but I decided not to say anything.

I went to the cabin to collect my duffel bag. When I returned, James offered his hand to help me off the boat. I headed for the clubhouse to change into jeans and a shirt. It could be cold by the ocean at night.

After Kaia left, Grant punched James playfully in the ribs. "Do you really have a date with her tonight?"

8

"No date. She asked me to be her guardian."

"That's a new one. Bet you're going someplace secluded."

"She's my student, Grant, not my girlfriend."

"And she's hot!"

"Grant, Candi's my girlfriend, remember."

"Kaia suits you."

"And what does that mean?"

"Just saying what's best for you."

James went forward and began to pull the blue cover over the Genoa. When he finished, he returned to the cockpit and went into the cabin to change his clothing. Meanwhile, Grant secured the furled mainsail with short pieces of rope. After he finished changing, James returned to the cockpit and looked toward the shore. Kaia stood on the shore at the end of the dock and waved to him.

"I'll finish," Grant said. He winked. "Have fun."

James shook his head at the comment and walked toward shore. He met Kaia and accompanied her across the parking lot to her dazzling navy blue Corvette convertible.

"Nice car," he said.

"Granddad had it specially modified for me."

She walked to the rear of the vehicle and pointed out the changes. The rear of the trunk curled upward and split at the end, a spoiler that resembled an orca tail. Below it was a chromed, orca fin-shaped plate. It replaced the original Corvette logo. "I call my Corvette, Orcinus, after the orcas. They're masters of the sea, and this car is master of the road. Get in."

Grant worked the blue cover down over the furled mainsail and began to secure it in place. While he worked, he watched Candi strut down the dock toward him. He knew if Candi even suspected James was with Kaia, there was going to be trouble. He glanced at James and Kaia in the parking lot. *Hurry up you two and get out of here.* Then he quickly lowered his eyes to his work.

It was easy to see why James was attracted to Candi. She wore her usual marina outfit. She was squeezed into short shorts and wore a tiny bikini that struggled to contain her overly large breasts. Every guy she passed on every boat stared after her. But Grant knew Candi better than James realized. James deserved better.

"Hi, Grant," she said with a sensuous smile. "James around?"

"Nope."

"Know where he is?"

"He's been hired for the evening."

"Well then, may I come aboard?"

Grant reached out a hand to help her. She took it and he helped her aboard. As she stepped aboard, she put her other hand on his chest and held it there a moment. Grant brushed it away. When he did, she turned to face the parking lot. Her eyes suddenly turned icy gray. "Is that James with Kaia Stone?"

Grant turned toward the parking lot. His face momentarily flushed.

"That slut," Candi said. "Damn her. She won't have my man."

"Candi, he's been hired to be her guardian tonight."

Candi didn't listen. She jumped off the boat and hurried away from him and toward the parking lot. Eyes on other boats followed her all the way down the dock. Some looked back at Grant with a question written in them. He shrugged his shoulders.

At the Corvette, I attached my seat harness while James positioned himself in the passenger seat.

"Buckle up."

"You drive sanely, I hope."

Did he challenge me? I race cars. This is my turf. Yours is the sailboat. I smiled, revved up the engine and spun the Corvette around in a full circle before I squealed out of the lot and onto the Cersea Marina driveway. James clung to his seat.

"Damn it, Kaia, you did that in front of the security cameras. Dad will be furious. I'll catch hell when I get back. So will you."

I slowed down once we were on the road. "I'm sorry. You're right. I'm a bit of a showoff at times. I'll apologize to your dad."

"A simple apology won't be enough for Dad."

He was right about that. His father ran a tight ship.

Candi ran toward the parking lot and fumed over Kaia's antics in the Corvette. What a showoff - Kaia and all her toys. Rich bitch, you won't have my James, damn you. Candi reached her Mustang, jumped in, and started after them. When she arrived at the end of the marina driveway, she looked to the right and to the left. There was no sign of the Corvette. Shit, I should have asked Grant where they were headed. She turned her car around and returned to the lot.

It doesn't matter. Kaia's inept with men and I know how to keep my man warm. She'll be sorry she ever messed with me.

We drove the Corvette north, stopping only once, at a store to purchase drinks and something for dinner. It was late afternoon when I parked in a seldom used overlook, hidden from the main road by a small hill. We got out of the car and stood in the lot to view the ocean from our perch, on its cliffs, high above the shoreline. The skies were still clear and the wind drove a cool breeze inland. It intensified as it rose up the cliffs. Our jackets flapped wildly. We were sailors, and the wind felt good. It invigorated us and made us long for the ocean. My feet twitched with that thought.

There was a gravel trail off to the north side of the parking lot. We took it downward in switchbacks until it joined a seasonal creek. The trail then cut through tall cliff walls as it wound downward along the creek and through a micro-climate of thick hanging vines, ferns, and old moss lined trees. It finally opened to the rock and gravel shore. The little sand present lay around the mouth of the creek and was piled around a huge tree trunk that had been washed up during a storm. The creek then meandered around the trunk until it reached the surf. The trunk was off to our right. On the left, and closer to the cliffs, was the black rock, a boulder. It was flat on top, but rounded on its sides and about three feet above the gravel. It was broad enough to seat two people comfortably.

I looked in the direction of the black rock. Waves broke on distant rocks and washed around thin black spires further out to sea. Then they smashed upon the shore. Gulls winged back and forth and sandpipers ran up and down the surf line, dodging waves. Driftwood, tossed ashore by storms, littered the beach. The wind was less here, at the base of the cliffs, and carried with it the tang of salt spray. I listened to the breakers and breathed in the salt air. This was home. Still, the compulsion to swim in the ocean assailed me. Now that we were here, my feet began to throb, and the itching in my ankles intensified. What in the heck was happening to my legs?

We planned to cook a dinner over a bonfire. James pointed to the large tree trunk that was wedged into the gravel and rocks. "That might do."

He was right. The trunk was about the right height to sit on.

11

By the looks of the charred wood next to it, someone had built a fire there not that long ago.

We walked toward it. Empty beer cans and broken bottles littered the fire site. James glared at the mess.

"This is senseless," James said. "When I was seventeen and near the end of the summer, I stepped on a can hidden underwater at a public beach. It sliced open my foot and required eight stitches. Since the stitches were on the bottom of my foot, I couldn't put weight on it. It healed slowly, and I had to hobble around on crutches for weeks after I went back to school."

"We can pick up their trash."

"We shouldn't have to."

"I know. You can't stop people from being stupid and inconsiderate."

"I wonder if they'd feel the same way if they sliced their foot open like I did."

"James, just how do you get anyone to change their bad behavior?"

"I don't know, Kaia."

It took only a couple minutes to clean the beach around the fire site. Then we lit a fire and heated hotdogs stuck on wooden sticks. It would be a hotdog and potato chip dinner, but we did purchase two prepared salads.

"I'd rather have salmon," I said.

"Sure, I'll just wade out in the surf and catch you some."

He stood up and turned toward the ocean. I grabbed his arm and laughed.

"You're right, I could have bought salmon when we stopped at the store, but how would we have cooked it?"

"You heat rocks in the fire, wrap the salmon in foil, and then lay it on the rocks at the edge of the fire to cook."

I thought about it, and the taste of salmon lingered in my mouth a long time. For some reason, that remembered taste eased the growing agony in my legs and feet.

We sat around the fire and talked about everything and nothing until the fire faded into dark embers. James smothered what embers were left with the nearby wet sand. That done, we moved to the black rock, sat on it, and looked westward. The sun, now a red ball, lay on the horizon and was slowly swallowed by the sea. We watched the deep red skies slide steadily into darkness. Finally, just as the sun dipped below the horizon, the Zodiacal lights arched high. It signaled nightfall. Soon it was dark and the full moon was already visible above the eastern cliff tops.

"Years ago," James said, "You could still see the bones of the wrecked ship over there." He pointed up the shoreline to the north. "Dad has a picture of it on the wall of his office. There's a newspaper clipping framed with it. It said the bodies of sailors washed up on this shore. People think their ghosts still haunt this place."

"One of them was your grandfather, wasn't it?"

James nodded. "He died in that shipwreck, but his body was never found."

James became silent, lost, I guessed, in melancholy thought.

The wind died shortly after sunset. A light mist formed offshore and was pushed onshore by the cool air. The mist became trapped between the ocean and the tall dark cliffs that framed a wall far behind us. It thickened. Tall, thin, rocky spires from four to six feet high jutted upward near the shore. They faded in and out of vision with the movement of the mist. It brought to mind the legend that this shore was haunted.

"I guess in this fog, these rocks could seem ominous to someone with an active imagination," James said.

That brought us both a nervous laugh.

We continued to sit on the black rock for hours. Sometimes we were silent and listened to the waves; sometimes we talked about our lives. Later, the mist dissipated and the moon rose mid-sky, lighting the breakers in soft silver light. The tips of waves flickered and went out, one after another, as they rose and broke. The breeze blew stronger now, in from the sea, cold knives that stabbed through our light jackets.

I had told James about the text message, that someone would meet us tonight. It was unusual, but he went along. So we waited. He watched the trail from the cliffs. I watched the sea.

It was now midnight. A drumming sound came from the water. He quickly turned.

"Hush," I said, "something is moving."

Chapter 3 - Choices

A private business jet cruised high above the Pacific Ocean. Kaia's parents, Jake and Lana Stone, sat opposite each other at a table in the cabin. They had just finished a meal and their plates were being cleared by a stewardess.

"One of your girls?" he asked.

"Of course."

"I thought so. She's quite distracting."

"Efficient too. All my girls are efficient."

Jake set a folder on the table and pulled out a document.

"I've been over this dozens of time," Jake said. "Our corporate attorneys assure me that it's well written."

"It should be. I negotiated the terms."

"Still, I'm concerned."

"We've done deals like this before."

"Not quite the same. Dumping toxic waste in the ocean - we'll be in violation of International Law."

"Not true. Didn't you listen to our attorney? The shadow company we're setting up isn't in a country that was a signatory to the treaty. They violate no law."

"But we own the company and will be held responsible by our government."

"I thought of that. On paper we'll show a thirty percent minority stake with another thirty percent owned by principal investors in their country – all government and military officials. The other forty percent will be held in offshore accounts – our accounts, but untraceable. We control the company, but invisibly, and all the right hands are greased."

"Still..."

"It's a sweet deal, Jake. We supply the containment vessels and sell them the ship. They do the dumping. We only facilitate them. We're clean."

"Lana, I agree about the containment vessels. Our scientists tell us the technology works and is reliable."

"Would I get us involved if it wasn't? Even if it failed, who would know? Whose fault would it be: ours for building the containers or theirs for not properly sealing them, or their carelessness while lowering them to the sea floor? Any failure would be tied up for years in court, and we could financially bail out at the first sign of trouble."

"You've thought this out."

"That's why we make a good team. You're the responsible conservative business leader. I'm the one who gets things done. Really, there's nothing to worry about. Everything is ready. I've dealt with all the right people. We'll be praised for bringing business to this impoverished country."

"But they don't know how to handle hazardous substances."

"Look, it's jobs for them. It lifts the workers and the economy. And, it's good for the international community. People in their country will have money to purchase goods from our country and others."

"Their government officials and their military will take most of the money."

"They have to spend it, and that lifts the economy."

"That's trickledown economics, Lana. The rich get even more powerful, while the poor get their leftovers."

"Jake, it's their country, not ours."

Jake looked out the window a moment and remained thoughtful. After a moment he spoke. "What will Dad say?"

Lana laughed. "I see - you're still worried about the old man. Well, he won't know. Every man has his weakness. I co-opted his representative on the board. Your father will only know what I want him to know."

Jake dropped the document on the table.

"Still, we're missing Kaia's birthday."

"I'll buy her something nice before we return."

"It's her eighteenth birthday, Lana – that's special."

"She starts college in the fall. Perhaps she should intern with our company."

"She's our daughter. I don't want her involved in your business."

"My business?"

"You know very well what I mean. Anyhow, it would be best if she wasn't raised in our business culture. She should intern with a supplier or a customer. That way she gets the experience without the special treatment she'd surely receive as our daughter. I'd prefer a customer since she could provide us with feedback and also learn to think like a customer would. That will make her an asset when she joins our firm."

"I know just the company."

"You've co-opted someone?"

"Oh yes, in this case, the president of the company."

"We'll talk about it when we get back home."

"Jake, I've been meaning to talk with you about Kaia for a while. You know I'm uncomfortable with her sailing lessons. She's at an impressionable age..."

"What, Charles Cersea is practically a brother to me. We were raised together in the same house. He's a good businessman. His son is quite respectable. They're a good family."

"Kaia can do better."

"Are you suggesting they'll have a relationship?"

"It's possible. She'll inherit our company someday. She'll need a sharp and aggressive companion. James Cersea doesn't strike me as the type."

"What are you suggesting?"

"We need to start circulating her around the eligible business people we're grooming."

"You're grooming, you mean."

"Have it your way. Most of them would be attracted to a pretty young girl like Kaia. Think of the alliances we could build."

"Lana, she's not a bargaining chip."

"Of course not, dear, I just want to make sure she has many to choose from."

Lana got up from the table and walked behind Jake. She started to rub his neck and back. "Come on, let's go to bed. We've got a long day ahead of us."

Jake leaned back. He thought about his childhood home and his Grandparents. That had been a long time ago. He hadn't thought about them in years. It brought a smile to his face and deepened his concern about this business venture. Perhaps, he thought, it's them and their love of the ocean I will betray in this deal. At that moment, he desired their favor more than any profit this venture would generate. Was there any way to back out now?

Then he thought about Kaia. Maybe Lana was right, but it was Kaia's choice, not theirs. Someday it would be her company. Wouldn't it be better if she wanted it?

James sat beside me on the black rock. The drumming sound from the water grew louder. It boomed like the surf but had an unusual cadence to it. We remained motionless, scarcely breathing. Something was moving, something in the water, but near the shore. At first a hump, like water flowing over a rock, disturbed the waves. A woman's face with long black flowing hair rose above the surf. She moved steadily toward the shore. Then she was on the beach. Her figure glistened silver-white in the moonlight. Rivulets of silver water ran sinuously down her body. She stared directly into my eyes and only briefly looked aside at James. She paused to remove something from her neck, and laid it on a rock near the shore. It shimmered, bright silver-gold, in the moonlight.

"She's not human!" James said.

I laughed at his incredible revelation. "She's a selkie, James."

"A selkie?"

"They're shape-shifters, originally from the Orkney Islands. In selkie legends, they would come to shore sometimes, and could be taken by men as wives, if their skins were stolen."

"No, she's the siren who wrecks ships on this shore." James roughly grabbed my wrist. I resisted. "Look, I'm here to protect you," he said. "We're leaving." He began to drag me away.

"Kaia," a musical voice called.

James responded to her voice by loosening his grip on me. He turned toward the selkie. I noticed an enraptured smile spread across his face. He continued to stare at her, his mouth open in amazement.

"Who are you?" I asked.

I left you the message. You came. The words weren't spoken. I heard them in my mind.

"You're LS."

She smiled, *Lady of the Sea.*

"But why all the messages?"

I've watched you for years, Kaia. Today you've come of age and must choose.

"Choose what?"

To dwell on land or in the sea.

Suddenly, the reason for the apprehension I'd felt all day stood in front of me. I knew, deep down inside, I already knew, knew all day long that I must make this choice. At that moment, I realized I wanted to remain a child.

17

Once more James grabbed my arm and tugged me toward the cliffs. This time I wasn't so sure I wanted to stay.

Kaia, why is this male with you?

"Granddad thought I needed protection."

Surely not protection from me?

I sensed the sincerity and truth in the Lady of the Sea's telepathic words and guessed that telepathy makes it difficult to lie.

James turned toward the selkie, then back toward me. "Did she say something?"

"I hear her thoughts," I said.

The male must not come closer. It's dangerous for both of us.

"She wants you to stay back," I said.

"I'm here to protect you."

Males, are they always so stubborn?

James didn't move, so the selkie started to sing. Her melody rose and broke like tall foaming waves and tugged at James like the oceans undertow, seeking to drag him out to sea. Kaia heard only a song filled with vowel sounds accompanied by a sophisticated rhythm reminiscent of the music of Polynesia. She watched the music transform James. His smile grew broader, his face became blank. He turned toward the selkie. His face flushed and he walked slowly toward her in a trance-like state. The Lady stopped her song and James turned quickly back toward me.

"She's definitely a siren," he said.

I won't harm him, but he must wait for you by the log. She pointed to where we ate dinner.

I told James what the Lady of the Sea said.

"I'm responsible for your safety," he said. "I won't leave you."

I don't want to do this, but he may interfere. It's necessary for you to choose of your own free will.

The Lady of the Sea sang once again. It was a similar melody but stormy. It rose in swells and crashed upon the shore. "Go to the tree stump and wait." She repeated the words over and over and wrapped them into her melody. The enraptured look returned to James face. He turned away from me and went to sit on the tree stump. He turned back with a plea on his face. I could tell he fought her command and wanted to return to me, but couldn't.

"I see why Odysseus had to be tied to the mast," Kaia said. "How did you do that?"

Selkies are female. We depend on human males to reproduce. The males had the advantage. It was a risky proposition until we developed the voice. Now we decide who we mate with. I came ashore to talk with you. The male doesn't make that easy. Still, there's something familiar about him.

I told James to relax. There was nothing to protect me from. I watched James. He clung to the tree stump and dug his nails into the bark. He clawed at it but couldn't free himself.

"Some Odysseus," I said. "I just don't understand males. Don't they think? Are they all driven solely by their passion?"

He doesn't trust me!

"Guess not. There are ghost stories about sailors drowned on this shore."

It was a storm, not any of our distant relatives.

"One of them was his grandfather."

I'm sorry. The Lady turned away from me and looked at James. Her gaze paused there, and she studied his face. *He must be James Cersea. Curious he's the one you brought here.* The Lady studied James a moment longer then turned back to me. *This must be difficult for him, still you must choose.*

"Why now?"

Because you are one of us: a child of the sea, but also a child of the land.

"How is that possible?"

What do you think happens to the offspring of a selkie and a human?

"My mother certainly isn't a selkie."

The Lady of the Sea smiled and laughed long and hard. *It stays in a family for generations, sometimes skipping generations.*

"Who then?"

Your Great-Grandmother.

"My Great-Grandmother..."

Forsook the sea for your Great-Grandfather and his love for her. You have been born a creature of both worlds. You're of age today. You must choose. It's our way.

I thought about my great-grandmother and great-grandfather. I'd been told so little about them. To me they were almost mythic people. Granddad, on the other hand, had been like a father to me.

Kaia, do you feel legs or a fluke?

My legs itched and my feet hurt. Was that what it meant to

have a fluke?

"What about my aunts and Granddad?"

Only females can choose. Males are forever bound to the land, although many become sailors. Your aunts both chose the sea.

"But Shelly lives with Granddad."

She cares for him.

"So selkies can be both sea and land creatures."

No, child. Shelly suffers for her use of legs. She must return to the sea frequently to recover. What is your choice?

"Why did Shelly choose the sea?"

It was easy for her as it was for her older sister.

"What happens to those who don't choose?"

They become pitiful creatures: forever unhappy and unfulfilled, forever out of place. They hope but are never complete. They are forever listless, never at home, desiring, but never attaining, without closure, lost, unsure. They swim too deep. Eventually they drown. They forget to breathe.

I turned away from the Lady of the Sea toward James. He sat unhappily on a log. Then I turned toward the sea. The Lady pointed north, toward to the dipper, the celestial clock of the night.

The handle of the dipper points to one o'clock. You have until dawn.

"But it's after midnight, I turned eighteen yesterday."

You were born under the stars. The next day begins at dawn. It has always been thus for those of the sea.

I walked away from the Lady and James to stroll southward along the shore, near the surf line, near, but not touching the wash. I still remained afraid of what lurked in the surf, what called me to drown my humanity.

James watched my silver shadow as it moved in the bright moonlight against the phosphorescent sea.

I knew the sea as well as I knew how to breathe, at least the sea near the surface and the shore. I began to earn my NAUI scuba license when I was eight. I finished when I was fourteen. Underwater and weightless, I felt at home. I thought about the swim fins I had worn on my feet and wondered what it would be like if they were permanent.

"Is that what happens?"

No, the legs grow together to form a fluke. It's more efficient.

I continued to stroll along the shore.

I will leave you to choose.

The Lady of the Sea turned away from Kaia and toward James. He sat alone, but his eyes continually followed Kaia. The Lady realized there could be a dangerous link between the two. Could that be the reason behind her apprehension for Kaia? His presence could influence Kaia in unpredictable ways. Still...

Her thoughts of James were interrupted by a sudden movement deep in the ocean. She felt it much as a human could hear a bell. It was loud and demanded her attention. From deep in the sea a new sea current rose toward the surface. She thought of the ancient myths and her eyes widened. She went from watching James to studying him. Perhaps, she wondered, there was a reason he was here. Ancient powers could be at work. The sea was seldom wrong. *I must go with the waves and follow the currents where they take me.* With that thought, she decided to break one of her long standing rules - not to talk mind to mind with a male.

James, do not fear us. We helped ashore those who survived the shipwreck. We found your grandfather, but too late. He was buried at sea with honor. Your grandmother wanted to spare your father seeing his body, didn't want him to know.

It was a shock to hear the Lady of the Sea in his mind. At first it frightened him. But her words were calm and assuring. He realized this must be what Kaia was hearing in her mind.

"Why is Kaia pacing the seashore?"

She's part selkie, James. Today she comes of age and must choose the sea or the land.

Now he understood what had distracted Kaia all day. He let his initial panic subside. The mental communication broke the spell he had been under. For the first time he was able to see her as she was. She wore no clothing but felt ancient and strong. He was not in the least aroused by her... so long as she didn't sing.

Don't fear for her, James, she will choose what she must. Whether she chooses sea or land, I suspect you will still see her. The Lady of the Sea smiled and patted the black rock. *Come sit beside me and be patient.*

James rose from the tree stump and walked to the black rock. As he approached it, he watched Kaia, who had turned, and now paced northward along the seashore.

Your grandfather loved the sea, your father also.

21

"You knew them?"

They did not sail unnoticed by us.

"I'm most alive when I sail."

We know. You, and many like you, still respect the sea. Selkies watch and hope. We are meant to be the shepherds of the sea. Will your kind let us?

"But why are you unknown to us?"

Not unknown, rather those who know us seldom speak of us to others.

"Wait a minute. I know Kaia's parents. How can Kaia be a selkie child?"

She is the result of a selkie-human mating.

"I don't see how that's possible."

It's been that way since before the great ice, before your Stone Age.

"Then it must be detectable in their DNA?"

The Lady of the Sea remained silent for a moment. James felt her lightly probe his mind for an explanation, and in turn, he visualized the dual helix in detail he had never noticed before. He watched it twist and turn in various patterns and saw how each movement modified the actions of different genes. Each action caused the body to modify in different ways. She turned away from James and watched Kaia, whose pace now quickened. Kaia kicked at the water and turned toward the cliffs.

It's an interesting question. I suppose it must.

"My DNA contains traces from port towns all over the world. I wonder whether my ancestors were all sailors."

James said those words, but at that precise moment, the Lady of the Sea felt movement again in the depths of the sea. This time it was a surge. With sadness she recalled Atlantis and the great wave that destroyed it. A different type of wave was forming. This time would it build or destroy? She nodded her head toward the ocean.

James, your presence here was unexpected, but I suspect not unanticipated.

"I don't understand. There's no selkie in me."

There's something else. I can only guess at it. The ocean has become restless with your presence. She was silent for a moment and stared out over the waves. *You also have choices to make. I begin to see them in the currents of the oceans.*

"Choose what? I can't choose like Kaia."

22

The Lady of the Sea nodded. *I don't know why, but mother ocean, has spoken. You may deny it, but she has tested you and found you worthy. I can see it in your eyes and feel it in your heart.*

James looked away from the Lady and toward Kaia who now sat on the tree stump and faced the cliffs.

Kaia felt the breeze. It blew over the sea and land. It created the ripples and waves on the water. It rustled through the grass and bent the trees. It was nurtured both by the sea and the land. It would remain the same no matter what choice she made. All her wealth, all her experiences, all her skills meant nothing now. She was born into the world with nothing. She had nothing now to help her choose. She could not buy her way or drive her way out of this choice.

Kaia, it's two o'clock.

Did she have to die to her life and experiences and become something else, perhaps something alien? All she remembered, all that she knew came from her life on land. She loved the ocean, but to choose it had a cost. Could she afford it? She would lose her friends, her family, and her hopes, but not her dreams. No, those dreams began with that first birthday text. Those dreams, sometimes nightmares, took her into these deep waters. Now she knew why. She no longer feared, but welcomed the ocean. She rose and walked back to the surf. She saw James seated next to the Lady of the Sea.

"What have you said to James," she asked the Lady of the Sea.

Like you, he can't remain unchanged by this night. He also has choices to make for the good or ill of all.

"Does my choice affect his?"

It's hard to say. Something stirs deep in the ocean. It responds to James. Will he flow with the current or fight against it?

"Then you must see the consequences of our choices."

No, child, I can see the currents and possible destinations, but there are many eddies along the way. The future remains uncertain. On one side there is darkness and death, on the other hope.

"Hope, is that all we can wish for?"

Darkness is the lack of hope.

"What do you want of me?"

Your choice.

"I can't choose."

You have until dawn.

23

Kaia turned away from the shore and walked up to the cliffs. She stood where the trail and seasonal creek met the rocky shore. The cliffs were solid, unmoving, and dependable - like her former life. They were there yesterday and they would be there tomorrow. She gently touched the delicate fonds of the ferns and smelled the fresh earthy scents. This was the world she knew. She heard the breeze as it funneled up the cleft created by the creek. It sang a lullaby. A little water flowed and it gurgled over the rocks. She rubbed her hands over the plants and rocks and treasured them as precious jewels she might have to surrender.

She turned away, once more drawn toward the sea. She reached the surf and bent down to touch the wet rocks. She smelled salty air. She heard her heart beat faster and felt the rush of the blood in her arteries. Her face flushed and her feet started to burn. She kicked them in the waves, but they did not cool. Water rushed over her feet, and she wanted, right then, to rush headlong into the waves and never return. But she remained conflicted between the land and the sea. She pulled herself back, painfully, and forced herself to take one step after another toward the cliffs.

Sensations overwhelmed her. The sea beckoned. The land nourished. The waves tugged. The grass and trees called to her in the breeze. She was torn between the land that sustained her, and the sea that demanded her. She looked at James then at the sea, the sea, then at James. She heard voices – voices that whispered, voices that demanded, voices that cajoled, that taunted, and seduced. She spun back and forth between sea and cliffs and held her hands over her ears. She screamed. She knelt in the sand and gravel. She screamed again. Tears streamed down her cheeks.

The Lady of the Sea and James both jumped up from the rock and turned toward Kaia. The Lady took hold of James' arm to restrain him. Her first inclination was not to let him interfere. But if Kaia couldn't choose, she'd be lost. She couldn't let that happen.

James, Kaia's drifting away.

"Can't you help?"

She needs a place to anchor herself, either to land or in the sea.

The Lady released James and he rushed over to Kaia. He knelt beside her and put his arms around her. He pulled her close in a hug, a simple desire to shelter her from harm. She stilled and then looked into his eyes. The tears ceased. She was still tossed by the

24

storm, but he provided a welcome calm. She didn't question her actions and returned the embrace.

"Kaia, I'll miss you," James said. "You must do what you feel is right."

She stared at James. "You think I'll choose the sea?"

"I know you will."

Kaia broke the embrace and walked toward the Lady of the Sea. James followed.

"What do you want of me?" Kaia asked.

"Of us," James added.

Are you ready to choose, Kaia?

"I can't."

Kaia knelt before the Lady of the Sea and tears once again trickled down her face. "What choice serves the most?"

The eyes of the Lady of the Sea opened wide and a salt tear ran down her cheek. She remembered the day she had to make her choice. It had been difficult, like Kaia's. She had asked a similar question and had become an uncommon selkie. Her memories flashed back to the shores of the Orkney Islands. The ice had retreated. Then she realized, these weren't her memories, but the memories of former Ladies of the Sea, memories acquired from the Shell of Knowing. Could the myths be true? She mopped the tear with her right hand. Memories - could she share them with Kaia?

Do you freely wish to serve land and sea?

"Yes, Lady."

The Lady of the Sea took a moment to study them both. Then she spoke to Kaia. *If you choose the sea your destiny will be forever bound by the waves. If you choose land, you will become our ambassador.*

"Ambassador?"

Yes, we need a guide, a go-between with man.

This time the words in Kaia's mind were accompanied by images. She saw generations of selkies and a rapid sequence of images that highlighted the so-called advances of mankind. The images started with the industrial revolution and ended with the present. She saw choking smoke and swam in toxic waters that used to flow pristine. She witnessed the slaughter of the seals and whales from their perspective. She saw the selkies change form - many were no longer seals, but orcas, and learned it was necessary for their survival. Sadly, many of the other images concerned the use of weapons, the sinking and decaying of ships, and sailors sucked into the deep to drown. Man's destruction of his environment embarrassed and saddened Kaia.

It overwhelmed her. "Could I return to the sea later?"

If you choose land, you will never be able to return to the sea.

"Why do you need an ambassador?"

The sea is dying, child, even those on the land should feel it.

Kaia started to cry for she knew the truth of it. In response, she felt James put his hand on her shoulder. She could see the images that the Lady's words conveyed. This time when she saw the poisons that flowed into the sea, she watched the death struggles of those who swam into it. She could feel the pain in her heart.

"I need the sea," Kaia whispered. She paused; it was difficult to frame the words. "But I understand... the greater... need."

Without help we will all perish, and with the sea so goes your life, and the life of man.

"Lady of the Sea, the ocean means everything to me. The soul of the ocean touches me. I feel it has always been my destiny."

Do you think I don't understand that longing? I once lived on the land for a human lifetime. Every day I craved to feel the sea, our mother, embrace me.

Tears filled Kaia's eyes and she bowed slightly to the Lady of the Sea. "I will do what I must for you, for all."

You make me proud to be a selkie. You are strong and are sustained by the spirits of both worlds. You will always be able to talk to us. We promise to come when you call.

"How?"

Your thoughts. When dealing with man, we will defer to you.

"I'm only a child. You trust me that much?"

You're the ambassador and born of both worlds. Your choice makes you an adult. Who knows better?

"Why me? Isn't there another?"

The Lady didn't answer. She turned and walked away, picked something up from the rock, placed it around her neck and disappeared into the ocean.

Once she was gone, Kaia turned to James. "I chose land."

"I would have chosen the sea."

Kaia grinned. "Together the two are one."

You have chosen well, Daughter of the Sea.

Chapter 4 - Chrysalis

Kaia shivered in the cold wind that blew inland from the sea, and her body swayed to the slow rhythmic wash of the waves. She couldn't free herself from the call of the ocean. Too much had happened in too short a time. She wasn't ready to make a commitment, but she had. Why couldn't she be just human? Why did she have to be something else? A quick forced decision, and childhood was over, forever. No going back.

What am I becoming? I chose land but I still desire the ocean.

She knew the truth of it. Her mind remained in a heightened state from the recent telepathic connection with the Lady. Internally, she not only heard, but felt the crash of each breaker. It rolled inside her heart. She tumbled with the waves. She felt the ebbing waves pull her outward far into the sea. The call was still there. The ocean wanted her. She took a hesitant step away from James and toward the shore. She struggled to a stop and reached toward James. She lightly bit her lip. Her new connection with the sea was strong, almost too strong. Waves, the heart-beat of the ocean, entangled her in their ebb and flow, and dragged her deep into the undertow. She imagined herself afloat, washed in her salt-water womb, ready to be reborn a different creature, something strange – something alien. Each wave pulled: "Return to me...return to me." The soul of the ocean enticed, but her choice had been made.

It was a struggle, but Kaia turned away from the ocean and toward James. She knew she must leave this place before it consumed her, before it drove her crazy. She walked up the rock and pebble strewn shore. James walked beside her in silence. They climbed past the pebble beach into rocks and boulders and continued upward toward the creek, the trail, and her car.

They reached the creek.

"What made you choose?" James asked.

Kaia stopped and James turned around to face her.

"I almost left you alone on the shore. How would you have explained that?"

James smiled. "I hope you would at least occasionally swim beside my boat, maybe even talk to me."

"You could always dive in and swim with me."

"Too dangerous, the boat could drift away and I could drown."

"Do you think I'd let that happen?"

"We could always meet on the shore."

"At the black rock."

"Do you read my mind?"

"I don't think so, James."

"The Lady did. When she was in my mind, I could keep no secrets." He blushed.

"Well IF I had chosen the sea, and IF we met along the shore, I wouldn't be naked like the Lady. I'd wear my bikini."

James laughed. "You're naughty. We're good friends and I'm taken."

"Taken by whom?" He blushed again. "Okay, keep your little secrets. I don't know who she is, but I don't need to read your mind. It's written all over your face."

He turned away from her, and she stared at the ocean, remaining motionless and watching the waves.

Finally he turned back and spoke. "Then the Lady's gone, out of your life."

"No, James, I agreed to be the selkie ambassador."

"Ambassador?"

"The sea is dying and I must convince people to stop the murder."

"That won't be easy, Kaia, but you're not alone. I'm on your side. Grant will be too. His Norwegian kin respect the sea, and Dad brought me up the same way."

"It's a start."

They continued the climb to the car. The itching had ceased the moment she chose. It was replaced by heat that began in her toes and spread to her feet. Her legs slowly stiffened. She had difficulty balancing on her toes. She slipped once, then twice, but caught herself both times. Then her legs stopped walking automatically. Each new step became uncomfortable. She began to stumble. In response, she mentally instructed her feet to lift, move forward, step down, lift, move, and step, over and over again. It took nearly all her concentration to do a simple thing - walking.

James noticed Kaia had slowed down. He watched her slip and bend forward to grasp something. James reached out his hand

and caught hers.

"Do you mind if I lean on you?" she asked.

"No. Legs bothering you?"

"Maybe it's the incline. I don't know. I feel I'm stepping on hot coals. Help me get to the car."

"Sure."

After a slow and arduous climb, they reached the Corvette. She didn't stumble once while he supported her. Kaia let loose of James and limped to the driver's door. She opened it and leaned on it for support. James took hold of her arm and turned her toward him.

"Just let me drive?" he said.

"Because I had a difficult climb, doesn't mean I can't drive my car."

"Kaia, you need your legs to drive."

"It's my car. Get in."

Kaia struggled into the driver's seat. James had no other choice. He was her passenger. Initially, Kaia drove with the same confidence he'd witnessed on the way to the black rock.

"I've been meaning to ask you," he said. "Where'd you learn to drive?"

"Dad sent me to professionals for training. He said it was for security and situation avoidance. If endangered on the road, I could always outdrive my pursuer."

"Your father's concerned about your safety?"

"He's got enemies."

James nodded. "Don't we all."

"The first rule for professional driving is safety. Other drivers do enough stupid things I have the skill to avoid. On the track it's different. All the drivers are professional."

"You've been at this a while?"

"Dad started me on the track long before I had my driving permit. I still go there once a month to practice."

"And you're taking sailing lessons from me."

"Granddad said you're one of the best."

"That's a nice compliment, but I know a lot of others more qualified than I am. I don't know what it's like to survive on the open sea. My grandfather, as skilled as he was, still died in a shipwreck."

Kaia flinched.

"Leg cramps?" he asked. "You should drive home. I can call Dad to get me."

"Definitely not, Mom and Dad are overseas."

"Then what's the plan for tonight?"

"I'm supposed to stay with Granddad."

"And where's that?"

"Back the way we came."

"Still."

"No, James, we go where I take us."

"Stubborn."

They continued to drive, but every so often he noticed a spasm. Kaia's legs would twitch, and her face would momentarily grimace. Kaia slowed and drove with extra caution. James noticed the frequency of the leg spasms increased. He began to check them with his watch.

"Turn around," he said, "drive to your granddad's. I'll have Dad come and get me."

"I'm not a baby, James. I'll drop you off at the marina then drive to his house."

James threw up his hands. "Are you always so stubborn?"

"Only when I'm right."

James wanted assurance that Kaia was out of harm's way, but she continued to drive, and the spasms continued to distract her – and him. Just before they arrived at the marina, she let out a loud moan, then switched feet and put her left foot on the accelerator. She moved it to the brake and they slowed down to enter the marina parking lot. She pulled up next to James' Jeep, parked, and turned off the engine. James' Jeep was opposite her driver's door, but since the lot was nearly empty, she left an extra space between the two vehicles. It was three-thirty in the morning. The parking lot lights near the clubhouse were still lit. Those further out toward them had been turned off. The descending moon bathed them in bright silver moonlight.

"Maybe you should stretch your legs," he suggested.

Kaia yawned and stretched her arms before she opened the car door. She momentarily stood. Then she winced. Her knees buckled and she grabbed the car door for support. "Oh, shit. Shit... shit...shit. It won't stop." The fire in her feet spread to her knees, then her thighs. She felt spasms crawl down her legs like some wild biting animal.

She cried out.

James hurried around the car toward Kaia. "Lean on me for

support."

With one hand she pushed him away. "No, I can handle this."

"Then get in my Jeep. I'll drive to your granddad's."

Grant sat in the marina office watching the security cameras. It had been the usual, uneventful night, until he saw James and Kaia arrive. It was the only thing happening, so he looked at them. He was only casually watching until he saw Kaia push James away. Were they fighting?

Kaia's spasms momentarily eased, but the tension in the legs remained. She gritted her teeth and forced herself to smile. She turned toward the car and made an effort to enter it. James put his hand on her shoulder to stop her. "You're in no condition to drive. I have been timing the spasms. They're closer together now, like you're in labor with a child."

At that comment Kaia's eyes opened wide. She clung to the car door with both hands. "I'm the child. The labor is about my choice. The Lady didn't warn me."

"Warn you about what?"

"I wanted the sea, but I chose land. She didn't warn me there might be consequences."

Kaia let go of the car door and took two steps toward the Jeep. James followed close behind her. It was a stupid maneuver for both of them. She felt the pain begin at her feet and shoot rapidly up her legs. She turned back toward the Corvette, but it was too far away. Her legs gave out and she felt herself fall. James was behind her and quick. He wrapped his arms around her, and eased her down toward the pavement. It was an embarrassing moment for both of them. When he grabbed her, his hands ended up around her breasts. To let go would mean he would drop her.

She blushed and immediately another spasm struck. He continued to lower her gently to the pavement. She looked up at him. He knelt down beside her.

Grant stared at the monitors. What the hell! Did James really do that? What are they doing behind the car? Oh my God, and on a

31

first date too?

"I'm sorry," James said. "I...nothing was intended by it."

"Thanks for catching me," she said, then the pain stuck again. She curled up into a fetal position and moaned.

"You're definitely not going to drive."

"Just give me a minute." Kaia rolled on her back and bent her knees. The pain subsided a little.

"Give me your phone, Kaia. I'll call your granddad. You'll have to listen to him."

"He's probably worried anyhow." She quick-dialed Granddad's number.

He promptly answered. "Everything okay?"

"Okay...nothing's okay, no damn thing is okay. Nothing about tonight has been okay. LS, The Lady of the Sea, is a selkie. I'm part selkie. Why didn't you tell me?"

"Tell you my mother is a selkie? I told you about them."

"You didn't tell me I had to choose on my eighteenth birthday."

"You chose land, I assume."

"You knew. You knew all along."

"Both of my daughters chose the sea."

"Why James?"

There was a long pause before Granddad replied. "Ah, that, well James and the Lady of the Sea met."

"Why? Was it necessary?"

"I'm sure she has touched James' mind, and by now she's curious. I'd love to know what she thinks."

The spasms hit once again and she yelled into the phone. "My legs are in pain, I can barely move."

"That shouldn't happen." There was concern in his voice. "Where are you?"

"In the marina parking lot with James."

"With James, that's good. You must not drive. You hear me, no driving." Kaia heard Shelly say something to her granddad but couldn't make it out. He came back to the phone. "Shelly says you need to lie down right now and relax your legs."

"I am lying down."

"You trust James, don't you?"

Up until the last few moments she knew the answer, but now she was conflicted. He was her teacher. He'd been her guardian tonight, but he'd touched her... "I think so," she said.

"That doesn't inspire my confidence. You need to stay with him tonight."

"What!"

"The best place would be his boat."

"I'll drive home."

"Kaia, do you want to end up like me, and be confined to a wheelchair the rest of your life? Ask James right now."

Crippled. Not able to drive...or sail. Kaia looked up at James. "Granddad says I should stay on your boat tonight. That's really a dumb idea, isn't it?"

"That won't work. I'll call an ambulance." James said.

"Kaia, give your phone to James," Granddad demanded.

"He wants to talk to you," she said.

James took the phone. "This is James Cersea. Kaia's in pain. I think I should call an ambulance."

"Don't. Absolutely not. It won't help, and it would turn out very...embarrassing ... for all of us."

"Your voice sounds familiar. Do I know you?"

"Of course, you visited me with your father last month."

"Mr. Atwater. You're Kaia's grandfather! But Atwater's not her last name."

"My son changed his name when he left home, but so did my father when he left the Orkney Islands with my mother. I don't even know our former name. I sense Dad wanted it that way."

"Kaia needs help," James said.

"Think about it. Medical science doesn't know how to treat a selkie. Do what I say. Take her to your boat. Let her sleep...if she can. Bring her to me in the morning. You remember the way, I assume."

"Yes, sir."

"No need for formality, son, call me Ervin."

"Okay, Ervin."

"Mom had similar problems. So does Shelly. Kaia needs to stay off her feet tonight. Your boat is close, so take her there. The Lady will feel Kaia's pain. When she arrives you must avoid her at all cost."

"Not necessary. We've talked."

33

"Talked?"

"Telepathy."

"Really. With you...a male! Maybe Shelly will explain it to me."

"Okay - you want Kaia in the harbor so the Lady has access to her."

"Yes. I'll make preparations for tomorrow." He hung up.

Kaia looked up at James. "Granddad's decided then. I'm to sleep on your boat tonight."

"Yes, and you should expect the Lady."

"I hope she has a cure."

"Me too, but I'm worried. What will people think about you staying on the boat with me."

"I'm no longer a child."

"That's not what I meant."

Grabbing my breasts was bad enough, and now we're going to sleep together!

Grant continued to stare at the monitor. They'd been between the cars far too long. There was no way he could turn any of the cameras for a better view. Well, James, old boy, she must be good.

Kaia grabbed hold of the Corvette for support and pulled herself up. A strong spasm cramped her legs. They buckled. James caught her once again. This time they were face to face and he grabbed her around her back in a tight embrace. She muffled her cry and clutched her legs. "Put me back on the ground, please."

Grant saw them stand and embrace. *Sure looks like they've enjoyed themselves. Bye bye Candi.*

James softly lowered Kaia to the pavement. "What now?"

"I'm part selkie, James. Selkies have flukes, not legs. I'm sure it's why my legs hurt. The ocean flows in my veins. Didn't we talk about that?"

James nodded. "If I hadn't seen the damn...selkie...myself, I'd drive you to the nearest hospital for a mental evaluation."

"James, I can't lie here on the pavement all night."

"Look, this is awkward for both of us."

"Nobody other than Granddad need know. Nothing will happen, right?

"Kaia, I give you my word. I'm really sorry I grabbed you earlier. It was an accident. I'll put you in the front berth. I'll keep watch in the galley."

She looked up at James. "I can't walk. You'll have to carry me."

He looked up at the moon. "This just gets better and better. I hope it's too dark for the parking lot security cameras to identify us."

They must be enjoying themselves, Grant thought. They went back for more. I don't want to be a voyeur. Security...it's my job. Oh, God, what are we going to do about the recording. I don't know the codes. Damn. Maybe James does. He watched James lift her. They moved away from the cars. What now? It's clearly them on the monitors.

"God that hurts," Kaia said.

"It's the best I can do. Can you manage?"

"I'll...have...to."

They stopped several times for James to rest. Eventually they made it across the parking lot and finally up the dock. When they arrived at the boat, he set her down and they both rested. Kaia lay on the dock and attempted to relax her legs.

"A little better?" James asked.

"For the moment."

"I need your help, Kaia. Could you put your arm around my neck and help me carry you aboard?"

With her help they crossed from the dock to the boat. The boat rocked slightly under their combined weight and he staggered.

"Whoa, don't drop me."

"Don't worry, you're safe with me."

Just how safe am I? Kaia wondered.

"I would never take advantage of someone," he added.

"I trust you, James." She said that with faked confidence.

She knew she had no other choice.

James maneuvered Kaia across the cockpit to the cabin door and opened it. He flipped on the lights. With her help they went down into the galley. He bent over to set her down on a bench near the front berth.

Oh great, they've moved to the boat. Grant reached for his cell phone. Better wait, give him a few minutes.

James motioned to Kaia. "I'll need to prepare the berth for you."

He looked into her eyes and noticed that they had changed. They were now the color of the sea, and sparkled like the tips of waves in the moonlight. James shook his head to clear his thoughts and entered the front berth. They'd spent the afternoon and the evening together. They were closer now, better friends, and ...the selkie...what did she want of them? What was happening to their lives?

While she waited, Kaia rubbed her legs in an effort to ease the pain. She peeked through the doorway to watch James make-up the roughly triangular-shaped queen sized bed. She looked around the galley. She had been here occasionally during her lessons. She knew James lived on his boat. It had a small and efficient built-in kitchen. Unlike on previous visits, the front berth door was now open. There was a picture attached to the inside of the door. It was a six by eight inch photograph of a blond in a bikini. She knew the girl - Candice Desdemona.

Kaia winched at the memory. Kaia had a close friend in high school, Ken. He was gentle and intelligent; her close companion, at least until he met Candice. When Candice was through with him, she tossed him aside. By then he had changed into a bitter young man and, despite Kaia's best efforts, remained that way. It was just another of Kaia's high school failures and Candice's successes. Kaia may have excelled in her classes, but she failed miserably in her relationships with fellow students. They either resented her wealth or tried to cozy up to her because of it. Thank god for the advice from the Lady. It helped her avoid too many mistakes.

"James, seriously, you're not dating Candice, are you?"

He stopped tucking in the sheets and turned toward Kaia. "Um...yes."

"What do you see in her, anyway?" She blushed. She knew the answer. "Have you had her on this boat?"

"Maybe once or twice."

"Not in this bed I hope."

"What kind of guy do you think I am?"

"I know what she is, what she does, and what she likes!"

"She's good-looking and fun."

"Sure she is, James, even without her clothes."

"You...you don't know her."

"Oh yes I do. I went to school with her. She hasn't changed - except for the worst. She's man-hungry. She's crazy. She eats men alive and tosses their broken bodies away. There's nothing else to her. She's even had breast implants recently. Surely you noticed that."

He blushed. "Look, what business is it who I date?"

It wasn't her business, so she stopped, but her bitter memories of Candice and high school continued. She was concerned for James. He came out of the berth red-faced.

"I'm sorry," James said. "That was rude of me, especially after what we went through tonight."

"I don't want her to hurt you the way she has my other friends."

"Thanks for caring. Bed's ready. Get some rest." He reached down toward her. "Do I need to carry you in?"

She rudely pushed him away and rose from the bench but fell to her knees and began to crawl through the doorway.

"Don't be stubborn," he said. "It's awkward for me, too. At least let me help."

He scooped her up and set her down on the bed. She would have struggled, but that would only have increased the pain. She turned on her side and clutched her legs. Another spasm struck. She lay still a moment. James waited in the doorway.

"I hope the Lady will hurry!" she said. Then she waved him away with a flip of her hand.

James left and closed the berth door behind him. He sat on a galley bench near the door and listened to Kaia on the other side of the wall. It was clear she struggled with her pain and wasn't able to sleep. Was there anything he could do to help her?

After her legs calmed, Kaia thought about the situation. James was obviously attracted to sluts like Candi. *I'm not at all like her. I won't throw myself at any man. Besides, he wouldn't be attracted to someone like me.* It gave him a bad reputation, at least in her mind. The situation caused her conflict. James had always been a gentleman with her and it really had been an accident. That was the logic, her emotions were something else.

James cell phone rang. He stood up. *Who'd call this hour?* Caller ID said Grant. *Is he on duty tonight?* He mentally went through the schedule. Yep. Better answer this.

"Grant," he said into the phone.

"James, I need you in the office right away."

"I'm with Kaia."

"I know. That's the problem."

Better not embarrass Kaia, he thought.

"What does Grant want?" Kaia asked.

"He needs my help. I'll be back in a few minutes."

James entered the office.

Grant looked up. "Do you know the codes?"

"Codes?"

"We need to erase the recording?"

"What recording?"

"You and Kaia having sex in the parking lot."

"What?"

"Oh, come on, James, I could hardly avoid noticing it on the monitors. You know what your dad will say."

"Do you think I'm that stupid?"

"Oh, so you flirted in the parking lot and took her to the boat for fun and games?"

"Dammit Grant, we didn't do anything."

"That's not what it looked like to me."

"She was having leg cramps, and I was only trying to help."

"Sure, that's why you grabbed her the way you did. It's all right good buddy, we can fix this."

At that point James realized that everything that happened in the parking lot with Kaia was recorded and must look bad. Grant didn't jump to conclusions. Dad mustn't see this."

"The codes, James, I need the codes."

"I don't know them."

"Oh shit, you're in a heap of trouble."

"You should have disconnected the feed."

"Oops..."

"Too busy watching..."

"My job is security, James."

"Okay, okay. What can we do?"

"It is a security system, after all. There's no way to access it physically without breaking down a few locked doors. We could address it electronically, but apparently only your Dad knows the codes."

"Yeah, just don't point last night out to Dad. I'll bring it up at dinner."

"You know how strict your father is. I can't afford to lose my job."

James put his hand on Grant's shoulder. "Okay...it's my responsibility. Tell Dad, but at least wait until morning. I'll talk to him about it. Just remember, it isn't what it looks like."

"Sure, good buddy, sure."

James went back to the boat.

If Grant tells Dad in the morning, I'll be taking Kaia home when he finds out. That leaves Dad most of the morning to get worked up over it. He won't call. It's not his style. He'll just stew on it until I return. By then he'll be ready to give me a good scolding. Well there's nothing I can do about it. I did nothing wrong, and before I see Dad, I need to make sure Kaia is back with her grandfather.

At five in the morning he felt the boat softly nudged toward the dock. It was an unnatural motion. He knew something large in the water had pressed up gently against the boat and hurried up to the deck. He arrived in the cockpit as the Lady of the Sea climbed up the stern ladder.

She looked up at him. *It would be best if you left us.*

James nodded.

You may care for her when I leave.

He immediately went to the shore. When he arrived, he waved to the cameras for Grant to see. Then he sat and watched his boat. The Lady went inside.

Kaia, I'm here.

The Lady entered the berth. Kaia held out her hand and the Lady took it.

"I'm in pain," Kaia said.

It's the price of legs and feet.

"But why, I chose land."

You've made your choice with your head, not your heart. You need to accept your choice, not waiver. Go with the flow. Go with the flow.

"My heart can't turn away from the ocean."

You're conflicted. It's why you found it hard to choose.

"You make that sound easy."

It wasn't for me when I made my choice. I was also conflicted. It wasn't easy for me while I lived on the land. I know your pain. A fluke is more natural than legs.

"How do I get rid of the pain?"

Commit yourself to your choice - then you can find relief like your great-grandmother did.

"How?"

Recuperate in her bed when your legs hurt.

"Will Granddad let me?"

He understands.

"How do you know it will give me relief?"

It helped your great-grandmother.

"You knew her."

I know her.

"She's still alive?"

Selkies live a long time. Surely Ervin's told you about the last day by the black rock when his mother left him and returned to the sea. She's with the other selkies now.

"Granddad never told me the whole story."

Focus on your task and learn how to accomplish it.

The Lady of the Sea reached up to her neck. Around it hung two necklaces: a golden one with a small golden conch shell and a silver necklace that contained a small silver conch shell. She removed the silver one and placed it around Kaia's neck.

The sea calls you through this. Wear it and be comforted.

"What do I tell my parents?"

You are who you are.

"You'll help me?"

James wasn't supposed to be on the beach with you. That wasn't my plan. It's become complicated.

"What does that mean?"

I can't yet see the whole story. I can't even see the beginning. It's lost too far in the past. If he learns to swim with the current, he's on our side and that's good. If he fights the current, he may drown more than himself.

"You didn't answer my question – will you be there to help."

Child, something is coming. I don't have a clue how to help. Your choices, and maybe James' as well, mean more than they seem. She rose from Kaia and turned toward the door. *One more thing, have James bring you a bucket of sea water when he returns. Rub it on your legs.*

The Lady of the Sea left Kaia and stood a moment on the deck of the boat. She looked down the dock at James. Their eyes met. *She needs you now.* Then she dove into the ocean. Moments later an orca fin swam out into the harbor. He returned to the boat and entered the galley. Arriving at the cabin door, he knocked and entered when Kaia spoke.

"James, I need a favor. Could you bring me a bucket of sea water, please."

"Sea water? I have fresh water on tap in the galley."

"It must be sea water."

He took a clean bucket from the galley and drew water from off the stern of the boat. He returned with it to the berth.

"It's not the best, it's only harbor water." He placed the bucket beside the bed.

"Still, it's salt water... You'll have to leave and shut the door. I'm going to bathe my legs in it."

He left and closed the door. Moments later James heard her groaning, interrupted by sharp cries.

"Do you need my help?"

"I'll get my pants off myself, thank you!"

By six in the morning, the boat was quiet. James checked on Kaia. She lay curled up and sound-asleep. Her hands clutched a silver necklace. She appeared calm for the first time since they left the black rock. He looked down at her and smiled. She seemed comforted by the slow rock of the boat and the light chiming of the boat's rigging. Despite what had happened at the black rock, she was still a sailor. He pulled the covers over her naked legs. Before he left the room, he tore Candi's picture from the door. Then he settled himself on a bench in the galley.

Chapter 5 - Sea Bed

A t seven in the morning James urgently rapped on the cabin door. In my dream I was swimming. Something pulled me deeper and deeper into dark water. I struggled to breath. I forced my eyes open and pushed away the dream. My legs ...

"We need to leave before Dad gets here," James said through the door.

He was right. No one should see me in this condition. I was tired, but the treatment with sea water had mitigated the leg spasms. Still, the dream disturbed me. I couldn't pull myself away from it. It lingered - so did the pain. My legs ... my legs hurt – a constant dull pain that sometimes became sharp teeth that chewed on my bones. It made me flinch at inopportune times. Were my bones trying to reshape themselves into something else – something selkie? I was scared and dressed in discomfort. I could walk only if I leaned on James for support. James flinched every time I did. We managed our way down the dock with a minimum of staggering and reached the parking lot. Fortunately, only a few people stirred on their boats. Most of those were fishermen, preoccupied by preparations for their day at sea. If they saw me at all, they must have thought I was just another drunk being helped ashore.

I couldn't drive, but there was no way I'd let James drive my Corvette. This time I didn't argue when he offered to drive me home in his Jeep. It was a vehicle that suited him - a green two door with a beige rag top and a roll bar behind the front seats. It stood tall next to Orcinus. Before we left, I rubbed my hand over Orcinus and told her she'd be okay in the parking lot today. Then James helped me into the passenger seat of his Jeep. I buckled up while he took the driver's seat. Then we drove away from the marina.

"No need to get us into more trouble by spinning my wheels," he said.

"James, I said I was sorry."

"Somehow, I think our problems with Dad are worse than that."

Something in the way he said that made it feel ominous.

I liked his Jeep, but for me the ride was uncomfortable. It wasn't the vehicle, it was me. No position was comfortable. I constantly fidgeted in my seat, rolling my hips one way then the other. I tried to lean back and put my feet on the dash. No position worked for very long. Every bounce brought new pain. I was exhausted but couldn't sleep, not even relax – the pain was too intense. I wished we had brought a bucket of sea water and then blushed. That would mean I would have to be half naked, at least sitting next to him in my underwear. I shut my eyes and said little. James pulled off the road and offered me a pillow he kept in the back seat. I put it under my back. It helped a little, and I ignored the possibility that Candi might have used it. I just appreciated the relief. I had to believe what the Lady had said to me about great-grandmother's bed.

Even with my eyes closed, I was aware of James and his concern for me. He frequently looked my way. Every time we hit a bump in the road, and I jerked, he apologized. If only he could take away the pain as well. But he was human, with all his human limitations and I was ... am becoming something different, a selkie. Where would that journey take me? Would I care in a year or two?

When we arrived at the driveway to Granddad's estate, the old ornate wrought iron gate was open, held prisoner by overgrown vines. It reminded me that I'd better get out the clippers and cut them back. I laughed mentally despite myself. I would have to get my legs back first.

The house isn't visible from the entrance because the driveway is lined with trees and rhododendron. The driveway turned to the right, and I saw Granddad's house, a three story brick Victorian with a broad white front porch that faced the circle driveway. An attached round turret stood three stories high on the right side, the side toward the ocean. It was crowned with a multifaceted cupola. I'd never seen the view from the top of that tower, for that was the forbidden floor. I imagined it must be spectacular.

This was my home away from home, and I could tell we were expected. Shelly stood on the porch and waited for us to arrive. I looked at her as we drove into the circle. She stood still while James parked the Jeep. I had so many questions for her. Shelly was a selkie. She must know what is happening, what would happen to me. I needed a guide.

Welcome home, came the telepathic voice from Shelly. Beneath the words I sensed Shelly was troubled, no, there was something deeper...something I couldn't quite grasp. She was trying to keep something from me. Then her voice was gone.

It seemed so natural to communicate by telepathy, but I couldn't do it. I didn't know how. Maybe Shelly would show me. I responded with a mental *Thank You* and waited, but no response came. Shelly's mind was closed. The Lady of the Sea heard my thoughts, but Shelly seemed not to hear. Why? Was she purposely blocking me out?

James got out and walked to my side of the Jeep. Meanwhile Shelly wheeled an old wicker wheelchair down the ramp to the driveway.

It's the best I could do on short notice.

"Thank you," Kaia said, out loud this time.

James helped Kaia out of the Jeep. "More telepathy?"

"Yes, my aunt's also a selkie."

Shelly held the wheelchair while James helped me sit. Before I was seated in the chair, Granddad Ervin drove himself out onto the porch in his modern powered wheelchair.

"Damn legs. I don't get a choice like Kaia does."

"Choice?" James said.

"I'm part selkie too, but males don't get to choose. We're stuck on land. As I get older, I have to put up with these damn legs. Seawater no longer brings relief."

Shelly wheeled me up the ramp, and James followed. We reached Ervin, who held out his hand to James. They shook hands.

"Thanks for taking such good care of my Granddaughter."

"I had no idea what I was getting into."

Ervin returned a huge belly laugh. "You talked to the Lady of the Sea."

Shelly spun around to face James. "He did?"

"Telepathically."

Shelly's face turned icy. "She never does that with males!"

"She did last night."

Kaia spoke. "The Lady told me James' presence disturbed the ocean."

Shelly and Ervin turned to look at each other. Something must have passed between them, because her expression changed from disbelief, to puzzlement, and then to wonder.

Ervin took hold of James arm. "Well, James, I always thought you would turn out well. You've been like a grandson to me."

"Grandson?" Kaia said.

"In a way, James' father, Charles, was raised in this house with my son. So the Cerseas are part of our extended family, the same way all selkies are."

"You never told me," Kaia said.

Ervin looked up at James. "I tried to keep those lives separate. Maybe that was a mistake. It doesn't matter now. You've met the Lady of the Sea. You know what we are. You share our secret. Now become part of our family as was your grandmother and grandfather."

"They knew?"

"Of course."

"The Lady said they found Granddad too late, that he was buried at sea."

"It's true, lad. I was there. My mother, Oceana, was distraught that many others were rescued, but not your namesake. She insisted we give him a burial at sea with full selkie honors. That was a sight, lad. Your grandmother, Odessa, kept it a secret from your father. She moved into this house as nanny and helped raise both my son and hers."

"That's why you wanted James to go with me, isn't it? His family already knew what we are."

"Not all of them, Kaia. James's parents don't know. Funny thing is - Charles always wanted to see a selkie."

"He's seen me."

"He's also seen Shelly."

"Should I tell Dad?" James asked.

"What does your heart tell you?" Erwin said.

"I should wait."

"Then wait. Won't you come in?"

"I think I better go home."

"So soon?"

"I need to talk to Dad."

Ervin put on a wicked smile. "He already called. You better go face the music."

"What music?" Kaia said.

James face flushed. "Grant watched us last night."

"Watched us how?"

"It looks worse than it was."

"What did it look like?"

James flushed a bright red.

"It was the security cameras," Ervin said. "I feel some responsibility for this because I asked James to go with you and to take care of you at the marina last night." He turned to James. "I'm sure it wasn't as bad as it looked."

"What wasn't?" Kaia asked.

Ervin spoke reluctantly. "There was a lot of embracing and something happening between the cars."

Kaia reached over and slapped James.

"I didn't deserve that."

"Grant should have covered for you."

"Remember, Grant called. We couldn't erase the recording, Kaia - we tried."

"Then that's for Candi, since you like sluts so much."

"Easy, children," Ervin said. "I can vouch for you. I was on the phone with you while Grant was watching. I'm sure there's a misunderstanding. Either way, James must come back tonight."

"Why."

"If for no other reason than to bring your car back."

"Hell would roll over before I let him drive Orcinus."

"Kaia, James knows our secret. We need him on our side. Let's be calm and talk about this tonight over dinner. I'm sure Charles will be rougher on him than you ever could."

"You know we didn't do anything."

"I believe you...but no one else will."

"Okay, but can I lock him up in the dungeon until he shows some sense."

"We don't have a dungeon."

"Darn, couldn't we set aside part of the basement."

Ervin gave Kaia a stern look. "James, off now. I'm sure Charles will understand why you need to be here tonight. Shelly will make dinner."

Kaia tossed James the keys to Orcinus. He caught them in the air. "She's delicate but powerful. Treat her gently and she'll respond like a lady should. She's not a whore like some SUV."

"Kaia, watch your language."

James got into his Jeep, and I watched him drive away.

"Did you get any sleep last night?" Ervin asked.

"Very little. James came in to check on me."

"Didn't I say you could trust him? You shouldn't have treated him so badly."

"No! Do you remember when I talked to you about Candice Desdemona?"

"From High School?"

"Yes, James is dating her."

"That Candi!" Ervin broke out in a smile, then laughed. "That won't last long."

Aunt Shelly wheeled me into the foyer, and Ervin followed in his motorized chair.

"Shelly will take you up to Mother's room. Rest there until dinner."

The third floor had always been off-limits to me. It was the floor of mystery, the floor of dreams. It was inhabited by imagined ghosts and ancient treasures. At least that's what I thought when I was a child.

"There were too many secrets for a child up there." Ervin winked. "You've made the choice. It's time you learn your heritage. Shelly's prepared Mother's bed for you."

"Thanks, Granddad."

Shelly wheeled me away from Ervin and behind the foyer stairs to the elevator. This was the first time I'd been allowed in the elevator. Shelly pushed the button for the third floor. While we went up, I recalled as a little girl I had often tried to sneak up the stairs from the second to third floor. Shelly was always there to catch me. As I grew older, I wondered what sixth sense she had. Now I knew - she really could read minds.

The elevator doors opened on the third floor. In front of the elevator door hung another large painting of the black rock. This one was different. Shelly let me study it.

"It's the black rock as viewed from the sea," I said. "The one in the study views it from the land."

"This one is the viewpoint of the selkie," Shelly said. "It's a pity we all don't see the land from the viewpoint of the ocean."

I thought about that comment then, and knew I would think about it for years. From the elevator we turned left into a hallway. Its walls were filled with framed photographs of the sea, except for one. That one showed old stone ruins.

Stone Age ruins on the Orkneys, Shelly said.

Many of the photographs were black and white. A few were in color. I suspected the older photographs came from the Orkney Islands. Newer pictures included wooden and old looking sailboats with people on board. I recognized Granddad and Grandma in one of the pictures. I looked further and they were in most of the pictures, frequently with others. In one of those pictures a man with long white hair and beard stood beside a woman with long black hair. She held the wheel of the sailboat. His face was clear, but through some trick of the light, I could not make out her face.

"My Great-Grandparents," I asked.

Shelly nodded.

"Who are the others?"

James Dylan Cersea and his wife Odessa. Odessa was your Grandmother's best friend.

"Have the Cerseas been family friends that long?"

Shelly laughed. *Charles Cersea and your father were the best of childhood friends.*

Shelly moved me further down the hallway. We reached the front of the house and turned left. Shelly opened what I thought would be the bedroom door. I was surprised when we entered a large sitting room.

"Oh, this is just like Granddad's suite downstairs. The bedroom's through that door, isn't it?" I pointed left to the other door in the room.

Shelly nodded. She let me visually examine the sitting room. Its walls were covered with wallpaper that had a sand and sea shell motif. It must have been specially commissioned. The sand near the bottom was black and the sand further up the wall, tan. A border of shells surrounded the room at the ceiling. The room was furnished in, what one might call an eccentric and eclectic style. There was an old padded sofa adjacent to the bedroom door and an ornate wooden desk along the western wall. The desk was centered on a window. One corner of the room was round. I realized this was the top of the turret tower. The outer walls of the tower were all curved glass. There was a single chair in its center. It was fashioned of driftwood and had a simple kelp-colored cushion. It faced west toward the sea.

"Shelly, please take me over there."

I pointed, and Shelly pushed me next to the chair. While I sat, Shelly pulled back the lace curtains on the western side. In the far distance I could see the ocean lit by the late morning sun. I looked out and mused.

"I feel close to Great-Grandma now."

"She's a great lady."

"You must tell me about her. I know so little."

"Maybe later, after you recuperate. This is your room now. I've moved your clothes into the bedroom closet. To make room, I dragged out Grandmother's trunk and put it at the foot of your bed. It's been in the closet ever since she left."

"Can we go into the bedroom now?"

Shelly winked. "I hope you're ready for this. It can easily overwhelm."

At the time I thought she meant Grandma's bed. Shelly opened the door and pushed me into what could only be called a fantasy bedroom. I quickly changed my mind about that. This wasn't a fantasy bedroom at all, rather a room designed to make a selkie feel at home.

The bedroom floor was tiled in a mosaic. It had a translucent quality and disoriented me at first. I felt I could look down through the surface of the tile into the ocean beneath. The floor molding around the room was sculpted to look like waves, although they didn't move. All the walls had murals. The wall that faced the foot of the bed was painted with a rock island. Selkies, with human torsos and black flukes, sat on a rock. They all wore shell bras and were adorned with black conch shell necklaces. They held tridents. One of the selkies faced the bed as if she watched over the one who lay there. The wall to the left was a mural of the open ocean all the way to the horizon. A pod of orcas swam in the middle distance. Gulls wheeled through the sky. The wall to the right was also a mural of the ocean with black cliffs in the distant background. A sailboat moved parallel to the shore. A woman with long black hair was at the helm.

Kaia looked up at the ceiling. It was high above the floor and painted a light sky blue with white, lacy clouds.

There are tiny lights embedded in the ceiling. They can be turned on at night to look like stars.

I noticed a round sphere hung high in the center of the room.

That's a marvel. It has an internal mechanism that allows it to take on the appearance of the phases of the moon.

I turned toward the bed. It dominated the room and was on a platform raised about three feet above the floor. It had broad curved steps on the side toward the door. The platform itself was irregular in shape and fashioned to look like a small rock island, similar to the island in the mural. It was carpeted in black. The mural behind the bed showed the shoreline of the black rock as seen from the sea, but the black rock itself wasn't visible.

I was speechless.

"It's almost too much to take in at one time, isn't it?"

"It must feel like sleeping on an island out in the sea."

"Your Great-Grandfather built this room for her. It's a tribute to his love."

Shelly pushed me over to the massive four poster bed and pulled a ramp out from under it. I crawled off the wheelchair and onto the ramp. I reached the bed but found no relief from the pain.

"The Lady said Great-grandmother's bed would bring relief."

Not that way. The bed has a secret and requires a key – a small conch shell, like the one around your neck.

"The Lady of the Sea gave this to me last night."

"She told me she gave you Grandmother's necklace. You should be able to use it." Shelly had switched from telepathy and spoke instead. Once again, I sensed Shelly was holding something back.

"How does it work?"

"There's a small indention on the headboard in the shape of your conch shell. Press it in there."

I crawled around on the bed and searched the headboard. "Care to give me a clue?"

You need to learn these secrets yourself in order to grow.

I ran my hands over the headboard in search of some irregularity. It took time because it was skillfully hidden. It was part of the larger conch shell engraved into the center of the headboard. I took off the necklace and inserted my tiny conch shell into its place. Two things happened simultaneously: the bed started to slowly rise, and I heard the sound of running water. I pulled out the conch shell and replaced it around my neck.

"You might want to slide off the bed while you still can."

Despite the pain, I rolled over to the edge of the bed and slid down the ramp. I eased myself onto the floor and took hold of the frame of the rising bed. I held on to keep my balance. The bed continued its ascent. The sound of running water increased. A fresh scented breeze wafted from under the bed. I smelled salt air, and my pulse quickened. When the bed had risen three feet, I looked underneath. There was a pool with thick glass walls under the bed. The pool extended down what looked like another three feet. It was filling with sparkling bright and swirling salt water. The bed continued to rise. I looked up.

"I can see why this room has a cathedral ceiling."

The bed didn't stop rising until it was six feet off the floor.

"How do I get in?"

"May I help you use the ramp?"

"No, I can manage." I said it bravely, but I wasn't so sure. I stood and held onto the side of the pool. Meanwhile, the gnawing pain in my legs increased. I gritted my teeth. I will do this myself, I resolved.

Shelly shook her head and left. At that point I realized I couldn't undress and hold onto the bed at the same time. I considered going into that pool fully dressed but decided against it. I tried to hang onto the wheelchair and undress at the same time. It rolled away from me and I almost fell. I clung to the bed with one arm and the wheelchair with the other. It felt like my legs would collapse at any moment. I let go of the wheelchair and turned to the ramp. I nearly fell but managed to sit on it. If I had stood any longer, I knew my legs would have turned to jelly.

It was easy to remove my blouse and brassiere while I sat on the ramp. I tried to reach my feet but found it difficult. To bend my legs and bring the shoes within reach brought spasms of pain. I tried twice. Then I realized I needed a different strategy. The ramp wasn't helping. I needed to be on the floor. I tried to stand, but my legs no longer supported me. I fell. The pain was intense. I rolled into a ball until it eased. I screamed loudly in my mind but only a gasp escaped my lips.

Is being a selkie worth all this pain?

I lay on my side and managed to untie and then remove the shoes that pinched my feet. That quickly brought some relief. I left my socks in place and tried to remove my pants. I managed that by rolling on the floor, one way then the other. When my pants reached my ankles, I could see the skin on my legs. From the calf downward, it had changed color and texture. It was gray and turning black. I rolled back and forth in rapid succession until I kicked off my pants.

What's happening to me? I looked at my legs and then my feet. I screamed - out loud this time. My feet grew larger. The socks tore open and webbed feet emerged. My feet continued to grow and the texture change in my legs now extended up my thighs. I grabbed my calves and screamed again.

Shelly burst into the room and froze. She stared at my legs. I knew from Shelly's eyes that something was wrong.

"You chose land, didn't you?"

"Yes."

"This would be natural for a selkie who chose the sea." *Get into the pool...now.*

Shelly reached down and lifted me on legs that could no longer hold me upright. The change in my legs had now reached mid thigh.

"What have I done wrong?"

Shelly didn't answer. She rolled me onto the ramp and pushed me into the pool. I immediately went under water and floated weightless. Warm salt water swirled around me. I felt the water massage my skin, and with it, the pain diminished. I began to swim eagerly around the pool. In the water my webbed feet felt natural. My head bobbed out of water when I rose to breathe.

You should be able to control the change.

"How?"

You should know inside whether to feel feet or a fluke.

"So I should think feet?"

It's not exactly a thought, something deeper, and something primal, a knowing.

"I need to <u>know</u> feet. I've always known feet!"

Shelly tried to convey something deeper than words. She sent images with her thoughts, but they were unlike those the Lady had sent. I could not understand them.

Until today, I had only known feet. Images of my past flashed through my mind. I used feet to walk, feet to sail, feet to dance, feet to drive my car. Without feet I couldn't walk, couldn't run, couldn't hike the forest and mountain trails. I floated in water and rubbed my fins but they stubbornly refused to change back into feet.

"Look at me," I said. "I'm a freak. Come people, come to the freak show. Oh look, see what we caught off the coast of California."

"Relax," Shelly said. "You aren't a freak. Let the pool soothe you. Let the salt flow through you. Go with it. Only then will you be able to master it."

"Why is this happening to me? I chose land."

"Grandmother was special in her own way too. She learned how to be an orca instead of a seal. It must be in our genes."

"The Lady said I wouldn't be able to swim with the selkies if I chose land."

"It appears she was at least partially wrong. Your arms don't hurt do they?"

"No, why?"

"Perhaps you'll only transform from waist down."

"Oh great, I'll be a damn mermaid."

That made Shelly laugh, and she laughed long and hard.

"There's nothing funny about it."

"Yes there is. Mermaids are part fish. They have scales and a fin rather than a fluke. Selkies are mammals. There isn't a word for what you'd be."

"Freak, that's the word - a freak. This isn't very comforting."

"Look at your legs," Shelly said.

I did. My thighs had returned to their normal color.

"You're returning to yourself."

"I still don't know how to control it."

"Then you'll need to be careful. I'd think you'd want to avoid a transformation in front of humans."

"That could happen?" A wave of panic flashed through me.

Shelly nodded. "Practice, Kaia. Use this pool for practice until you perfect it."

Perfect it! How in the hell am I supposed to do that?

Shelly left, and I pushed away those negative thoughts. Waves of relaxation drifted through my body. I floated in the pool and slowly, ever so slowly, my legs returned to me. The pool provided peace. It soothed me with happiness. It lifted me with joy. I felt I could stay in the water forever. It was close, as close to the ocean as I could get on land. The transformation no longer frightened me. I brought my legs together and wondered what it would be like to have a fluke. I moved them together and kicked them slowly up and down.

"Ah, thank you Great-Grandmother," I softly muttered. Then I noticed the mural behind the headboard. With the bed in the raised position the mural behind the bed centered on the black rock. A common conch shell laid on top the rock. This was all hidden with the headboard in the down position. It was only visible with the bed raised. It was the same image of the black rock that had appeared in my phone.

What's so important about the black rock and the conch shell?

Shelly entered the library. Ervin sat in his powered recliner and gently rubbed the large conch shell that normally sat on the table beside him. He looked up at her.

"You've been concerned about her," he said. "I can tell."

"Yes, she troubles me. I...I was made to see...she was unformed...I worried about what she might become. I'm more worried now. And the Lady's constantly in my mind. I'm afraid, afraid for her, afraid for us, afraid for the entire world. She said...she said Kaia could change the future. She's so young, so undependable. What kind of future will we have?"

"How's Kaia?"

"Better now. It was quite a scare and totally unexpected."

"Yes. It means she can live in both worlds."

"Maybe, but not without pain I'd guess. You've talked with the Lady?"

"For some reason she found this amusing. She called Kaia 'Daughter of the Sea.'"

"That's a very old myth," Shelly said. "The Lady shared it and many other things with me. It was something talked about by the Orkney shamans when the selkies and humans lived together on the shore of the ocean."

"Will you tell me?"

"With all that is happening, you need to know."

Chapter 6 - Appearances

Ileft Kaia with Ervin and headed back to the marina in my Jeep. The Lady of the Sea and Kaia had jarred me out of complacency. They had replaced it with a storm that swirled around my life. My sails were torn, and my ship swung out of control. How was I going to explain myself to Dad? The stress put me on an adrenalin high. The past, present, and possible future all clashed for attention. They wove a web of knots that were impossible, even for a sailor, to untie. The more I struggled with them the tighter they got. I needed to concentrate, but my mind flipped erratically from one complication to another. I needed to find answers before I faced Dad.

Kaia...everything was rational until last night. She was a student - I was her teacher. After meeting a selkie, I'll never look at the ocean the same way again. Less than a day, less than twenty-four hours, and my life has been turned inside out. Why did I go with her? The answer was clear enough. She asked...and, to tell the truth, I wanted to go. But before she asked me, Ervin asked her to take me along, and he knew the Lady would be there. Was I set up?

It doesn't matter. I must take responsibility for my actions. I was with Kaia, and how will I explain my actions to Dad? That's a big problem. I can't tell him everything that happened last night. I guess I can say we went to the black rock, but that's a hangout place for couples. Would he believe we just went there for a picnic? Probably not. There's just no way to explain she's a selkie. Worst of all - how do I explain that I didn't have sex with her. The recording will make him think I did?

How do I get myself out of this mess?

Kaia's my student...was my student yesterday afternoon. That was before the selkie complicated things. What are we now? Before the selkie arrived, I thought we'd become close friends. Now, Ervin wants me to be part of their family. She's definitely not a sister, not that I don't want one. Maybe. Can I talk to her about personal things? I don't think so. She went ballistic when she found out about Candi. There's too much history between them. Candi? Is she what I think she is, or just a good lay? What did Grant mean when he said I would be better off with Kaia? Does he know something he's not telling me? Grant's my friend. We've been close for years. At least we can talk about it. Maybe after I talk to Dad.

Oops, I'm speeding. No cops anyhow. Slow down, James. Compose yourself. Remember to breathe. Stay out of deep water. I was there when Kaia made her choice. I was there when the Lady of the Sea walked out of the ocean. I was there when the Lady of the Sea told me about my grandparents. Too much, too fast. Do I have two families now – a human one and a selkie one? Am I comfortable with that? I guess that depends on my relationship with Kaia. Too much to think about right now. Dad...I need to be prepared for Dad.

Dad will be angry. It's his marina, and he's drilled that in all my life. I still have the mental scars. He expects me to set a good example, but last night went wrong from the beginning. I chose to go with Kaia. That's right, it was my choice. Kaia pulled her stunt in the marina parking lot with me in the car. Dad's going to chew me out over that, and I'll just have to take it. He's not just Dad, he's also my boss. I'll apologize, but that will fall short, because once again I'll have set a bad example. It will be the umpteenth-thousandth time I'd get that lecture.

It's not that I don't try. Dad sets his standards too high. Nothing less than perfection will satisfy him. Maybe that's why I've rebelled so often. Yes, that complicates my life. I want to please Dad, but I also need to live my own life. It isn't because I don't have someplace else to go. I've got a bachelor degree in marine engineering and another one in business. I could work anywhere.

But this marina is my home. It has been home all my life, except when I was away at college. To stay means I have to please Dad. Just how do I do that? I'd disagreed and insisted on my way too often in the past. Unfortunately, Dad has the irritating habit of being right, and I have a disturbing way of being wrong. It makes me feel like I'm still a kid, at least in his eyes. I'm not. I'm twenty-four and on my own. When will he realize that!

Then there's the other problem, the one I can't tell Dad, at least yet. He would think it's a bizarre excuse. Excuses never work with him. You take the lecture, and the punishment, and move on. I'll have to lie, or at least not tell him the whole story. He knows I left with Kaia in her Corvette. Did he know where we went? He'd have talked to Ervin. What did Ervin tell him? I'm sure Ervin left the selkie part out. Still, I have no idea what Ervin said. It makes lying difficult. Dad must know I had Kaia on the boat overnight. How am I going to explain that to him? She's eighteen. At least Dad can't accuse me of statutory rape.

I pulled in the lot and parked the Jeep next to Orcinus. They could keep each other company while I got beat up. Her car keys in my pocket rubbed against my thigh. It was tempting. I could jump in and drive away right now. Maybe even squeal her tires out of rebellion. That won't work. Damn, I feel like a little kid caught with his hand in the cookie jar. That's not a good analogy. Best try to think positive.

By the time I got to the office, my knuckles were white from being clenched around the wheel. Breathe. Don't swim. Don't sweat. It will be over in a few minutes, and I can drive away.

I walked in. Dad sat behind the desk. He was watching the video. My throat closed. I'd already seen it with Grant.

"Just what were you thinking?" Dad asked.

I couldn't speak.

"This is the fifth time I've looked at this and tried to understand what in the hell you were doing. Grant says you weren't having sex. How can I believe that! I keep looking for another possible explanation."

"Dad, we didn't. I know. I was there."

"So Ervin says. He told me you were on the phone with him, while you and Kaia were on the ground between the cars. I can't believe he'd cover for you. But the recording."

"Do we have to sit and watch it, Dad? It's embarrassing enough, don't you think?

"Not nearly enough."

I'm in for it now. Here it comes...

"Son, someday you'll inherit this marina from me. I've spent a lifetime building this business and my reputation. Reputation. It's important. Appearances mean everything. I'd like to leave the marina to someone who cares about it as much as I do."

"Okay, Dad."

It was the beginning of the all too familiar lecture. Dad set the stage and the stakes. The only comfort I had was that it will all act itself out over the next few minutes.

"This is difficult for me, Son. It shouldn't be my business, but your reputation is. I'm concerned that you're dating Candice Desdemona."

What the hell? "Candi?" What did she have to do with this?

"Candy is it? That should give you a clue about her. She doesn't have a very good ... reputation. She'll ruin yours."

"You're right, Dad, it's none of your business."

"Remember, you can learn either by listening or when life kicks you in the groin, but you will learn."

"So you think Candi is a slut?"

"I know. Don't you ever watch her? Here, let me show you her on the monitors with about every male in the bar. She's even hit on your best friend Grant."

Candi is a flirt. I know that and I...I like it. But, did she really flirt with Grant? Was she sleeping with others? That would be betrayal.

"Grant said nothing about it."

"What do you expect? He's your best friend. He won't say anything to hurt you. But he must be conflicted over it."

"Is that all?" I moved toward the door.

"No. Sit. We've much to talk about."

I stood. Maybe it was rebellion, but I stood. Everything that happened since I left the marina with Kaia yesterday flashed through my mind. Kaia's life had changed. Now, talking to Dad I realized - so had mine. Things could never remain the same. Still it's no good to argue with Dad. He looked at me and patiently waited. I sat.

"With some help I might be able to salvage your reputation."

"With Candi?"

"Candi's bad enough. Would you marry her if she got pregnant?"

"Pregnant. No, Dad. I've been careful."

"So you did have sex with her."

"Dad, you're not usually so blunt."

"You usually listen better. What makes a good wife?"

"Um...someone who's compatible."

"Let me make this clearer. Would Candi make a good mother?"

I hadn't thought of her in those terms. This was an entirely new perspective. "No...she drinks and she's wild – well, not a good example for children."

"Right. You're old enough to use your brains in relationships, not just your glands. When you marry, and you will, you'll want someone who'll be a good mother, so date accordingly."

"I'll be careful."

"That's not enough, Son. Sex isn't love. That's the danger of it. Sex is highly emotional and short lasting. A relationship based solely on sex will fail just as swiftly as it starts. Love grows out of close companionship, a connectedness that takes time to build. If you have sex, at least have it for the right reasons."

"Okay, I think I understand."

"Then what makes your mother a good wife?"

"She takes care of you?"

"Not the right answer. We take care of each other. Let me help. To the outside world your mother is a lady. How does everyone view Candi?"

"Okay I get the message."

"No you don't. What did you do last night?"

"Last night?"

"You took Kaia to your boat. Did you have sex with her too?"

"No, Dad, absolutely not. She was in pain and needed to recuperate."

"But you left her on the boat in the middle of the night?"

That caught me by surprise. "Kaia had a visitor."

"I didn't see anyone."

"She came by water."

"Oh. Who was it?"

"A distant relative."

"Okay, so you had good motives, and someone checked up on you. What about Kaia's reputation? Do you know what her father would do if he even thought you had sex with her?"

"No."

"He'd send his guards to make sure you got the message. They've been known to break legs."

"He's out of the country."

"I know. I can explain your courtesy to the person who saw you put her in your Jeep at seven this morning. Did you even think about the security cameras?"

"Yes, Dad, I did. I would have erased them if I could."

"That's why I never allowed you to know the codes. I'll do us both a favor. I'll remove last night's recording. You were more than a little friendly when you grabbed her from behind the way you did. What was that, aggressive flirting?"

59

"Dad, it was an accident. Her legs gave out. I caught her by instinct."

"Some instinct," he laughed. "When you got up, the two of you hugged."

"She would have fallen again."

"So, despite all that apparent love making, you took her to your boat. Do you have any idea what it looks like?"

I did.

"It's about appearances, Son. Think, before you do something stupid again."

"Dad, Ervin insisted I take her to my boat to avoid further injury."

"Ervin, you've used the name twice."

"He told me to call him by his first name."

"I see. It makes some sense. I used to call him Dad, although he wasn't my father. Well, I talked it over with Ervin. You did what was required and even decent. Others might not see it that way. I also talked with Grant. Did you know that Candi saw you leave with Kaia and chased after you?"

"She did? She's possessive, I guess."

"Until someone else comes along. She's a climber, Son. She's the type that uses men to achieve her goals."

That hurt. I'd seen Candi in action. Yes, she manipulated the men around her. Was my relationship with her an illusion built on sex, not love? Would she change her behavior if I asked her? *Can a seagull turn into a swan?*

"I see what you're saying, Dad."

"Sometimes truth hurts. Will you be staying with us tonight?"

"No. There are things I need to do."

"Care to tell me?"

"It's kind of personal, Dad."

"If you were younger, I'd ground you."

"Okay, Dad. I'm going to break up with Candi and then go back to Ervin's."

"Ervin's? Well, you're old enough to make your own choices."

"Thanks for the vote of confidence."

"I didn't say your choices were good. This may not be the time to break up with Candi."

"But you're right about her, Dad. Do you expect me to act like I still care?"

"You always will, at least at some level." It was almost a whisper, the voice of a possible confession.

I turned toward him, expecting more. "Some more cryptic advice?"

He gave me a forced smile. "Base your decision on logic. Emotional decisions usually lead to disasters."

"Then it's best I end it now."

"Women like Candice won't take no for an answer. They can't conceive of a man turning them down."

"What do you expect me to do, live a lie?"

"There's no easy way out for you, Son. You should have thought about that before you started the relationship."

"Well, I'm going to do it and then go to Erwin's for dinner."

"Kaia's there."

"Yes, Kaia's car is still in the parking lot. I need to return it to her."

"Well, at least Ervin can vouch for you to his son. Be careful."

That night James was late for dinner. Shelly had set the table formally with china plates. A large platter sat in the center of the table. Shelly lifted the cover in preparation to serve the meal. It contained grilled salmon garnished with steamed mussels and a medley of vegetables. Everyone was seated around the table.

"Shouldn't we wait for James?" Kaia asked.

"No, Ervin said, "let's eat before it gets cold. Charles said he was on the way. We can always warm some up for him when he arrives."

"I think I'll call him," Kaia said and placed the call.

James answered. "I'm sorry I'm late. It was unavoidable."

"Where are you?"

"I'm almost there."

"James, are you okay? You don't sound yourself."

"It's done. I'll be fine, once I get there."

"What's done, your Dad...?"

"I'm tired and sore. Just let me get there. I'll explain when I arrive."

Seven minutes later the doorbell rang. Shelly got up from the table and pointed at Kaia. "Stay there," she ordered. Ervin placed his hand on Kaia's shoulder and made her sit back down.

"Something's wrong," Kaia said, "I can feel it."

Shelly went to the front door. Kaia heard her gasp then jumped up. This time Ervin grabbed her arm and wouldn't let go. "Wait," he said.

Shelly returned with James. He had a black eye and three ugly scratches on his cheek.

Kaia pulled away and rushed over to him. "What happened? Are you okay? Is Orcinus okay?"

"The Corvette's okay, but I had a wreck of sorts. I broke up with Candi."

"And she did that to you? That bitch!"

"Mind your language, Kaia," Ervin said.

"But that's what she is. James didn't deserve this."

"It was a mistake to date her."

Despite the situation, Kaia broke out laughing.

"What's so damn funny about it?" James asked.

"I bet you're the first guy to ever say no to her."

"Well, she's got a mean temper when she's riled."

"I could have told you that!"

"Why didn't you?"

"Why did you date her?"

There was silence...they both blushed.

"Children, this is the dinner table. Take talk like that outside."

"Sorry," they both said.

Kaia left to get a cold pack for James' eye. Meanwhile, Shelly went to the kitchen and warmed up James' dinner. While they were absent, Ervin asked James about his meeting with Charles. So James told him. In conclusion James said, "What happened last night didn't exactly look good on video."

Kaia had returned during the story. When James finished, she provided her own version. Ervin asked an occasional question. They finished.

"That can be awkward," Ervin said. "Charles said it looked like the two of you had sex in the parking lot."

"We didn't," Kaia and James replied simultaneously. Then they looked at each other and began a nervous laugh. After that they both blushed.

"I trust both of you."

"Dad said he'd delete the recording, but he's worried what Kaia's dad may do if he thinks we actually did something."

"Don't worry. I'll take care of that. It was my decision to have her stay on your boat. I can explain why it was necessary, and why you are trustworthy."

"Dad won't understand," Kaia said. "There's no way to explain the Lady to him."

"You're probably right," Evin said. "He won't acknowledge what his heart surely tells him."

Kaia moved to seat herself, but James rose. Ervin briefly rose off the wheelchair. James moved around the table to help seat Kaia.

"That's not necessary," she said.

"It may be old fashioned, but it's the way I was raised." He seated himself. "It looks like you're legs are better."

Kaia nodded. "I'm more worried about Mom. Dad's at least rationale. Mom's all hormones and overreaction. Of course, she might sic Bill on James."

"Ah, Bill," Ervin said, "Lana's henchman. He's one mean SOB."

"Oh great!" James said. "Something else to look forward to. Candi was bad enough."

"Bill should be in jail for the things he's done," Ervin said, "but no one dares to testify against him."

"I think Mom pays them off," Kaia said.

"Or threatens them," Ervin said.

"Wonderful," James said, "Now I have to deal with a sadistic psychopath. So how do I get on Lana's good side?"

"I've wondered that for years," Ervin said. "I've never succeeded."

"Great, maybe I should leave right now for Alaska."

"Can we go together?" Kaia said.

Ervin stared at them. A smirk flashed across his face. "What do you think that would look like?" They blushed again. "We'll solve our problems one at a time. First, James needs to stay with us until his wounds heal."

"I should go home," James said.

"Reconsider," Ervin replied. "Your injuries will only add

credibility to what appeared to happen in the parking lot, only it will look like you raped her."

That hit James like a punch in the face.

"More importantly, you're part of our family now – you know our secrets."

"Just one lone human in a fine family of selkies," James said.

Kaia laughed but Ervin remained serious.

"I'm not sure what you are, James," he said. "You've talked with the Lady of the Sea – unusual all by itself. She said you have some unexpected connection to the ocean. Not a selkie, but I think not precisely human either."

Kaia turned towards James with a renewed interest.

"Not human?" James said.

"Perhaps that's a bit too strong...different, if you prefer. I began to suspect your family history after your grandfather and I became good friends. I sought, but found, no concrete answers, only this unshakable feeling."

James smiled at Kaia. "Can't be anything compared with being part selkie."

"Perhaps. Did you ever wonder about your love of the ocean? It's been part of your family for as many generations as I can trace."

"You know my family history? Dad doesn't even talk about it."

"He doesn't know, and I can only guess. I can't take your ancestors back four thousand years or more, but the Lady of the Sea might be able to. I'm curious about who sired your family that long time ago."

He paused and had the full attention of both James and Kaia.

"Are you going to tell me?" James said.

"Only my suspicions – do you know the story of Odysseus?"

"What has that to do with it?"

"Perhaps everything. Your last name is Cersea, curious. Ever wonder about it?"

"No."

"Odysseus stayed with Circe for several years. His son supposedly married her."

"So there's a similarity with my last name."

"No, James. If his son married Circe, they must have had children."

"You can't be serious?"

"James, I can't prove it. When the Lady of the Sea met you she sensed something odd and very old. She inquired of me through Shelly. I told her my suspicions.

"Shelly talks with the Lady?" James said.

"Regularly, Shelly and her sister, Mera both chose the sea. They went to the Orkney Islands. When I became crippled, Shelly returned to care for me. "

"Shelly," Kaia said, "Do you have problems with your legs too?"

"A selkie who chooses sea and lives on land always has problems with her legs. They are unnatural appendages. I have to return to the sea frequently to ease the pain. I was on the shore only a few days ago."

"Then you can teach me."

"The Lady wants me to teach you all about selkies."

"Back to James," Ervin said. "The Lady decided, if possible, to find the truth. Besides, she believes James caused the movement in the ocean depths. I lack the proof, but I think you descend from Odysseus and Circe, if not Odysseus, then his son. I don't know what that might mean, but it firmly ties you to the ocean."

"Just like a selkie," Kaia said.

"So we're in this together?" James said.

She nodded and they became silent around the table.

Ervin broke the silence. "James, Shelly has prepared your father's former bedroom for you."

"I'm in Great Grandmother's bedroom," Kaia said. "Can I show him later?"

"It's your room. There's a trunk in it. You may want James to help you open it...tomorrow."

Dinner was over and they adjourned to the library. Once there, Shelly helped Ervin move from his wheelchair into his recliner. Kaia sat down next to Ervin and noticed, for the first time, a large common conch shell sat on the end table next to his right hand. Conch shells on the necklace, on the bed, and on the rock in the bedroom painting. Shell wallpaper in her sitting room. *Other than decorative taste, what has this to do with selkies?*

"Tonight I'm going to tell you a story," Ervin said, "my relationship with James Dylan Cersea, James' grandfather. When we were still in our teens we met by chance. At least it seemed that way. Now that I'm old, I'm not so sure chance plays any part in our lives. I think we're chosen for our tasks, and we either succeed or blunder blindly through our lives.

"James and I both loved adventure and sailing. We laughed a lot, played a lot, and in the course of things fell in love with the same woman. We both dated her and vied for her love. I asked Sedna to marry me, and she accepted. That would destroy most friendships, but James loved both of us. He was the best man at our wedding, and I was best man at his, when he married Sedna's best friend, Odessa. The four of us were inseparable. We worked together, sailed together, and vacationed together. Then that wicked storm wrecked James' ship on the black rock reef. It broke Odessa's heart. Mother heard of it from the other selkies, as it happened, and went into the sea. She retrieved his body. We buried him at sea in an ancient selkie tradition."

"You've already told me Dad doesn't know." James said.

"Yes, Odessa felt it best to list James as missing, to spare her son the grief. There were already too many rumors of sirens drowning sailors and orcas helping others ashore. That's the source of the so-called black rock haunting. Sedna grieved with Odessa, and Odessa came to live with us. The three of us together raised Charles and Jacob. Your father is like a son to me, and if you turn out half the man your grandfather was....."

There was a knock on the door.

"Who at this hour?" Ervin asked.

"I'll go," Shelly said and left the room. She went to the front door and opened it. Two men stood in the doorway. They listened from the Library.

"Hi, I'm....it's you!" one said.

Shelly gasped. "You remember?"

"Yes. It seemed a dream until now."

"It was supposed to be."

He reached under his shirt and pulled out a black conch shell on a chain. "No, you were there. We were under fire. You rescued me. You gave me this."

"Ervin is my father."

"And he risked you in a firefight."

"It's not that simple."

"But he's your father. You've been here all this time. I wish I had known."

"David," Ervin yelled from the library. "Something serious must have happened to bring you here at this hour."

"I'll show you to the library," Shelly said.

David placed his hand on her shoulder, and she didn't object. They entered the library. Calvin followed.

"I apologize. I would have called ahead, but it was too risky. I think Lana's having me followed. Cal drove me."

"It must be important."

"It is."

"Tell me."

David looked around at the others in the room. There was concern on his face. "To everybody?"

Ervin looked at his family and James. "David is my representative on the corporation board. Calvin does discrete investigations for me. David and Cal, Let me introduce my family. You know Shelly, my daughter. This is Kaia, my grand-daughter, and James Cersea, who might as well be my grandson. Anything you say affects all of us."

"What happened to James?" Calvin asked.

Kaia glared. "He had an altercation with his girlfriend."

"She's got mean claws." He looked at James. "I'm sure it will heal ... eventually."

David looked at Kaia. "Are you sure about Kaia? It concerns her mother."

"What a surprise," Kaia said.

David laughed. "Okay, Lana thinks she has compromised me. One of her girls..." He looked up at Shelly. "I didn't...but they made it look like I did."

"Didn't what?" Kaia said.

She uses her girls to sexually compromise her targets, Shelly said to Kaia's mind.

Kaia turned toward Shelly and blushed. "My mother - what a shock!"

David looked at Ervin. "When is that boy of yours going to learn - Lana runs the company, not him. She owns or has compromised all the board of directors, most company officers, and some of it managers. She hires and fires at will. The workers call her the Dragon Lady."

"Nothing new there," Ervin said.

"I'm here because I received an email with an attached

recording. I believe it came from a waitress. Lana and your son are up to no good."

He held out a memory stick. Ervin looked at Shelly. "Put it in the computer please, and bring it up on the television." Ervin then turned back to David. "How'd she know who to contact?"

"I don't know. We have friends in many places."

Kaia and Shelly exchanged glances.

"True, but it's a problem, Cal. We need to find out who's behind this."

"Yes, sir."

"Is this real or are we being set up."

"I understand. I'll get my men on it."

"Thanks."

Shelly started the video. Jake Stone talked enthusiastically about the future of hazardous waste disposal. They could tell by the surroundings he was in a foreign country, probably pacific rim, in a closed meeting with government officials and military officers. Jake talked on about the deep sea trenches, calling them a desert, devoid of life. Hazardous waste could be stored there without any environmental risks, wastes that industrial countries would be eager to get rid of. Besides, the trenches were subduction zones. The waste would eventually be buried inside the earth's crust, offering a permanent solution.

"I just want to slap him," Kaia said.

"He's crafty," Ervin said, "but stupid. He's found a way around the law, but the sea isn't a dump, and it's anything but a desert. There's life in the depths, strange life, but life nevertheless. Does he really think the waste will stay where he puts it?"

"Of course, it isn't safe," Kaia said, "but the company will hire all the scientists it needs to make people believe it's the truth, or at least create enough doubt to avoid any punitive action."

"Kaia has a good understanding of modern business," David said.

Ervin pointed to the screen. "Notice Lana in the background. Here's a lesson for you, evil always hides in the background. It requires an honest, but deceived man, to front for it."

"You've never talked about Mom that way before."

"She's only been wicked so far - never this evil."

"And she's put the company at risk," David said. "They tried to keep me in the dark, but here's what I've learned. Unless the company has hidden offshore accounts, Jake and Lana have used their own money, and I suspect hidden offshore accounts to set up this puppet company. They hid the fact that our company has run up a huge debt over the purchase and retrofit of the ship and the development of the containment vessels. We'll recover the cost of the ship as soon as it is sold to the puppet company. The cost of the containment vessels is another matter."

"Damn her anyhow," Ervin said.

And I thought I had problems, Kaia thought.

Shelly turned to Kaia. *It's part of the problem we have to face.*

"I've got to stop them," Kaia said. "The Lady of the Sea says the ocean is dying."

"The Lady of the Sea has joined us," Shelly said.

"What?" Kaia said.

"This involves her kingdom. She's in my mind."

"What's going on?" David said.

Ervin looked at David and Cal. "I have a few secrets. Remember our retreat under fire?" They nodded. "We had help, female help..." He looked up at Shelly who took David's hand. "Selkie help. My family is all part selkie."

David gripped Shelly's hands tighter. "That explains the conch shell..."

And the reason for the dream, Shelly said to David telepathically. "You remember now."

"We both do," Calvin said.

"Are you both still with me?" Ervin asked.

"You...and the selkies...saved our lives." They both saluted him.

"We have to work together to stop them," Ervin said.

"You own a lot of stock," Kaia said. "Make him listen."

Ervin was silent. He took a sip on his drink and leaned back in his chair. Everyone else waited. The silence became painful. "Jacob and I have been on a separate course for years. I've given him free reign of the company, even though I disagree with him on many things. But this goes too far. Unfortunately, David is correct. Lana has control of the company. I can't stop her by myself, not without a scandal that will destroy everything."

He paused and took the opportunity to look each of them in the eye. When he reached Kaia, tears formed. "I waited and hoped for the selkie Ambassador and now you're here."

What shall we do? All heard the Lady of the Sea in their minds.

"We must stop them," Ervin repeated.

"Yes," James said.

What would you have us do, Ambassador.

"I'll give Dad a piece of my mind," Kaia retorted. "Then I'll tear that damn ship apart with my bare hands."

"Kaia, that won't work," James said.

"Why not?"

"We'll end up in jail."

"Okay by me as long as it stops them."

Shelly added, "Kaia's not ready. She's overconfident. Too many things can go wrong."

"I have to try," Kaia said

"Wait," Ervin said. "We can approach this on many fronts. Don't rush into confrontation, Kaia. Let me plan this out."

They all turned to Ervin.

Do we all agree? The Lady asked.

They did.

Chapter 7 - Treatment

The meeting ended, and it was late. David and Shelly excused themselves and went outside. They sat together on the porch swing and talked. Calvin stayed inside and met privately with Ervin concerning the inquiry Ervin had requested. They shared a drink in the library. When they finished, Calvin went to the porch and reminded David it was late, and they had a lot to do in the morning.

"Shelly and I were just talking about that," David said. "I could stay here tonight. She'll drive me to the office in the morning."

"I'm sure it's all right," Shelly said, "but I'll check with Dad."

They went back inside. Ervin wasn't in the least surprised at her request and suggested David be put next to James, in what was the girl's old room. Calvin left in his car. David sat in the library and shared a drink with Ervin while Shelly prepared the room. The parlor was located next to the library at the front of the house. James and Kaia went there and sat together on a loveseat.

"I think Shelly has a boyfriend," Kaia whispered.

"I think you're right," James replied.

They drank lemonade while they waited for Shelly to return. When she did, Ervin invited them to join him. Shelly took David up to his room. A few minutes later, she returned.

"He's making himself comfortable," she said.

"Then the rest of us best be off to bed," Ervin said. He winked at Shelly. "I know you have a lot of catching up to do. Don't keep him up too late."

Shelly helped Ervin move from the recliner into his wheelchair. Then he drove off toward the elevator. Kaia and James waited for him to leave and then followed Shelly to the foot of the stairway.

"I'll show James to his room," Shelly said, "then I'll check on Ervin and you."

The three walked up the stairs together. Ervin waited for them on the second floor. Hallways ran down both sides of the stairwell. Each hallway ran toward the front of the house and the flight of stairs to the third floor.

"May you dream of starlight and salmon," Ervin said. "Come along Kaia." He turned around and drove his wheelchair toward the hallway on the left.

Kaia glanced at James' wounded face and wished him a good night. Then she followed Ervin. James and Shelly waited at the top of the stairs until Ervin entered his room and Kaia turned the corner to climb the next flight to the third floor.

James whispered. "You're a selkie, but your voice isn't seductive like the Lady's."

"It can be, but selkies learn to control it."

"The Lady didn't."

"And you weren't supposed to be there."

"That's supposed to explain it?"

"Initially. Once she learned who you were, she changed her mind."

Shelly abruptly turned toward the hallway on the right of the stairs and went to the first doorway on the right. "This is your bedroom. David is in the room toward the front of the house. It was originally the girls' bedroom, and this was the boys' bedroom. Our nanny, Aunt Odessa, slept in the room between them. I shared the furthest room with my sister. Charles and Jake shared this room."

"You look too young to be my Dad's age."

"Why thank you. Selkies, especially those who choose the ocean, live a very long time."

"Kaia chose the land."

"Perhaps. I wonder what she chose in her heart."

"I don't understand."

"Neither do I. Kaia chose land but acts like she chose the sea. The Lady calls her Daughter of the Sea. It evokes an old myth from the Orkneys of the selkie who could fully be of the land and the sea."

"What does that mean?"

"I'm not sure. I suspect Kaia will develop in unpredictable ways."

"Like what?"

"Be careful of her voice, James. She's young and untrained."

What did that mean? Would she become seductive like the Lady? I'd spent the summer teaching her how to sail. It was a tutoring arrangement and sailing is an act of teamwork with the wind and water as both allies and potential enemies. It reveals character. It develops life-long kinships. I knew Kaia's likes and dislikes, her strengths and her weaknesses. But there are always surprises. Last night was a big one. Now our kinship had a new dimension.

"Where's your room?"

Shelly laughed and pointed up. "I'm on the selkie floor. My room is across the hall from Kaia's. My bedroom is about the same size as yours but it's at the front of the house. There's a large room over the entrance to the house and it's attached to my room. It has a Jacuzzi tub that fills with salt water. The long soaks at night allow me to stay on land as long as I manage."

She led me into my room. It was spacious enough for two boys. The color scheme was beige and brown. There were two windows on the north wall with two desks beneath them. One of them must have been Dad's. There was one window to the east side, the back of the house. Beneath it was a nightstand with twin beds on each side. There were two dressers along the inside wall and a closet along part of the other wall.

Shelly pointed to a door next to the closet. "It leads to the bathroom."

"Thanks Shelly. Which bed and which desk were Dad's?"

Shelly pointed them out and left, closing the door behind her. I sat down on the bed closest to the doorway - Dad's bed. Over the years, I'd been in this house many times, but never suspected Dad was raised here. Why didn't he tell me? Was there a reason to keep it secret? We'd often had dinner with Ervin or sat long hours with him in the library to swap stories, discuss politics or the environment, and sometimes to ask Ervin for advice. Ervin was one of those rare people who listened carefully and had both wisdom and the right words for the situation. Now I understood. Dad went to Ervin for advice, like a son went to his father. Ervin had replaced Dad's lost father. I never knew my grandfather, but I'd known Ervin all my life. I'd gladly call Ervin grandfather. He's the only grandfather I'd ever known.

I went over to Dad's desk and sat down. I opened the drawers, but they were empty. I rubbed my hands over the surface and felt the occasional dents and grooves. Dad once sat here and studied. I looked at the other desk and imagined another boy there. I'd never had a brother or a sister. Grant was as close as I'd ever come to having a brother. I went back to the bed and lay down. Dad must have laid here. I felt I belonged, that this house was part of my heritage...my grandfather's house. It was a house of selkies, and I belonged with them.

My face stung, so I went over to the mirror and looked at it. My eye was worse. I'd last seen it in the rear view mirror when I arrived. It was only swollen then. Now in addition, it was black with purple edges. There were three ugly red streaks down my left cheek. I rubbed them. They still burned. The adventures and misadventures of the last twenty-four hours crashed on me like giant waves. They pounded me into the gravel and rocks until I felt bruised and broken. Too much had happened – the sailing lesson, Dad's criticism, the selkie, and finally Candi's rage.

Then I realized I should have brought another cold pack with me. It was too late now. I'd disrupt the family if I went back downstairs.

I had a pressing need to talk with someone, so I called Grant. I told him I'd broken up with Candi and what had happened as a result. He wasn't at all sympathetic.

"I'd guessed as much," Grant said. "She wrote 'I hate you' on the mirror in your boat with her lipstick. I cleaned it up, packed up everything that I thought was hers, put it in a bag, and left it on the hood of her car."

"Thanks."

"Sure buddy. Wait till I tell everyone about Candi's claws."

"No. Don't...don't. Grant, you must promise me not to tell anyone."

"But why?"

"It's complicated. Please...don't."

"Kaia?"

"The whole thing is more complicated than you can imagine. Would you mind looking after the boat until I return?"

"Sure thing. Is it all right if I sleep there?"

"Be my guest. There are clean sheets in the closet. Would you mind washing the ones on the bed?"

"Sure."

We finished, and I decided to call Dad and tell him what had happened. Dad agreed with Ervin's assessment. If I showed up at the marina with visible injuries, it would be harder to control the rumors.

"Stay there a week or two. I'll tell everyone that you're out on an assignment."

"Dad, I didn't bring any clothes."

"I'll have Cardea pack your duffel bag tonight. Grant can bring it to you in the morning."

"Could he bring my Jeep?"

"So, you're using your brains again! Good - if it's gone it will back up my story. I have your spare set of keys. I'll have Grant drive it and ask Ervin to have Shelly drive him back to the marina."

"Dad, Candi blamed Kaia for the breakup. Candi didn't believe Kaia wasn't my girlfriend and said some very nasty things about her. That was before she took out her anger physically on me."

"Does she know Kaia?"

"Kaia said they went to high school together."

"Then allow me to make an educated guess. Kaia has wealthy parents who lavished her with all the latest toys and gadgets, like her Corvette and the professional driving lessons, scuba lessons and anything else she fancied."

"Dad, Kaia said she'd apologize for misbehaving with the Corvette."

"I'll accept it, but I'll have to make a public example of her. I can't tolerate that kind of behavior. Kaia may have the skill, but others don't. Someone will get hurt. Now, please don't interrupt me. Let me finish. Candi's not poor. She wouldn't be at the marina if her parents couldn't afford it, nor would she have attended a private school with Kaia. But Kaia's parents are very wealthy. Candi probably thinks Kaia can have anything money buys and resents it. She wants the things that wealth can buy, but will have to grab for it by seducing her way into it. I didn't want you to be stuck with her."

"Well it's over, and I've felt the consequences."

"Son, it isn't over, not a bit. Candice will blame Kaia. She may fight to get you back. So think twice before you ever provoke a woman again."

I thought the phone calls would help but I was wrong. I had planned to sleep on the boat tonight, not stay here. I had no pajamas. Well, I'd slept in underpants before. I undressed and hung my pants and shirt over a chair and then crawled under the covers. I guessed that David had to be satisfied with the same solution.

I couldn't sleep. It wasn't only the pain. Seduced...I thought I had seduced Candi, not the other way around. Candi was sweet and entertaining, in a sensual way, but she showed her true claws tonight. The scratches and black eye were bad enough, but she'd kicked me hard in the groin before she left. I'd crumbled and lay on the ground in the parking lot while she stomped away. I'd planned to enjoy driving the Corvette. Instead, I drove it in pain.

I played the past over and over in my head. If I did this or that, would it have led to a different ending? Could I somehow take back that first date with Candi? Lost in thought, I lost track of time. I drifted into that strange realm between sleep and awareness.

They were interrupted by a light tap on the bedroom door. Instantly I jerked awake. "James, can I come in?" It was Kaia's voice.

"Yes," I whispered back.

There was another tap on the door, slightly louder. "James, are you awake?"

I didn't want to wake everyone. So, I got up and grabbed my pants from the chair just as the door opened. I quickly held my pants in front of my legs. She chuckled, "I've seen you in your swim suit. You are wearing underwear, aren't you?"

"Do you think I sleep in the nude? I didn't have a chance to pack."

She wore sweat pants and a tank top. Well, I'm a sailor, so I adopted sailor etiquette. I turned around and pulled my pants on.

"Nice butt...feel comfortable now?" she whispered when I turned back to face her. I didn't expect it, but I felt embarrassed.

"What are you doing here? Wasn't last night bad enough for our reputations?"

"I've come to apologize. If I hadn't asked you to the black rock, none of this would have happened."

"I'm glad I went. It's complicated my life, but it's exciting in a scary sort of way."

"What's so scary?"

"What does the Lady expect from me?"

"I keep asking myself the same question."

"And how are we going to stop your parents?"

"I could try to reason with Dad."

"Really," he said. "And when was the last time that worked?"

"Whoa, are you bitter over something?"

"I had a run in with my Dad before dinner. It was pleasant compared to the encounter you'll have, if you argue with your parents."

"I have to try."

"Of course you do, but you could end up damaged like I am."

76

Kaia moved close and examined my injuries. "I'm sorry I mentioned Candi. I shouldn't have pried into your private life."

"That's what friends do – they look out for each other."

"Friends, is that what we are?"

"No, it's more than that. Dad was raised with your father. We're related in some strange way."

"I've always wanted a big brother to look out for me."

Was that what I was now, a big brother? "I wish it was that simple. I feel we've been tossed together by the Lady."

"So, you feel that too?"

"We're bound up in this together, wherever it takes us."

"Good, I need all the help I can get. Now, sit down on the bed and let me care for you."

"I can take care of myself."

"Don't be a baby. It's the least I can do. I feel responsible for what happened."

"You're not. It was bound to happen sooner or later."

"Are you going to sit and let me take care of you, or do I have to take you downstairs and wake the whole family."

"Kaia, haven't we done enough to our reputation for one day?"

She put her hands on her hips and glared at me.

I knew her stubbornness. "Okay, have your way."

I sat down on the bed and she bent over me. Then she opened a bottle of peroxide. She poured some on a cotton cloth and began to wipe the scratches.

"Shit, that burns."

"Shush, you big baby. Take it like a man."

She repeated the process, and this time I only winced.

"By the way, I met David on the stairs. He went up to Shelly's room while I was on my way down to yours."

"What did he do when he saw you?"

"He laughed and wished me a good night."

"Dang, Kaia...our reputation."

"I don't think he'll say anything, except maybe to Shelly."

Kaia finished cleaning the scratches.

"I'm glad that's over," I said.

"We'll need to repeat the treatment in the morning. Now for your eye, I brought some warm water to soak it and another cold pack."

She sat on the bed beside me and began to soak my eye. I watched her with my other eye while she treated my injured one. I'd never been this close to her face before or felt the warmth of her body against mine. She was distracting. Her eyes were indeed the aqua of the sea and sparkled with its swells and mystery, but the expression on her cheeks changed rapidly as she tended to my wound. One moment she showed concentration, the next concern, and then anguish. It flicked back and forth between these emotions. Water ran down my cheek and splashed on my chest. She casually blotted it up. Her touch sent currents of electricity through me. I had to remind myself she was my student, but I knew we were closer than that by now – kin of some sort. *Remember Shelly's warning - beware of her voice.*

"I can do this myself, you know," I said.

"You could, but I'm better at it."

"So, I should just shut up and enjoy it?"

"If you're smart and don't want to risk waking up the rest of the house."

I remained quiet for several minutes. Her closeness continued to bother me, more and more as time progressed. Our relationship had changed today. I had met a selkie and had become a holder of family secrets. I'd learned my family and the Atwater's had been intertwined for generations. We were all in the service of the Lady. I tried to think of Kaia as a cousin, but that wouldn't work. Grant would make more of the relationship. I could already hear him say, "Sure, a kissing cousin."

She finished soaking my eye and began to examine my chest. "Any other injuries?"

She must have seen me blush.

"Okay, what else did she do?"

I shook my head briefly. Should I lie? No, she's too perceptive. Could she read my mind - possibly? Once more she put her hands on her hips. There was no easy way out. "She – um - kicked me in the groin."

This time Kaia blushed. "You probably deserved it."

"Hard, Kaia, it's still tender."

"Well, I'm not going to kiss it and make it better."

I blushed and noticed she did also.

"I don't know why I said that. I'd better be going." She tiptoed to the door, opened it cautiously, and left.

The next morning, Shelly knocked on my door to wake me for breakfast. I dressed in the only clothes I had and met Ervin in the hall. He motioned for me to ride down in the elevator with him.

"Kaia visit you last night?" Ervin asked.

There was no way to deny it. "She came to apologize and treat my injuries."

"I trust both of you, but you're the one who must remain responsible."

"I am."

We got off the elevator and went into the dining room. Kaia was already seated. So was David, and Shelly was waiting to serve them.

"James," Shelly said, "Last night I should have asked what you wanted for breakfast. Are bacon and eggs okay?"

I looked around the table. Ervin had a bowl of oatmeal and Kaia was eating yogurt and granola. David had bacon and eggs. She'd made the same for me.

"You don't need to do anything special for me."

Kaia got up, walked over and touched my cheek. "She must have dirty fingernails. It's worse than it was last night."

"I heard someone up and about last night," Shelly said.

"Kaia visited James," Ervin explained.

"So, I didn't imagine it," Shelly said.

Kaia stared at Shelly. David squirmed slightly in his chair.

"There are no secrets in this house," Ervin said.

That made David squirm even more. He looked at Ervin, curious as to whether Ervin referred to him as well.

"Hey, I only went there to apologize," Kaia said.

"And I thought you were my nurse," James said.

Kaia turned her head sideways and stared into me eyes. "I can't wait...to give you another peroxide treatment... <u>everywhere</u> you hurt."

"Children, behave," Ervin said.

Then they all laughed.

"Are the eggs all right?" Shelly asked.

"Yes, thank you," James replied.

"We've had a slight change in plans this morning," Ervin said. "Grant is bringing James' clothing and his Jeep, so David has to stay until he arrives."

That seemed to please David.

"James will be with us a while," Ervin said. "So, I've got a challenge for Kaia and him - my mother's sea chest. She left Kaia some things in it. She can have them if she can figure out how to open the blooming chest."

"You don't have the key?" Kaia asked.

"It doesn't have a keyhole," Shelly added.

"Then how do I open it?"

"That's the challenge."

"Do you want me to bring it downstairs," Shelly asked.

"No, leave it upstairs," Ervin said.

"At least let me move it out of Kaia's bedroom and into her sitting room," Shelly said. She looked at me when she said it.

"That's okay with me," Kaia replied with a slight smirk.

Shortly after breakfast, Grant arrived in my Jeep with my clothes. He greeted Kaia with a wink. So like Grant! She looked at me and rolled her eyes. I shook my head side by side in agreement her and introduced him to Ervin, David, and Shelly.

Grant looked at my face with a wicked smile. "I used to think you were handsome."

"It's my war paint," I replied.

"Did you win or lose?"

"Where's Custer when I need him?" I took my duffel bag from him.

"So you lost!"

"Hey, I didn't say it was the Little Big Horn or whose side I was on."

Grant laughed and put his arm around me.

"Come upstairs and see my room," I said.

"Your room? You have a room here?"

"I'm in Dad's old room."

I could see the surprise on Grant's face, but said no more of it until we got upstairs. Kaia and Shelly climbed the stairs with us.

"James, I'll help Kaia move the sea chest out of Kaia's bedroom. You and Kaia can work on it after I leave to take Grant back to the marina and David back to work."

"Could I treat you to lunch?" David asked. Shelly nodded in agreement.

Kaia and Shelly vanished down the hallway and passed up

the stairs to the third floor.

Once we were inside my room, I tossed the bag on the bed and started to unpack. While I put my clothes in the dresser and closet, I told him about the death of my grandfather and how my grandmother had become the nanny in this house.

"Let me get this straight, your father and Kaia's father were raised together. That's good. It means you and Kaia have an excuse to spend time together."

"Grant..."

"I'm not stupid. You broke up with Candi to be with Kaia."

"That's not what happened."

"If you say so. Candi really did a number on you, didn't she."

"No kidding."

"And you have to stay in the same house with Kaia – tough duty."

"Grant ..."

"Hey, I'm only stating the obvious."

It was anything but obvious, but I'd never convince Grant. If I couldn't convince him, what about everyone else?

Chapter 8 - Secrets

While James was downstairs with Grant, Shelly and I moved the old sea chest away from the foot of my bed. It was heavy, but together we managed to carry it into my sitting room. We placed it in the turret where the driftwood chair formerly sat. Last night, the chest had been a curiosity. Now, I knew it held gifts from my great-grandmother. I wanted to explore it.

I knelt. It was a large old tin and wood sea chest painted with a sky blue background. It didn't have a domed lid like some chests I'd seen. It was rectangular and flat on all sides, like an old traveling chest. Scenes of different shorelines from around the world were painted on its surfaces. There were a few irregular dents from rough handling over the years. It was free of engravings. On the front face was the painting of the black rock as seen from the sea. The black rock itself was embossed outward about three eights of an inch. There were hinges on the opposite side but no visible latch.

There was no keyhole.

"It's a challenge," Shelly said.

"Do you have any idea what's inside?"

"I suspect some jewelry and maybe her journal."

"It's too heavy for that."

"I thought so too. As you sure you want James to help you?"

"I'm scared, Shelly. What if my legs transform? What if it happens in front of him?" It was a terrifying prospect. I imaged myself flopping around on the floor like a fish out water while he laughed at the spectacle.

"Make sure you spend time daily in sea water, at least until you learn control."

It didn't help. The thought made my leg start to itch. I remembered what happened last time…the itching turned into pains that felt like chewing...the chewing into a fluke. It brought renewed panic. I didn't want Shelly to notice.

We went back downstairs. Shelly left in Ervin's car with the two guys. She'd be gone most of the day. Granddad said he could take care of himself until Shelly returned. "Try to open the chest," he advised.

So, I took James up to the third floor. He paused to study the photographs, just as I had yesterday. I pointed out his grandfather and grandmother in one of the pictures. They were on a sailboat with a much younger Ervin and his wife, Sedna. James touched the picture. He put his finger on the woman with long black hair who stood at the helm.

"Kaia, that must be your great-grandmother."

She reached out and ran her finger over the image. "I think you're right. It's a shame we can't see her face."

"I wish I could have sailed with them."

"Me too."

We went into my sitting room. I showed him the sea chest, and we both knelt down to examine it from all four sides. He lightly thumped it in a few places.

"No obvious trigger," he said.

I smiled. "I tried yesterday. I've got something else to show you." I got up and opened the door to my bedroom.

He looked up at me with questions on his face. He hesitated. Was he was afraid for some reason? He certainly acted strange. I stood in the doorway with my hands on my hips. "Come on James, the room won't bite." He got up and followed me through the doorway. I heard him sharply draw in his breath when he entered..

"The selkie room," I said.

His eyes flashed around the room. "Incredible, those selkies in the mural - they're so life-like. They have flukes instead of legs. You chose land, so you don't get a fluke?"

"Why, do you like mermaids?"

"Just asking."

"What would you do if I could have a fluke?"

"We could swim together."

"With a fluke I'd be better than you."

That was a relief. James wouldn't be offended by my fluke. I could be myself with him. I relaxed and pointed up at the ceiling. "You should see it at night. The ceiling has tiny lights that look like stars, and the ceiling fixture takes on the phases of the moon. I tried it last night. I felt I was laying outside on a rock in the moonlight."

James smiled and looked into my eyes. I could almost read his thoughts. I'd all too innocently invited him into my bedroom tonight. Oops. I stared up at the ceiling. *Did I use the voice?* It wouldn't be right to do that. *Is he aware I might use it on him?*

We were silent. I guess he was trying to figure out what I meant and while I tried to figure out if I used the voice.

James broke the silence. "I've sailed a few times at night. The stars are incredible once you are away from the city lights."

"There's more." I touched a switch beside the bed. The room filled with the soft rhythmic sounds of waves washing on the shore. James sat down on the translucent floor and closed his eyes. A peaceful and soothing feeling washed over me. It felt like I lay on a warm rock on the seashore. I could lay there forever.

"There's music too." I said and turned it on. Now, in addition to the wash of waves, we heard the distant sounds of drums, strings, and a flute. It was accompanied by singing. I didn't understand the words but felt the music at the center of my soul.

"It isn't African," James said. "Similar complicated rhythm. It reminds me of something." He thought about it a moment. "It sort of sounds Samoan."

"What would that have to do with selkies?"

"I just thought it sounded similar."

James turned to the murals on the two adjacent walls. He smiled at the pod of orcas and walked up close to the painting of the sailboat. "A black haired woman at the helm again. Could she be your great-grandmother?"

"Perhaps - it seems a theme."

"I thought selkies dwelt in the sea. Why would they sail? Yet from the pictures in the hall, your great-grandmother appears to be a competent sailor."

"Maybe that was Great-Granddad's doing."

I suggested we return to the sea chest. James lingered in the room. "Come on," I said, "it's a challenge. Let's find a way to open the chest."

We left the bedroom and sat on the floor with the sea chest between us. The obvious latch was the black rock. James tried to push on the black rock from various angles. That didn't work, so he tried squeezing it top to bottom, then sideways. Nothing worked.

"Try twisting it," I said.

That didn't work either. "Maybe it requires a feminine touch," James said.

I tried pushing, pulling, squeezing, and twisting but nothing happened.

"Maybe it has a hidden trigger, sort of like the latch to a car hood."

I took out a nail file and probed around the lid and hinges. I couldn't feel anything. I handed him the file. "You're the engineer, see if you can find something."

Nothing worked.

"Maybe there's a ball inside that has to be rolled just so to undo the latch," James said. He put his fingers under the sea chest and tried to lift it.

"I can't imagine my Great-Grandmother being able to lift this by herself."

James agreed. "Maybe Ervin would let us x-ray it."

I shook my head. Too scientific. Too practical. It had to be something simple. We just needed to reason it out. That afternoon we researched latching mechanisms on the Internet, but it was useless. Everything we tried failed.

At dinner we confessed our failure. Granddad didn't seem surprised. "Take a break, perhaps a picnic to the black rock." It sounded like a great idea, but James was reluctant. He asked Granddad if the music in my room was Samoan.

"It doesn't come from Samoa. I admit it's similar. I was there once. The music is much older than you can imagine."

James and I cleared the table while Shelly moved Granddad into the Library. Once the dishwasher was loaded, Shelly got all of us drinks, and we sat in our usual story positions around Ervin.

"The music," he said, "comes from a very ancient time, a time when the world was young and uncomplicated, a time when there were few barriers between man and the spirit world he lived in, a time when he did not question the strangeness of the selkies. They were just another part of the world.

"The Orkney Islands were such a place. Hunter-gatherers dwelt on the islands and lived off the sea. Ancient selkies also subsisted on the sea life around the islands. It was natural they came into contact with each other. When they did, they learned from each other, shared their knowledge, and an advanced Stone Age culture was born. The men built stone houses with many rooms and running water for their latrines. They lived much closer to modern man than the wandering, club wielding hunter-gathers on the mainland. Sadly, the climate changed and the settlers disappeared. Modern man wonders where they have gone.

"They are still with us. Their female children took to the sea. All living selkies come from them. The music you hear is the music that used to echo throughout those stone houses and along the shore as man and selkie celebrated the harvest of the sea."

I had to ask. "What about the Daughter of the Sea myth?"

"Of course you're curious. It's natural, now that she's given you that name. There were shamans in that Stone Age settlement. It is said that one was a strange male. He wore a fluke instead of legs. He was crippled by it. He was at home neither on the land nor in the sea. He said the day would come when a selkie would be born, one who would be able to be both human and selkie, one who would be at home both on the land and in the sea."

That's why they worried about my legs transforming into a fluke. I shouldn't be able to do that. Would I end up a cripple, just like that shaman? Did that explain why Granddad was crippled? I shared Granddad's genes. It could happen to me. It reinforced the panic that gnawed away at my confidence. One way or the other, I had to learn to control the transformation, or I would end up crippled, or worse, just another freak.

It should have been easy, but it wasn't. The sea chest stubbornly refused to reveal its secrets. And James didn't want to be out in public until he healed. So, every day for a week, we tried to solve the puzzle. Evenings, I treated James' injuries in his room. He confided he was scared I might use the voice on him. I confessed that I was scared of that, too. We both worked to avoid the complications the voice created, and in the process, denied our changing relationship.

After the nightly treatments, we sat together in his room and talked for hours about our lives and aspirations. We kept few secrets from each other. I told James about high school and the antics of Candi. James listened but wouldn't talk about Candi. It embarrassed him, and it was too much fun for me to rub it in. I couldn't resist. I trusted that someday he'd become comfortable enough to tell me. Probably not when I still rubbed his nose it in.

Ervin was right, James belonged in our family. He not only could keep our secrets but cared about our concerns.

At the end of the week, we were back at the sea chest. We tried everything over for the umpteenth time. Squeezing, twisting, probing, shaking, or lifting still had no effect. We even tried singing to it or playing the ancient selkie music. The chest stubbornly refused to open. I was frustrated, but I wouldn't let James take it apart with a power saw or a hatchet. I knew he was only teasing -

but that's how frustrated we were.

"We've tried everything over and over again," I said.

"I still say I should borrow a saw from Ervin and cut off the damn hinges."

"You think he'd let you? You think I'd let you. This is a sacred heirloom. Besides I don't want it damaged."

"There's no dang keyhole and no hidden triggers I can find."

"There must be a simple solution, James. Relax. What haven't we tried?"

"Selkie mind control?"

"You think telepathy opens this?

"It would be telekinesis, not telepathy."

"I don't think it's possible. The Lady never showed any telekinetic ability. I can't find a way to use my conch shell either."

"What? You think a conch shell could be a key?"

"It unlocks my bed."

"Your bed?"

"My bed isn't just the bed you see, James." I gave him a broad smile. "Come on, it's about time I showed you."

I removed my conch shell necklace and led James into my bedroom. Then I climbed up on the bed and crawled to the headboard. He kept his eyes fixed on me and it made me a little nervous. Once there, I inserted the conch shell into the indentation at the center of the headboard. The bed started to rise. I removed the shell and dropped off the bed.

The bed began to rise. "The bed moves? What's under it?" he asked.

"Just watch."

He moved over to the bed. There were four posts at the corners of the bed. James held one of them. "They vibrate," he said. Then he put his ear to a post and listened. The posts slowly extended. "It must be activated by hydraulics...clever." A minute later the bed stopped eight feet from the floor. James looked into the swirling pool of water.

"It's salt water and must be special," she said. "It heals my legs."

"Shelly told me she has a salt water Jacuzzi in her room. Maybe Ervin does too."

"I don't know about them, but Great-Grandmother used this for her legs. It works." I pointed to the mural behind the headboard.

"With the bed raised, the black rock has a conch shell resting on it."

We both looked at it a moment, then I activated the mechanism to close the bed. "There's no conch shell on the trunk. So how could I use my shell?"

"It must be a clue. Why would she have two separate keys?"

"That makes sense."

James looked at me and focused his eyes on my conch shell. "Could I see your necklace?" he asked. I handed it to him. "How do I remove the shell?"

"Why?"

"There's an embossing of a black rock on the center of the chest. It lacks a conch shell. The embossing has a small shelf about the size of your conch shell. What would happen if we placed the shell there?"

"Let me do it." I held out my hand, and he dropped the necklace into it.

"Must we always do things your way?"

"I'm the princess."

"And what am I, your serf?"

"No, you're my teacher, unless you want to be my serf."

"That's crazy. How could I teach you and serve you at the same time?"

I placed the tiny conch shell on the small shelf. Click ... shhssss ....creek .... shsss ... thunk. "I think we did it."

Together we lifted the lid of the trunk. It bent over until it rested at an angle against the back of the chest, held in place by two straps. Inside, it was remarkably clean, considering it hadn't been opened for a very long time. There were no spiders or other creepy and crawly things. There weren't even any webs or dust. It looked like it had been closed only yesterday. The chest held a shallow wooden insert covered in deep green velvet. The velvet remained in remarkably good condition, considering it had to be well over a hundred years old. The insert was divided into several compartments. Most had lids.

"Her jewelry must be in here," I said and lifted the lid on the larger closed compartment. Inside was a royal blue silk satchel. I lifted it out and carefully opened it. Inside was a string of large black pearls. I held them up against my neck. "These must be worth a small fortune." I replaced the pearls in their satchel and put them back in the chest. Then I opened the next compartment. Inside was a clamshell shaped ring box. I opened it and found a matching set of bands with sapphire stones. "Great-Grandmother's and Great-Grandfather's wedding rings?"

"It makes sense. The third ring must have been her engagement ring." That stone was a small black pearl.

"Granddad said there was a tradition of black pearls in our family, all except for Mom that is. She wanted a huge diamond from Dad. I'd prefer the pearls."

The next compartment held another conch shell necklace. It was plain, unlike my silver one. The conch shell chain looked like a sailor's rope, only it was made from a fine bronze colored metal with stands all twisted together. "This looks like it's meant for a sailor, I wonder if it was Great-Granddad's?"

I took the conch shell and rope necklace and returned to the bed. This shell activated the bed. "James, I want you to wear this."

"Why?"

"In case we need another key. Here, let me put it on you." I draped it under his neck and latched it. "Don't take it off."

"Is that a royal command?"

I glared at him. "I'm a princess of the ocean."

He shook his head. "Right! I don't think I can be one of your subjects."

"What do you want to be, my prince?"

"I think we should be equals."

"Just wear it for me, won't you?"

"Yes, Kaia, I'll do it just because you asked."

Inside another compartment was a necklace. It contained a small vial. "Perfume?" I asked. I opened and sniffed it. "It's only seawater."

"Seawater helped you earlier."

"It helps me in the bath too."

"Maybe it's for emergency use."

I put it back in the chest. "What else is in the trunk?"

There was a pile of small shells in a large compartment. James rummaged through it with his hands. He stopped and pulled something out. It hung between his hands. "Look at this, a shell brassiere. I never saw one before. Your Great-Grandmother had a shell brassiere!"

"She was a selkie. Don't the selkies in the mural wear them?"

"That's true, but I thought it was only an artistic license. The

Lady of the Sea doesn't wear anything."

"Maybe she didn't expect to be seen by you." I let him stew on that for a while. "Let's see what's hidden under the insert."

James tried to lift it out, but it wouldn't move. I tried next but couldn't move it either.

"More secrets?" James asked.

"We'll have to try later. It's time for dinner."

Before we left, I picked up the blue silk satchel that contained the string of black pearls.

At dinner, we told Ervin we had opened the chest.

"What's the trick?" he inquired.

"It's the conch shell on my necklace," I said. "The paintings of the black rock were the clue. Set the shell on the black rock embossment, and it unlocks the chest." I went on to explain we couldn't lift out the jewelry tray. Ervin inquired about the contents and I described the jewelry to him.

"Well, we still have a week before James needs to go home. And, you have my birthday present."

"The Alaska trip?"

"The plane leaves tomorrow morning."

Of course. In all the excitement I'd forgotten. "Could James go with me?"

"Sorry, the trip is booked up. He can drive you to the airport though. I have something else for James to do. James, would you let me hire you for the three days that Kaia is on her trip?"

"What do you need?"

"I've purchased some state-of-the-art solar panels. They're flexible. Would you install them on my boat? You can stay there overnight if you like."

"Ervin, I've never seen your boat."

"Oh, you'd like her. She's a fifty foot sloop, broad beam, rigged for both genoa and jibs. She can sleep six in comfort. And she's designed for weeks at sea. I like solar power - means you don't have to carry lots of gasoline or diesel fuel. The solar array I purchased will cover the cabin roof. You can do this, right?"

"It would be my pleasure."

"Pleasure, hell, I'll pay you for it."

"Not necessary - consider it my rent for living here."

"Let's not haggle - I'll give you a fair wage."

Kaia piped in. "Boys, behave yourselves."

They looked at her. James made a deep bow, and they burst out laughing.

When he finished smirking, Ervin added. "You and James can try to find a way to remove the tray when you both return."

"What should I do with Great-Grandma's things?" Kaia asked.

"She left these for you. Shelly, what do you think? Should they all be Kaia's?"

"I think Grandmother wants it that way," Shelly said.

"You can't be serious - the black pearl necklace alone is worth a small fortune."

"It's nothing," Ervin said. "Perhaps this is the right time to tell you. My parents, your great grandparents, left you an inheritance. I've managed the investments for you, and they've grown substantially over the generations. Your mother and father know nothing about it. You don't ever have to depend on them for support."

"But I still have to go home and deal with them."

"You'll be away at college by fall. That will get you out of their house. James will be going back to school too."

"Dad told you?" James said.

"Yes - he said you needed additional courses in public relations. You know why."

James glared at him. "There are no secrets." Ervin laughed.

Kaia held the black pearl necklace against her chest. "Granddad, I don't know what to say. Great-Grandma's things are so beautiful."

"And the shell bra is yours too?" James said. He dangled it from his hands. Ervin raised his eyebrow. "What, you've never seen your mother in it?"

Ervin shook his head back and forth in denial. "I thought there were no secrets in this house."

That brought a laugh to all of us.

"How would it look on you?" Shelly asked me.

"I don't know. James, help me put it on." He blushed. "Over my clothes, silly." That brought another round of laughter. He stood up from the table and lowered the shells over my chest. He tried very hard not to accidentally touch my breasts. They already knew his touch, so why did it bother him now? I anticipated the thrill of a slight brush, but he was careful. I held the shells against my breasts while he tied it behind my neck, and then behind my back. I turned around and modeled it. James couldn't take his eyes off me. I kissed him lightly on the cheek. "You like this?"

"You won't wear this on my boat, I hope."

"Why not?"

"Because every man out there won't take his eyes off you, that's why."

"So you want to keep this image all to yourself?"

Ervin and Shelly laughed loudly. "James, Kaia always was an incorrigible tease," Ervin said.

And you're practicing with the voice, Shelly added in my thoughts.

I was? "James, would you take this brassiere off!"

He helped, but when he finished, he lightly kissed the back of my neck.

"Did I give you permission?"

"One good tease deserves another."

That led to more laughter. "Kaia, I think you've met your match," Ervin said.

"James is full of surprises," I said.

You deserved the kiss. He resists the voice better than most. Perhaps the Lady is right about him.

We finished dinner and gathered, as usual, in the library for some after-dinner drinks and to watch the news on television.

"Granddad, there was a second conch shell necklace in the jewelry compartment. I gave it to James to wear in case I need a second key."

"Does his work?"

"It worked for the bed."

"Oh." Ervin pulled a conch shell necklace from under his shirt. It had a rope chain like James, but his shell and chain were silver. "I wonder if mine works too. I think Shelly's shell must work because she keeps the room clean."

"I didn't know it would work for the trunk," Shelly said.

"Now we all know," Ervin said.

"Are all your mother's things hers now?" Shelly said.

"Yes, why?"

"What about the secret closet?"

"Oh, that. Show it to them when Kaia returns."

Chapter 9 - First Test

The next morning I was on my way to Alaska. James dropped me off at the airport. He gave me a brief hug and went north to begin work on Granddad's sailboat.

I took the plane to Anchorage, then a shuttle to a cabin on the bay. When I arrived, I was curious about my fellow travelers so I checked the tour list. Candice Desdemona was on it, but she wasn't on the plane. I was apprehensive all afternoon and evening. But she didn't arrive that evening. Good, I didn't want a scratching and clawing fight. I was quicker, but unlike James, I wouldn't hold myself back. I could give as well as take, especially where she was concerned. It wasn't like her to miss an opportunity for confrontation. If she skipped this trip, where was she, and what she was up to? Perhaps she's already found another guy and was working her crafty little fingers into his life. I felt sorry for him. Poor tortured soul. But maybe he deserved her? Despite the old saying, likes do attract each other where relationships are concerned.

The next morning I was on a sightseeing boat off the coast of Alaska and feeling anxious. If I thought this trip would be a pleasant and relaxing experience, I was wrong. Little fingers pricked at my mind and tactile sensations ran up and down my legs. They itched, they felt warm, and they twitched. I knew where that led. My legs, weren't acting like legs should. They forced me to concentrate. *I have legs, not a fluke. I have two legs, two knees, two ankles, and ten toes. I will not become a freak in front of all these people.* I breathed in and out slowly and concentrated on my surroundings. I desperately tried to ignore what could only be a call from the ocean.

I sat in the cabin with several people. Some were former classmates who must have booked this as a graduation present. They clustered with other students from other schools. Two passengers were on their honeymoon. Five senior citizens were present. They clung together in a clot surrounded by the boisterous teens. The boat was big compared with James' sailboat. We sat in an enclosed cabin lined with windows down each side. Benches ran down both sides of the cabin beneath the windows and across the back.

Much to my consternation, our tour guide had been speaking, but I hadn't been listening. I should. She looked like a native

Alaskan and should be a better tour guide than the non-native ones.

Toward the bow of the boat there was a separate cabin with the captain and another crew member. Doors on the starboard and port sides led out to a deck that ran along the side of the boat. The deck also surrounded the captain's cabin. There was also a bigger deck at the stern. All decks were surrounded by guardrails. So far, the weather on our sightseeing tour had favored us. The sea was relatively calm, and the skies free of clouds. Still, it remained cool on the deck, definitely jacket weather.

Liz, one of my former classmates, sat beside me on the bench and examined photos taken with her digital camera. Eric, another of our classmates, sat opposite us and reviewed the news over the Internet on his smart phone. He exclaimed, "Look, a bunch of dead fish have washed up on the Jersey shore."

"Who cares," Liz said.

"I care," I shouted without a thought. The cabin became silent and the other teens stared at me. At first I glared back, but, when my legs twitched, I turned away from them to look out the cabin window. The senior citizens looked at me with interest. The newlyweds...they were off in their own world.

Dead fish, just one more piece of evidence that the sea is dying. Not one of these people care. I felt like screaming at them but realized that wouldn't change their insensitivity. How could I change their opinion? They're my age. They should understand. She looked at the couple on their honeymoon. These teens and young adults, as well as their children, will be the first to suffer if something isn't done.

Conversation returned, but I ignored it and continued to look out the window toward the endless blue horizon of the ocean. I daydreamed about sailing toward that horizon with James, and I became lost in the dream.

Liz tapped me on the shoulder and jerked me back to reality. "What a waste of time and money," she said. "We've only seen humpbacks, and I want to see killer whales."

"Yes, where are the killer whales?" someone yelled.

That was enough. I stood up and turned toward the group. "They're orcas, not killer whales."

"Who cares what they're called," Liz said. "I just want to photograph them."

Our guide intervened. "They are properly called orcinus

orcas, but it's too early in the year for them to be here in Alaska."

That saddened me. I also yearned to see them. I reached inside my jacket and pulled out my conch shell. I must have unconsciously rubbed it. The touch soothed me. I looked back outside. The flow of water around the boat sang to me. It gurgled and splashed. The sounds became louder and the chatter of conversation diminished. Then I heard nearby humpbacks. That drew my thoughts further away from the ship.

Once again, Liz put her hand on my arm and broke my reverie. "That's a lovely shell, what is it?"

"It's a miniature conch shell."

"Are they all silver colored?"

James had a common conch shell and Granddad a silver one. What about Shelly? Her image blurred away to be replaced by the Lady of the Sea, only this time the Lady wore golden pearls and a golden shell. She smiled and I felt a deep longing for my family.

Liz interrupted my thoughts. "Hey, you tripped out or something? Your eyes went all glassy."

"Sorry," I said, "you made me think about my family."

"What has that to do with, what did you call those things...conch shells?"

I laughed out loud. "We all wear them. It's a family tradition."

James, where are you? I need you right now. I'm stuck here with the half-dead, and you're the only one who cares.

Disgusted, I turned away from Liz and looked out the window. I let myself drift with the waves until I once again heard the humpbacks. This time, I allowed myself to move up and down with the motion of their flukes as they swam. Suddenly I saw rivers of salmon moving through the sea. Sounds of echolocation flooded my ears. The salmon were chased by two orcas, a male and a female.

This time Liz shook me. "Are you all right?"

"Fine."

"You were kicking your feet together. It was kind of weird."

I panicked. *My legs, what if my legs suddenly turned into a fluke in front of all these people?* I imagined myself flopping helplessly on the cabin floor like some fool fish. I couldn't let that happen. I must learn to control the change or else avoid being with humans when the ocean calls. Human, that's what I once was, still am, at least in part. The other part of me – it's alien to everything these humans know, especially the half-dead who share this boat.

I'd had enough of the complacency of the other passengers. "Two orcas are there," I said and pointed about thirty degrees off the starboard bow.

"Who in hell do you think you are?" Liz said, before she turned to the guide and asked her, "Will we see orcas?"

"No," the guide laughed, "I already told you, it's too early."

It was my turn to laugh. "One male and one female are thirty degrees to starboard. We'll see them soon enough."

The guide replied, "I've studied orcas for years. It's unlikely they'd be here this early."

Remember, Kaia, never argue with those who can't hear and can't see. Was that the Lady's voice or just a memory of it?

I turned away from everyone and looked through the window on the starboard side. If this was a test, I was ready for it. The cabin became close and confining. I needed sea air and got up. I opened the door and walked out on the deck of the ship. With closed eyes, I pictured the male and female orca at play near and around the ship. The engines sped up and the boat turned slightly to starboard and then accelerated. I opened my eyes.

They're here.

Two orcas swiftly chased salmon off the Alaska coast.

"Why are we here, Siku? It's been days since we left our pod."

"Aga, my mate, selkies said the fish would be here."

"Good, you know I have to eat a lot before I can have a calf."

"That's why we are here.... Wait... She's calling us."

"Who?"

"The Daughter of the Sea."

"She's here?"

"We must to go to her."

"But Siku, I'm enjoying my meal."

"You know why we must go – the Lady of the Sea told us we must go to her whenever she calls."

I overheard the entire conversation as clearly as if the orcas were human and stood beside me on the deck.

Several minutes passed before the ship slowed down. It stopped and a black fin appeared above the waves. It was small at first, but as it came closer it grew in size and appeared to be about six feet above the waves.

The cabin door swung open. Most of the passengers joined me on the deck. I turned as Liz ran giddily out and tried at the same time to open her camera case. She slid on the deck and almost knocked me overboard. I smashed into the guard rail and grabbed the camera with my left hand, then caught the loose camera bag strap with my right hand. Then I steadied myself. Thank my sailor reflexes worked. If I were a landlubber, I'd probably be in the water, and the crew would have to rescue me. Then I had a horrible vision. I saw them pulling out a person half human and half sea mammal. It was terrifying. Whatever it took, I must not let that happen.

"Thanks for saving my camera," Liz said.

No apology? That's all you care about? *I almost went swimming with the orcas thanks to you.*

One orca suddenly jumped out of the ocean in front of the boat and gracefully reentered the water.

"I got the picture, look!" Liz held her camera out for me to see the preview image. "Oh look there's two." Liz said as she frantically snapped more photos.

Obviously, duh, one male and one female.

The orcas continued their play. The male dove under the boat and the boat rolled slightly from his wake. The female tried to join him, but, before she dove, he returned to her side. Then they both disappeared. Slowly the face of the male appeared above the water. I smiled at him. *Thank you for coming, Siku. Thanks for the entertaining dance.*

"See everybody," I said, "they aren't killers, they're orcas and they love to play."

Liz continued frantically snapping pictures. It irked me. *You can't capture their spirit in photographs. You have to feel it flow through you.*

"How do you tell them apart?" Liz asked.

"The taller fin is the male; the shorter and slightly curved fin is the female."

"That's right," the guide said.

"Which one is she?" Aga asked.
"The one with the black hair," Siku replied.
"What about the other one next to her."

97

"She's dumb and insensitive - like most of the two-legged."

"She's bigger than a salmon and looks like a yummy seal."

"She's not a seal, dear. We don't eat the two legged."

The orcas continued to swim around the boat. The female repeatedly raised her head in and out of the water while Liz, snapping furiously, photographed everything.

"What's that orca doing?" Liz asked.

"It's called spy hopping," the guide said.

The orcas disappeared under the water.

"Liz never learns," I whispered to myself.

The male orca returned and raised its head near Liz and then opened his mouth showing his numerous sharp teeth.

"Wow, look at that!" Liz said.

No Siku, she's not dinner.

We don't eat the two-legged, Daughter of the Sea, but she angers you. What would you have us do with her?

I noticed Liz bent over the rail taking pictures of his open mouth. *Oh the temptation!*

"Liz, back up," I said. "He's angry with you. Go inside, now!" I reached over and grabbed her camera. "I'll toss it overboard and into his mouth if you don't get inside."

"Okay, okay. I believe you. You know more about killer whales than our guide. You've been right about them so far."

Once inside, I returned the camera to Liz.

Thank you for answering my call, Siku. May the salmon be plentiful.

May the selkies prosper, Daughter of the Sea.

Both orcas rose beside the boat one last time. They spy hopped, then raised both of their tails simultaneously above the water and slowly flopped down. Then they were gone. I whispered a goodbye and felt them swim away toward the salmon. The boat turned away from the orcas and toward the shore. They rest of the passengers went inside and sat down.

"You predicted that two orcas would be here?" Liz said. "How did you know?

"I just know some things," I replied.

After the vacation, I headed home by plane, and James met me at the airport.

"I'm so glad you came to pick me up," I said.

"Did you see any orcas?"

"Yes, Aga and Siku."

"They have names?"

"It's what they called themselves. I talked with them."

"You had a conversation...with orcas?"

"More than that, they came when I called them. They called me Daughter of the Sea. Once again, that name. I thought it was a legend, but it seems to be some kind of title. I don't understand."

"Maybe the Lady of the Sea will explain."

"She seems amused by the name. I suspect it's something she wants me to learn by myself."

"You talked to her then?"

"I saw a mental image of the Lady, but this time she wore golden pearls and a golden conch shell."

"So you can talk with orcas as well as selkies?"

"Orcas are intelligent and civilized creatures. I didn't know they were telepathic, but I'm not surprised considering the size of their brains." By then we had reached the car. "You drove Orcinus?"

"I thought you'd want to drive it back home."

"Get in James. Buckle up."

"You're not going to do anything crazy are you?"

"Watch me!" I started the engine and sped out of the parking lot.

"You must have had a fun time."

"Yes and no. Liz was there. I need to get her and the other half-dead out of my system. God I detest her."

"What's her problem?"

"It's not just her. They're all insensitive. There was a fish kill, and they didn't give a damn. They thought the orcas were only an amusement. They are mammals, and they are as intelligent as man."

The Lady spoke in Kaia's mind. *Release your anger; let it melt like ice, lest it consume you.*

"Most humans don't care," James added.

"James, how do we change that? How can we get people to listen?"

We arrived home for dinner, and I thanked Granddad for the Alaskan trip. Over our meal, I told him and Shelly about the Alaska trip, my callous classmates, Liz, and the orcas: Aga and Siku.

99

When Shelly heard I had talked with the orcas, she exclaimed, "You can do it! I shouldn't have worried. Few selkies who have chosen land have the ability to talk with those of the sea. I feel better now - you can reach us anywhere and anytime."

"Shelly, the orcas addressed me as Daughter of the Sea. It's a title. I'm sure of it. What does it mean?"

"All selkies are daughters of the sea," Shelly replied.

"But Granddad told us the legend."

"It's only a legend."

"There must be more, I heard Siku say the selkies told him the salmon would be in Alaska, yet he called me Daughter of the Sea. I wasn't just another selkie."

Perhaps that's what they wish you'll become, Shelly said to me telepathically, *the Lady too.*

We finished dinner. "Kaia needs some time in the pool." Shelly said. "I'll get her ready after I settle Dad in the Library."

"I'll clear the table for you," James said. He got up and started to bus the dishes. Kaia headed for the stairway.

"James, meet me in the library when you're finished," Ervin said. Shelly left to make him comfortable in the library. Then she went upstairs to tend to Kaia.

Ervin was resting in his recliner when James finished busing the dishes. The library was one of James' favorite rooms in the house. He loved books, and the walls of the room were covered in bookcases, except for the one narrow and tall window in the center of the outside wall. The books were an eclectic mix of modern and classic stories. Many dealt with the sea. One whole section dealt with ocean science and another with sailboats, both historical and current. A model of James' Grandfathers' ship sat alone on one shelf. Next to it were two novels: *Mutiny on the Bounty* and *Men against the Sea.* Ervin's recliner faced the window. There were end tables on both sides of his recliner. Three chairs were set in a semi-circle facing his. It was his arrangement for storytelling.

"Pour us both a drink, won't you," Ervin said. "I'll have the usual."

James went to the bar and returned with two drinks. He motioned to the chairs. "Story time?"

"Not tonight, the girls are busy. Sit beside me."

James pulled up a chair next to the end table. A large common conch shell always sat in the center of that table. Ervin picked it up and held it to his ear while James sipped his brandy. Ervin set the shell down and sighed. "I'm feeling old. I yearn for the ocean, but, with these damn legs, I'm stuck on land. The ocean rolls through the shell and gives me at least a little relief."

"Like Kaia in her pool?"

Ervin shook his head in disagreement. "The shell touches the mind; the pool soothes the whole body. It's quite different."

"I thought the baths helped?"

"Not much these days. Time's slipping away, and there's too much left to do."

"But the baths refresh Kaia."

"And Shelly."

"Is there something special about the water?"

Ervin chuckled and took a sip of his drink. "So you think there's some sort of selkie magic at work. Well, there isn't. It's just plain old sea water. If you think about it, our blood is mostly sea water." He set down his drink and put on a serious face. "I talked with Charles while you cleared the table. The recording has been destroyed. If necessary, I'll confront Jake about any rumors. A scandal would hurt the company, so he'll listen."

"Thank you."

"Charles and I also talked about you and Kaia."

"Oh." James leaned back in his chair and took a long drink while he studied Ervin's face. It didn't look like he was in for a scolding. "What did he say?"

"He's concerned about the rumor and about Candi."

"You know the whole story?"

"He filled me in."

"Ervin, my reputation, Kaia's and my reputation, is spiraling downhill, certainly not the way I expected it to go. I'm innocent with Kaia, and everyone believes I'm guilty. No one said a word when I was with Candi, and she doesn't have a good reputation at all. The world's upside down."

"James, like a river or sea current, life flows in only one direction. You can't change the past, only learn and go forward."

"Just how do I do that?"

"It all depends. Are you in love with Kaia?"

The old man stared intently into James eyes. Perhaps there was something of a selkie in Ervin, James thought. He can see truth even when it's hidden. James slowly nodded his head. "Yes, perhaps

I am. I've been trying to sort out my feelings for her. Thinking of her as a sister or cousin just doesn't work. Do I care for her because of who she is, or because she's a selkie."

"You're concerned about the voice."

"Oh yes. Once you've encountered it, you never forget it. How do I know my true feelings?"

"What did you feel while you worked on my boat?"

"What has that to do with it?"

"She wasn't there - she couldn't have used the voice on you."

"I see. That's when I should be aware of my true feelings. I truly missed her."

Ervin smiled. "So you haven't committed yourself to her."

"We just haven't talked about it." He thought about his many conversations with her. *Oh, maybe we have, but I wasn't listening.* "We got to know each other when we sat together on the black rock. I know we've been thrown together by circumstance, yet I want to be around her, wherever this task takes us."

"Thanks for being honest with me, James. I've watched you grow up, and you're like a grandson to me." He reached out and put his hand on James sleeve. A tear rolled down Ervin's cheek, and he wiped it away with a sweep of his hand. "I'm sorry to have to ask this James, but is Kaia still a virgin?"

Surprise swept over James' face. He suddenly realized that Ervin was having a man-to-man talk with him. "Everyone thinks we have, but we haven't."

"Good, then we only have to deal with appearances. Keep it that way. The rumor can be squashed if she can prove she's a virgin."

"Have you talked to Kaia about this?" James said with alarm.

"No, that's why you and I are having this talk. I'd be uncomfortable telling my granddaughter she has to stay a virgin."

"You mean I have to do it? What about Shelly."

"If you care, you'll have the conversation."

Later that night, I returned to James' room to treat his wounds. He looked uncomfortable, reticent, and deep in thought. It disturbed me. *What had Granddad said to him?*

"We talked about my trip at dinner," Kaia said. "You said nothing about Granddad's boat."

That brought a huge grin. "You should see her - she's a

102

beauty. I'd like to take her for a sail someday. Do you think he'll let me?"

"Maybe if I asked him and go along to see you don't hurt her."

He looked up at me while I cleaned his cheek.

"Hurt her? Never. Well, I've finished the job for him, and I'm almost healed. Dad will need me back at the marina soon."

"Not yet! I'm still concerned about the surveillance video, aren't you?"

"Dad destroyed it, but someone else may have seen us. I'm worried what your dad might do to me."

"Granddad said he'd take care of that."

"I'm not sure your dad will listen to him. I really don't want to be beaten up."

"So you're going to dump me?"

"Dump you? Are you crazy! We're in this together. We'll continue our lessons. If we stopped, everyone will assume something really happened between us."

"So everything will be just as it was - nothing else?"

"Kaia, nothing remains the same."

"So, you agree, something has happened."

"We'll need to be very careful when we're in public. If we misstep there'll be gossip."

"Candi will gossip anyhow." Kaia said.

"So, we'll prove her wrong."

"Is that what you want - to show her nothing has happened between us?"

I noticed that James struggled to answer. He was having trouble defining our relationship. What about me? What did I expect? There was no other man I could confide in, perhaps none other I ever would be able to. We'd been thrown together by unexpected events. We would continue, but as we were before? I doubted it.

"I made a mess of things," James said. "I never should have dated Candi, but I can't undo that. I'll take my lumps. I just don't want gossip to ruin your life."

Gossip? Just what do you think our lives will be like? I'm a damn selkie. The Lady has placed demands on both of *us*. Nothing about our lives will ever be normal. *Are you ready for that, James Cersea?*

Chapter 10 - Into the Water

At breakfast the next morning, everyone except for Kaia sat around the table. Ervin and Shelly started to eat. James waited for her.

"Eat," Ervin said.

"Where's Kaia," James replied.

"She got up early and wanted poached salmon and eggs for breakfast," Shelly said.

James raised his eyebrow. "A bit unusual."

"You have that talk with her last night?" Ervin asked.

James looked at Shelly and squirmed.

"Don't worry, James, this house has no secrets."

"How can a human be at home in a house full of selkies?"

Ervin laughed. "It's easier than you think."

"Think - they can read thoughts."

"It's impolite," Shelly said. "One of those things selkies are taught not to do."

"Oh, but Kaia seems to know what I'm thinking."

Ervin gave a huge belly laugh. "Women, James, any woman, human or selkie can read a man's face. We're transparent to them and unarmed."

"Your words of advice for today."

"You'd be wise to heed them. Did you have the talk?"

"No, sir."

"Get on with it, son."

They finished with breakfast. Before Shelly cleared the table she told James that Kaia would like to see him.

"She's out of bed?" James asked.

"I dressed her," Shelly replied.

James got up from the table and turned toward the doorway.

"Remember what I said," Ervin said.

James left the room, passed through the hallway and jogged up the stairs, taking two steps at a time. When he arrived at her room, the doors to the sitting room and bedroom were open. He stopped and knocked at the bedroom door. "Kaia, may I come in?"

He heard a splash. "I've been waiting for you."

The words hung on the air like music. James peeked in. Kaia raised herself out of the water chest high and peered over the pool at him. She wore a sea blue shell bra. Rivulets of salt water ran down her chest and across the shell. She looked dazzlingly beautiful. He walked over to her.

"Nice color shells."

Kaia rolled sideways and raised her black orca fluke out of the water. *What the hell?* James thought. "How'd you grow a tail?"

"I wanted you to see me as I truly am. See, I have a fluke." She raised it out of the water and smacked it down. Water splashed over James, and he jerked backward. "I just learned to control this," Kaia said. "It's fun."

"I guess I deserved that," he said. He wiped off his face and brushed the water off his shirt.

She stared into his eyes. "Well, do you still like me, tail and all?"

He remembered his admission to Ervin. How could he tell her anything when she was being so playful? "Like you? I think it's more than like. You're special."

"Yes I am. You've never seen someone like me." Once again she waved her tail at him. He moved back to avoid being splashed.

"This isn't permanent, is it?"

"No, silly, I've learned how to switch back and forth. It's a little painful, but it works. Why?"

"Oh, the old sailor fantasy - being in love with a mermaid."

"Mermaids are part cold blooded fish - yuck! I'm not the least bit cold. I'm all mammal - one with legs or a fluke. So, do you fantasize about loving a mermaid?"

"No, just you."

"You sound serious."

"I am. I want you to be my girlfriend." He'd gotten too close, and she splashed him again.

She laughed and her laughter was strong and sensuous. "Care to swim with me?"

Again music accompanied the words. "I don't have a fluke or a suit."

"I could loan you a shell or two." James blushed, but at the same time felt a strong desire to swim with her. She continued. "Shells are so appropriate, don't you think. I'll have Shelly make you something for you. Let's see would it take two or three? Maybe four?"

He turned bright red, but she still didn't let up. "This is what it's like to be a sex object. If I wear shells, so do you."

"Kaia, obviously you're feeling better, a little cocky, but better."

She propped herself up on the side of the pool. He watched her fluke flip back and forth underwater like a cat twitching its tail while stalking a bird. "Sure you don't want to swim with me?" she said.

"It'll be a bit crowded."

"No different than a jacuzzi or a hot tub." She lifted her fluke out of the water and waved it at him. "Jealous?"

"I'm happy for you, Kaia." He reached toward the fluke. "May I touch it?"

Kaia nodded, and James ran his fingers along the side of her fluke. She laughed. "That tickles." He stopped and backed away. "No, I was just kidding. It's rather sensual."

He backed further away and stared at her. The music in her voice continued.

"I'm not using the voice."

"Are you sure of that?"

"No...I'm not sure...It's something else I need to learn."

Still the music hung on the air. At least he was aware of it.

I need to have the talk with her, James thought. Meanwhile, Kaia studied his face. He took a deep breath. "Kaia, this is a bit awkward for me. There's only one way to prove nothing sexual happened between us. You must stay a virgin. It's one way to stop this rumor before it grows out of control and destroys us."

She slapped her fluke hard on the water and splash the wall behind the pool. "That's too embarrassing, and I won't do it unless there's no other way."

"I'm sorry I mentioned it."

She dropped into the water and floated, barely moving her arms or fluke. James drew close to the pool. When he reached the side, Kaia reached out and grabbed both his arms then bent backwards, rolled over, and pulled James into the pool. He came up spitting water. She wrapped her fluke around his legs and kicked. He went under again and pulled himself back up.

"That's enough," he said. "How can I go downstairs dripping wet?"

"I'll call Shelly to bring a towel when I'm ready for you to leave."

The music in her voice became intense to James. She put her arms around his head and pulled him close. He responded with a kiss. He stood on the bottom of the pool and wrapped his arms around her. She wrapped her fluke around his legs. They fell beneath the water and he felt the roughness of the shell bra through his shirt. They kissed a long time underwater then broke the surface to breathe.

"How do you stand the shell bra? It's so rough."

"It's padded on the inside."

"So it can chafe on the outside. My chest will be raw if we keep this up."

"Are you suggesting I take it off?"

She kissed his neck, unbuttoned his shirt and then moved downward to his chest. "Is this where I chafed you?"

"Kaia...stop...virgin... remember."

"I'm only playing, playing, playing," she sang.

James recognized the musical tones of a selkie. He could not resist her words. She called him and he was enraptured and enthralled. He grabbed her in a tight embrace. Suddenly, she pushed him away.

"James, I'm sorry. I didn't know I used the voice. Forgive me."

"Forgive what?" he said as he started to untie her bra.

"Out of the water, NOW."

He got out and dripped water on her carpet. "I don't know what got into me."

"I do. I'm so sorry. It's my fault. Now I understand what selkies do to males."

"Kaia, I forgive you. I wanted it too, but I promised to control myself."

"James, that's why this is so difficult. I must control myself and not let the selkie control me, and you through me." She looked at him dripping wet, a puddle forming around his feet. She pointed to the bathroom. "Inside's a towel. You can undress and borrow my robe."

She waited until he closed the door and then transformed back to human form. Getting her legs back was easy now that she knew the trick. But she was naked from the waist down. She grabbed the towel she'd laid by the headboard and wrapped it around her. A few minutes later, James appeared in her white terrycloth robe. He'd wrapped his wet clothes in a plastic bag.

"Go to your room and change," Kaia said. "I'll meet you downstairs."

"How about a picnic by the black rock," he suggested.

"Are you asking me out on a date?"

He looked at her and smiled.

A date. We were actually going to have a date. I wondered what it would be like to swim in the ocean with my fluke. I was about to find out.

This time we packed salmon and a metal pan to cook a late lunch over a bonfire. We rummaged through the pantry and added a bag of toasted chips and salsa with some cookies for dessert. James arranged everything neatly in a picnic basket with plates, silverware, cooking utensils and a several bottles of water. I went to the wine cooler and returned with a bottle of Riesling and two glasses. We said our good-byes to Ervin and Shelly. When we got to the circular drive, we fought over who would drive. I won as usual and drove Orcinus.

It was a beautiful sunny day with only a trace of clouds in the sky. Traffic was light and the drive up the coast, relaxing. We parked in our usual place, out of sight from the road. James took my hand, and we walked hand in hand all the way to the shore. He carried our blanket, towels, and the lunch box in his other hand.

Is this what it feels like to have a boyfriend, I wondered. He fits into my life the way my hand fit into his.

We spread the blanket next to the tree trunk. James walked the shore to gather driftwood for the fire while I sat on the blanket and prepared to cook lunch. Once he had a neat pile of driftwood, he added some kindling and lit it with a paraffin fire-starter. "From my charcoal grill," he said.

It took a while for the fire to burn down to coals. While we waited, James opened the bottle of wine and we drank, saluting the day, the ocean, the black rock, and being together. After the fire was ready, we began to cook. We talked about my sailing lessons, my parents, selkies, but most of all what we might do to stop my parents from polluting the ocean. Every proposal was more preposterous than the last. Not one of them had a chance to be successful.

After the meal, we cleaned up, repacked the picnic basket, and bagged our trash. Then James picked up the blanket, and we moved to the black rock. Curiously, there was a single common conch shell sitting on the rock. It was the image from the text messages. "Was that there when we arrived?" James asked.

"It must have been."

James picked it up and held it to his ear. At first he heard the sea rumble. Then he heard the sound of drums. Strings and flutes joined them. It was like the music in Kaia's bedroom. What the hell, James thought. The sounds became more demanding. He started to dream. There was a fleet of ships with square sails and rows of oars....

Kaia, take the shell from him, NOW. The Lady said in her mind.

"James, give me the shell," I said. *Did I just use the voice? That's right, you have.*

He handed the shell to me, and his vision stopped. When I took it in my hands, I began to hear the drums and flutes. I had a vision of a seal morphing into an orca.

You're not yet ready for the Shell of Knowing. Put it back.

I recognized the command voice of the Lady and carefully set the shell back on the black rock.

"What is it?" James said.

"It's a selkie thing. The Lady called it the Shell of Knowing."

"Knowing what?"

"The truth I guess."

"Why'd you put it back."

"She said we weren't ready for it."

He looked longingly at the shell. "This is like the temptation in the Garden of Eden. What did you see? I saw ships. I think I imagined the fleet that sailed to the Trojan War."

"Wishful thinking, or knowing?" she asked.

"If it's the Shell of Knowing then there must be some truth in it. What about you?"

"I saw a seal morph into an orca. For some reason that bothered the Lady. I felt it was most urgent. She did not want me to learn more."

James reached for the shell. I grabbed his hand. "I want to know the truth too, but she said we weren't ready. We aren't. Let's not be like Adam and Eve." He pulled his hand back.

"Then why did she leave the shell here?"

"To tempt us? I don't know."

There is one who must take the shell when she is finally

ready, the Lady said.

We needed to get away from the rock and the shell. "Let's go for a swim," I suggested.

The sea had calmed, but waves still washed around the rocks. James considered it. This was not the best place to swim. It was a bit dangerous.

"You wore your suit, didn't you?" I asked. He started to take off his pants. "You better have."

"What did you think? Where's your suit?"

"I wore my top."

"And?"

"I'm going to wear my fluke."

"You're not going to transform in front of me, are you?"

"Politely turn around until I'm in the water."

"Must I?"

"Do I need to use the voice?"

"Can you?"

"Yes. I did it to you moments ago."

He turned around, and I walked toward the ocean. When I told him he could join me, he turned back. I'd left my clothing lay near the surf line. I was already beyond the surf and flipped my fluke at him. He looked at the breaking water and the rocks. I waved back at him. He moved over to the mouth of the creek where there were fewer rocks and a sandy bottom. He waded out into the water to join me.

Five selkies appeared in the water in front of him. They all wore black conch shells and pointed their tridents at him. He backed up and they came forward, forcing him back on shore.

"Whoa ladies, she invited me here."

"It's okay, he's my boyfriend," I said.

Not until the Lady of the Sea says so. It's our duty to protect the Daughter of the Sea.

"I don't need protection from James."

He's your toy then?

Despite myself, I laughed.

"What?"

"They asked if you were my boy toy."

"Is that what selkies think of males?"

"I don't know. It's not what I think of you."

"Tell them to go away."

"They won't. They say it's their duty to protect me."

"From me? Ask the Lady."

I reached out into the ocean. First I felt the surf, then the swells. The currents swept me across the ocean. Then I felt the Lady. *Why?*

You chose. He has yet to choose. I cannot trust him until he does.

But I want to swim with him.

And where will that lead?

He promised not to.

Is that enough?

Yes.

You trust more than I. Candi was in his thoughts when we met.

That's over and done.

Is it? He must choose, and he must commit before I will call back the guard.

Watch. I made sure I didn't use the voice. "James, would you turn around so I can come back out of the ocean?"

James turned around. I walked out of the surf and put my clothes back on.

See, I said.

We will see, the Lady replied.

"You can turn back now, James."

The selkies were gone.

"What was that all about?"

"The Lady doesn't trust you. She said you must choose, and you must commit."

"To what?"

"She didn't say."

"Boy, that's helpful! So they only time we can swim together is in a swimming pool?"

"I wouldn't count on the guard not showing up."

The next morning Shelly showed us the secret of the closet in my bedroom. It looked like a normal walk-in closet with clothes hanging on both sides. The back wall had been built of red cedar. Shelly led us inside and removed her necklace. It was the first time I'd seen it. The chain around the conch shell contained a string of black pearls. Her conch shell was solid black.

"You're no ordinary selkie," I said.

"I'm a selkie, Kaia. All selkie's wear a conch shell necklace."

"Still, you're no ordinary selkie."

"Selkie blood runs in your veins. You're no ordinary human."

"You wear the black conch shells like the selkies in the bedroom mural," James said. "Those selkies that chased me out of the water wore them too. Kaia's great-grandmother even had a set."

"Shelly, what do the black pearls and shells mean?"

Shelly looked at both of us. She acted like she didn't want to answer.

"Is it some kind of secret?" I asked.

"No." She turned away to face out the closet doorway at the bed and the mural behind it. When she spoke, it was a whisper. "Those who wear the black are the Queen's guards."

"But they guard me too."

"You are the Ambassador."

"I think it's more than that."

Shelly turned quickly away. She obviously didn't want to say more. She shoved her conch shell against a knot hole. The back wall swung inward, and Shelly pushed on the open end until the doorway was open. We entered a large attic room. It held eleven sea chests and a set of twin beds covered in dusty sheets. There were boxes of books and a wooden box of very old National Geographic magazines. Another cedar closet was adjacent to the doorway to the room. I opened its door. A number of formal gowns hung off one wall in storage bags. The other wall had a rack with conch shell bras of various colors and configurations.

Formal wear, one for land, one for sea. Okay, I get it.

James interrupted my reverie. "You said you had to go home tonight for a birthday party. We still don't know how to get into the bottom of the sea chest."

"You're right. Let's work on that."

"Kaia, wouldn't you like to try on one of the dresses?" Shelly said.

I ran my fingers over the nearest dress. It was soft and silky. I ran my hands over several of them. Each dress was more beautiful than the last. Yes, I wanted to try one on. "James, would you mind waiting for us in my sitting room? Work on the sea chest by yourself."

James left, and I picked out a pale blue full length dress.

Shelly carried it into the bedroom. Then I picked out matching shoes. I joined Shelly, and she helped me dress. The gown fit perfectly around my chest, my waist, and was the right length. The shoes fit too.

"It looks like it was tailored just for you," Shelly said.

"Am I that much like Great-Grandmother?"

"More than you realize. Let me fix your hair."

When we finished, Shelly left for a moment and returned with the string of black pearls from the chest. I had left them in my dresser. She hung them around my neck. I looked at myself in the mirror.

"Gorgeous," Shelly said, "just like Grandmother."

A little lip gloss finished the job.

James waited in the sitting room while Kaia dressed. Before he could work on the sea chest, he was interrupted by a phone call from his father. He was needed at the marina that evening to help with security during the party. He was still talking to his father when Kaia walked into the sitting room. He closed his phone and gaped at her. Kaia watched his eyes sweep over her body and turned around to model the gown for him. He remained speechless.

"Isn't she beautiful?" Shelly said.

He walked over to Kaia. "You're beautiful in a way I've never..."

"You've only seen me in my jeans and bathing suit, never as a lady."

"You can say that again." A lady, he thought. What was it his father had said about a lady? Yes, Kaia looked every bit a lady, was a lady. He thought of her as both a lady and his girlfriend. I took him several moments to gather his thoughts. "I've got bad news. Dad called. I need to be at the marina tonight."

"When must you leave?"

"Soon."

"Then we'd better try to open the bottom of the chest."

"Shouldn't you change?" Shelly asked.

"I'd like Granddad to see me in this gown."

James opened the chest with his conch shell and tipped back the lid. Kaia reached down and easily lifted the tray out of the chest.

"How did you do that?" Shelly asked

"I don't know," Kaia said.

"Something's different," James added.

"I closed the jewelry compartments before I went to bed."

"That must be it. When the lids are open they engage a lock."

"Let's not put the tray back. We can try the lock after we examine the trunk."

The bottom of the chest held a strange assortment of items. On top of an assortment of rocks were a large round box and a leather bound journal. There were also carved pieces of driftwood in the shape of porpoise, orcas, and various types of whales and fish. Shelly picked up one of the rocks. "Orkney Island," she said.

"How do you know?" Kaia asked.

"I went there to live in the selkie home waters after I made my choice."

Kaia lifted the journal. It was secured by a black leather band. It had a conch shell seal but no keyhole. Kaia toyed with it and tried her conch shell. It wouldn't open.

"Another mystery," James said.

Shelly lifted out the sculptures. "I remember these. Grandma used them to teach us about the creatures that inhabit the sea. Those were such sweet days."

James reached in and withdrew the box. He unbuckled it and lifted out a black pearl tiara with silver highlights. "That's just what your outfit needs." He stood up and placed it on her head. Shelly rearranged her hair behind her ear. "Go look at yourself in the mirror."

Kaia walked to the mirror, and James stood behind her. She saw herself and imagined she was a princess. Then she looked at his reflection, and his image shimmered. It twisted and reformed. He reappeared in ancient leather armor. She felt a sea breeze and saw behind him a square sailed ship with multiple oars on both sides.

"Let's show Ervin," he said and broke the spell. They went downstairs into the library, and she modeled it for Ervin.

"You're a beautiful granddaughter, Kaia, a lady, definitely suiting your rank as the selkie Ambassador."

Kaia made a brief curtsy to Ervin. He smiled and turned towards James. "Charles just called. I know you have to leave, but before you go I'd like to hire you again. Would you upgrade the battery system on my sailboat to power the refrigerator?"

"How much do you want to spend?"

"I've already ordered the batteries."

"How soon do you need it?"

"Soon. It's best to be prepared. Leave your clothing. Rest assured you'll be back. I'll have Shelly wash them."

"In that case, I should leave now."

"So soon?" Kaia asked.

"Dad needs me for security. I originally was supposed to be a guest."

"You planned to take Candi, I suppose." I regretted the question as soon as I asked it.

His eyes flickered a moment, then he turned toward me and smiled. "That was before. In that dress, you'd be the envy of every guy. I'd ask you to accompany me tonight, but that would only add to the rumors."

"If Candi's there, things are going to turn out bad, even in my absence. James, I want to go with you, but my parents scheduled a birthday party for me tonight. Granddad, is there any way for me to skip going home."

"No, I can only go so far against your parent's wishes."

"Don't worry," James said, "Grant will keep me safe." He turned and walked toward the front door. I hurried after him and grabbed his hand. Ervin came behind in his wheelchair.

"Call me if you need me," I said. James turned and gave me a hug. I returned it.

"Hmmm," Ervin said, and we broke apart.

"He's my boyfriend, Granddad."

"So soon?"

"Really, Ervin, that's the way it is," James said.

"There are no secrets in this house," Ervin said.

"There are nothing but secrets in this house," James retorted, and everyone laughed at the truth of his statement. Just before James entered his car, he turned toward me.

"We still have a lesson tomorrow, don't we?" Kaia asked.

"Bright and early."

Chapter 11 - Parties

I drove Orcinus home for the birthday party I dreaded. My home, what a joke, I hadn't lived at home since elementary school. Most summers had been spent with Granddad and the rest of the time at boarding school. The new house isn't even the house I grew up in. When Mom and Dad moved, they casually tossed away my childhood and left me in a sterile empty home. My past life and past house were long gone. They existed now only in dreams, intangible, things I reached for but could never touch, in a way forbidden. I felt it before I met the Lady, but she had been warning me since my twelfth birthday. I'm still on land, but in my heart, I'm a selkie. Only the sea could be my true home. This house...their house, has become a prison and the gateway to hell. I no longer have much in common with Mom and Dad, save blood, and even that is getting thin. In their latest endeavor, my parents made it clear they are enemies of my kind and the sea.

It's their home, not mine. Oh sure, I still have a bedroom, and it is filled with my things. Stuffed toys and childhood treasures represented my past, but I'm no longer a child. The things I hold dear are elsewhere, on the seashore and in the upstairs bedroom in Granddad's house. His house, my home, is the only land bound home I ever want to know. I am restless now, like the sea, uncomfortable in familiar places, ready to move on to someplace, anyplace else, certainly not here.

I parked Orcinus in the five car garage next to Dad's Mercedes. When I got out, Bill the Stalker watched me from the doorway. He had the same evil grin he always wore when Mom and Dad weren't around. I finally had to admit it might not be entirely his fault. I'm part selkie, and the selkie in me might make me irresistible to men, even jerks like Bill. If that's the case, how do I drive this repulsive slug away?

Bill watched me get out of the car. He grinned widely and marched toward me with a gleam in his eye. "I don't have any bags," I said. "Go tell Mom and Dad I'm home for the party." Bill stopped. His grin disappeared. *So, he doesn't like taking orders from me.* He paused - stood there motionless. I became impatient. "Do I have to repeat myself?" Maybe it was the tone of my voice. Maybe it was something more. Did I use the voice on him? His face became a mask of confusion. Then he turned around and entered the house. Thank God, at least I can get past Mr. Paws.

I entered the dining room without incident. Bill stood behind my mother, Lana, and near the kitchen door. He leered at the young maid who carried a platter of meat to the table.

"She's new," I said.

"They don't last long," Lana replied. "It's so difficult to get decent help these days."

I watched Bill while I talked with Mom. He smiled at me while he patted the maid on the rear. She jerked. It was clear why the help doesn't last, Bill drives any decent one away. It's comforting to know I'm not the only object of his ... attention. Then Bill pinched the maid while he stared at me. The maid squirmed but managed not to drop the platter. This charade was all for my benefit. Mom and Dad were oblivious as usual.

"Come, give your Mommy a big hug," Lana said.

I walked over to her and let her wrap her arms around me. I remained limp. *I'm not the daughter you wanted. I should be sorry, but I no longer care.* I extracted myself from Mom, walked over to Dad and gave him a big hug.

"It's good to have you home again," he said. "My you've grown. You're eighteen now. That's wonderful."

"Yeah, Dad, I'm an adult now. I can make my own choices." Did he understand the ordeal I had just gone through? I held out my hope, but he didn't react.

"You'll always be my little girl," Lana said.

I still hugged Dad. I rolled my eyes. He smiled back.

"Dear, Kaia's a young lady now."

I turned around and saw Mom frown. *Thanks, Dad, for your support.*

"We would have invited some of your friends to your party," Lana said, "but we don't know any of them. I hope you don't mind spending this occasion with us."

Jake continued the thought. "I invited my old friend Charles and his son James, but they have a party of their own tonight."

"That was thoughtful, Dad."

"Yes, James," Lana said with a hint of sarcasm. "How are your lessons going?"

Oh wonderful, has she heard the rumors? "I'm learning lots,"

I said. It seemed the appropriate thing to say until I realized it could be taken many ways. Mom frowned.

Bill left while we ate. Mom started the conversation on ocean dumping. I wondered if she did it to antagonize me. The Dad talked about his overseas conquest and how much money they could make when they encapsulated the world's toxic trash and then deposited it in the ocean depths.

I remembered what Granddad said and tried, very hard, to ignore my feelings. The more he talked, the more difficult it became. I was about to lose it.

"Are you sure it's safe?" I asked as calmly as I could.

Lana set down her fork and glared at me. "Are you questioning your father?"

"No, Mom, I'm questioning the safety of the enterprise."

"What's got into you," Lana said, "You've never been disrespectful before."

"Mother, there's too much at stake here."

"Your father knows what he's doing."

"Does he? And if we poison the sea, what then? It'll be too late to say we're sorry."

"Kaia, stop this right now," Lana said. "The enterprise you question supports your lifestyle."

"I'd rather be poor and know the sea is safe."

This time Lana started to rise from the table, but Jake motioned her to sit.

"Kaia, I'm not rash," Jake said. "We've spent years researching the safety of the encapsulation technology. There is so little land and so much sea. My scientists say it's safe."

"Have you tested it?"

"We've put it thorough years of accelerated laboratory tests."

"But you haven't tested it in the ocean."

"Kaia you're naïve. I can't wait until everyone agrees the technology is safe. Then I will have too many competitors. That's just the way business is. We make our profits by acting before our competition is ready."

"And if you are wrong, then everything in the sea suffers."

"Do you think we haven't made a risk analysis? The sea's a big place and any hazardous waste would remain highly localized."

"I suppose you tested that too?"

"Stop this," Lana said. "You will not question our business

decisions."

"Granddad can," I blurted out. "He can make you listen."

Lana rose from her chair and stood over me. "What's gotten into you? Is it James? Is he responsible for your disrespect?"

"James has nothing to do with this," I retorted. "I care about what happens to the sea." I turned toward Dad. "You should too."

"I do care," Jake said. "Why don't you believe it's safe?"

"I know it isn't, Dad. I just know it. I can feel the pain."

Lana started to laugh. "That's your reason - you just feel it. You lack facts and, of course, feelings trump the science. Grow up, Kaia." She went back to her chair and sat.

"How about a cake and Kaia's present," Jake said. He motioned to the serving girl who returned moments later with a cake lit with eighteen candles. She set it in front of me, and I blew out all the candles.

"What did you wish," Lana asked.

"That Dad would listen to reason."

"That will be enough," Lana said. "Perhaps you'd like your present." She handed me a long skinny package, one skillfully wrapped and tied with golden ribbons. I opened it and set it on the table. I tried to hold back my tears.

"I know how you like orca's," Lana said. "It's a whale bone carved into the shape of an orca."

"It's horrible!" I stood up. Lana slapped me hard across my face. I turned and fled for the door. Jake stood up and grabbed Lana's hand.

"I'm leaving. I'll be with Granddad until I go to college."

Lana started after me, but Jake held her tightly and turned her toward him. "Let her go," I heard him say.

I left.

Jake and Lana continued their conversation after Kaia left.

"Stop this, Lana. I was eighteen when I ran away from home. I had a fight much like this with Dad. She's her own person now. You'll only get her back with honey."

"I can't stand her being disrespectful. Look at everything we've done for her."

"She's just going through her rebellious stage. Give her time, Lana. She'll come around."

"I'll convince her, Jake."

"Lana, she's not one of your girls. She's your daughter. She needs your love, not threats. Don't you dare act rashly."

Lana hugged Jake, "Of course, dear, but Kaia's not the sweet innocent child you think she is. I've received word that Kaia spent the night with James on his boat."

"She's an adult, Lana. Charles is my friend. I'm sure there was a good reason."

"She had sex with him, Jake, I just feel it. It's behind her disrespect."

"Now you're talking just like her. Where's the facts?"

"Don't you care?"

"Of course I do. At least she's not doing it with some low-life."

"She should wait until marriage."

"Did we? Or don't you remember?

"She's our daughter, Jake. Would you be happy with James as a son-in-law?"

"Yes I would."

"Need I remind you that Kaia will inherit the company? She needs someone who can run it. Do you think James will be capable?"

"He's got degrees in engineering and business. I'd say with some experience..."

"Please...let me introduce her to some up and coming executives."

"Just as long as you let her make her own choice." He pointed his finger at her. "So your dislike for James was behind your scheduling this party at the same time as the marina party."

"Dear, would I do a thing like that?"

"Yes. May I remind you, she's our daughter, and Charles is like a brother to me. Don't treat me or Kaia this way again."

Charles Cersea sat behind his desk at the marina and watched the security monitors on the opposite wall. He looked over at James who sat in a chair beside the desk. They watched the guests arrive and made sure the boats stayed secure.

"When I started this business," Charles said, "we didn't need security cameras or security staff. Boating people were respectful of each other."

"Most of them still are."

He nodded in agreement. "But we need to protect them from those who aren't. I know you planned to attend the party tonight. I'm sorry, but I need you here. You were going to bring Candi, weren't you?"

"Dad, if it weren't for the circumstances, I would have asked Kaia to accompany me."

"Really?"

"We've gotten close over the last two weeks. You should have seen her in one of her Great-Grandmother's formal dresses."

"Oceana's?"

"You've met her?"

"Of course. I was raised in her house. She was a beautiful lady, Son. Kaia reminds me a great deal of her."

"So you wouldn't object if I dated her?"

"Don't rush things. You need to get this Candi thing behind you first."

"Dad, I want your approval because I'm worried about what Kaia's father would say."

"Jake, well, we still meet for lunch occasionally. I suspect it would be alright with him, but Lana will be a problem. She probably already has plans to marry Kaia off to some rich and useful person."

"Dad, arranged marriages went out with the dark ages."

"Not according to Lana."

Charles returned to the monitors. "We'll talk about this later. There are too many guests and strangers here tonight. I don't trust all of them, the strangers especially. People will get drunk and act badly."

I laughed. "When I was sixteen, you wouldn't let me attend. The next morning I found a halter top on the floorboards of my boat. I can guess what happened there during the night."

"Things like that occurred, still do, but things didn't get stolen or damaged."

"Maybe so, Dad, but if the halter top was left behind, what did she do, sneak about topless?"

"She'd get caught on camera these days. Son, I've got the docks and parking lot covered tonight. I need you and Grant inside. You'll probably only have to deal with a few drunks. If anything significant happens, I can turn over the surveillance recordings to the police."

Something on the monitors caught my attention. "Wait, Dad, there's Candi." We watched her enter the bar on the arm of a marine.

"That's Ken Worth with her," Charles said, "he's just back from overseas."

"His dad has that huge yacht. Dad, I was a fool. Candi goes for the money, doesn't she?"

"Well, you've finally learned to look at her with more than your dick."

Ouch.

We focused our attention on Candi. "Shouldn't we ask Grant to keep an eye on her?" The words were barely out of my mouth when Candi suddenly turned around. She momentarily left her date. We picked her up on another monitor when she joined a conversation with two seated men. She talked with them for nearly a minute and then turned back toward the camera. She mouthed the words, "Bastard."

"What's that all about?" I said.

"Looks like trouble. You better go talk to those two." He tossed me an ear-piece. "Join Grant on the floor. I'll listen. If she causes any trouble, I'll have her escorted out."

The office was located behind the bar and down a hallway that contained the bathrooms. I left the office. A drunk staggered into me and bumped me into the wall. I maneuvered around him and got past the bar. Grant saw me. I pointed to Candi, and Grant moved toward her. Candi was surrounded by several women. She talked to them with agitated arm motions. Grant screened me from Candi's view, and I made my way across the floor to the two men I'd seen talk to her.

"Gentlemen," I said when I arrived. "Candice was just here and had a conversation with you. It seemed to upset her. We don't want problems. What did you talk about?"

They looked at each other and then back at me. Neither spoke. They turned again to each other and then tried to engage in a conversation with another guest. A fourth guest, a stranger, got up and walked over to me.

"I overheard them," he said. "They gossiped about this fellow James. He apparently had Kaia Stone on his boat overnight. She's under age isn't she?"

Oh shit, I thought and turned away from him. "Dad, did you hear that. We've got big trouble."

"Get off the floor, immediately."

I rushed toward the bar. From nowhere a hand grabbed my shoulder and spun me around. I briefly recognized Candi's face before she slapped me. My head hit the bar, and I fell on the floor.

"You had Kaia on your boat before you broke up with me. What's she got that I don't?"

"She was injured. I took care of her until morning, and then drove her to her grandfathers, nothing more."

By this time, Grant had his hands on Candi's shoulder. "You need to leave, Now!"

Candi's date took hold of her hand. "Come on Candi, this party isn't fun anymore."

"That's right, James, throw me out of your club."

I got up and turned around. The room was suddenly silent. Everyone stared at me.

"It's the truth, everyone. Kaia was injured. Her grandfather asked me to watch over her until the morning. I did - nothing more. You can check with him if you like. Stop this stupid gossip."

I turned and stomped toward the office.

Dad wasted no time. As soon as the door closed he began. "That was a real bone-head mistake denying everything in front of everybody. Stupid...stupid...stupid. That guarantees everyone will talk about it and nothing else. They'll gossip about it. And gossip takes on a life all its own. It no longer matters what you did or didn't do. What matters is the gossip and who hears it." He pointed his finger at me and waved it wildly. "You will take a course in public relations when you go back to college and you will get an A. Is that clear?"

There was no use to argue.

"You stay here and watch the monitors. I'll go out on the floor to salvage what I can."

I sat down at Dad's desk and watched. People were gathered in groups, and they were all talking, gossiping I supposed. There was nothing I could do about it. Dad appeared on the monitors. He approached one group. They stopped talking and began to listen to him. Soon people were nodding. Then Dad went to another group. He spent the next hour moving around the floor and talking with the members and guests.

Meanwhile, Grant had to escort a couple of drunks to the door and ensure they had someone to drive them home or else get someone to walk them to their boats to sleep it off.

Dad didn't return to the office until midnight, when the party began to break up. "I did what I could. I told everyone I'd talked with Kaia's grandfather and that you were only following his instructions. And you'd driven her to his house in the morning. Now take care. We must put this rumor to bed."

I moved to the chair next to his desk, and he took his usual place behind it. We sat in silence as he carefully watched the remaining people leave. Finally, everyone had left, and Dad told Grant to go home.

"I think it worked," Dad said. "Now get to your boat and get a good night's sleep. You've got a sailing lesson in the morning." In all the excitement, I'd forgotten about it. "With Kaia," he said. "You'll be watched. Make sure you two behave."

I left the office and walked slowly down the dock toward my boat. I was totally sober - security doesn't drink, especially at parties. I felt like a cold beer, but it was too late for that. The marina was sound asleep. Most of the lights in the parking lot had been turned off, and the windows of all the boats were dark. The soft clang of ropes against rigging was the only sound I heard. It was music to my ear but a nuisance to many others. I got onboard my boat and checked the bungees that kept my ropes from clanging against the mast. Then I went down the steps into the galley.

I flipped on the light in the galley. It was a warm and humid night, so I stripped down to my underwear. Then I turned off the light, opened the door to my bedroom, and crawled into bed. The covers moved. I tried to stand but bumped my head on the low ceiling.

"James?"

"Kaia? What are you doing here?"

"I ran away from home. I thought it would be okay to stay here tonight."

"No, no that won't work. You've got to leave." I knew as soon as the words came out of my mouth that wouldn't work. "No, stay. Your car's in the lot?"

"Yes."

"I hope no one will notice."

"What's wrong?"

"Just about everything." I told Kaia what had happened at the party. "If anyone sees you leave there will be no end to the gossip."

Kaia told me what happened at her birthday party.

"So we each had another memorable evening," I said.

"But we're together," she said.

That gave us both a weak laugh but didn't resolve our problem. A little light from the parking lot came in through the portholes. "Are you in your underwear?" Kaia asked.

"What do you think?"

"Me too – t-shirt and panties."

"But you're under the sheets, I'm not. I'll sleep in the galley. I'm setting the alarm for five o'clock. We'll leave under the cover of darkness."

Kaia patted the bed. "Be comfortable...sleep with me."

"Kaia, things are bad enough. Shelly told me to be careful about your voice, and I made promises to Ervin and Dad. Please understand, I can't lie down next to you." *Sleep next to her in our underwear!* Not now, not after what happed earlier tonight. She's a selkie. Did she use her selkie voice to invite me to bed? How would I know? She'd be warm. She'd be up against me. I'd feel her even if I rolled over with my back to her. I knew where that would lead.

"Get some sleep," I said. "We'll creep out of the harbor before anyone wakes." Then, I left for the galley and slipped into some light cotton lounging pants.

Chapter 12 - Lessons

Neither James nor Kaia got much sleep that night. Both were troubled - Kaia, by her parents' insensitivity and James, by yet another encounter with Candi. Images of the day spun around in their minds and tormented their rest. James woke early. His body demanded sleep, but that was out of the question. He knocked on the cabin door and persisted until Kaia woke. Dawn was a few hours away. They dressed, went quietly up on deck, and carefully released the mooring lines. James turned on the battery powered motor, and they slipped out into the harbor with a minimum of noise. They weren't completely alone. Some of the fishing boats also headed out. They could make out the running lights of other boats and reasoned that, other than their running lights, there was little to distinguish them from any other boat. They were out of the harbor and in the ocean before the sun rose.

Candi didn't sleep well either. She spent the night fuming and contemplating revenge. She knew Kaia had a sailing lesson scheduled for the morning and wanted to make another scene. All lessons by the staff were posted on the staff board. She had checked it the previous evening before she and her date left. She arose at eight o'clock, rolled away from her date and dressed. Then she went up on the deck of his father's yacht. It was moored only a few docks away from where James kept his boat. She took a quick look down the docks. James boat was missing. Damn, she thought, Kaia's already with him. She felt the anger swell and grimaced. *Just wait until the two of you get back!*

James and Kaia motored at a slow pace off shore. They ate a cold breakfast in the cockpit while the boat drifted and watched the sun rise. It was time to set sail. James turned the power back on and steered the boat into the wind.

"Time to graduate," he said. "You're in charge today, Captain."

"Then heave to it and get the mainsail up."

"Yes Captain, sir."

I scowled at him. "Get serious, we're being watched."

"I took care of that last night."

"Really, somehow everyone seems to think I'm guilty of something."

"We are, ...they think we're guilty."

She looked at the fishing boats. Many had moved uncomfortably close and other pleasure boaters were on their way out of the harbor in their powered boats. There were no other sailboats out this early.

"In case you haven't noticed, everyone is watching," Kaia said. "So behave yourself."

"I always behave myself."

"Right, I seem to remember someone's picture fastened to your bedroom door."

"It's past. It's done. Forget it."

"Maybe for you, but what about Candi? Is it over for her too? She slapped you last night. That means she still cares."

"Cares, she's probably already sleeping with someone else."

"That could be her form of revenge."

Kaia let him think about that for a while. While she did, she set sail on a port reach heading further out into the ocean. Some of the power boats followed. The breeze was brisk but not overly strong. It would have been a great day for sailing except for Kaia's foul mood. The boat moved up one wave and down another as it sliced through the water. A fleet of fishing boats floated near the western horizon. Everywhere they sailed they seemed to be accompanied by a fleet of boats.

"They're watching us with binoculars, aren't they?" James said.

Kaia gave him the 'why yes' look. "Then let's sail up the coast toward where Granddad keeps his boat."

"You're the captain."

"Then ease out the lines, mate."

"You're letting this go to your head, aren't you?"

"Hey, this is my lesson. I'm in charge today."

"Yes, Sir, Captain Sir."

Candi continued to sit on the deck of the yacht and seethe.

127

There was nothing she could do at the moment except to plan her revenge. There were so many ways she could punish Kaia - so many ways to get James back. *How mean should I be?* She was in the middle of plotting when someone caught her attention. Toward the dock where James kept his boat, a stocky looking guy appeared. He walked toward the spot where James kept his boat. Candi lifted the binoculars and watched him. He wasn't dressed for the marina and looked totally out of place. The way he was built, and the way he acted reminded Candi of someone who had military training. Maybe he was a security guard. She continued to watch. He walked out to where James kept his boat and looked out at the ocean. She clearly saw him mouth, "shit." He turned around and headed toward the clubhouse.

Now that's interesting, she thought. What's his connection?

James and Kaia sailed miles up the coast. They had taken turns napping to make up for the lost sleep of the previous night. They were now far from the rocky shoreline.

"Remember," James said, "We have to tack back, so leave plenty of time."

"We're offshore from the Black Rock, aren't we?"

"First rule, check your charts before you go sailing."

"Okay, I studied them. I know there's a reef a quarter mile off shore."

"Okay, good job."

Kaia looked out to sea and searched from shore to horizon.

"Looking for something?" James asked.

"See any orcas?"

"You think the selkies are someplace around here?"

"I think I'd know it if they were, James"

"Another selkie secret?"

"I dreamed about the Black Rock for years before I spent the evening there. In my dreams, it was always a mysterious place. There was always someone just outside my vision. I originally thought it was the Lady. Now I think it was you."

"I didn't have a choice to make."

"But you did, you agreed to go there with me."

"I did, didn't I? What would have happened if I hadn't gone?"

"I would have become lost. Without you, I couldn't have

chosen."

"Why me?"

"I don't really know. It just is."

For Kaia, it was an admission that she wasn't as perfect as she thought.

They sailed further north, but now they watched the shore. Nothing was unusual. Gulls winged in and out. No whales of any sort were visible. They moved along in silence with the wind blowing their hair, the sounds of the wave striking the bow of the boat, and the light creaking of the rigging.

James broke their silence. "If I had asked you, would you have gone to the party with me last night?"

"I can imagine what the rumors would have been like if I had. Could you imagine me in a fight with Candice? It wouldn't have been pretty for either of us. That's what would have happened. You would have been forced to throw us both out. Think what the rumors would be then."

"If there were no rumors, would you have?"

"James, wise up, I can't escape being a selkie, and we can't escape the rumors."

"Look, I understand all of that. Can we put that behind us? You're my girlfriend. I'd like to know if you would have gone with me."

He was right, but he was also wrong. There was no way they could avoid either her being what she was, or the rumors that were probably spinning out of control by now.

He seemed to understand what she was thinking. "Do the rumors matter? Do we pretend we don't care for each other? We have to go on with our lives. I'd like to know you'd be with me despite any of the problems we face."

When he said it, Kaia realized that he had decided to be with her despite the problems she faced as the selkie ambassador. She had fled from home, not to her granddad, but to James. They were in this together.

"Your life wasn't the only one that changed at the Black Rock," he said. "My life changed too. It was a date that wasn't a date. Would you have been my date for the party last night?"

Kaia looked into his eyes. "Yes, I would have. I would have faced down Candice and everyone else."

James knew they were finally alone. He moved toward Kaia

and placed one hand on the wheel opposite hers and placed his other arm behind her back. He drew her close, and they kissed, slowly and hesitantly at first. James thought, it wasn't like before in the pool. Kaia was playing then. She had used the voice - not now. He made the choice to approach her. Then their desires kindled a fire. This had to represent her true feelings, he thought. The boat started to heel sharply to starboard.

"Whoa. Someone needs to keep their hands on the wheel." James said.

"Remember the Captain is in command, mate," she said with a mocking laugh. She turned the wheel and corrected the course.

James backed away and saluted, "Aye aye, Sir"

"Get serious, James."

"You kissed me back just now. I didn't imagine that."

"We kissed before in the pool."

"Yes, but you were using the voice. You aren't now. So is this your true feeling for me?

"Did you kiss me like that because you like me or because I am a selkie?"

"The way you are, of course."

"James, I'm only part human, and the selkie part has power over human males. How will I ever know the truth?"

"Time, Kaia, time will tell. Your great-grandparents must have had the same discussion and look how that turned out."

"Hmmm."

"Just answer one question for me, Kaia, are we a couple or not?"

"I want us to be a couple...but we need to keep our relationship secret."

"Why?"

"I've enough eyes prying into my life."

"Do you care? I don't any longer. I want us to be together. Are we in love or not?"

"There's more to consider - Bill, Mom's henchman. Mom didn't want you at my party. She made that clear enough. I don't think she likes you. It's probably not you, you're just not the one Mom has chosen for me. By now Mom has heard the rumor. That means she'll probably send Bill to make sure you stay away."

"Dad thinks your father wouldn't mind if we dated."

"You talked about us to your father!"

"I asked his advice, so I didn't screw up...again. You're not angry with me are you?"

"I guess not. I just can't imagine having a conversation like that with Mom."

"Not close?"

"She's not the nurturing type."

"We talked about this before at Ervin's."

"And we talked about Bill as well. If we're going to be together, you should know that Bill is obsessed with me."

"That makes me a rival."

"And makes him dangerous. It may be my fault."

"I don't understand."

"Shelly told me the subconscious selkie in my early teens may have enticed him."

"Great."

"Unfortunately there's more. The Lady sent me a text on my twelfth birthday. It was the first, and she cautioned me not to cross Mom. She advised me to see how Mom treats those who anger her. I paid attention. Mom's ruthless. She destroys those who get in her way."

James was silent.

"Still want to date me?" she asked.

"Your parents are committed to poison the ocean. Even if we didn't date, we'd be together in that conflict with them."

"So the answer is - yes?"

"Then we're a couple, and we'll face this together.

Candi was curious about the stranger, but she couldn't act immediately. She had to have breakfast with Ken. It dragged until she was uncomfortable. Finally, she told him she'd have to go to her parent's yacht to change her clothes and take care of a few things. She promised to return in the evening and gave him a passionate kiss before she left. At her parent's boat, she dressed in an outfit that looked respectable but showed a generous amount of her cleavage.

She knew the stranger had gone into the clubhouse. *He must be a member or connected with one, or he wouldn't have gotten in. Somehow he's involved with James or Kaia.* She circumspectly entered the clubhouse, noticed him at a table and sat at the bar. She positioned herself, so she could watch him while she was being served. An empty glass sat in front of the stranger, and he downed a second glass of beer. She leaned over to the bartender and nodded her head in the direction of the stranger. "Who's he?"

"He's one of Stone's guards, name's Bill."

"Kaia's family?"

The bartender nodded. "He asked me when James usually gets back."

"He's checking up on them?"

"I guess. You made quite a scene last night."

Candi smiled. "I'd apologize, but James is a jerk and Kaia's a slut. What's Bill drinking?"

"I'll pour two and charge it to your tab."

"It's amazing how well you read my mind."

He poured the glasses and set them in front of her. "It may be none of my business, but I suspect you still love James."

"He's an asshole."

"People act out the way you do, because they still care."

"It's Kaia's fault."

"So you took it out on James." The bartender shook his head. "Not the best strategy." He nodded toward Bill. "What are you going to do now, consort with the enemy?"

"You'd be surprised what you can learn from people like him."

"Careful, they're powerful people. I've heard a thing or two about him. You might get hurt."

Candi smiled, picked up the two glasses of beer and left the bar. She set one down in front of Bill. "I'm buying," Candi said, "mind if I join you?"

He looked up, stared at my chest, and smiled. He was my type. This was going to be all too easy.

It was late afternoon. James and I were still about an hour from the marina. Other boats had crowded near us for the last two hours, so we kept our distance from each other and behaved as teacher and student should. That ended suddenly. I felt my heart rate increase. It was accompanied by disorientation. My senses suddenly became acute. I could see farther into the distance, and I smelled distinct odors from the ocean I'd never noticed before. I could hear sounds echo from under the water.

"James, take the wheel," I yelled.

"Are you okay?"

"No."

We were on starboard tack when James took the wheel. I went to the starboard side of the cockpit, grabbed the rail and stared out to sea. I closed my eyes and felt the pain flow like rivers up my legs. With it came an intense longing for the ocean. I was scared. Would my legs change, right here in front of James, in front of all those people on the other boats? I longed to jump overboard and had to clutch tightly to the rail to restrain myself. I opened my eyes and saw a pod of orcas in the distance.

"Orcas," she said.

"Selkies?"

"Probably not."

"Why don't you sit down? Rest a minute. I'll get us back to port."

My awareness of the orcas grew. I knew how many were in the pod and the number of calves. I sensed the salmon they chased and fed on. I could hear the echolocation. I learned their names. I was losing myself. The ocean demanded me to come to her. I used all my will to pull back. When I did, my legs started to throb. I turned away from the sea and toward James. James is my land and my anchor. I must believe I can do this.

My legs said otherwise.

"James, my legs hurt. I need to get back to Granddad's."

"Take the wheel. I'll handle the sheets."

"Lend me your strength, James."

James turned his attention from the sails. "What do you need?"

"Your strength."

"You already have it."

"You are the land to me. My legs want the sea. Help me stay on the land."

"You've got my love Kaia, but this selkie thing just gets weirder and weirder."

"Help me."

"If I'm going to help, I need to know what to do," James said.

"Just love me. Build the connection. Strengthen me."

"How do I do that?"

"Love between soul mates is deeper."

"Is that what you think I am?"

"Don't you feel it?"

"Apparently not as strongly as you do."

"And I'm the one who's conflicted?" I said. "Make your choice, James, is it land or sea?"

He stood confounded for a moment. "I get your point. I choose the sea."

"I chose land. Together we are complete."

Done...the choice is made, the Lady of the Sea said.

I realized then, that's what she was waiting for - his commitment to me and the ocean.

My legs still hurt when we docked the boat. I was able to walk, but with difficulty. I staggered slightly and onlookers snickered. I knew they must think I was drunk.

"Lean on me," James said.

"Are you kidding? I've got to do this myself."

"The hell with them all. I'm taking you to my Jeep."

Orcinus was parked next to the Jeep. I insisted on getting in Orcinus. He disagreed. He stood next to the car while I buckled myself in and lowered the convertible top. I was about to say goodbye when I looked in the rear view mirror and saw Candi and Bill come out of the clubhouse together. They both looked at us and then turned to talk excitedly with each other. Bill broke off from Candi and started to run toward us.

"James, get in the car, now! Bill looks like he's ready for a fight."

James turned around and saw Bill. There wasn't time to go around the car, so he put his hand on the side of the car and vaulted into the passenger seat. He quickly belted himself in as I started the engine. I spun the wheels on the Corvette around then sped out of the parking lot. James turned around to watch Bill. Bill changed direction and headed toward an SUV.

"I think you got Dad's attention with that stunt. Bill's heading for his SUV."

I turned on the main road and raced down it. "I can outrun him."

"I'll call Dad," James said and placed the call while I wove in and out of traffic on the four lane highway. "Dad," James said.

"What in the hell do you think you're doing," Charles said.

"We're being chased, Dad, see if you can get the plate of the car that's behind us. It's Bill, one of Stone's guards. He's a dangerous man."

"Don't I know! Are you going to be all right?"

"Kaia can outdrive him. If the police stop us, we may need that video to prove we were threatened by him."

"Take care, Son. Remember, this time he's messing with us. We can't be bought or threatened, and I grew up with his boss."

"Kaia's a skilled driver, I trust her."

I looked at James. He was jolted back and forth in his harness every time I swerved around cars. The adrenalin rush brought my legs back to normal, but I suspected I would pay for that later. I glanced at James. If it wasn't for his adrenalin rush, I doubted he would have enjoyed my driving. He looked backwards.

"I see Bill. He's behind us."

"I can watch him in the mirrors. Damn, I wish traffic was lighter. We're in trouble if we get caught in a clot."

I honked at a Chevrolet truck about to pull into the left lane then zoomed by him. He gave me the finger and swerved into my lane behind me. He accelerated - possible road rage. Two were chasing me now.

"You're popular," he said. "How many will we have chasing us before we're through?"

"As many as it takes."

Moments later, Bill rushed up on the rear of the Chevrolet truck and tailgated him. Bill honked his horn over and over, but the driver of the pickup wouldn't budge. Bill swerved over into oncoming traffic. When he was beside the truck, Bill turned sharply right and forced the truck off the road. The pickup hit a guard rail and scraped along it. The passenger door flew off before the pickup came to a stop.

It delayed Bill and allowed us to race ahead.

"He's one mean bastard," Kaia said.

"The pickup didn't have a passenger, and I saw his air bag inflate," James said.

"Good thing I've got speed rated tires. I doubt Bill does." The traffic remained moderately heavy, and the pursuit continued for several hectic minutes.

"Someone must have called the police by now," I said.

"Can we avoid them?"

We reached the turnoff to Ervin's and continued north, toward the Black Rock. Bill was far behind but still visible. It was twilight, and it would be dark soon.

"I've got to do something, James. Darkness will make the chase too dangerous." We could easily out-drive our headlights. I scanned the road ahead. We were northbound, and there was a large break in traffic in the southbound lanes created by a slow semi trying to pass another slow semi. Bill was still locked in place by the current southbound traffic.

"Let's see if he can match this," I said. I braked hard and spun the Corvette around into the south bound lane and then accelerated hard southward. Bill didn't have time to react. We were abreast when he tried to repeat my maneuver.

"SUV's weren't designed for high speed turns," I yelled to James.

Bill skidded sideways and would have rolled the SUV except he was too close to a Lincoln. He sideswiped it. The impact caused Bill to cross over into the empty southbound lane. He ended up off the road with the nose of his SUV stuck in thick bushes. The Lincoln ended up off the road on the other side. It didn't look like the impact caused serious injuries.

"I'll call 911," James said.

"Don't. It will place us here."

"We must do something."

"Look, others are stopping. Let them call. I'll bet Bill's been drinking. He'll end up in jail."

I slowed down but kept a large gap from the traffic behind us. I didn't want someone to record our license number. Just before we reached the turn off to Ervin's, I saw three police cars headed north with their sirens on. Once they passed us, I turned off toward Ervin's and slowed to the speed limit. I looked at James and patted his hand. "You look white. Did I scare you?"

"I have more respect for race car drivers now."

"You can always ride with me next time I practice."

"I think I'll pass on that."

I chortled. James called his father to report what happened.

"Tell Kaia I'll hold the recording," Charles said. "Turning it over to the police would implicate her...and you. Tell her I won't tolerate any more stunts in my parking lot. The two of you are drawing far too much attention to yourselves."

"I'll tell her, Dad."

Twenty minutes later we arrived at the Atwater estate. Ervin and Shelly waited for us on the front porch. I parked and we got out of the car. Then we walked up the steps hand in hand to meet them.

"Well," Ervin said, "did you have enough fun for one night?"

"You know?" James said.

"Shelly watched everything through Kaia's eyes," Ervin said.

"It was scary and disorienting," Shelly said. "I normally wouldn't do that," She touched her black pearl necklace. "I was ordered to protect you."

"Well, we made it here in one piece," I said.

"Thanks to her superb driving," James added.

"It's a small matter, Granddad, but I'll need a new set of tires."

James put his arm around me, and we both laughed.

"Come on in, you two," Ervin said. "It's time to freshen up for dinner."

We had dinner as usual in the Atwater dining room. Ervin sat in his wheelchair at the head of the table and near the door to the kitchen. Shelly sat to his right and I sat to his left. James sat next to me. My legs still hurt from the encounter with the Orcas, but I insisted on being seated in a chair. So James seated me. As usual we had fish for dinner. Tonight it was Tilapia. The conversation was light and cheerful throughout most of the dinner. Toward the end Ervin asked what happened at both parties. "I want to understand why Bill was chasing you."

I went first and told him everything that happened at my birthday party, including Mister Paws and the serving girl. I continued through the argument and how Mom slapped me.

"Granddad, Mom's birthday present to me was whale bone scrimshaw carved with Orca's."

Shelly stopped eating. "How horrible, don't they have any respect."

"Then I ran away from home," I said.

"Kaia," Ervin said, "don't end up like your father. Jacob and I had a big row when he was eighteen. He said some very unpleasant things and then left. I still helped him finance his business. We talk about business occasionally, but he never returned home. I miss the son I used to have."

"I can't live with Mom, she's a monster."

"Do you feel that way about Jacob too?" Ervin asked.

"He's always been there for me in the past. When I wanted to learn to drive, he took me to the track and started me out in little race cars powered by souped-up lawnmower engines. He couldn't always be with me, of course, and I couldn't take myself, so his driver took me. But Dad was there as often as he could and seemed to be thrilled with every new skill I learned."

"So you can at least trust your father."

"No. He's changed. Last night, all he talked about was money and the power it brings. I think Mom's infected him with her disease. At dinner, Dad went on and on bragging about the money he'd make when he dumps toxic waste in the ocean. The Lady told me not to argue, but he's so wrong."

"Kaia," Ervin said, "it's hard to change businessmen when they see a profit and think what they are doing is correct."

"He believes in it?"

"Of course, Kaia, you don't think he'd do it for spite, do you?"

I hadn't considered that possibility. "Then I should be able to show him why he is wrong."

"As I see it," James said, "some businessmen see the profit and then find some way to justify their action to themselves and others."

"You're making them sound like sociopaths," Ervin said.

"How can anyone with a conscience act the way some of them do?" James said. "Don't they see the damage to society or the pain they cause individuals and the environment?"

Ervin interrupted him. "Kaia, you ran away from home. You didn't come here. Where did you go?"

I blushed and both Granddad and Shelly turned toward James. "It wasn't his fault. I surprised him. I was asleep in his boat when he arrived after his party."

"The two of you," Ervin said. He pointed his finger at us. "You keep drawing attention to yourselves. Kaia, you know better. You should have come here. Why didn't you?"

I had to think about that, and James didn't make it easy. He smiled and looked deeply into my eyes, anticipating the truth. "I thought James would understand."

"And we wouldn't," Ervin fired back. Then his expression mellowed and moved from my face to James. "Well then..." Shelly lightly laid a hand on Ervin's arm. He looked at her then back at me. "Well then, you've run away from home. Do you intend to stay with James or with us?"

Stay with James? I looked at Ervin, and he stared back at me. I couldn't read his mood and that disturbed me. "With you, of course, Granddad."

"Kaia, why didn't you come here?"

"I had a sailing lesson in the morning."

"And that excuses it? Weren't the rumors bad enough?"

"Hey, we behaved ourselves!" Well mostly...we did.

James blushed. I looked at him, remembered the sailing lesson and blushed too. Ervin studied our faces. "Okay, so keep your secrets."

I looked at James, and he looked back at me. He smiled at me and winked. I nodded to James. We had made an agreement. We would live with our complications. "James is my boyfriend, Granddad. AND we are behaving ourselves."

"So how is Bill involved?" Ervin asked.

"He was with Candi," Kaia said. "He ran across the parking lot after us, obviously looking for a fight. He's mean. Mom lets him hurt people. I didn't want him to hurt James."

"Does anyone know what happened to Bill?" James asked.

He's been arrested, the Lady of the Sea said in all their minds.

"You eavesdropped," I said without thinking.

There is a first generation selkie at the police station. She chose land but can still talk with me.

"What's going to happen to Bill?" James asked.

Bill failed the breathalyzer and arrived at the station in handcuffs. He complained he was a Stone Security Guard in pursuit of stolen Stone Company secrets.

"What bull," James said.

He was asked why he didn't call the police or FBI. He said there wasn't time and the secret was too sensitive.

"Yeah, right," James said.

"Lana will get him off," Ervin said. "She'll verify his story and toss money at the owners whose vehicles he wrecked. It will silence them."

139

"What about the drinking charge?" James asked.

"Ah, that may stick," Ervin said, "unless she finds a way to bribe the officers or the judge."

"She'll do it," Kaia said.

"Well, either way he'll spend the night in lockup."

"Serves him right," Kaia said.

Ervin nodded in agreement. "But, you didn't listen to me or the Lady. Now he's become a problem. I thought you weren't going to argue with your parents."

"I couldn't help myself."

"I thought we agreed I'd do the planning."

"Yes...but."

"Then let me help."

"What do you want me to do?"

"I can accomplish little by myself. We need to know your parent's plans. That means we need a spy who can get inside, someone who can swallow her anger and go home."

"Granddad!"

"Kaia, you don't have to stay there, just drop in for dinner and instead of arguing, ask innocent questions and listen. He'll be happy to tell you."

"You don't understand."

"You asked for my help. I will try if you help me."

"Granddad, isn't there another way?"

"No."

"Can't Shelly eavesdrop?"

Absolutely not, the Lady of the Sea said in their minds.

"But you listen in on our conversations," Kaia said.

You're selkies.

"James isn't."

He's family.

"I don't understand. You have the ability, but you refuse to use it, even with this much at stake."

Kaia, it's a short distance between eavesdropping and controlling a person's mind. Never take away a person's choice, no matter what's at stake. It's our law. We only use the voice when we may be assaulted by males, or our lives are at stake. Even then, we take great care.

There was no way to argue with the Lady of the Sea. I was trapped and I knew it.

Chapter 13 - Candi's Revenge

Bill proved as easy to manipulate as any male I'd ever known. I flirted with him, and he eagerly responded. It was all too easy. We got to know each other over a few rounds of beer. He drank two beers for my every one, but that was my usual strategy - let myself appear drunk when I'm really not. I was surprised. He could hold his beer fairly well. He was a big guy after all. Once we got to know each other, I asked what brought him to the marina. He mentioned James Cersea. I told him I used to date James. He locked eyes on me when I said it. We spent the next few hours talking about James and Kaia. He was quite interested in what I had to say. He got up and walked to the door, stood there a while, then returned to the table. I could tell he was angry, and that's just what I needed. A hint of a few special favors bought me an interview with Lana Stone, Kaia's mother. Step one in my plan for revenge - turn the mother against her daughter. To do that, I had to learn what motivated the mother. I had a few ideas from my conversation with Bill.

Early the next morning. Bill called to tell me Mrs. Stone wished to speak with me.

I followed Bill's directions and arrived at the gate to the Stone mansion. I lowered the car window to reach for the intercom button. Before I touched it, the gate started to open. I looked up, saw the camera and smiled. I repressed the desire to wave (best appear professional). I lowered my window and drove through the gate. At first, the driveway ran through a wooded area. Then it turned to the right, and I could see the mansion in the distance. I grew up in a McMansion, in one of the gated communities outside the city, but the Stone mansion was obscenely huge, certainly too much for one family. I felt out of place, but I wasn't about to be intimidated.

There's some money here, I thought. Toss a little my way - don't waste it all on Kaia.

I drove up to the garage. Bill stood beside it, dressed in a black shirt and a black suit. A maroon tie completed his outfit. He motioned for me to park, and I followed his arm motions. After I parked, Bill walked over to the car and opened the door for me.

"Mrs. Stone awaits you in her office. Let me escort you there." He sounded and acted so formal when he opened the door, taking my hand to help me out. Then he patted me firmly on the rear. I didn't even squirm. He was mine. A few favors and he'd do anything I'd ask.

"Thanks for helping me with the invitation," I said.

"Mrs. Stone is <u>most</u> anxious to meet you."

Good, a little manipulation and I'm on my way to revenge.

Bill escorted me through a side door and into Lana's office. I looked around when I entered. The office walls were lined with framed newspaper clippings and a series of shadow boxes with an eclectic collection of bizarre and unrelated items. It looked odd, perhaps eccentric.

How do I use this to my advantage? Maybe she'll let me read a few of the newspaper clippings.

I quickly focused my attention on Lana. I didn't want her to think I was easily distracted. She sat behind an ornate wooden desk, and was dressed in a business suit. The formal setting exuded power. I swallowed hard. Patience, I needed patience. Men are one thing, women are quite different. A woman with this much power could be quite intimidating.

Lana flicked her hand casually at Bill. "Leave us," she commanded.

He formally bowed his head and left, closing the door behind him. While he left I had a chance to study Lana. I was left alone with Lana. She was middle aged but extremely attractive. She had long black hair, brown, almond shaped eyes, and a tanned skin tone. She was medium height and slender with overly large breasts for someone of her stature. They pushed up out of her dress. A large gold pendant with red stones sat on top of her cleavage.

It was clear from a casual look that there was very little of Kaia in Lana, except for the good looks. Kaia's eyes were prettier, but her mom's boobs were more enticing.

"Have you studied me enough?" Lana said.

That caused me to pause. Lana was far too observant to be easily manipulated. She was going to be quite a challenge. Well I was up to it. I must pay close attention, hear every nuance, and understand what isn't spoken.

"Sorry, ma'am. It's just, well, I'm a little overwhelmed."

Lana smiled. "Candi, I know why you're here. You want revenge on James. It's such a short focus. You need to think about your future. You'll find he's just a passing interest. You want money and power - all of the things I've earned."

Does she see right through me?

"You can do much better than James. What will he inherit - a marina? Sure, it's a big one, but if you work with me, you could turn the head of a multi-millionaire CEO."

Lana paused and studied me. I tried to keep a calm and expressionless face, but the conversation so far intrigued me. Connections, she might have the connections I could use.

"Candi, you're what I call a Bad Girl. I don't mean that in a derogatory way. You own your sexuality. You're no man's puppet."

"I don't understand."

"Oh, I think you understand quite well. You want it all and will do anything to get it. You need to realize that James stands in the way. He has money but isn't aggressive about seeking wealth and power. He'll never take you as far as you could go."

She's manipulating me and I thought I was going to manipulate her. "What's this all about?"

"It's about you. It's about me. It's about money, power, and control. Oh, sex too."

"I don't follow you."

"Sure you do. I was just like you when I was younger, and I had your looks too."

"You still have them, ma'am."

"Call me Lana, because we're going to be good friends. Now Candi, your real name is Candice isn't it?"

"You've checked up on me, haven't you?"

"Of course, my dear, I always do thorough investigation before I recruit someone. I know every affair you've had, with whom, how long they lasted, and why they ended, all the stuff that makes a good scandal. What you lack is someone to show you how to manage your conquests successfully."

Interesting, perhaps I can learn something from this woman.

"I saw you admiring my trophies. Yes, that's what they are, trophies of rumors, conquests, scandals, mishaps, acquisitions, and mergers. All manipulated by me and my girls."

"Girls?"

Lana laughed. "I'm altruistic. I generously support an orphanage, with all those poor homeless girls so hungry for a better life. Where do you think I get my girls? You're different. You grew up with money and power and have a thirst for more."

"What does your husband say about this?"

"We have a good partnership. That's why we are so powerful and wealthy. By the way, Candi is such a low class name; it's the name for a slut or a stripper. Candice on the other hand has exotic appeal. You will use Candice from now on."

"Are you recruiting me?"

"Are you're interested? I have a banking CEO we need to remove and replace with our candidate. A nice scandal would do. He's attracted to young women and is a sucker for big boobs. You fit the profile of his predilections in many ways. All you need to do is seduce him and arrange to be caught with him in embarrassing situations - the more sexual, the better. After a few hints from me to his wife that he's having an affair, and she'll call for the private investigators. All I need to do is find out who they are, and we can act out our game for them. The resulting scandal will bring him down."

"I'm good, but I'm not that good."

"Oh, by the way, he's also a bit kinky and needs a strong hand. I can teach you what you need to know. Are you in or out?"

"What do I get out of it?"

"You'll find I can be very generous to those who successfully carry out my plans - money and power, if that's what you want. I can even arrange for a marriage to someone rich and powerful, someone who's part of my cartel."

"It sounds interesting."

"Good. There's a downside. I know you want it all - but remember I'm the one in charge. Don't ever oppose me. You do exactly as I say. Bill's my enforcer, and he enjoys hurting people. Don't ever fail me."

I suddenly remembered the favor I had hinted to Bill and panicked at the thought. Lana must have seen the expression on my face.

"You flirted with him and to me a hint is as good as a promise. Keep it. You need him on your side. I suspect he'll only insist on handcuffs. I won't allow him to permanently harm you."

"You know about my flirting with him?"

"There are no secrets between us. I'll want to know just how good you are, so, do your best for him. I expect a very good report."

I realized then that I had been stupid. If she could bring down a banker, then it would be nothing for her to destroy me. There was no way to back out, not now. I created this situation and now I was trapped. I'd have to put up with Bill's aggressive sex play, but...I'd be on the inside with Lana and there were so many new possibilities.

Now it was my turn for manipulation. "Does Kaia know about your...occupation?"

"She suspects, but wouldn't approve if she knew."

"She must have learned something from you. Look what's she's done to James. He flipped over her."

Lana stared at me with icy eyes. "Did they have sex?"

"I wasn't there, but I know James."

"What do you think happened?"

"I think he took advantage of her on his boat."

"So you think it's James' fault?"

"Yes."

"Candice, you went to school with Kaia. Help me out. I can't figure out what to do with her. She's always been difficult and such a rebellious child. I think it's Ervin's fault. He gives her too much freedom."

"You could reprogram her."

"Reprogram?"

"Yes, like in some of those cult churches. Brainwash her. Turn her into the obedient daughter you always wanted."

"What a brilliant idea! I like you already. You're almost as devious as I am. Yes, I think I could arrange that, but only as a last resort!"

Chapter 14 - A Pearl Necklace

Early the next morning, James and I ate breakfast with Ervin and Shelly. Then we left for the marina. When we arrived, several cars pulled into the lot near us. Four people got out of a nearby car and eyeballed us together in my Corvette. I pulled in and parked next to James' Jeep. We got out and I began my act. I put my hands on my hips and frowned at James. "Remember – appearances," I whispered. Then I glared at him. "Who's your girlfriend now?" I said it quite loud and in an accusatory way. The four people turned toward us.

He smiled wickedly, "Who I date is my business. Are you my student or not! Let's get down to the boat. We've got a lot to cover today."

It looked like we were fighting. The four people left. Then we quietly walked to the boat.

"We arrived together," I whispered while we walked. "How will we explain that?"

"I told you yesterday - we shouldn't try. Every time we do, something goes wrong."

I laughed. "Let's get on the boat before we tempt fate."

There was a commotion near the clubhouse. I turned in that direction. James followed my lead. Charles charged out of the clubhouse and stomped toward us. Everyone's eyes followed him. "Wait right there," Charles yelled. We stopped. When he got close, he pointed at me and shook his finger, but he winked. Then he spoke loud enough for everyone to hear. "You squeal your tires in this lot one more time, young lady, and I will ban you from this marina."

"I'm sorry, sir," I said meekly and winked back.

Charles smiled in spite of the situation. Then he quickly returned to his frown. "As for you, Son, I don't want any more bad reports. Now get back to work."

"Yes, sir."

"Well, what are you supposed to do?"

"Ervin bought additional lessons for Kaia. We were about to go sailing."

"What lessons?"

"He wants us to cover more advanced skills such as sailing

with limited or damaged equipment and survival techniques."

"Good idea. Get to it!"

He waved them off with a shake of his hand and stomped back to the office.

"What was that all about," I asked.

"A lesson in Public Relations...for my benefit, of course."

"Is he angry with me?"

"Let me put it this way - don't squeal your tires again. He understands why you had to do it yesterday, but he may have to punish you so that others behave."

We got to the boat and set sail. A short time later we cleared the harbor and sailed northward along the coast.

"What's the lesson plan for today?" I asked.

"How to sail without a Genoa," James said.

"Why do I need that lesson? I'd be with you."

"What would you do if something happened to me, or the sails tore, or any other number of things went wrong?"

"James, I can always jump in the sea and transform."

"You'd abandon me?"

"No. You're right, I need to learn."

Sailing without a Genoa causes the boat to head reach. The boat wants to turn into the wind, and it takes a strong hand on the wheel to make the boat stay its course. I had other plans. I wanted to see the orcas. So we talked about it. James didn't care whether or not we began our lessons today, so we sailed offshore from the black rock. I felt an orca pod would be there. James realized by now if I sensed something, he had to take into account my selkie paranormal abilities.

Sure enough, an orca pod was nearby. I reached out with my thoughts as I had in the tour boat. I felt the slow motion of their flukes as they moved together in a family. Looking into the pod, I noticed mothers and their calves. I thought this might be Aga's and Siku's pod. James set a course straight toward them. I decided to try to call them. I pictured them in my mind and felt their contact.

"Daughter of the Sea, what do you wish of us?"

"Are you Aga and Siku's pod?"

"They are part of us."

"They are still far north in Alaska. I talked with them two suns ago."

"You must swim swiftly."

147

"Through the air."

"Is such a thing possible?"

"The two legged make it so."

"They also harm the water and take too many fish."

"Kaia," James said. "You seem to be preoccupied."

"Give me a second. I've called an orca pod to come here."

"Orcas or selkies?"

"Orcas, James."

"Good, I won't have to worry about the selkie voice."

"Selkies are the caretakers of the ocean. James, we need to drop the sails so the orcas can approach us."

We dropped sail, and moments, later a pod of black fins swam alongside the sailboat. They took turns spy-hopping to peek at me. Two calves playfully rubbed up against the boat and pushed it one way and then the other.

"Playful, aren't they?" I said.

"Playful until they sink us," James replied.

"Calm down guys," I said. Then I dove off the boat and into the water. Moments later I popped up and smiled up at James through my teeth. "I didn't think that through," I said.

He looked down at me and surely noticed I had transformed my legs into a fluke. He looked puzzled until I tossed my bathing suit bottom up on the boat. It had shredded during the transformation.

"Oh," he said and started to laugh.

"It's not funny."

"You brought a spare didn't you?"

"No, it never occurred to me I might need one."

"I've got a spare."

"Not Candi's, I hope."

"No, mine."

It was my turn to chuckle. "So you're going to let me get into your pants."

He shook his head at me. "Are you using the voice?"

Was I?

"You could drop me a towel when I'm ready to get out of the water."

"I'll go get one."

He went into the cabin and returned moments later. He set a beach towel down on one of the molded seats. I dove beneath the waves and waved goodbye with my fluke. Moments later, I rose out of the water holding onto the fin of an orca. I sat sideways with my fluke toward James. The orca dove. About a minute later I rose out of the water on the back of a different Orca. I waved to James and then disappeared again. Next, I spy-hopped on an orca with my back to his fin. Each time I rose out of the water I looked at James. My antics and the entertaining orcas amused him. He stood by the rail and watched. I thought about having one of the orcas splash him, but they might throw too much water into the cockpit and rock the boat. James could fall and maybe hurt himself. I was having fun, James should too.

I disappeared below the surface for over a minute. Then, all the orcas rose in unison with me riding one. I waved to James. Then, we all dove in unison before I breached on the back of a male. The orca was very close to the boat. It tossed the boat and splashed James. He still clung to the rail as I disappeared under the water. I hoped he was okay. Despite my plan, I had both tossed the boat and splashed him. It was time to stop. I came up by myself, and the orcas swam away.

James leaned over the side. "I felt left out."

"Then join me."

"You know the answer to that. Safety first. Someone has to stay in the boat. The wind could blow it away faster than we can swim toward it."

"Aw shucks, you're missing all the fun." I dove once again and then breached, arching high in a flip before re-entering the water. Then I swam to the rear of the boat where the ladder was located. "Toss me the towel."

He tossed it down to me. I grabbed it and wrapped it around myself. Then I transformed. I realized James must have seen my naked butt distorted by the water. I looked up and watched him turn away. He must have seen and was trying to be polite.

"I didn't flash you, did I?"

"I'm sorry. I didn't mean to watch."

"You're all right with my naked fluke."

"I'm uncomfortable with your naked butt. It makes me feel like I'm a Peeping Tom."

I finished wrapping the towel around myself and climbed the ladder. When I reached the cockpit, I headed toward the cabin. "Where do you keep your underwear?"

"In one of the plastic storage bins under the cushions in the galley."

"It's going to be fun rummaging through your things."

"Hey. Don't be too inquisitive."

"Will I find something embarrassing?"

James thought about it, 'God I hope she doesn't find the condoms.'

He barely finished the thought before she said, "James, how many boxes do you have in here?"

"Ah, you found them then?"

"Found what."

"Um, maybe I'd better help you."

"James, really do you have to have so many."

"Safety first."

Kaia started to laugh, and James nervously joined her. "So many kinds and colors" she said. "How do you choose?"

"Um... whatever suits my date."

"I'm talking about the underwear, what are you talking about?"

"Underwear?"

"Can I use the red ones."

"Use any you want."

"Even the ones with the little hearts that say 'kiss me'."

James thought, 'Damn, I should have pitched the ones Candi gave me.' "What-ev-er."

Moments later, I joined him on the deck wearing my shorts and my t-shirt.

"You look nice," he said.

She turned around and modeled it for him. "Your underwear doesn't show, does it?"

"You can't tell."

"Good, shall we get on with our lesson?"

"Not today, I checked the forecast when I got the towel. There's a storm brewing. We've got plenty of time, but we should head back to port."

I reached over to James and kissed his neck. He turned toward me. I saw panic in his eyes.

"Do you know what you're starting?"

"Starting?" I said, "starting...starting... starting..."

"Kaia you're using your Selkie voice."

"James, I'm sorry. I was just playing."

"With the orcas and now with me. I don't think any guy could resist if you use that voice."

"Then you're fortunate because you're the only one I want to use it on."

"Remember what Shelly said about freedom. Doesn't my choice mean anything? I imagine your great-grandmother and great-grandfather must have had this same conversation."

"They worked it out, and we can too."

"Okay, I'll think about it. James, when the Lady came out of the sea you couldn't resist the voice. Now you recognize it. Will you eventually be able to resist it?"

"I don't think so. You have no idea how compelling it is."

"Then tell me when I use it, James. I want you as my boyfriend not...how did the selkies say it...my boy toy."

"You don't need to use it on me, Kaia. I don't need to be seduced. I love you the way you are."

I looked to the west and the thickening clouds. "Shouldn't we raise the sails?"

"Wait a moment. I'd like to give you a late birthday present just in case things get hectic later." He went below deck and returned with a small wrapped package. I carefully unwrapped it, and then opened the box. Inside was a black pearl pendant in a platinum setting. I held it and ran the chain through my fingers.

"Can I put it on for you," he asked.

Tears ran down my cheeks.

"What's wrong," he asked.

"This is way too much."

"You're worth it."

"Do you mean it?"

"Of course I do."

"Then I accept."

Chapter 15 - Parental Plans

The sailing lesson was over, and Kaia had to return home. That was the agreement, and it took a lot of courage to carry it out. They needed a spy, and she was the only candidate. Ervin and The Lady made it seem so routine, so simple, but it wouldn't be. Kaia already sensed that. She would have to listen carefully, ask innocent questions, and control her temper. It was the last item that worried her the most. She cared. How could she act like she didn't? Learning to control the selkie transformation of legs into a fluke was easy by comparison. And that took her a long time to master.

She found herself gripping the car wheel too tightly and pushing the throttle a little too heavy. It was the anger building inside her. She had to control it. Last time she was home, she ran away - to James. At least she now understood why - they were a team. Her life was changing too quickly. A few days ago she was a child, but those days were over. Now she was the Selkie Ambassador and Daughter of the Sea (whatever that meant). The latter title sounded important and made her feel she headed a conspiracy to save the oceans. It shouldn't have to be a conspiracy, she reasoned, it's just that people don't listen. Like global warming, the death of the ocean was bad science. Unfortunately for humanity, the two were interrelated. A few days ago James was only her teacher. Now he was her teacher, her co-conspirator, and her companion. They were going to be together a very long time. That, at least, made her smile. She took one hand off the wheel and clutched the black pearl pendant. Yes, James, yes.

There were other surprises and worries. The selkie voice was one of them. She slipped into it too easily. If it weren't for James' comments, she wouldn't have acknowledged it. At least now, when she used it, she sensed it...most of the time. She had no control over it. Just one more thing to worry about tonight. If she slipped into the voice when talking with Dad, Mom would surely notice it.

While Kaia drove home from the marina, Lana and Jake sat in the study around the fireplace and sipped on wine.

"I told you she'd come back home if we treated her with respect," Jake said. "Take care, Lana. I want her to feel comfortable tonight."

"This is her home," Lana replied. "She belongs here."

"No, it isn't, not any longer. You have to realize she no longer belongs here. We have to let go. Kaia's an adult now. She must be free to make her own choices, just like we did."

"She talks like your father. She's disrespectful to everything we've accomplished. I think Ervin has had too much influence on her. She acts as if the world is black and white, and we're on the side of the bad guys."

"Life will teach her otherwise," he said. "It's all a spectrum of gray. There are a lot of companies worse than we are. We don't make bullets or guns or things that kill people. We make chemicals and devices that make life better and more productive. She'll come around."

"She knows nothing about our company."

"That's why we've talked about her interning with a customer."

Lana nodded her head in agreement and smiled. Her idea of an entry level position was far different from the one Jake suggested.

Kaia arrived home and parked Orcinus in the garage next to her father's Mercedes. She had driven home straight from the marina and still wore her shorts, shirt, and deck shoes. She got out of the car and walked confidently to the door. Bill waited. He opened it for her.

"Lost your driver's license, I hear," Kaia said with a chuckle. "You really should take driving lessons before you hurt somebody."

Bill glared at her.

I didn't need to egg him on like that. First words out of my mouth, and I've already let my anger out. Control, Kaia, control.

Bill returned to the obedient servant role.

He'll never be a gentleman, but I've got to hand it to him, he sure can act his role.

"Your parents await you in the study."

"Thank you, William, that will be all," Kaia said with a smirk. She turned abruptly away from him and stepped through the door. She sensed his hostility when he slammed the door behind her. *I've gotten just a little under his skin. Better cool it.*

Kaia entered the study and immediately hugged her father. She turned to Lana. "I just came from sailing. I need a shower and a change of clothes before dinner. May I be excused?"

She caught herself. Those last words had carried with them the selkie voice. Her Dad nodded, but her mother fixed her eyes on the black pearl pendant that hung around her neck. She swallowed hard. She shouldn't have worn it home. It was too late now. She quickly turned and rushed upstairs to her room.

After she left, Lana turned to Jake. "Did you buy her that necklace?"

"No, maybe Dad did."

"It's lovely, a black pearl in what looks like a platinum setting."

"A black pearl, are you sure," Jake replied.

"Yes."

"Hmmm, it looks like our little girl has grown up."

"I bet she's stunning in a dress with that necklace."

"Of course, dear," Jake replied. Then he leaned back in his chair and thought about his sisters and their black pearls. He hadn't seen either of them for years. Dad said they went back to the Orkney Islands. *I wonder if they're still there.*

Well Mom had seen the necklace. There's nothing Kaia could do about it now. Why not just flaunt it. She knew she couldn't hide the necklace now that Mom had seen it, so she decided to take the opposite approach. After her shower she put on a low cut blouse and a matching skirt and let the necklace hang prominently two thirds of the way between her neck and close to her cleavage, just like Mom wore her gaudy red thing. She went downstairs and joined her parents for dinner. Bill was conspicuously absent. Kaia preferred to keep an eye on him and wondered what sinister thing he was up to.

At dinner, Kaia congratulated herself for not arguing, although she seethed at many of the comments made by her father, and even more so by the insensitive comments of her mother. She learned that the ocean dumping was proceeding, but outfitting the ship would take time. That was good news. Kaia and her friends needed time to plan their actions. By accident, Kaia also learned that dead fish had washed up near one of her parents' chemical factories.

Jake assured Kaia the plant wasn't responsible, but he admitted the EPA would conduct an investigation. They were already being prodded by environmental do-gooders.

"Environmental terrorists," Lana said. "Not to worry."

Jake appeared a little taken back by Lana's comment. "At worst, our scientists will disagree with their scientists and then we'll call in some independent scientists to conduct their own inquiry."

"Who'll pay them?" Kaia asked. *Oops, the voice again.*

"We will," Jake replied.

"Our money buys our result," Lana added. "If the science doesn't work, we can always toss a few million to some government officials and like magic, the problem goes away."

Kaia smiled, despite the agony that ate away at her insides. Her temper was now eleven on a scale of one to ten. It was time to chomp down on her tongue before she said something she'd later regret. To her this was a business lesson. Too much money and too much power begot too many wrongs. No wonder the world had become a miserable place. The people who suffer are powerless against those who use their position to continue the status quo and enrich themselves in the process.

They ate dessert, and Jake complemented Kaia on her necklace. "It's lovely. Who has such good taste to give it to you?" he inquired.

"James Cersea. He said it was a late birthday present."

"It's beautiful." He smiled broadly and gave her a wink. "I want you to know I approve."

Did Dad just say what I thought he said? Kaia turned toward her mother. Lana's expression had changed. She wasn't smiling. She had a cold look on her face. It wasn't a look of motherly love, more a look of calculated evaluation. Her gaze stopped and lingered at the new necklace. Then Lana smiled sweetly. It seemed so forced.

"Tonight you and I can have a nice mother and daughter conversation," Lana said.

Great, Kaia thought. There's something to look forward to! We've got nothing in common, Mom. What are you going to do, belittle and badger me some more. You don't like James. I'm sure you'll want to rant on about him.

After dinner, Kaia went to the place that used to be her room. She sat on the bed next to the shorts and shirt she had worn when she arrived home. She picked them up and neatly folded them on her dresser next to her purse, intending to put them in a bag when she left. She put James' underwear on the bottom of the stack. Then she picked up her cell phone. She briefly contemplated a call or at least a text to James. Something stopped her - a selkie sixth sense, perhaps. She must not give her role away. She must wait until she was out of the house. She set the phone down on the nightstand and looked around her room. A terrible thought ran though her mind. Bill may have been in her room going through her things while she was at dinner. *Bill may even have bugged my room.* Maybe there were hidden cameras as well. It would be just like that pervert. I won't search for them. It would give Mr. Paws too much satisfaction. Where was Bill anyhow? *Had he peeked in on me when I showered?* The thought gave her cold shivers.

There was a knock on her door. "Yes," Kaia said.

"May I come in?" Lana said.

Do I have a choice? Then she remembered she should try to be nice. She forced herself to smile so the words would come out right. "Sure, Mom."

Lana walked in and sat down on the bed beside Kaia. She turned toward Kaia. "You're eighteen now. My how you've grown!" She reached forward and took Kaia's necklace in her hand. "It's absolutely lovely, expensive too, and babe, you're certainly worth it."

The comment made Kaia uncomfortable. Not everything was about money - at least with most people. She'd never had a conversation like this with Mom before. Lana had always been critical of her. Kaia never measured up to Lana's expectations. The complements from Lana seemed phony, and Kaia wondered where the conversation would lead. A panic began to set in. There was a whirlpool and her mother was spinning it. It began to suck her in. Kaia suddenly wanted to be anyplace else than here.

"James Cersea, gave it to you," Lana said. "He's a good lad and a real catch for someone. He'll inherit the marina from his dad someday, so he's not poor."

"Mother, everything doesn't have a price tag." *Remember, Kaia, the voice doesn't work on women.*

Lana put her arm around Kaia. "Naïve, but honey, I'm proud of you. You must have done something very special to earn a trinket like this."

"Mother!"

"You don't need to lie to me, Kaia. I had a nice long conversation with Candice not that long ago. She told me all about you and James. So don't try to make up stories. I know you spent the night with him and have been with him quite a lot since. I imagine he's quite good because Candice is insanely jealous of you, and Candice is very good at it herself." Lana paused a moment before she smiled. "I didn't earn a trophy like this until I was twenty-one."

"Mom, it's not a trophy."

Lana got up from the bed and paced around the room. She walked over to where Kaia had stacked her clothing. She started to move it aside and suddenly stopped. She held up a piece. "This is male underwear," she said. "And it has little hearts on it."

That was too easy, no accident. Bill must have been in my room and told her.

"I tore my suit and James loaned me his underwear."

"You have his underwear and you say you haven't been intimate with him."

"We haven't..."

"Sure, baby, Mother understands. I used to worry about you, but now I see you've really got it. Good going, kiddo."

Danger signals flashed in Kaia's mind. She imagined she could here sirens wailing. Pull over, get out of the way. Kaia recalled one of the Lady's texts and heard it in the Lady's voice, *don't ever argue with your mother.* Kaia couldn't help herself in the past. She argued, and she'd learned the hard way. Each argument with Lana always ended in grief and pain, Kaia's grief and pain. No, she thought, believe what you will, Mom. I know the truth. It's not worth an argument.

Now I've got to get out of here as fast as I can.

She leaned into her mother's arms and pretended to be the good daughter. Inside she seethed. She wanted to push her mother away, to run someplace and hide. Her mother's arm felt like a snake wrapping itself tightly around her, ready to squash her without hesitation.

"You like James, I assume."

"Yes, Mother."

"I liked your father from the very first. He had the drive to become successful. I've helped make him wealthy and became wealthy and powerful in return. You can do the same."

"Yes, Mother."

"Well, you're no longer a virgin, so..."

"Mother!"

"Don't interrupt me when I'm giving you advice."

"Yes, Mother."

"I've seen how Bill hangs around you, so you must have an allure I don't understand. I don't see you in action, but I see the results."

"You let Bill stalk me?"

"He knows better than try to sample you, I'd cut off his dick if he tried."

"Mother!"

"I really would, with a dull knife, and he knows it."

"Why do you put up with him?"

"He's very useful, my dear. He keeps...others...from disobeying me."

The thought disturbed Kaia. That her mother used some sick bastard to enforce her will on others was the ultimate in her depravity. It was sick and wrong. What had they said at Ervin's about freedom and enslavement? Her mother used Bill to enslave others to her will. That was too much. But Kaia was trapped. She knew she must appear to remain the good daughter, at least until she got out of the house. This bitch could turn that monster loose on her own daughter if she thought it would help. Bill would rape her and enjoy it.

"There's something I want you to do?" Lana said.

"What, mother?"

"I've noticed there's a young CEO who can't keep his eyes off you. He's someone we need in our company. I want you to encourage him. You might even find him ...well, enjoyable."

"Mother, I'm ...."

"Don't be prudish about it. James doesn't need to know. Of course, Jake and I share everything, so maybe even James will come around to this arrangement. You'll find you can obtain lots of presents if you choose to offer yourself appropriately."

Kaia seethed inside. Her mother wanted her to prostitute herself for the good of the company. No, no, NO! She wanted to use the selkie voice, but she knew it would be pointless. Kaia pulled back from her mother's arms. "Mom, are you telling me Dad knows you have affairs?"

"My dear, I usually don't, but my girls do. Enough of this.

158

Jake and I will attend an industry conference next month. You'll go with us. I'll make sure to introduce you to our target. Then you take over. Seduce him. Influence him. Make him ours. You'll think about that won't you?"

"Yes, Mother."

"If you need advice or training, come to me."

Not likely, Kaia thought.

"Do be a dutiful daughter. Candice gave me such a good idea in case you decide to be rebellious."

If it came from Candice, it can only be something mean and vengeful.

Kaia had schooled herself for six years. She hid her feelings deep inside in a sacred place, a selke place. Her mother wouldn't sense her true feelings. But she knew for certain the spying was over. She'd never return to this house again. 'Thank goodness,' she thought, 'I have a sailing lesson with James in the morning.'

Her mother left her alone in her room to ponder the situation. Once again Kaia picked up the cell phone to call James, and once again she set it back down. She had to continue to act the dutiful daughter. She picked up James' underwear, folded them, and put them in her overnight bag. *Well, James, our luck continues - we keep finding new ways to cause difficulties for ourselves.* Kaia wanted to leave in the most desperate way - to run away for good. Coming home had been a mistake. But she couldn't run. Running would only incite her mother. *Why did I let myself be talked into this - I knew better.* The worst thing about it: she'd have to spend the night in this room. She thought of Bill spying on her and decided not to change into her pajamas. She'd sleep in her clothes and leave before breakfast. *James, I wish I could be in bed on your boat.*

That thought would have to carry her through the night.

Chapter 16 - Troubled Waters

James was waiting for Kaia in the parking lot when she arrived for her sailing lesson. She kept the car running and lowered her window. "James, let's skip the lesson today and go see Granddad."

"Why?"

"I'm in serious trouble."

James turned slowly around. He visually scanned the marina to see who might notice. There were several people around the clubhouse and the docks. They came and went from their boats or stood and talked with each other. One or two walked around carrying an early beer.

"We're probably being watched," he said.

"You said it yesterday but I disagreed. It doesn't matter anymore. I'll never go home again. I've got to hide from Mom. I really have to run away this time."

"That serious!"

"Yes. I don't want to talk about it here."

James moved to the passenger door and got in. He did it casually so no one would notice. "Before we go anyplace, I need to let Dad know we won't be sailing today."

He sat down in the passenger seat and called. He told his father there was an unexpected problem, and he would be away with Kaia during the day. Charles said he would cover for him and let Grant know.

Before she started to drive, Kaia reached down and lifted her black pearl pendant from around her neck. "I made the mistake of wearing this home."

"Why does that make a difference? I already know your parents hate me!" He buckled up, and Kaia drove slowly out of the lot. This time she didn't want to be noticed.

"Not to Dad. He liked it and approved. But Mom's convinced you and I had sex, and she insists I seduce a young CEO for her. She threatened to punish me if I didn't go along."

"Seriously, your mother did that! Unbelievable."

"We need to talk with Granddad...now!"

Kaia continued her conservative driving. She kept at or

below the speed limit. Along the way to Ervin's, Kaia explained her predicament to James in detail. If it were possible, James was even more appalled than Kaia was.

"I never thought Mom was this bad. It's obvious she doesn't care about me. I don't think she even cares about Dad. She only cares about herself, and how she can enrich herself at the expense of others, including me, her own daughter."

"Does your father know?"

"Mom said she shared everything with Dad."

"I can't conceive of that. Did she tell the truth?"

"I don't know, James."

"A person like her would tell lies, maybe even believe them."

"That sounds like Mom."

"What will you do?"

"What can I do? Run away."

"You know I'll go with you."

Kaia took her left hand off the driver's wheel and wrapped her fingers around the black pearl pendant. She turned briefly toward James and gave him a smile. "I knew you would want to." She handed James her cell phone. "Call Granddad for me."

James called and began to explain, but once Ervin realized the serious nature of the situation, he said, "Not here. This matter involves the whole family. We'll meet at the black rock."

James told Kaia what Ervin said.

"He can't walk," she replied. "How will he get from the parking area?"

James asked Ervin that question and relayed the answer to Kaia. "He says that's his problem, and it has an easier solution than yours."

Kaia was near the interchange that led to the Atwater estate. She glanced at it and passed it by. She headed toward the ocean. They didn't know how long it would take to put the meeting together, so James suggested they stop for some fast food in the village down the road from the black rock.

Kaia and James were first to arrive at the parking lot and walked hand in hand down the trail to the shore. They sat together on the black rock and waited. This time the Shell of Knowing wasn't there. "Good thing it's missing," Kaia said with an edge to her voice. "I know too much already, and much I'd like not to know."

"It's a tangled web we find ourselves in."

"And all we wanted to do was make the world a better place."

"We should have expected this. People who want to change things always meet resistance."

It was midmorning, and the surf seemed to be especially agitated. "It's almost as if the sea senses my mood," Kaia said.

"Or mine," James replied.

They sat and listened to the booming of the surf for a while. Very little was said. Kaia leaned into James arms and they sat side by side in a perpetual hug. The ocean in front of them seethed in turmoil. Kaia and James resonated to its mood. Kaia suddenly pulled away and turned toward the breakers. "They're coming, I can feel it."

James looked out over the waves. Pod after pod of orcas appeared offshore. An uncountable number swam back and forth along the shore. One pod broke away from the others and swam inland. It approached the surf line and disappeared. Moments later the Lady walked out of the ocean, but she was not alone. Nine selkies accompanied her. They all wore black conch shell necklaces and carried tridents. The Lady wore a string of golden pearls and a golden conch shell just like Kaia had seen in her vision. She waved her hand and four of the selkies headed away from the sea toward the trail up to the parking lot. The Lady smiled at James. "You no longer have to fear us," she said, "You've committed."

That didn't help James. The Lady couldn't totally eliminate the charm in her voice. James looked at the congregation of selkies and wondered if he could stay beside Kaia and remain sane. Kaia tightly grabbed his wrist. The Lady approached Kaia and put her arm protectively around her. They put their heads close together and locked eyes. All the while they talked telepathically. The conversation lasted quite a while. James felt left out and hoped the Lady would find a way to calm Kaia - a way for them to escape this mess. The remaining selkies stood near them but ignored James. Well, at least they weren't pointing their tridents at him this time.

After a while, James heard a noise near the trail. He turned and saw Ervin. He sat in a chair on a platform supported by two poles. Four of the selkies carried him. Shelly followed on foot. "He looks like a prince," James said without thinking.

"Yes, a prince," the Lady repeated.

The selkies set Ervin on the ground beside the black rock. "Now we council," she said.

Kaia related what she learned when she was home with her parents. She told everyone her parents weren't ready for the ocean dumping. The ship needed some additional work. That meant they had a little time to stop the ocean dumping, but her parents were responsible for the fish kill. She told them about the remarks made about the EPA. Ervin commented that congress had long ago gutted the EPA by limiting enforcement funds. "The EPA tries to regulate, but they've lost their teeth."

"After what Mom demanded of me, I can't ever go home," Kaia said. "I don't see any other choice than to run away. I'm not safe anywhere. Please let me change my mind and join you in the sea."

"If I could, I would spare you this pain," the Lady said. "But the choice, once made, is final."

"What can we do?" James said.

The Lady turned toward him. "I thought this was Kaia's problem?"

"This is our problem," James said.

The Lady spent a moment looking back and forth at both of them. She noticed the black pearl necklace that hung around Kaia's neck and smiled. "I see."

"It's a problem for all of us," Ervin said. "I should have anticipated this."

"You did the best you could," the Lady said.

"I can't find a single solution, except for her to run away."

"Perhaps that will be necessary."

"It takes time to create a new identity. I don't know if it can be ready in time."

"There's another way," The Lady suggested. "Kaia could use the Selkie voice to enthrall the CEO and avoid sex with him."

"No," Kaia said. "That's not right. I would control him and then dash him on the rocks. No. It's immoral and wrong." *And it wouldn't be fair to James,* she added telepathically to the Lady.

The Lady laughed long and sensuously. "Yes. We are evolved creatures after all. We have morals, too. You are right, it is great wrong, but a wrong you may have to commit to prevent a greater wrong."

"Is there no other way?" James asked.

Ervin put his hand on James' shoulder. "I understand how you feel, but you may need to let this happen."

"No," James said and glared at them.

Kaia took his hand. "I love you, James. Don't ever forget that."

"We're done then," Ervin said. "I'll have Cal establish new identities for Kaia and James should they be needed."

"I see a flaw in this plan. How do I control the Selkie voice?" Kaia asked.

"She knows how to use it," James added.

Kaia blushed.

"You've practiced?" The Lady said.

"Not intentionally, but it does have an effect on James and my Dad."

"Then you know how it feels. You pull it from the depth of your soul. When you use it, human males desire to obey you. Be careful, it doesn't work on most females."

No kidding. "How do I control it?" Kaia asked. "I don't want to command James. I don't want an obedient slave, but someone who truly cares for me."

"You'll learn to distinguish what comes from your heart and what comes from your mind." The Lady raised her hand and four selkies approached Ervin's chair. He made a quick bow to her and then was carried away.

She took hold of Kaia's hand and briefly touched the pendant. "It may not be necessary, but hold tight to James when we leave. He's spent too much time with us and may desire to follow."

Kaia took James' hand and became his anchor when the selkies left. She watched James as his eyes followed them. He smiled but looked into Kaia's eyes. She sensed he could resist their call. When they were gone, she pulled him close and kissed him.

"They're gone," he said.

"Yes."

"I hope I didn't embarrass you," he said.

Kaia laughed and they hugged. The orca pods offshore still swam back and forth in an agitated sea.

The sea will remain restless, The Lady said.

Kaia wondered – does even the sea obey my commands?

No.

Then James heard the Lady's voice in his head. *You should understand; Circe was a sea witch.*

James returned his thought to her. *Am I indeed a*

descendant?

The river of DNA flows and has many branches. It is difficult to find the source, but I know this, you are unlike other humans. You feel the ocean flow in your veins. The ocean feels your emotions. Kaia is fortunate to have met you. Together you give me hope.

After they returned from the Black Rock, they dressed for lunch and met in the Atwater dining room.

"What do we do until we have new identities?" James asked Ervin.

"You're set on running way then."

"I certainly don't want Kaia toying with some CEO."

"I don't like the idea either," Kaia said.

"You have two choices," Ervin replied. "You can hide, or you could pretend that nothing has changed."

"I'm not going back home!"

"I'm not suggesting you do. You've run away but your parents don't know it. That buys us time. Sooner or later Jacob will call me to see how you are doing."

"He'd suspect I'd be here?"

"Of course, where else would you be?" He paused and looked at the black pearl necklace hanging around Kaia's neck. "From James?"

"Yes."

"Lovely. Well then, I'd recommend against hiding because that will only encourage Lana to do something stupid."

"So, we just continue with our sailing lessons and stay here at night?" Kaia said.

"Both of us?" James said.

"Maybe James should spend most of his time at the marina," Ervin said. "That would make Lana think everything was going as she planned."

The next morning they went sailing. Once they cleared the harbor Kaia steered a course due West. It was windy. To compensate, the sails had been reduced. The mainsail had been replaced with a smaller and more rugged mainsail and the Genoa replaced by a jib. Still the boat heeled sharply, and they moved up each wave and down each trough. The boat jerked each time the bow bit into a wave.

"This takes more skill," James said.

"And more strength," Kaia added.

"Only if the sails aren't balanced. Too much mainsail and the boat will steer into the wind. Too much jib and the boat will turn downwind. Either way, you will fight the boat with the wheel. You need to learn where your boat balances under all weather conditions."

"I get the physics, but what do we do about it?"

"How does the boat react?"

"It wants to steer into the wind."

"Then we either need less mainsail or more jib. We could reef the mainsail but that's difficult and not necessary unless the wind increases. The jib is equipped with roller reefing. I can let it out a little."

James rolled out some jib, secured the lines and then trimmed it.

"How's that?" he asked.

"Beautiful," Kaia said. "What a difference."

"I learned the hard way," James said.

"Why do you think Granddad wants me to learn to sail under these conditions?"

"Where will you go if you run away?"

"I don't know," Kaia replied.

"You're a selkie, you need the ocean. You're not going to hide in the middle of some continent."

"Do you really think we'll have to run?"

"Do you see any other course?"

"The Lady said I could use the voice to control him."

"We both know that's wrong and I sense you don't know how to control it."

"It's true. I can't control it. Using it I'd cease to be me and become some sort of monster. If I did that, I would take a big step toward being like my mother."

"Then what choice do we have?"

Chapter 17 - My Prison

I walked into a room I've seen many times
Slammed the door and started to cry
My house may look like a mansion
But it's a prison
The people who live here look happy
But it's a mask
An illusion
I'm the princess trapped inside these bars
I can't follow my dreams
Once there was a time
different
from this one.
A time of freedom
A time of hope
A time of choice
My prison won't take these from me.

Bill walked into Lana's office. She sat behind her laptop and had just reached for the phone. She paused in mid-motion, looked up at him and glared at him with narrowed eyes. Her lips drew up in a snarl. She shoved the phone back in its cradle. "My patience is growing thin, and you're no help. I didn't tell you to chase her or assault James. You know better!"

She reached in her desk drawer and took out her knife. She used it occasionally as a letter opener. She gestured with it at Bill while she spoke. Bill stared at the point each time she shook it at him. A trickle of sweat ran down his face. "What in the hell were you thinking," she said. "Jake sent her to executive driving school. Do you think you can match that...in my SUV. You wrecked it. I will take that out of your pay. Do you know how many people I had to pay off? I sometimes wonder whether you're worth it."

"Ma'am, you're right. It's just the things Candice said to me. They riled me up. I got angry."

"You got drunk, you bastard. Don't you dare blame Candice for that!" Lana paused and took a deep breath. She jabbed the knife into a pad of paper on her desk. "Don't think on your own. Don't even think you're going to think. If you're going to act stupid, do it on someone else's time. Not on my payroll. Don't involve me." She looked at him and twisted the knife from the paper. She waved it at him again. "I know you...don't you dare take this out on any of my girls."

"Yes, Ma'am."

"Thanks to your stupidity, you've been grounded by the police until we bring your case before the right judge. You need you license to drive - idiot. Surely your men can handle things until then."

This was the opening Bill waited for, an opportunity to change the subject. "They've been occupied acquiring the items you requested, ma'am."

"You'll be ready then, should they be needed?"

"I will be ready *when* they're needed. I'll get them set up in the guest house."

"Good, get over there and supervise."

"It will be my pleasure," Bill said with a gleam in his eye.

Bill hurried out. He didn't want to incur any more of Lana's wrath. Besides, there were things to occupy him, things that needed to be set up, things he couldn't wait to use on Kaia. When he left, Lana rummaged through some papers on her desk before she made phone calls. The judge she had in mind required the attention of some of her girls - the younger ones. They'd be his reward, but they would carry a message that Lana had enough evidence to create a scandal anytime he failed her. Shortly after she finished the arrangements, Candice arrived.

"You're late," Lana said and rose from her desk. She still held the knife. She looked at it and set it down. She walked up to Candice. Candice sensed her foul mood and shrunk back.

"You wanted me to spy on Kaia," Candice blurted out. "She didn't go sailing yesterday. I overheard Charles tell Grant to look after the boat because they went to Ervin Atwater's."

"That meddlesome old fool. Well at least I'll know where she is."

"But she went sailing today."

"Tell me, Candice, how does Kaia do it? What's her allure? I don't understand it, but just look at Bill. She's probably responsible for his stupid car chase. He can't keep his eyes off of her."

"Or his paws."

"He'd better not touch her."

"He paws and pinches everyone...hard, and he doesn't limit it to the butt. I still have bruises from him."

"Imagine what he could do to anyone who disobeys me. Do you understand that lesson?"

"But you keep Kaia off limits."

"She's my daughter."

"Is she really? Does she share your interests? Does she share your goals? Is she like you at all?"

Lana slapped Candice hard across the face. Candice backed away from her but didn't leave. The threat of Bill was far too real. Lana turned away from Candice and returned to sit at her desk. She sat a moment and then looked up at Candice.

"I won't apologize," Lana said, "but you're right. Kaia needs a change of attitude. Spy on her, but keep your opinions to yourself."

"Yes Ma'am."

After Candice left, Lana picked up the phone and called Bill. "Do it," she said. "I want Kaia here tonight. I'll be at a charity event this afternoon. Do it while I have an alibi."

That afternoon, Lana sat next to Jake in his Mercedes on their way to a charity performance in the city. They regularly attended these events and provided financial support to worthwhile causes. Jake would mix with the businessmen and bankers while Lana gossiped with their wives.

"I've been thinking," Jake said. "Maybe Kaia's right? We need to thoroughly test the containment vessel. I'd like to know it will maintain its integrity a thousand years or more."

"Are you second guessing your scientists?"

"No, I just have a feeling."

"First Kaia, now you," Lana said. "Decisions are made on facts, not feelings."

"I could put Kaia into the science department as a trainee. She would learn firsthand."

Lana turned away. She gritted her teeth and glared out the passenger seat window. Jake drove on while he contemplated Lana's comment. Facts were important of course. Truth was important, but what was the truth? That's where feelings came in. It was the conscience - the ethical arbiter. Truth was never complete. One always had to contend with the law of unintended consequences. Further testing was reasonable, even necessary.

Lana interrupted his thoughts. "You know James and Kaia are having an affair," she said.

"That's not the way I heard it from Charles. I've checked James out. He's a good lad."

"Jake, you're blind to what's going on, as usual. You noticed the necklace she wore last night?"

"The black pearl, of course I noticed it. James gave it to her."

"Men don't give women things like that without a reason."

"She could do worse than James."

"Are you saying you don't mind?"

"James comes from a good family. If he's in love with Kaia then I'm happy for her."

"Do you remember when you gave me that first necklace?" He nodded. "It was after a weekend of hot sex. Do you really think Kaia is still a virgin?"

I gave you a diamond, not a black pearl. It doesn't mean the same thing. He laughed. "You're not one to preach morality. She's eighteen and old enough to make her own choices. I'd rather she waited to have sex until she's married, but she's an adult. We've taught her what we can, but she's on her own now."

"I don't want her stuck on the first guy she screws. There are others who can take much better care of her."

"Did Kaia admit to having sex with James?"

"She wouldn't confess to it, but a mother knows."

"Those are feelings, dear...not facts," Jake said. "I recall..."

"Candice told me about James. They had an affair until James broke up with her over Kaia. He's not as good as you make him out to be."

"I wasn't either. You knew that, but I've been faithful to you from the day we met."

"Jake," Lana said with a tear in her eye, "she's my little girl, and I only want the best for her."

"Then drop it. Don't spread dirty rumors, dear, especially tonight with your so-called friends."

"I know how to behave," Lana said, but her voice dripped with acid.

They arrived at the performance and were escorted into the building. Once inside, they greeted others in their circle. Lana saw Candice in the crowd. She shared a drink with a young man in a military uniform. Lana smiled. Candice would soon move on to their target.

"I see Richard, where's Candice," Jake asked.

"See the military uniform. She's the blond."

"I'd like to meet her," he said.

"You've never wanted to meet one of my girls before."

"But she knows Kaia. She may be able to help."

"Later, dear," Lana whispered. "Richard might suspect a connection if we're seen with Candice."

Lana left Jake to join a party of smartly dressed women. She talked with them and listened to their comments, but she positioned herself to watch Candice. Lana had counseled her young assistant not to rush things. Tonight Candice needed to spend just enough time with the banking CEO to gain his interest. Lana knew all about his sexual fetishes and had trained Candice to play right into them. All Candice had to do was to give him a way to contact her.

This was going to be a profitable evening after all.

It was near sunset when Kaia and James docked the boat. Grant met them at the dock as was usual. "Can we get a drink?" Grant said.

"I'll pass," Kaia said. "I'd rather avoid the image of the two of you getting drunk."

"I don't drink to excess," James said. "At least let me walk you to your car before I join Grant."

When they stepped off the dock, they parted from Grant and walked across the nearly deserted parking lot to Kaia's car. Before they reached it, a black van pulled into the parking lot and drove slowly past them. Kaia gave it a brief look and turned away. It pulled quickly into a nearby parking place. The doors opened.

"Something's wrong," Kaia blurted out.

The words were barely out of her mouth when she and James were each hit by a tazer. They both collapsed on the pavement. Two figures in black rushed over, picked up Kaia, tossed her into the van and then sped away.

"Grant," Charles yelled over the loudspeaker. "James is down in the parking lot. Kaia's been kidnapped. I'll call the police. Grab the mechanics and see to James."

Charles immediately called the police and gave them a description of the vehicle. Then he called Ervin.

171

"I should have expected this," Ervin replied. "There won't be a ransom note. Kaia's threatened to run away from home. Her parents are likely behind this." Then he told Charles the whole story, but left out the selkies.

"I'll still have to call Jake," Charles said.

"Be cautious."

Jake was driving home with Lana when he received the call. "Charles, what's up."

"Kaia's been kidnapped."

"What?"

"They attacked James and Kaia but left with her."

"Attacked both of them?"

"I've already called the police. I have the abduction on video."

"I'll call the FBI."

"Okay."

"I'll send them to you for the video, and Charles, I'm sure you and your son will do everything possible to get Kaia back." He hung up.

"What's happened," Lana asked.

"Someone's kidnapped Kaia. They'll probably want money or some of our secrets."

Lana smiled. *He's bought it - hook, line, and sinker.*

Charles finished talking with Jake and immediately called Ervin to convey what Jake had said.

"Jake may not be involved," Ervin said, "but what about Lana?"

"You still think it's a family matter and not someone out for a ransom."

"Either way, I'll find out." He couldn't tell Charles the whole story. Shelly was already searching for Kaia. The selkie guards had already been alerted. All selkies, land and sea, were looking for her. "We'll get her back, Charles. Meanwhile, look after your son. He gave Kaia a black pearl pendant."

"He did?"

"The question is," Ervin said, "does Jacob know and what's his opinion?"

Kaia awoke from her nightmare. 'Chloroform?' she wondered, 'or something worse.' Her fogged mind started to clear. She felt restraints on her wrists, and that suggested caution. She would not panic. There was a gag in her mouth. She slowly pulled on the restraints to test them. She was attached to something, possibly a bed. She could move her feet. She opened her eyes and would have screamed if she could. Bill stood over her and leered down at her. This time she struggled to free herself and banged the cuffs against the metal bed.

"No one will hear you," he said in a casual but sinister voice. "Relax; you're going to be here with me for quite a long time."

She wanted to use her voice and tell him to go shoot himself. But no, she needed him to free her. *If I can use my voice, I can protect myself.* She knew it was wrong, but she thought about trying to control Bill. She wasn't ready, but she had to be. The only training she had was accidental use on James. She could fail, and then worse things could happen. This was Bill, and he was an SOB. She was helpless. No, she wasn't, she could rely on the voice. It gave her renewed strength. She could control this situation, as bad as it seemed to be.

She started to hum. The gag didn't prevent that.

Bill backed up. "You little minx, you're enjoying this."

Hell no, just take the gag off, will you?

She continued to hum, and he bent over her. He ran his hand up her thigh.

"I've been looking forward to this a long time," he said.

She didn't struggle. When he was close enough, she kicked him with all her might in his groin. He flew away from the bed and landed with a thud on the floor. She struggled to free herself and listened to him moan. Finally, he got up.

"You'll regret that, bitch."

Just take off the gag, Dodo. She raised her feet, ready to strike at him again. He jumped back when she tried to kick.

"Ah, you're making a game of this. What fun. Do you need tighter restraints? I can arrange that."

He grabbed rope and sat on her so she couldn't kick, then started to tie the rope to one ankle. He was in the middle of securing one leg when Lana walked into the room. "What do you think you're doing?"

"Securing her legs. She kicked me in the groin."

"Good. I'll do worse to you if you hurt her. We're here to program her, not damage her."

Kaia recognized her mother's voice. *Program me? For what? Oh, so I would become her perfect little daughter.* Kaia knew what that meant. *You won't succeed, Mom.* Kaia noticed her father wasn't present. *Maybe he doesn't know. Where am I, anyhow?*

Bill backed off, and Lana approached Kaia.

I need to play Mom against Bill.

James sat in his father's office and answered questions for the police. They'd already reviewed the tapes of the kidnapping and taken them for evidence. Charles objected because the FBI had been called in. The police said the FBI could contact them. This was their jurisdiction.

"James, why did you walk her to the car?" a policeman asked.

"It's polite. Is this about me or Kaia? I was tazed too, you know. What are you doing to find her?"

"We were given an anonymous tip you were involved."

"Oh sure, I just love being tazed!"

"You have a motive. The source said you had her on your boat overnight and she was underage."

"Dad, do you want to explain this? They don't seem to believe me."

Charles replied. "Kaia had severe leg problems and couldn't drive home. On her grandfather's advice she spent the night on his boat with James to protect her. You can verify this with Ervin Atwater if you like. By the way, it was her eighteenth birthday, so she wasn't underage. Everything else is gossip and has no foundation in truth."

"We'll check with Mr. Atwater. Is there anyone else you would suspect?"

"Yes there is," James said. "A guard from the Stone household threatened me because I was with Kaia."

"I can show you the tapes," Charles said. "He chased after them from the parking lot."

"Do you know the fellow's name?"

"It was Bill. I think he was recently arrested for drunk

driving."

"Tackling the Stone household is out of my league. I'll toss this up to my superiors."

"Maybe you should let the FBI handle it," Charles said with a caustic tongue.

Lana pointed her finger at Bill. "You bungled it, you bastard. James was supposed to be blamed, not attacked, idiot. Your men were too quick. Now the police are interested in you. Get out of my sight before I really get angry. Make yourself useful and come up with an ironclad alibi. Or do I have to do everything myself."

"Ma'am, it was my guys that bungled it, not me."

"You planned it. No excuses."

He left, and Lana removed Kaia's gag. "Sorry we have to do this dear, but you have your priorities all wrong."

"Bill groped me, Mom. That's why I kicked him. He threatened to tie me down and rape me before you came in."

"He did, did he?"

"I wouldn't lie to you."

"It'll be just you and me. I'll keep him away."

No, I can't use the voice on you.

"Mom, please don't gag me. You can make Bill behave, and I can call for help if he gets out of hand."

Lana had to think about it. Bill was a problem but she needed him. He was the only one who knew how to use this equipment. "Okay," she said, trying to sound reluctant. "I'll have a monitor installed."

"Where am I anyhow?" Kaia asked. "This isn't part of our house."

"We're in the basement of the guest house."

My house, my prison.

Chapter 18 - The Black Rock

Alone figure sat stationary by the seashore. His gaze stretched out to the horizon. He felt insignificant beside the vast expanse of the turbulent sea. He was crushed beneath a slate gray motionless sky and remained mesmerized by the foaming breakers that rhythmically groped the shore. He sat on the black rock, far back from the reach of the waves. He'd been rigid and silent for hours. Even the gulls, resting nearby, and sandpipers, poking and playing about his feet, considered him a permanent fixture of the landscape.

His face was vacant and expressionless, and his eyes hollowed by some phantom. Only his hair and jacket moved, driven by the cold, relentless, and sometimes gusty, wind. He felt a storm brewing. One was already tossing inside his mind. The sea and sky expressed echoed his brooding mood. They moved together with his thoughts. Anger and frustration built inside him like the waves and the oncoming storm. James watched the next wave rise as it approached the shore. Slowly, it grew higher and gained a lighter blue-green crest with a darker underbelly. The crest curled over and fell upon itself, turned white, and then crashed, shattered on the rocks, until it touched the pebble strewn shore. Then it reached up, far into the shore, until its energy was spent. It left pools and rivulets that hastily tried to return to the mother sea. For hours, he'd watched the sea breathe in and out the emotions of his life. It should be calming, but it wasn't.

It was hopeless. It had been hopeless from the beginning. Now Kaia herself was gone. Two days, and the police were no help. They'd been given a suspect, Bill, but they hadn't even brought him in for questioning. James had gone to Kaia's house to talk with her parents, but thugs had driven him away at gunpoint. He was outnumbered and powerless against them. He had an ironclad alibi, but the police still suspected him. With his father's blessing, James took a vacation away from his duties at the marina. While he was gone, Grant cared for his boat.

He wanted answers. This rock, this very rock, was the place where he spent one quiet evening beside Kaia, quiet, until the Lady of the Sea walked out of the ocean and made Kaia choose. Her choice forever changed both their lives. He wanted Kaia, wanted to spend the rest of his life with her, and now she was gone. How could he get her back? He wanted action, but to act, he needed to know who kidnapped her and where she was. Then, just let someone get in his way.

Damn the Lady. She was indeed a siren, intent on smashing his life on the shoals, for that's what she'd done. He sat beaten and broken on this rock as if he were a piece of driftwood tossed there by the uncaring sea. He wanted to take back the meeting with the Lady and all that resulted from it, but he knew, without hope, there is never a way to take back the past. But, without the Lady, would he be in love with Kaia? He thought, briefly, what life would have been like if he hadn't broken up with Candi. She would have made his life miserable with all her affairs. Why didn't he see that when they met? He'd been a fool. Trust must be the foundation of any successful relationship. There was no way he could ever trust Candi.

James continued to stare vacantly at the breakers, but now the pattern of the waves changed, scattering around something new in the water. There wasn't a rock there a moment ago. He was sure of it. His expression changed. His eyes focused on that spot and quickly dilated. His pulse increased, and he immediately rose from the rock. The object in the water grew larger and moved forward, closer to him with each wave. First, he saw her long black hair, then the waves breaking around her unclothed torso. The Lady was here, and he was unprotected. *What could she possibly want from me?* He turned to flee, but she started to sing.

Why do you run? The Lady said in his mind.

"I want answers, but I'm not sure I want yours."

The song continued. He heard the longing call of the sea, the call for the waves to return to their mother. He was lost, lost to her siren call. His mind screamed at him to flee, but the sensuous nature of her call demanded he turn and go to her. Still he fought it. He pushed images of Kaia to the front of his mind. It helped. It strengthened him and made the Lady make her call more insistent.

Nine of the guard walked out of the sea behind her.

We each seek the same thing, James.

Involuntarily, he placed one foot in front of the other and walked toward her. She awkwardly walked toward him until they were about six feet apart. She stopped her song, and it broke the enthrallment. His eyes flicked frantically one way then the other, to search for an escape route, but there was none.

Relax, we will not harm you.

Running from her was useless, she'd only sing again, and draw him back to whatever she would demand of him.

"What now? Kaia's gone. What more can I do?"

"It is for Kaia's sake, and yours, that I am here," the Lady said. Her voice was musical, as before. It carried that same vestige of siren enthrallment, although to a lesser degree. It demanded he remain intent on her every word, unable to miss any beat or any nuance, unable to avoid its erotic call. He put one foot forward toward her and then pulled it back. She smiled, and he heard a musical laugh.

"What happened to her," he demanded. "Where is she?"

"Kaia needs to talk to you. She's in my mind. Speak to her. I will be your conduit."

He knew selkies could communicate telepathically with each other so he spoke directly to Kaia. "Kaia, where are you?"

"Mother kidnapped me," the Lady said, but it was Kaia's voice he heard. "She wants Bill to turn me into the perfect daughter Mom always wanted."

"They're trying to program you?"

"Yes."

"That's dangerous. Are you all right?"

"For now, but I don't think violence is out of the question. That's why we need to act quickly."

"What can I do?"

"I've been practicing with the voice but using it hurts my legs. It's made me weak. I can barely walk. I'm...I'll try to make Bill take me to the hospital. The Lady will know when. Don't try to rescue me! The Lady will take care of that. As soon as possible, we need to run away. Go to Granddad and work it out."

Kaia's voice was gone, and he once again faced the Lady. She didn't speak, or worse, sing, and he wasn't giving ground.

She grinned back at him. *I see - your love for Kaia is greater than your fear of me. Do not fail her. Do as she says, her rescue and your escape requires all of our family.*

Then she turned and walked back into the dark swirling waters. This time, he didn't need Kaia to help anchor him from his desire to follow her into the ocean and to his doom. Moments later, he saw her fin appear when she swam away into the distant ocean.

Six members of the guard followed the Lady into the ocean. The other three had already walked up the trail toward the highway.

He turned around. With renewed energy, he jogged upward toward his Jeep. When he reached it, all three were seated.

I am Mera, Shelly's sister. Take me to my Dad.

"Buckle up ladies," he said. The other two looked confused.

"Mera, would you show them how, please."

He drove and quickly realized his unusual predicament. There were three attractive naked women in his car, and they were driving down a heavily traveled four lane highway. This was strange, even for California. *I'll never get used to selkies.* Everyone else on the highway noticed, the males gawked at them, but it didn't seem to bother the women. He observed a few women punching their husbands in the arm.

Damn, I'm going to get arrested.

Gawkers nearly caused numerous accidents. The worst were the truckers who swerved into their lane as they looked down from their high perch into his Jeep.

Thank God, I didn't leave the top down.

They arrived, and Mera rushed out of the Jeep to give Shelly and Ervin a big hug. The other two followed her. They all went inside.

Great, a house full of selkies.

Shelly turned toward James. "Ervin waits in the library."

She and the other selkies remained in the parlor while he went to Ervin. Ervin already had two drinks poured and waved for James to sit beside him. The conch shell that usually sat on the table now lay in his lap. James sat.

"Now we wait. That's the hardest part of any mission - the wait before the battle. Kaia must make the first move."

"And if this doesn't work?"

"Then we take bolder action. In Kaia's plan, no one gets hurt; no innocent bystanders get in the way."

"I wish I had your confidence."

"We have a secret weapon."

"Yes, the selkies. But I want to help."

"Don't. It may seem illogical, but the hardest part is played by the officer in charge who must stay behind and hope everything works out as planned. You must stay. The police already suspect you. Don't give them hard evidence. Let the rest of us do the work."

"I understand the logic, but my heart says otherwise."

Ervin chuckled. "When you're my age, you learn to think both with your heart and your mind. You need to plan your escape. First we get Kaia, and then you both leave. I insist you take my boat."

"That's why you had me work on it?"

"Contingency planning, if you will."

James realized that running away with Kaia was a suicidal mission. It meant spending the rest of his life in flight and hiding.

"How quick can we get our new identities?"

"If you want this done well, it takes time. You don't want the first custom official you meet to arrest you, do you?"

They moved into the dining room where a big map was laid out on the dining room table. All of the hospitals were marked, as was the Stone estate.

"All we need to know," Ervin said, "is which hospital."

"We have some selkies who have chosen land at one of them," Shelly said. "They are still connected to us."

"The three of us can cover the others," Mera added.

"I'll drive," Shelly said, "drop you off, and station myself to go to either place."

"Let's go," Mera said.

"Wait girls," Ervin said. "Don't you think you should get dressed first?"

Mera blushed. "Sorry, Dad, I've forgotten what it is like to be human."

"I've got some clothes that might fit," Shelly said. "A couple of you might fit into Kaia's things." The girls left and went upstairs.

"What about me?" James asked.

"You stay here for the moment. We need to talk. Then you go home and remain very visible. "

"Why?'

"They want to pin the kidnapping on you. Don't help them."

"Kaia could tell the police who really kidnapped her."

"She could, but her parents are rich and powerful. They will buy doctors who'll claim she's delusional."

"We know the truth."

"Oh, so you're going to tell them a selkie told you. No court on land will accept her existence. No, James, if you try to rescue her, it would implicate you in a further kidnapping. You'll have the police worldwide after you. Running away is one thing, kidnapping another. You must stay out of her rescue."

"I care too much."

"She already knows that. You showed it when you gave her the necklace." He paused. "You know black pearls have significance in this family."

"She said she liked black pearls."

Ervin laughed. "I don't know whether you meant it, but in our family black pearls signify engagement."

James remembered the black pearl engagement ring that was in the sea chest. He should have known. He recalled the conversation he had with Kaia when he gave her the necklace. "I've never asked her."

"The necklace speaks for itself."

"I should ask her father."

"If you talk to him, it could spoil everything. I suspect, however, he would accept you as a son-in-law. Call it a Dad's intuition, anyhow, you asked me for her hand."

"I did?"

"Sure, not in so many words, but I approve. You two were meant to be together."

"What about Dad?"

"I know Charles would approve."

"This complicates things, Ervin. I can't let her be controlled by Bill. Think about what he might do to her."

"Trust her James. That's the foundation of a relationship. She has control of the voice. He won't be able to harm her. If you go there, she will not be able to protect you."

"Are you sure she can control the voice? I'm not. I'll still go."

Don't make me force you to stay, the Lady said in his mind. *You know I can. But, it will compromise my ability to help Kaia.*

He was powerless to disagree. She could hear his thoughts, and they would betray him. He had to go along with their plan.

James dropped his arms by his side and sighed. "Fine, have it your way. But nothing better go wrong!"

"When Kaia disappears a second time," Ervin said, "you'll be a prime suspect. You'll need an unbreakable alibi and later, a place for both of you to hide. We'll set up the secret room behind Kaia's bedroom closet until I can arrange alternate identities."

"What will I do for an alibi?"

"You'll need to be around a lot of people when she's rescued."

"You want me to be around a bunch of witnesses?"

"You should go to the marina and stay there until called. You'll have to act out your part carefully. Stay around people until after Kaia's rescued."

"I see a flaw. Calls can be traced."

"You'll receive a text message with a time and a picture of the black rock. You'll understand, but the police won't. In case they pry, the number will be untraceable."

"Did you send the texts to Kaia?"

"No, I don't know how to use the danged technology. The Lady does it somehow. Call it magic if you will."

"So it's a call from the ocean?"

He laughed. "You'll leave by my boat."

"Why?"

"Yours can easily be traced. I'm counting on that. I intend to hire your friend, Grant, to take your boat. He'll be accompanied by Mera, who looks a lot like Kaia. Put her in Kaia's clothing and at a distance no one will know the difference. They'll leave the marina shortly after Kaia escapes."

"You think Grant will go along with your plan?"

"That's what friends are for. I was planning on giving my boat as a marriage gift to Kaia. I'll arrange for it to be stocked for a voyage, say to Hawaii."

"Your plan for the police to chase the wrong boat could put Grant in danger."

"He'll gladly do it for you. I'm sure you'd do it for him. Has your father ever told you the story about my marriage to Sedna?"

"You did. What has it to do with this?"

"Plenty. Greatness of heart runs in your family. You pick good friends. Trust Grant. He surely trusts you."

Before he left, James went upstairs into Kaia's room. He knelt in front of the sea chest. He stared at it a moment before he took off his conch shell. *I hope this works.* He set the conch shell on the black rock. *This has to be the right weight to work.* He heard a click and opened the sea chest. He reached in and quickly found the clamshell box. He opened it to check its contents. He smiled and slipped the box into his pocket. He would be ready this time.

Chapter 19 - The Cell

Kaia lay strapped on a hospital bed in the basement of the guest house. Electrodes were attached to her head, and her brain patterns were monitored by Bill. Lana looked down at her daughter and grinned. "Soon my dear, you'll be everything I ever wanted in a daughter." She patted Kaia on the head and handed a journal to Bill. "I think this is Kaia's diary, but I haven't been able to open it."

"I'll make her tell us how," Bill added. He went over to the monitors and sent an electric shock through Kaia. She jerked on the table and opened her eyes, but they were glazed. "Sleep deprivation is important. She'll be ready for more drugs soon. A few more days and she'll be putty, then we can remold her as we like."

"Take good care of my sweet daughter," Lana said. Then she left.

Bill walked over to Kaia and leered down at her. "Just try to sleep," he said. "I can't wait to dish out more pain."

Kaia's eyes met his. He smiled and winked. He enjoyed this assignment. It was the best part of the day. He bent over next to her ear. "I have my own plans for you, Kaia dear, and guess what, your mother will never know."

Lack of sleep and the drugs made everything hazy and dreamlike. She drifted in and out of a dreams state. At the moment, she thought she lay on the sea bed in her room and watched the paintings on the wall. She turned her head around and took in the scene on each wall. The room cradled her like the ocean. She could almost hear the surf gently caress the rock. She looked down at the floor. The carpeting was gone. Her bed lay on a slate black rock. She turned. There was no doorway. Her bed and the rock lay in the middle of the ocean. She turned back to the paintings. The attending selkies on the nearby rocks stirred and began to move like cartoon caricatures. One dove into the sea. While she watched, their caricatures sharpened. They morphed into living selkies. All wore black conch shells, and they all turned toward Kaia. The guard, my guard, she thought. A female orca began to swim circles around her bed. Others arrived and followed it. Soon she was circled as far out as her eyes could see.

She stared down into the oceans and saw into its deepest recesses. In response, the ocean seeped into every corner of her mind. She heard the speech of orcas and their dolphin kin. Then she heard the deeper songs of the humpbacks. The sounds grew until the ocean resonated with sound. All the creatures of the ocean spoke with each other, just the same as people communicated on cell phones. Kaia reached out with her mind and touched the salmon, and then all the fish of the ocean, all the way down to the zooplankton that floated in wide rivers. She watched poisons that flowed into the ocean from the mouths of rivers. She witnessed the overfishing of the ocean and heard sea mothers cry for their children. She saw the oil sludge lying on the ocean bottom in deadly pools. A sea worm crawled through the sludge and was eaten by a fish. She knew that poison would work its way slowly up the food chain. She felt the sea dying, and knew that man and his greed were to blame.

The Lady of the Sea walked out of the ocean and up to the foot of her bed. "Kaia, you're in danger. Don't let them burn your mind out. Stay with me. Let us instead awaken the sleeping selkie."

"I must escape from Bill."

"We must escape from all who would steal our skins and try to own us. We are the ones who choose. Men like him are the reason we developed the voice."

Kaia stared into the Lady's eyes and saw the ocean flowing back at her. She floated with it into the sea. Then she saw herself on the bed through the Lady's eyes. *That's it; let me be your anchor.*

"I know your true name," Kaia said.

"Your heart allows you to see the truth. Keep it secret. I am just the Lady of the Sea." She held out her hand. "Come join me."

Together the Lady and Kaia dove into the ocean. Kaia's legs turned into a fluke as soon as she hit the water, but it didn't end there. This time she turned into an orca and tried to keep up with the Lady as they swam deep into the mother ocean.

Pain began at her toes, erupted into fire at her knees, and consumed her legs. Kaia twitched, she rolled, she screamed, silently at first, followed by a long piercing wail. Her eyes opened with dry sobs. Bill stood over her with a syringe ready to give her more drugs. She knew it had to stop here, nut found it difficult to focus. *Help,* she screamed in her mind. The pain remained, but she felt strength grow like an ocean wave with each pump of her heart. The strength spread like water through her arteries. It began as a small fire, a candle flame, and then it flared and burned. It flowed outward and passed throughout her body, from her limbs into her chest. The power of the ocean rushed through her veins. *I am a selkie. I am the Daughter of the Sea. I am strong.* She began to hum. When she did, Bill lost his grin and stared, unblinking, into her eyes. She started to sing, "Bill, Bill, Bill, beautiful Bill, Bill, you're hurting my legs, Bill, Bill my legs."

She went on singing and watched his expression change. A sweet innocent smile wiped away his evil grin. He stared at her like she was the most precious thing in the universe. She knew that expression. She had seen it on James' face when the Lady sang to him. She had seen it in her bedroom, on James' face before she was aware she had used the voice. She continued to sing and Bill unstrapped her legs and then her other bindings. She sat up and rubbed her legs. She tried to stand. Her legs wouldn't work. She clutched the bed and sat back down. The room spun around, and she became nauseous. Time slipped away until she heard the whales sing. It renewed her. She sang again to Bill, this time sensually. Her song flirted with him, replaced his goals with desires, and made him want to bring a car to the guest house. In her song, she promised Bill a reward when he returned. He smiled at that thought. It was a risky test, but he had stalked her a long time. He left her alone in the room.

There were several minutes of anxiety intermixed with an inability to focus on her surroundings. She still floated in a drug induced haze and had to lay her head down on the table to remain conscious. The ploy worked. Bill returned flushed and expectant. She sang again and rewarded him, allowing him a touch of her ankle while he removed the dolphin anklet, the anklet her father had given her on her sixteenth birthday. Following her commands, he hung it on the inside doorknob of the bathroom and left the door open.

Kaia sat up and touched her chest. The conch shell and the small vial of sea water were still there, but the black pearl necklace wasn't. She immediately knew her greedy mother had taken it for herself. There was no way she'd leave without it. She sang Bill a promise of an even greater reward if he'd retrieve it.

It took a long time. Time enough for her to wonder whether or not her spell over Bill would hold. She was uncertain. Was Mom home? Would she interfere? Was this all worthless? Would she fail? She shouldn't have worried. When she sang, Bill became susceptible to rewards like a good little puppy. He was pliable, a victim to her words, carried on her song. There was no question in her mind about Bill. He was a sick, sadistic bastard. She needed to get away from him as quickly as possible. If he returned to himself, she would be in terrible danger. Trouble was - the bastard seemed to enjoy being a slave to her voice. She felt dirtied by having to use it on him.

Nearly an hour had passed, but he still hadn't returned. By then the drug induced haze had retreated a little. She could focus on the walls, but the room still seemed to move. She saw the journal where it lay in front of the monitors and made a mental note to have Bill return it to her. At least the nausea had decreased. She still couldn't think clearly, but now she felt the presence of the Lady in her mind. Kaia thanked her for her supporting strength.

No, dear child, the strength was all yours. You drew on it when you finally accepted your heritage. You're now a selkie, Daughter of the Sea. I've only taken the journey with you.

She had drawn on selkie power, but it had cost her the use of her legs. The pain was intense. Right now she wanted a fluke, not legs, but she was in the world of the land, not the world of the sea, her world. She could not afford to show her fluke. Would it always be that way? Then Bill arrived with the necklace. He held it out for her like a little child who had stolen something precious. He grinned and waited for his reward. Kaia permitted him to put it around her neck. She inquired and learned her purse was in an adjacent room. She had him fetch it without any promise of reward. He readily obeyed. She had him put the journal in it. Now she sang about her being close to him, his holding her close. He lifted her off the bed and carried her to the car. It hurt her legs, but it was the only way. It took him about a minute to seat her. Then she sang about the hospital.

A short time later, they arrived at emergency. Bill dutifully obtained a wheelchair and wheeled her inside. On the way Kaia softly sang to him. Go back to the guest house, lie on the bed, and wait for me to return with your reward. After he left, Kaia signed herself in. She felt the Lady leave her mind.

Well done, Daughter of the Sea.

Ervin sat up in his recliner when the Lady contacted him.

She's at the hospital. Call Charles. James needs to be especially visible the next few hours.

Kaia explained to the doctors that she had been able to walk until the last few days. She was uncertain what day it was. She told them she had been kidnapped and drugged and wanted to know if she had been raped. The doctors drew blood and conducted a full body examination. When they finished, they focused on her legs. She was taken for an ultrasound and x-ray examination of her legs and back. They indicated they were concerned about blood clots. When they examined her back and hips, Kaia noticed the technician looked at her strangely while she studied the image.

Does my fluke show? Would they find her some freak they would want to study? She knew she needed a quick rescue. *Some heroine I'd make. I can't even walk.*

They were reluctant to give her pain medication until the results of the drug tests were known. In pain, Kaia lay on the bed and waited for the results. Moments dragged into hours until a nurse unexpectedly entered her room.

"They're on the way."

"Who?"

"Mera and Shelly."

"Who are you?"

"One who has chosen land."

"Thank you, sister."

"Sister – I never thought I'd hear that from one of the sea. Thank you."

The nurse left.

It's time for the Lady to text Jacob, Mera said telepathically to Ervin. *He should get here a few minutes after we leave.*

"You'll leave something for him, right?"

Just as planned.

Moments later, another nurse rushed into her room. *I'm your Aunt Mera*, she said in Kaia's mind. A black conch shell hung around her neck. Aunt Mera looked enough like her to be her twin. She brought a hospital wheel chair with her. It took only seconds to get Kaia in it. They waited. Another nurse and a doctor appeared. They both wore black conch shells. That made Kaia smile. They

187

rushed her out the door and down the hall to an elevator. The door closed, and they enjoyed a brief moment of laughter then quickly suppressed it. They still had to get out of the hospital. When the doors opened on the ground floor, Mera wheeled her out. As soon as they passed through the outside doors, Shelly drove up in Ervin's car.

Two policemen walked past the car and toward the hospital. Kaia felt a moment of panic. Mera moved away from Kaia and softly hummed. She caught the attention of the policemen and accompanied them into the hospital.

While the policemen were distracted, Shelly got out of the driver's seat to help Kaia into the car. Mera returned and took Kaia's wheelchair to the hospital door. Then, she took the seat next to Kaia. Shelly drove away.

"Are the police here to check on me?" Kaia said.

"Probably," Shelly said. "No need to worry. They didn't recognize any of us."

"We've got to keep it that way," Mera said.

"Will my fluke show up in the x-rays?" Kaia said.

That caught them all by surprise. "I don't know," Shelly said.

"Then something could still have gone wrong."

"It doesn't matter. Our plans remain the same."

"Is it time to let James know?" Shelly asked.

"Have the Lady tell him an hour from now."

"Can't I talk with him?" Kaia said.

"Absolutely not. Calls can be traced."

"Not all calls." Kaia smiled and imagined herself with James on the sailboat off the black rocks. They clung to each other and kissed. *James, I'm free, and I miss you.*

I miss you too, came his reply.

Shelly looked at Kaia in the rear view mirror. *You're full of surprises.*

I am the Daughter of the Sea, she replied.

That gives us all hope, the Lady said.

The telepathy was costly to Kaia. She bent over and clutched her legs. Mera reached over and put her arm around Kaia.

"I've never known such pain," Kaia said. "I can't walk at all."

"It's imperative we get you into the sea bed without delay."

The pain will diminish once you're in the pool, the Lady said.

"I'm sure James will insist he sit by you once we get him to our house," Shelly added.

That dream, I just can't get it out of my head, Kaia said.

It was close, the Lady said, *but your mind is okay, enlarged a little, but okay.*

Enlarged?

Don't ever forget the dream, you need to remember what you saw and felt, Daughter. It's the reason we must all act.

When the police arrived at her hospital room, Kaia was missing. They immediately sent the floor nurses to search for her.

"She can't have gone far," they said. "She can't walk."

Detective Robbins picked up her chart. "Kaia Stone. Damn. Sergeant call headquarters and report that Kaia Stone is...rather was here."

The arrival of the police to talk with a missing patient quickly reached hospital administration. A representative rushed into her room. "I'm sure she's still in the hospital," he said. "She's probably out for some additional tests."

"A doctor and two nurses took her to the elevator," a floor nurse said.

"Did you recognize them?"

"This is big hospital. I don't know all the doctors and nurses."

The hospital representative initiated a thorough search of the entire hospital. While they waited, the policemen began their interview.

The hospital representative became spokesman, and the nurses became silent. "When the patient arrived, she stated she had been abducted, so we called the police. We followed the correct procedures – see to the patient's immediate needs and call the police."

"I'm not questioning your procedures," Detective Robbins said, "only your complacency. Don't you read the papers? You had Kaia Stone in your hospital and you merely called the police. Her kidnapping has been highly publicized. The FBI is involved. She was here, and you just let her disappear? How can that happen?"

"I'm sure we'll find her."

"Just how many nurses were at the nursing station?"

"Three."

"For the whole floor."

"No, just this wing."

"If an emergency comes up, then what?"

"They call for help."

"That didn't work very well, did it?"

"No, I guess not."

At that moment, Jake Stone arrived and walked into the room, "Where's my daughter?" he insisted.

Detective Robbins turned toward him. "Mr. Stone, we haven't met. I'm Detective Robbins and this is Sergeant Smith. We didn't know it was your daughter until we arrived, otherwise the Chief would have rushed over here. Seems like this hospital doesn't pay attention to the ... " He stopped and stared at Jake. "How did you know she was here?"

"A text," he replied.

"From whom?"

"I don't know. It just said KAIA @ HOSPITAL. I called, and they confirmed she was here."

"Do you know who called?"

"No. There was no callback number." He didn't want to tell them about the picture of the black rock and conch shell that accompanied the message. It reminded him of his family and seemed a private matter. "Now, where is she?" Jake Stone demanded.

"Missing, sir."

"You better tell me everything."

"She checked herself in and told the staff she had been kidnapped and drugged. They say they called the police right away."

"Any idea who kidnapped her?"

Just then a doctor walked in. He looked at the police and then at Jake. He turned toward the detective. "This was a serious case, so I brought her up from emergency myself. I tried to talk to her about what happened to her, but she seemed disoriented, probably some lasting effects from the drugs. She didn't say who kidnapped her. I have our initial test results with me."

"May I see them," Jake said.

"Who are you?"

"Her father."

The detective nodded, and the doctor handed the folder to Jake. "The blood tests confirm her story. She had been drugged." He turned to the detective. "I've saved some samples and my report for forensics. They might be able to tell what particular drugs were used. It looks to me like some witch's brew. Good news, though. She was worried about being raped, but we've confirmed she's still a virgin."

Jake's head jerked up. *What's wrong with Lana, James and Kaia have told the truth all along.*

"There's been no ransom note. Do you have any idea who might have a motive?"

It was time to end the charade. "I know you've focused on James Cersea because you think he has a motive. He didn't kidnap Kaia. I'm sure of it."

"Why?"

"We haven't announced it, but Kaia is engaged to him. He has no reason to kidnap her."

"Love does strange things to people," the Detective replied.

"Forget James, and find the damn kidnapper. That's your job, isn't it? So, was she taken again, right from the hospital?" He glared at the hospital representative while he said it then patted the doctor on the back. "I'm sure you did everything you could for her."

"Maybe you should go home," Detective Robins said. "She might contact you there."

Jake started out the door and made it part way down the corridor before he was stopped by a nurse. "Jacob Stone?" the nurse asked.

"Yes."

She dropped a black conch shell into his hand. "She left this for you."

A black conch shell, Kaia's black pearls, Dad's common shell, my old shell. Shells - a tradition or something more? Those who wear them are my family. Lana lied to me. What am I going to do about that?

James sat in the clubhouse at the bar with a crowd of people. He was running out of stories and jokes when he heard Kaia speak to him mind to mind. That unexpected contact disoriented him. He had stopped in the middle of a story. He smiled and put down his drink. "Sorry guys, I lost my train of thought."

"Maybe you've had enough," one of them said with a slur.

"It's only my third beer," James said, although he had nursed the same one for hours. He never drank to excess - the drunks he witnessed as a child were enough to cure him of ever wanting to be drunk. Besides, he needed to remain sober to carry this off.

The only person who noticed his break in concentration was Grant, and he was in on the plot. James took a few more sips. *How long would it take for Kaia to get to Ervin's? Too long. Way too long.* A few minutes later, James' phone rang. He read the text from the Lady. He closed the phone.

Ninety minutes to two hours - must I wait that long? James remained at the bar with his drinking buddies but kept checking the clock. James could no longer concentrate on his stories and Grant stepped in with some of his own. The hands on the clock dragged. Grant sat beside him and tried to cheer him up. It wasn't cheering he needed. This needed to be over. He wanted to be with Kaia. Finally, his father called him from the office.

"Excuse me," James said with a slur in his voice. He turned to his drinking buddies. "Dad wantss to seee me." He got off the barstool and pretended to stagger toward the office. Grant started to follow. James turned around and put his hand on Grant's shoulder. He leaned on Grant pretending he needed help to balance. "I'd like a few minutes alone with Dad." Grant nodded and returned to his drink.

James walked into the office and shut the door.

"Son, Kaia's been rescued and is back at Ervin's."

"I've talked with her, Dad."

"I thought there were supposed to be no cell phone calls."

"Dad, I didn't. I wouldn't jeopardize the plan. Kaia and I will be leaving as soon as we can."

Charles got up from behind the desk and walked over to his son. He put his arms around him in a hug. "Good. I'm proud of you, son. You've picked a good cause to support."

"Dad, I'll likely be on the run with her, maybe for years."

"Oh, I think Jake Stone will come to his senses before that long."

"You think so?"

Charles nodded. "I'm happy you and Ervin have trusted me with the whole story." He smiled at James. "Our family has always been seafaring. Now the sea has chosen you. Go with Kaia. The future of our world is far more important than our individual lives."

"Then you believe Kaia?"

"Son, I've heard about selkies from Ervin all my childhood. He used to tell Jacob and me the stories. I never thought they were real until now. As for the ocean – those who love it already feel its pain."

"But the risks, Dad. If we fight back, we could get hurt."

"If you knew there was a wrong and did nothing, how could I be proud of you? How could you live with yourself?"

There was a knock on the door. "Come in," Charles said. The door opened and a beautiful black haired woman walked in. She wore Kaia's clothes.

James looked confused.

"It's Mera, Son" Charles said. "I'd know her anywhere. We grew up in the same house. She just arrived in Kaia's Corvette." He pointed up at the monitors and winked. "I have her arrival recorded."

Indeed he had, and it must have been convincing because Mera looked a lot like Kaia.

"Kaia's aunt," Mera said in a musical voice that lingered on the air. She handed James the Corvette keys.

"You have the selkie voice," James said. "Does Dad know?"

"Trust me, son, I know all about it. I knew the moment she spoke, she'd become a selkie. Ervin told us enough stories about the voice."

"Then I'd better get Grant. Have they met?"

"No," Charles said.

James gave him a wry smile, laughed and turned toward the door. "This should be interesting."

"One moment, Son," Charles said, "before everyone gets involved.

James shut the door and turned around.

"Kaia's a lovely woman, so like her great-grandmother."

"So you approve?"

"Son, I don't know whether or not you believe in soul-mates, but each of you seems to complete the other in ways I've never seen before."

"Thanks, Dad."

James left the room and staggered over to the bar. He made it a point to chat with each person. He put his arm around Grant. "It's three-thirty," James said. "Time to get my boat ready."

One of the guys at the bar looked up. He looked drunk, but not wasted. "Did I see Kaia Stone walk in a minute ago? I thought she had been kidnapped."

Grant had seen her too, and watched her walk toward the office. "Perhaps," he said. "Perhaps not."

James and Grant walked away from the bar, but instead of turning toward the docks, they turned towards the office.

"That was cleaver," Grant said.

"But are they sober enough to remember?" James replied.

James escorted Grant into the office. There was a fourth person in the room, the beautiful dark haired woman of about twenty who had posed as Kaia moments before. Grant was in on the plot. He knew she was a selkie, but he'd never seen one before - except Kaia, of course. She looked like she could be Kaia's sister. He wondered about that. Do all selkies look like Kaia? He turned toward James with a huge smile. "James, this might really work."

"This is Mera, Kaia's aunt. You'll be on the boat with her for days. Make sure you call her Kaia if anyone sees you together."

"I should thank you." Grant said.

"For the company paid vacation," Charles said, "You're welcome."

"Ah...yes," Grant said. He smiled at Mera and turned to James.

"You're helping me out," James said. "Do your part, and we'll get together later."

"So, I just slip out and change into look-alike clothing?

"No, you could be seen. You'll have to change here."

"But...Mera's here."

That brought a round of laughter from James, Charles, and Mera. The music of her voice lingered after the others became silent.

"Aren't you being unduly shy?" James said. "Selkies are naked when they come out of the sea. It doesn't bother them. Besides, you're sharing a boat with her, and you'll need to change sometime in the next two weeks."

"I could turn around if it would help," Mera said and filled the room with her sensuous music.

Grant turned toward her and smiled broadly. "What a voice. Do you know many songs?"

"Um, Grant, you might think twice before asking her to sing. Just a suggestion, mind you."

"I'll sing to you if you like."

"Grant, there's something you should know. There are only

female selkies. They use their voice to seduce human males."

"I know how to behave," Mera said. But her voice suggested otherwise.

"I'm not worried about you," James said. "Remember guys, you're headed down the coast for Baja. Mera, I'm counting on you. Make sure he doesn't get distracted."

Mera did turn around and Grant changed his clothing. Then Charles dimmed the lights in the clubhouse. On schedule, a couple left the office and passed by the bar. Heads turned. Mera looked like Kaia, but Grant was taller and of fairer complexion than James. Mera hummed softly and whispered a song of enchantment over the crowd. Everyone thought they saw James and Kaia pass by. Grant put his arm around Mera. They walked out the door and down the dock. Charles and James followed their progress on the security cameras. Within ten minutes they set sail in James' boat.

"Good, they're away, and no one noticed the switch," Charles said.

"But you'll need to edit the recording," James said. "That's obviously not me."

"Son - it needs to be Grant and it's easy enough for me to explain it isn't Kaia."

"Okay, then I'd better leave. Anyone might come knocking at your door."

Charles got up from the desk, crossed the room and embraced his son. "Everything's going to work out. If anyone suspects you, they'll spend the next few days trying to find your boat. There's a lot of ocean to cover when you don't know which direction they went. Then when they get around to asking me, I'll tell them Grant rented it for a vacation with Mera. The paperwork is right here in my desk."

"So, I hide out in the kitchen pantry area until Shelly arrives."

"Yes. You can leave the office as soon as the cameras indicate the passage is clear. Lock yourself in the pantry. I'll trip the breaker so only emergency lights will be on. If the lights go on, it will be a warning to exit the delivery door. I'll flip them twice if you need to hide."

Oh great, more time spent waiting. At least Kaia is safe.

After James left, Charles sat in his office and daydreamed. He wondered what it would be like to join his son on his mission. It would mean he would have to leave his marina in less capable hands, but it could be done, if only Cardea would agree. She'd always been a supportive wife, but this would mean a great sacrifice.

The phone rang and interrupted his thoughts. He automatically answered.

"Charles, it's Jake Stone. I'd like to apologize."

"For what? We grew up together in the Atwater home. We've always been brothers."

"Please, this is difficult for me. I hate being wrong. I left the hospital a while ago. They confirmed Kaia is still a virgin. You were right, and I was silly enough to believe rumors."

"No need to apologize. How is Kaia?" Charles said to be deceptive.

"She's escaped from the kidnappers but has disappeared again."

"Then she must be running from something, or someone. Do you have any enemies?"

"You've got to be kidding. I stopped keeping a list years ago. There must be hundreds waiting in line for me to stumble. What about James?"

"He's probably on his boat."

"Kaia's not with him?"

"I don't know. Why would you think that?"

"Charles, he gave her a black pearl necklace. You know what that means."

"I do, but do James or Kaia?"

"I had hoped Kaia left the hospital to find James. Now I have to worry. There's been no ransom note.

"That's odd," Charles said.

"I thought so too. Why kidnap her if you didn't want something in exchange?"

"Indeed."

"I've pointed that out to the state police and FBI, and it seems to lead to a dead end."

"You said Kaia escaped from her kidnappers. It may still be dangerous for her. She may be running away from someone. My guess is she'll find a way to contact you."

"Or Ervin. I haven't been the best father to her."

"That can change. She needs you now, Jake, more than ever before."

"Charles, I want you to know that Kaia and James...well...they have my approval."

"Mine too..."

After they finished their conversation, Charles called Ervin. He repeated his conversation with Jake and added, "I don't think Jake was involved in Kaia's kidnapping. Lana must have acted alone."

"Charles, be cautious around Jacob. He's far too manipulative for my liking. I continue to hope he'll change. We must wait and see."

It was dark when Shelly arrived in Ervin's car. She drove around to the delivery door for the marina kitchen. She got out in a delivery man's outfit and carried a package into the office. Earlier, Charles had rotated the security camera, so the rear of the car wouldn't be visible. No one would be able to get the license number. While she was inside, James sneaked out the door and around behind the car. He knew how to stay out of sight from the cameras, and his father had explained how the cameras had been rotated. James waited by the passenger door. When Shelly returned and opened her door, he opened his and got in.

They drove into the parking lot and paused next to the Corvette. He slipped out the passenger door and lay down on the ground next to the driver's door and opposite the security cameras. Shelly drove away. He waited fifteen minutes then reached up, unlocked the driver's side door and rolled himself in. Seconds later he drove out of the lot.

Finally, I get to drive Orcinus. Last time wasn't any fun, thanks to Candi.

When Lana and Candice entered the basement of the guest house to check on Kaia, they saw Bill lying naked on the bed.

"I don't believe this, you stupid dick."

Bill quickly sat up, "Where's Kaia. She promised me a reward."

"A reward, for what, letting her escape?"

"I took her to the hospital. She couldn't walk. She said she'd come back."

"You took her to the hospital! Who's brainwashing whom? And I thought you were the expert. Hmm, let's see if I can work this out. You were stupid. Kaia outsmarted you. Kaia escaped. You were stupid. You really need to learn to think without your dick. Perhaps my knife."

His eyes opened wide. "Please, no," he pleaded.

Candice made cutting motions with her hands. "Let me."

Lana looked at Candice and smiled. "Perhaps, but not quite yet."

"Damn." Candice frowned.

"We've got to find her before she talks, and you still think you deserve a reward. Be a good boy and lay back down on the bed."

"What do you have in mind?" Candice asked.

"Help me strap him down."

"Hey wait a minute," Bill said.

"Bill, this is less severe than you deserve. So take your reward."

He knew better than to resist, especially since she held a knife. Together they strapped him down tightly.

"Bill," Lana said, "it's obvious you've been into the drugs. I can only image how she managed to get you to take them. I've underestimated her. She's obviously a very capable little minx. I don't know how she does it, but I've got to worry about damage control. Sleep it off."

She motioned Candice to the door.

"I didn't take any drugs," Bill screamed.

They walked out. As the door closed Bill screamed again, "Don't leave me here." The door closed with a thud, and he struggled vainly against his bindings. He cursed every curse he knew, and there were a lot of them. It was going to be a very long night, and he'd spend it thinking about his revenge on Kaia.

198

Chapter 20 - Another Black Pearl

Nearly weightless, Kaia floated above the bottom of her bedroom pool. It only took slight motions, barely perceptible, of her hands or fluke to keep her there. She peered through the glass sides of the pool at James. He had been her constant companion ever since he arrived. They were together again as was meant to be. He sat beside the pool on the carpeted platform that surrounded the bed. He held the Lady's journal in his hands and tried to figure out how to open it.

With a light flip of her fluke she rose to the surface and moved to the head of the pool. His eyes looked up from the journal and followed her. She scrutinized the wall murals and found comfort in the panorama on the walls of her room. The painted selkies at the foot of the bed kept constant vigil over her day and night. She'd seen them in action. In the side murals, orcas swam free in the ocean, and above them all a single boat sailed, steered by a lady with long black flowing hair. As a result of her imprisonment, Kaia knew these images weren't there by chance, or the whim of the artist. They carried a message to the person who occupied this room. *Three facets of the same life.* Selkies and orcas were linked together of course. And the woman on the boat - she was too.

Kaia swam to the side of the pool near James and grinned at him through the glass. He smiled back at her. She grabbed the glass sides with her hands and casually draped her fluke over the side. She dangled on the pool wall supported in front by her hands and in the rear by her fluke. Water dribbled off her fluke and down the outside of the glass. James carefully moved the journal away so it wouldn't get wet. He picked up a towel and sopped up the flow.

"You're feeling better," James said.

"It's taken a while, but I'm back to my normal self."

"Good, because we need to leave soon."

"I know. I talked with Mera. She told me the Coast Guard caught up with them this morning. Have you heard from Grant?"

"Yes, he called after the Coast Guard left. He wants to continue his 'vacation' with Mera for a few more days."

Kaia laughed, rolled backward into the pool and then playfully lifted her fluke out of the water and waved it at James. To follow that she dove underwater and turned cartwheels twice. Then she swam to the side of the pool and kissed him through the glass sides. Finished, she rose to the surface and leaned over it toward James. "Selkies are irresistible after all," she said.

"I know. That's why I'm worried. Is Grant safe with Mera?"

"He couldn't be safer. Relax, she isn't misbehaving...but she does enjoy his company."

"That's what worries me. He apparently enjoys hers as well."

"Do you seriously think we're the only human/selkie paring?"

"No, but ...well...I'd like you even if you weren't a selkie."

"But I am, James, and that haunting dream I had while I was kidnapped is still vivid in my mind. I see it in the walls around me. I feel it in the tug of the ocean currents. I've got to do something about it."

"You know I will be part of this too."

"Are you sure? Our lives won't ever be normal. We won't have a nice home in the suburbs."

"Let me think about it while you get dressed for dinner," James said. Then he got up, left the bedroom, and closed the door behind him.

News that the Coast Guard had found and boarded James' boat reached Lana almost as soon as it happened. Candice was in Lana's office when she received the call. Candice watched a dark cloud spread rapidly across Lana's face. It wiped away the confident smile Lana always wore. Lana slammed the phone in its cradle.

"They've played me for the fool," Lana spat. Her eyes narrowed and she grabbed a pencil. She stabbed it several times into the desk until the point was broken. She picked up another.

Candice took a step back. "Who did?"

"Kaia wasn't on the boat. Neither was James. The Coast Guard verified it was sailed by two people, Grant Gregson and Mera Atwater. Mera looked a lot like Kaia, but she had a passport listing her as a residence of the Orkney Islands."

"Do you think Kaia arranged this?"

"Damn it, Candice, it doesn't matter. They gave me a false lead. They've had three days to run. They could be anywhere by now."

"Kaia always runs to her grandfather, doesn't she?"

Lana lifted her eyes to Candice and grew a wicked smile. "They could have gone there. I think I should encourage the police to call on him in the morning."

James waited in the sitting room while Kaia dressed. He paced the room from the doorway to the turret, turret to doorway, and then finally settled in the lone chair in the turret. He looked out the window toward the distant ocean. Why on earth did it take women so long to dress? He got up and paced again. Finally the bedroom door opened and Kaia stepped into the room. He walked up to her and lifted the black pearl from her cleavage. "I didn't know what this meant."

"What does it mean?"

"Never mind - let me correct that now." He reached into his pocket and took out the clamshell box then knelt in front of her. "Will you marry me?"

"You took those out of my trunk didn't you?"

"Well, yes."

"They're mine, not yours to give."

"But I thought...I gave you the necklace, doesn't that count?"

"I did accept it, didn't I? Let me think about it. Come on - we're late for dinner."

They went downstairs and ate quietly while Ervin talked about how their ruse had been uncovered by the Coast Guard and how imperative it now was for them to leave the country. After dinner, Shelly got up to clear the table.

Kaia rose. "Wait a minute," she said. Shelly stopped and turned back toward Kaia. "James, did you take something out of my trunk without my permission?"

James stammered. "Yes...Kaia...I did."

"May I have it back...now?"

James stood up, took the box out of his pocket and handed it to her. She opened it and picked up the black pearl engagement ring. "Why did you take this, James?"

He flushed a bright red. "Because I want to marry you," he said. Ervin and Shelly burst out with laughter. "Well, will you?"

"Of course." She held out her hand, and he took the black pearl engagement ring, knelt, and placed it on her finger. The ring fit like it was meant for her. One more piece of evidence that she was just like her great-grandmother. Ervin and Shelly applauded.

"This calls for champagne," Shelly said.

"I've got a very old bottle in the wine cooler."

"We can clear dishes later," Shelly said. "Let's go to the library and celebrate."

"When do you guys plan to get married?" Ervin asked.

"Give me some time to enjoy being engaged," Kaia said.

"Let me suggest Hawaii, after you two arrive. That is, if you're still friends after being cooped up on a small boat for a few weeks."

"So, if we pass the test, we can get married?" James said.

"Does the Lady know?" Ervin asked.

"I'm sure she does now," Shelly replied.

"She'll want to be there," Ervin added. Then he thought about it. *Yes, she'll probably insist on a very special wedding for you, maybe one not seen for the past few thousand years. That should be a sight.*

Early the next morning, Kaia lay on her stomach in her bed. James lay beside her on the bed and gently stroked her hair. It was barely light and both were dressed in pajamas. They had set their alarms so they could meet early in the morning. This was the day for flight.

With pen in hand, Kaia wrote a letter to her father. James moved on to gently rubbing her upper back while he looked over her shoulder at the letter. "Are you really going to tell him you're a selkie?"

"He's part selkie too!"

"But he doesn't admit it."

"He needs to know the whole story."

"Then, are you going to tell him about Lana?"

"Everything."

"Ervin's still concerned about Jake. Lana has a strong hold over him. Who will Jake believe?"

"I left proof in the guest house basement bathroom. He'll believe me when he finds it."

"What about us?"

"Granddad said our fathers talked and that they both approve. So, I'll tell him we're engaged."

"That makes it easier. Will you invite your father to the wedding?"

"I want to, but we can't let Lana know."

"What will your father do about her?"

"He's always been the brains. I never understood what she brought to the firm."

"But she even tried to recruit you to her sordid business."

"Dad would be successful anyhow. He doesn't need the 'opportunities' Mom creates."

James lowered his hands and began to rub her middle back. "You're not wearing a bra."

"Of course not - women never do to bed. You should know that!" Kaia put her pen down and rolled toward him. He pulled her close and felt the heat when their chests met. He pulled her even tighter and passionately kissed her. "About time," Kaia said. "You're aroused."

"I can't help it." he said. "You're beautiful, and I love you."

"And that's why you wanted to snuggle so tightly this morning."

"I'm a guy, you're a girl, and we're engaged."

"In what?"

"Come on, you're not frigid are you?"

"You have a reputation, you know."

"Don't you feel anything?"

"James, I'm not cold. I do react to your touch. I even enjoy it, but ..."

"Okay, this is all new to me. I haven't been engaged before."

"I haven't either. All I know is I'm comfortable with you now."

"Are you saying I should take charge?"

"Only so far."

"How far is that?"

"Until I say stop. We're not having sex until we're married. Just let me finish the letter without any more distractions."

"Yes, princess, can we still pet?"

"After I finish the letter. Don't cloud my mind with sensations."

Kaia rolled back over and continued with the letter. James lay on his side and watched her until she finished it. She signed her name. "I'll give it to Granddad at breakfast."

James nodded and got off the bed. "See you at breakfast," he said.

"Get back in bed, honey. We're going to be together from now on."

Jake woke early from a restless sleep. For three nights he'd derided himself for focusing on work to the exclusion of his only daughter. All his accomplishments now seemed a trifle. He had been arrogant. Everything he'd done paled in comparison to Kaia. It had been three days, and she hadn't called. He wanted answers, and he wanted them now. Most of all he wanted Kaia home. At dawn, he called the police. The superintendent told him they were going to interview Ervin Atwater that morning.

"My father wouldn't kidnap my daughter," Jake said. "She's always cherished him."

"He's your father?"

"I changed my name when I went into business."

"We had a tip he knows something."

Jake thought about that. *He might know something at that. Kaia loves him. She's always taken her problems to him instead of me.* He picked up the black conch shell the nurse had given him and thought about home. *I should go see Dad.* Too many years had passed since he left home following that stupid argument. Dad usually looked after Kaia while he was away on business trips. It started when Kaia was a just a child, when Lana began to treat Kaia as an inconvenience. Strange he hadn't notice that until now. As a result Kaia had been cared for by a series of short term nannies and her grandfather. Lana even sent Kaia off to boarding school when she was ten.

What was I thinking? I should have reared my own child. Kaia's my daughter. Will she ever forgive me? How will I cope?

He knew he could use his father's advice and vividly recalled the fight with his father the day he left the house. It had been over goals and ethics - his father's ethics and his lack of them. He had considered his father old-fashioned. It was money and power that were important for his generation, not the old fashioned belief that we are part of bigger plan. That day, he threw his conch shell necklace at his dad. Now he wanted it back. He wanted that connection to Kaia. He wanted that connection to his family. Would

Dad return it?

Damn, my schedule, I'm going to see Dad this morning.

Shelly walked into Kaia's bedroom. "Time to get up," she said and stopped in her tracks. James lifted his head over Kaia's. "Oops, sorry," Shelly said, "I didn't know you were in here."

James buried his head in a pillow. Kaia rolled on her back and pulled the pillow away. "You look guilty."

"Of what, snuggling."

Shelly smiled and then chuckled. "Is that what they call it these days? I'll leave you two alone."

"We'll be down in a couple of minutes," Kaia said.

"Take your time." She left, and Kaia hit James over the head with her pillow.

"What did I do now?"

"You looked guilty."

"But...but...but."

"We know what we did and didn't do. Appearances James, appearances, remember - the number one rule!"

"Appearances – Kaia, we're in bed together...in our pajamas, no less!"

"Oh...yes we are, aren't we. Oops."

Then they hugged and kissed.

Thirty minutes later, they walked down the stairs hand in hand. Just before they entered the dining room, Kaia turned to James and whispered, "Now, don't look guilty." Of course, that made James anxious just as they joined Shelly and Ervin at the breakfast table.

Ervin looked at them and lifted his eyebrows. "Are you two lovers packed?"

"Our bags are in the pantry, near the garage."

"Good, Shelly will drive you to the boat as soon as she finishes dishes."

"I can help with the dishes," Kaia said.

"I'll clear the table when we're done," James added.

They all sat for the last breakfast they would enjoy together for a long time. It weighed on everyone. Ervin set the mood as they began to eat. "I haven't done all that I could," he said. "I'm partly to blame for the errors of the company. Jake doesn't own it by himself. He owns twenty-seven percent of the stock. I own another twenty-seven percent. Our fifty-four percent guarantee that we control the company. I've always voted with him before, so I'm in part responsible for the current board and this interest to dump toxic waste into the ocean. I can change that if I can build up enough support with other stockholders. I think they might listen carefully to the liability side of the dumping. No one wants to lose money on an investment. But that causes a very visible fight for control of the company. It could become a feeding frenzy. All the company's sins could come out. It would destroy any possible chance at reconciliation."

"I'm more worried about Mom," Kaia said.

"We need a way to neutralize her," Ervin said.

"Just how do you plan to do that?"

"I don't know. The whole dang thing is too complicated right now. I can't expose her without destroying the company."

"Then she's got the upper hand," James said.

"That's why we have to flee," Kaia added.

"My boat is ready. I've transferred the title to Kaia." He pushed the title across the table to her. She picked it up. "Consider it my wedding present," he said.

"Thanks, Granddad," Kaia said and then handed her letter to Ervin. "Could you deliver this personally? I only want Dad to see it."

"What does it say?"

"You can read it if you like. I told him everything."

"Even your intention to marry James?"

"Of course."

"That could be difficult. He'll want to give you away. Do you want that?"

"I'd like it, but can I trust him?"

"Well, that's going to be my challenge. Do you trust my judgment whether he's invited?"

"I trust you completely, Granddad."

"Good. I love a challenge, it keeps me young."

Breakfast was over. James bussed the dishes to the kitchen. Meanwhile, Kaia and Shelly rinsed them and loaded the dishwasher. They had just finished when Shelly turned sharply toward the front door. Kaia felt urgency from Shelly spread into her mind. It appeared as a dark cloud at the front door. Her adrenalin surged. Shelly whispered to James and Kaia. "Grab your luggage. Get upstairs and hide in the secret closet. Hurry and be exceptionally quiet."

James and Kaia rushed out of the kitchen and into the pantry, grabbed their bags, and climbed the old servant's stairs to the third floor. They rushed down the hall and arrived in Kaia's sitting room as they heard the knock on the front door.

Kaia peeked through lace curtains. "Don't move them," James said. "It may be seen." They both could see a police car parked in the circular drive in front of the building.

"Why are they here?" he asked.

"I don't know but it can't be good news. We need to get into the secret closet."

They carried their luggage into the closet, closed the door, triggered the mechanism, and entered the inner closet. They closed and locked the inner door and laid their luggage next to all the trunks. Then they moved toward the bed furthest from the door. It was awkward because they moved from bright light into a dimly lit room. A single small window high in the wall allowed a small ray of light in. It had been a foggy morning that threatened rain, so the light from the window was weak. It provided enough filtered light so they were able to see once their eyes adjusted. They lay down behind the furthest bed when a ray of light suddenly brightened. It fell on Great-Grandmother's Sea Chest and lit up the scenes on its surface. The image of the black rock stood out clearly in the bright light.

"Shelly put it here yesterday." Kaia said.

"Look where the light falls."

"The black rock, where it all started," Kaia said. "Appropriate."

"Who knows about this room?"

"Don't be concerned. This floor was always off limits. Shelly and Ervin would be the only ones."

"My dad and your father were raised here. Tell a child something is off limits and for sure they're going to find out."

"Okay, maybe they know what's on the third floor, that doesn't mean they know about this room. We had to be shown, remember."

"So we just wait this out."

"As long as it takes," she said and laid her head on his chest.

"I long to be on a boat with you, far away from all of this, "

James said.

Jake sat behind the wheel of his Mercedes on his drive toward his father's house. Once he made up his mind, he had called work and told them to cancel his appointments for the day. He cited Kaia's kidnapping as the reason. He wondered how many minutes would pass before Lana heard. He immediately turned off his cell phone. He didn't want an argument with her right now. He would explain later. He turned off the main highway and toward his father's house.

This business has destroyed my family. I've made a mess of it. None of this would have happened if I'd just listened to Dad. Would I have been successful in business, Dad's way? I could have chosen other paths, less ruthless ones. Instead of being feared, I might have been respected, like Dad. He was successful. Even his competitors said good things about him. Will he forgive me?

Shelly opened the door. The policemen provided their identification and asked to talk with Ervin. Shelly invited them in and asked them to wait in the hall. Acting as a dutiful maid or butler, she had them place their cards on a silver platter. Then, she took them to the library and provided the cards to Ervin who nodded and dismissed her to bring them to him. He knew they were playing for time, and this was such a fun game to play with jackass and dumdum. He looked at the cards. Which is which? Who is jackass, and who is dumdum?

"What can I do for you?" Ervin asked.

"I'm Detective Robbins, and this is Sergeant Smith. We understand that Kaia Stone spends a great deal of time here. What's your relationship to her?"

Now I know who jackass is.

"Seriously, you could have asked my son? You spoke to him at the hospital."

"Jake Stone? You're Kaia's grandfather?"

"Guilty as charged."

"How did you know about the hospital?"

"It's a long story. Jacob called Charles Cersea who called me."

"Isn't James his son?"

"I was close friends with Charles' father. After his father died, Charles was raised in this house along with my son. They are like brothers to each other."

Sergeant Smith spoke up. "Didn't Jake say in the hospital that Kaia and James were engaged?"

"So he did," Detective Robins recalled.

"Jacob hasn't announced it, has he?" Ervin said.

"Apparently not. So it's all one big happy family?"

"One could always hope!"

"How come your last names aren't the same?"

"Jacob and I had a fight when he finished college. He left home and changed his name."

"So you don't talk to Jake?"

"We're business partners. We better talk."

"I don't see any motive."

"Motive for what?"

"Her kidnapping."

"Why in the hell would I kidnap my own granddaughter?"

"Yes, why?"

"I think she escaped from her kidnappers and then ran away."

"That makes some sense, but why hasn't she contacted her father."

"That should suggest the problem begins at home."

"What are you suggesting?"

"Hear me out. She's an adult. It doesn't matter if she ran away from home. It's her choice. No crime is committed if she left. However, you still need to find and prosecute the people who kidnapped her in the first place."

"You're suggesting, if she escaped from kidnappers but won't go home, then somehow home is connected to the kidnappers."

"Precisely." *God, is this guy thick.* "Didn't Charles give you Bill as a suspect? Yet you never even interviewed him. I think if you dig deep enough, you'll find he was involved."

"Is Kaia here?"

"She was." *I'm not lying, she's not in this room.*

"So, you know for a fact that she ran away?"

"Yes, Kaia came here after she escaped from the hospital."

"Did she say who kidnapped her?"

"She said it was her mother, Lana Stone, with the help of Bill and someone named Candice. Proving it might be very difficult. Kaia was drugged and is afraid of her mother. I doubt she'll ever go home."

"Do you know where Kaia is?"

"On the run. What do you think? She didn't tell me where she was going, so Lana couldn't find out." *So what's a little lie?*

"Okay, since we're here, do you mind if we search the house?"

"This house has no secrets, gentlemen." He pointed toward his wheel chair. "I'm sorry, as you can see I'm crippled. I couldn't get by without Shelly. She's my help. I need her to get through the day. I'll ask her to show you through the house."

I think I've stalled them long enough and given them plenty to think about.

It had been too quiet in the secret room for James and Kaia. Time stretched out with no sounds and no idea what was happening downstairs. They lay together on the floor a long time in the near dark. They whispered concerns to each other while they waited. They were effectively trapped in the room. All they could do was to wait. There was no way to know what went on downstairs, or was there?

Shelly, what's going on? Kaia asked telepathically.

Remember the policemen that entered the hospital when we left? They're here. Ervin revealed that the kidnappers were Lana, Bill, and possibly Candice. They want to search the house, so be quiet until they leave.

Kaia whispered her conversation with Shelly to James. They lay still on the floor and listened to footsteps and conversations too muted to be understood. The footsteps and conversation came closer. They heard a creak when Kaia's bedroom door opened. Then they heard voices.

"Kaia's bedroom," Shelly announced.

"This is some bedroom!" Sergeant Smith said.

"The rich can afford to indulge themselves," Detective Robin replied.

Shelly abruptly corrected him. "This was Ervin's parents' bedroom. He's maintained it in memory of them. Kaia uses it when she's here."

The detective brushed his hands over a dresser. "It's clean."

"Not being used often doesn't mean I don't keep it clean," she said sarcastically.

"What's in the closet?"

"Clothes...duh! What do you think goes in a closet?"

"May we look?"

"This house has no secrets, Sir."

James put his hand over his mouth to stifle a laugh and thought, it has nothing but secrets.

Kaia and James heard the outer closet door open and crouched lower behind the bed. They heard the policemen search through the clothing.

"Those are Ervin's mother's dresses," Shelly said. "Treat them gently; they're very old and expensive."

Thank James for moving them there, Shelly communicated to Kaia.

The policemen left. Then Kaia wrapped her arms around James and kissed him. A few minutes later, Shelly let Kaia know the police had left. They could come out of the secret room. They picked up their luggage and went downstairs.

This would be a sailing trip, albeit a long one, but they still traveled light. James and Kaia each carried a duffel bag with their clothing. Shelly carried their smaller packs containing toiletries and small personal items. It took a couple of minutes to load these into the trunk of Ervin's car.

"Dad wants to talk with you before you leave," Shelly said.

"You've never called him that before," Kaia said.

"There's no longer a need to pretend."

They left the garage, passed through the cook's pantry and bar and entered the library. Ervin rested in his recliner. He held a conch shell to his ear and set it down on the end table when they entered. "Ready?" he asked.

Kaia rushed over and hugged him. James walked up behind her and laid his arm around her back. When Kaia released Ervin, he took James hand and shook it. "I know you'll take good care of her."

"Their luggage is in the car," Shelly said with urgency.

"Charles wanted to be here, but he understands our need for secrecy. He'll play his part. Kaia's boat is ready to sail. It's fully stocked, but in your travels you'll need money."

"We can manage," James said.

Ervin stared at him a moment, then laughed. "Still the old school, eh, the man must provide. James, take care of Kaia, keep her safe, be together, work together, love together. Don't let ego get in the way."

"Haven't you done enough, Granddad?" Kaia said.

"Not nearly," he replied. He handed Kaia an envelope. "There's cash in various currencies hidden on the boat. This tells you where. There's also a laptop with satellite link. This particular laptop has a special program. You'll see a conch shell on the desktop beside the other program icons. Click on it and you'll get a blank blue screen. That's for protection. Type "Black Rock". Nothing will show on the screen but it will activate a program that will take you to a Swiss Bank and enter the account codes to access the account. You'll be able to transfer funds anywhere in the world."

"Granddad, is all this necessary?"

"Ask yourself what you're going to do with the rest of your life."

The dream swirled in Kaia's memory. "I must do what I can to save the ocean."

"That doesn't come cheap. I felt even when you were a child that you would become the promised one."

"The what?"

"The selkie who would choose land but remain with the sea – the ambassador - the final hope of the ocean, the Daughter of the Sea, and that's just what you've become."

He turned to James. "I think it's time I confess it was my idea to push the two of you together."

James laughed. "It barely took a nudge. We sat together on the black rock. The longer we talked, the more I wanted to be with her. "

Chapter 21 - Family Ties

It was close now, Jake could feel it. He slowed down his Mercedes. There were more houses and driveways along this road than he remembered. Farmer George's field was gone. He wasn't sure where it once lay because houses stretched out to the horizon. But that was the opposite side of the road from his father's house. His side, strange that he should think of it that way, still had a few small fields. He remembered the old wood and brick houses that lined the road. Many were still present. A few had been converted into offices. Some were missing. Her house was gone, that blond he had a crush on in high school. He wondered what happened to her. It had been what, at least twenty years since he'd driven this road.

He found the driveway. The brick pillars looked older. Wild vines clutched to the bricks and the metal gate was permanently open, held prisoner to the chains of the vines. The house was set back. Jake couldn't yet see it. The bushes that lined the drive were overgrown and wild. He wondered who cared for them these days and laughed when he recalled the mess he and Charles made trimming them when they were kids. Jake turned around a bend in the driveway and pulled into the circle drive in front of his childhood home. The house looked the same, but aged. The bricks looked like they could stand a sandblasting to remove the mold and discoloration, but the house stood firm, rooted in place like the ancient trees that framed it.

He stopped the car and looked out the window. The trees where he and Charles used to play were huge and in need of pruning. The tree house and fort were gone. He expected that, but he felt wounded by it. In his memory, he saw Charles and himself playing pirates or Greek Warriors attacking Troy. Those were precious times, lost forever. Charles had done well with the marina, but a gulf had grown between them, created by their different businesses and interests. Yet Charles was still a friend, a brother Jake knew he could confide in.

The white trim on the house looked cared for. The front porch was expansive and inviting. He parked and got out of the car. He walked slowly to the porch while he surveyed the surroundings. He climbed the steps and crossed the wooden porch. When he arrived at the door, he wanted to walk in but stopped himself. This wasn't his home any longer. He picked up the old brass knocker. For the first time, he noticed it was in the shape of a shell. *Odd, I never noticed it before, but then time does strange things to memory.* He knocked, but no one came to the door. He rapped again. *Maybe I should have called.* He saw the old porch swing that hung at the end of the porch just the same as the day he left. He walked over and ran his hands over it. It had been kept in good repair. He sat in it and leaned back. He rocked the swing back and forth and recalled one of Ervin's many selkie stories. Then he heard Charles ask Ervin to read from the Odyssey.

Jake continued to rock and thought about other times, peaceful ones, before the hectic business life drove them away. *Maybe Charles does have it better. He can mix business and pleasure.* That made Jake recall sailing with his father and Charles. It was something that included the whole family; something they frequently enjoyed. He saw his older sisters, Shelly and Mera, with their long black hair blowing in the wind; his mother, the beautiful Sedna, clinging to his father's arm; and Nanny Odessa, Charles' mother talking with them and laughing. He turned back toward the helm and recalled his grandmother, with her long black hair, where she usually was, her hands on the wheel. A silver conch shell hung around her neck and swung loosely with the motion of the boat. Why hadn't he noticed that before?

The front door opened and Jake turned toward it. His father slowly wheeled himself out. "Good to see you, Son," he said.

Jake stood up. "Dad, a wheelchair?"

"It's been a long time, Son."

"Last time ... you walked with a cane."

"It's gotten worse. I can only take a couple of steps these days."

"I can arrange for help."

"No need. Your sister, Shelly's back. She's out running errands."

"She's returned from the Orkneys?"

"She's cared for me for the last few years."

"It's been that long?"

The old man nodded his head. "Come on in. Make yourself at home. There's coffee in kitchen or something stronger in the bar."

Jake held the door open for Ervin who drove himself in. Jake followed. Even after all these years he remembered the way. He glanced from the foyer into the dining room. The table was set as always, and looked just the way he remembered. He pictured Charles, his sisters, Mother, Father, and Nanny seated. Everyone was laughing. He smelled the salmon and saw the fresh apple pies made from their own apple trees. He and Charles used to pick them. A tear formed in his left eye, and he casually brushed it away. He must have recalled a special occasion, because Grandmother had returned and sat at the head of the table.

Ervin wheeled up beside him and looked into the room. "Memories, son?" Jake nodded and Ervin continued. "Some of those who sat here are gone. All I have are the memories." Jake thought his father's voice sounded sad, but Ervin had a broad smile on his face. "They live here," Ervin pointed at his heart and then at Jake's. "They all live here."

Jake understood. He felt them take up residence.

"Let's go to the library, son."

Jake followed and helped his father into his recliner. As he did, Ervin's conch shell slid out from under his shirt. Jake took it in his hands. "Silver? Dad, I recall you wore a common conch shell."

"Times change, Son."

"But the conch shell on the table is the same, isn't it?"

"It was a present from my mother on my eighteenth birthday."

"You gave me my conch shell on my eighteenth."

"Yes, Son, I did."

Jake picked the shell up from the table and held it to his ear. He heard the sounds of waves breaking on the shore accompanied by the whistling wind. They flooded his ear. Beneath it, there was an almost indiscernible voice, ethereal and enthralling. He held the shell a moment and let a smile melt across his face. Ervin smiled back at him. Jake removed it from his ear and set it back on the table.

"Sometimes," Ervin said, "I can still hear her voice."

Jake wasn't sure what to think. Were Ervin's problems with the legs the only sign of his father's aging? Was he becoming senile? Was dementia taking its toll? Jake wanted to recall his father as the strong man who guided his boat securely over rough seas. But that man did not require a wheelchair.

"Can I get you a drink?" Jake said.

Ervin smiled. "What are you having?"

"Scotch and Soda."

"Make mine Scotch and Water with a pinch of sea salt."

Jake went into the adjacent bar. Ervin could hear him open and close doors in search of the bottles. He took even more time trying to find the salt. While he waited, Ervin picked up the conch shell and held it to his ear. He moved it to his mouth and whispered two words. "He's here." He listened to the shell a moment then replaced it on the table. Jake arrived with both drinks.

"I don't usually have so big a drink," Ervin said.

"The bigger the problem, the bigger the drink," Jake replied.

"This one must be a whopper?"

"It is. Dad, I want to apologize for the terrible things I did and said before I left."

"I don't remember them. I only wanted you back home."

"I'm here now."

"Yes, I see. I can also tell something has been troubling you."

"Kaia."

"I thought so. She ran away, Jacob. Here, you better read her letter." Ervin handed Kaia's letter to Jake and slowly sipped his drink while Jake read it. Ervin watched Jake's face slowly change as the dark clouds of anger spread across it.

"I don't believe this," Jake said. "Lana?"

"You have Kaia's own words. Lana kidnapped her."

"She said she was kept in the basement of the guest house. She left the anklet I gave her there as proof."

"Then I suggest you recover it."

"Dad, what good will that do? If Lana is behind this...."

"We have a problem. Most importantly, though, Kaia is safe."

"You helped her escape, didn't you?" Jake said.

"She escaped from Lana all on her own. I merely gave her a place to hide."

"How could Lana do this to her own daughter?" Jake asked, but deep inside he knew the answer. Lana had grown increasingly ruthless as she gained wealth and power. She couldn't stand any adversary that stood in the way of their ... no, her road to wealth and power. "What can we do, Dad? A scandal of this magnitude will destroy us."

"A final reckoning for all the company's misdeeds."

Jake slowly nodded. "You knew." Of course his father did. He hung his head. "I admit to my part."

"We must do something about Lana."

"But what?"

"Do you want to divorce her, or see her in prison? I'm not going to suggest you have her killed."

"I want her out of my life and far away from Kaia."

"Prison and then divorce. We'll need ironclad evidence of the kidnapping and a way to avoid exposing the other crimes she's committed in the name of the company. We may need to buy her silence."

"This is beyond me."

"First, hang onto the letter. Better yet, leave it with me. I know a very good investigation firm, all ex FBI and CIA personnel. They're discrete and not easily dissuaded. They won't work for just anyone. They have to believe in the rightness of the cause."

"I doubt they'll work for me."

"They'll do it for me. One other piece of advice – a competitor who respects you is less dangerous than one who hates you. Build bridges. They won't trust you at first – like Scrooge, you'll have to earn it through kindness and generosity."

"Lana will fight me."

"Good point, you may have to wait until after she's in jail. I know you're angry with her. Can you still act your part?"

"I can, if it will get Kaia back, but how can I get around Lana?"

"You know Lana. I don't think you can trust the police either; they're undoubtedly in her pay."

"Then what should I do?"

"What you need is inside help. I will arrange a new executive secretary for you. You'll find she has excellent credentials. She's quite good at business and has a special gift — telepathy."

"It doesn't exist."

"Oh yes it does, Son, all selkie offspring are telepathic to some degree."

"You mean selkies are real, and you're actually going to put one in my office?" *Dad really does have dementia.* "How will that work out?"

"Both of your sisters are selkies, Jacob. Why do you think

they went to the Orkneys? Kaia, is a selkie. I'm part selkie and so are you."

"I don't feel it." *This conversation is crazy.*

"We're males and selkies are females who must make the choice when they are eighteen. Most choose the sea, but some choose the land."

"Kaia just turned eighteen. Did she choose the sea?"

"No, Kaia's a special case. She chose land but remains connected to the sea. Jacob, they made Kaia the selkie ambassador."

As crazy as it sounds, this is starting to make sense. "Is that why she fought me over the dumping of toxic wastes."

"Yes. She's young and inexperienced. She's weak now but growing stronger with each new challenge. She doesn't yet grasp the enormity of her task."

"Is that's where James comes in?"

"Ah, James, he complicates her task for the better I think."

"You think they are meant for each other?"

"Yes, they're soul mates, ancient souls or something like that if you believe in such."

"I used to think Lana was my lifetime mate. Boy was I wrong."

"Life isn't over, Son. You may still meet yours. Can you stay for dinner?"

"I'm sure Lana already has plans to interrogate me about this morning. I'll tell her that I saw you, that we had a business crisis, and it needed immediate action. It won't exactly be a lie."

"Tell her the crisis involves my disagreement on ocean dumping."

"How'd you find out about that?"

"An anonymous recording of your overseas meeting."

"Cell phone?"

"I don't know."

"It will surprise her that you know about it. All I have to do is continue Kaia's argument. That ought to set her off. Where's Kaia?"

"With James."

"Where?"

"I'm not exactly sure. They ran away together. I expect they want to get married."

"I want to be there."

"After what happened, she wonders if she can trust you."

"You must tell her it wasn't me. I could never treat her the way that letter suggests."

"I'll try," Ervin said.

"Dad, I have one other request. I threw my conch shell at you when I left. May I have it back?"

"That's not so easy, but I've an idea. The selkie will bring it to the interview so you know it's her and not an impostor."

The next morning Jake sat in his office. He lifted Kaia's anklet out of his pocket and dropped it on his desk. He found it exactly where the letter told him it was, behind the bathroom door in the guest house. When he was there he also saw the metal table and the electronic equipment. He took pictures with his cell phone and sent them to Ervin. Such brutality used on his daughter. It was unforgivable. Later he went back with a camera and took pictures he could send to the police or at least the private investigators. Somehow, he and his Dad needed to get them in the guest house as witnesses and to gather forensic evidence. Surely, there would be samples of hair, fingerprints, etcetera that would support Kaia's testimony.

He pushed the anklet around on the desk with finger, then reached out and choked Lana's picture. He put her picture face down in a drawer and wondered whether she ever loved him, or whether he was just another pawn in her game. He remembered how they met, their wedding, their passionate love, but he also recalled how she changed as she gained power. S*he's become a monster...but she's too observant.* He opened his desk and put her picture back in its former place. He slipped the anklet back in his pocket. He knew he must keep up appearances, but how? *The bitch kidnapped my daughter and confined her in that...that prison. How can I remain affectionate to her when I want to put my hands around her neck and choke her out of existence?*

The front desk interrupted his thoughts. "Mr. Stone, Ms. Doria Reynolds is here for her interview."

He sent an intern to bring her up to his office. While he waited he thought about the arrangement he had with Lana. She always had a say in those closest to him, his executive staff. Well, not this time. While he waited he caught himself drumming the desk with his fingers. He stopped and placed his hands under the desk. He picked up Doria's resume once again. She had excellent credentials. She graduated at the top of her class and had impressive job experience. Just how did his father find her on such short notice? Then he realized that crafty old man must have been planning this for a long time.

The door opened, and a tall woman with blond hair highlighted with streaks of black entered. She was power dressed in a conservative business suit. He stood up, walked over to her and shook her hand. She looked him straight in the eye. Unlike many in his family, she looked like she was of Norwegian or Swedish descent.

"Iceland," she said. "People always ask when we first meet."

"You look familiar. Do I know you?"

"We went to high school together."

"No - you're the girl from down the street."

"That's how I got to know your father. He gave me support, my first job, and followed my career."

That devious old man. He never did like Lana.

Jake motioned Doria to sit at a small conference table. "Doria. That's not the name you used in school. It was More...something."

"Morwenna. Doria sounds more professional don't you think?"

They sat. "What can I get you to drink?" he said without thinking.

She removed a conch shell on a chain from her purse and laid it on the table between them. "I'd like Sprite with a pinch of salt."

Of course, he thought, expect the extraordinary. He asked an intern to fill her order and bring him a coffee. The intern balked at the suggestion of salt. "Just do it," he said. Then he sat down across from her and picked up the conch shell. He rubbed it between his fingers then let it dangle from the chain. "It's my old shell all right, but it used to be on a string."

"A string doesn't fit someone in your position. I took the liberty to put it on a white gold, rope chain. I hope that's acceptable."

"Thanks, that's thoughtful." He placed the chain around his neck and fumbled with the latch. "How do you women do this by yourself?"

"Here let me help you." She got up and closed the latch. The conch shell lay around his neck and centered itself over his tie.

The intern knocked on the door and set the drinks down on the conference table. Then he left.

Doria took a sip. "Not the usual interview is it?"

"Are you really a selkie?"

"No, I'm the offspring of a selkie."

"That makes a difference? This may sound strange; you'd think I'd know by now, given that Ervin is my father."

"Selkies are all female, Mr. Stone."

"Jake."

"Selkies live in the sea. My mother is a selkie, so I'm first generation. Most first generation selkies choose the sea. At eighteen I chose land. The Lady of the Sea agreed it was my destiny. I'm content with my choice."

"What about male offspring, like me?"

"You don't get to choose."

"Then tell me what it's like."

"Usually one hears the heartbeat of the ocean in her soul. Those who do, usually choose the sea. Some feel the pulse of the earth as well. That's me. Both draw you and fill you."

"It's not something I've experienced, but then I'm male."

She gave him a broad expansive smile. "Females must make the choice, but males can also experience the connectedness - if they don't drown it first."

He pondered her comment. *Is that what I've done with my life, drowned my conscience?* He automatically picked up her resume. "You have impressive credentials: top of the class, excellent business experience, a long line of promotions."

"They're helpful, but not the reason you'd hire me. You've got a problem, one that requires my special skills."

He smiled and then laughed. She was clever and every bit his match. He realized it was the first time he'd enjoyed himself in quite a while. "Who's interviewing whom?" he said. "Okay, then tell me about your special skills."

"I can talk mind to mind with any selkie and with some selkie offspring who have chosen land. I can also hold an immense amount of information in my head and readily access it. That's a handy skill in business and probably why I excel at it."

"So you store things like a computer."

"Better. Computers can only regurgitate what they've been

fed. I can turn the data sideways and upside down, and then use my intellect to make sense of it for the problem at hand."

"Is that a normal selkie skill?"

"No. I don't know why I have it. But all selkie offspring have unusual gifts that begin to show up usually between the ages of twelve and eighteen."

"Skills like what?"

"First there is a growing sense of something larger than them, followed by the touch of the ocean or the land. It's a new awareness, like waking up to a brighter and more beautiful world, to more vivid colors and smells, an awareness of the minutia that was formerly unseen. At least that's what happened to me. Others say they suddenly feel the interconnectedness of life or an unexplainable confidence or power."

"That helps?"

"Not really. It happens in middle school or high school when children are most vulnerable. Most who receive these gifts find themselves outcasts. They don't fit in. Don't you remember what I went through my senior year?" I had few friends. I went to prom, but alone."

"I was an outcast as well."

"I know."

"I would have asked you."

"Why didn't you?"

"I asked someone else." At that moment he realized, if he'd gone with her, his life could have turned out differently.

"I watched you. Anyhow, those who must choose lead lonely lives until they make their choice. Some meet others with the gifts and form life-long bonds. Sadly, some reject the connection and deny its existence. They tend to lead mundane lives without ever finding the poetry of life."

"You must be talking about me. Have you been in my mind?"

"That would be rude and is an unforgivable act for a selkie. Because we can do a thing doesn't mean we should use its power to control others."

"Reading a mind isn't the same thing as controlling it."

"Yes it is. If I know what you're planning, then I can either assist or confront you. Either way I end up determining the results. It's about freedom, Jake. The pulse of the world beats freedom. The only evil is trying to control another. We can teach and consult, but ultimately everyone must be allowed to make their own choices for good or ill."

"You already know I've made a mess of it."

"Have you? Do you remember high school?"

"I don't remember a great deal. It wasn't a pleasant experience for me. I felt destined to greater things and was being taught junk. My attitude changed for the better when I went to college. I needed that knowledge and the skills I learned to get where I am."

Doria smiled and nodded. "What did you do for enjoyment?"

"You know. Charles and I used to sail. We even raced our sailboat a bit. I looked forward to those weekend regattas."

"You felt it then: the rush of the wind on your face, the flow of the water around the boat, the sense of being part of the greater world."

She was right. Once he felt all those things, but he had indeed drowned them. "Tell me, how many selkie offspring are there?"

"Uncountable. Consider there have been hundreds of generations since the late Stone Age. I'd guess that anyone with a family connection to the sea has some selkie blood in them."

"You're hired, of course. You're what the company needs right now. Take the adjacent office. When can you start?"

"Immediately."

"Good, I'll have personnel process you. Meanwhile use the office and bring yourself up to speed on our businesses."

A strong breeze blew out of the northwest. Grant and Mera continued to sail down the coast of California on a broad reach. The boat sped along at a brisk pace, biting into one wave and rising on the next. It was a clear day with only a few high cirrus clouds. The California shoreline was distant and unseen. No other boats were in sight, but a pod of orcas swam in the distance and followed their general direction. Both Grant and Mera had become deeply tanned. Mera was at the wheel, and Grant rested on the seats that formed the sides of the cockpit. Grant had just asked Mera about Kaia and James when Mera suddenly turned toward the California coast.

"What's wrong?" Grant asked.

"Trouble," Mera said. She pointed to a speck on the horizon toward the California coast. Something moved toward them at high speed.

"What now? Surely not the Coast Guard again."

"No, this is different."

"How?"

"It's feels wrong."

"I trust your intuition, Mera."

"You're too far from shore."

"Too far?"

"I can swim all day if I have to. What if they intend to sink us?"

"I didn't think to bring a gun."

"You better get the inflatable lifeboat out of storage."

"Right." Grant went below while Mera held their course. A short time later he came back up to the cockpit. "It's at the bottom of the stairs." He looked past her at what now was clearly an ocean racer. "Whoever's driving that is drinking gas like there's no tomorrow."

Grant noticed that Mera had been watching something off the starboard side of the boat and turned in that direction. The pod of orcas had turned and now moved toward them.

Moment's later the ocean racer pulled up in a course parallel to theirs. A person who looked ex-military pointed a rifle at them. "Drop sails," he demanded, "and prepare to be boarded." They had no choice. Even so, it took several minutes to comply. A sailboat can't stop suddenly like a powerboat. Mera turned the boat into the wind and Grant dropped the sails. They drifted, and the powerboat pulled up alongside and moored itself to them. The driver turned the engine off. The man with the rifle sat on the powerboat deck and kept the rifle pointed at them. Another person left the powerboat and boarded the sailboat. Grant was about to call out Bill's name, but caught himself. Best pretend he didn't know it was Bill. It might improve their chance of survival.

"Scared?" Bill asked.

"What do you want?" Grant said.

"Answers and don't waste my time with lies. You've already given me enough trouble. Where are Kaia and James?"

"We honestly don't know," Grant said.

Bill grabbed Mera, and Grant moved to protect her. The man

with a rifle fired a shot. Grant heard the bullet whiz by his ear. He stopped.

"Good," Bill said. "This is how it works. I ask the questions, you answer them or the lady gets hurt. You're lying. You're in James' boat just to confuse us. Isn't that true?"

"No. Mera Atwater and I rented his boat for a vacation. Charles has the rental papers. Go see for yourself. James said he had other plans. If he's with Kaia, it's news to us." When he mentioned Mera's last name, Grant noticed that Bill's face became confused, so he continued. "Mera's father is Ervin Atwater. She's the sister of Jake Stone. You're messing with some very powerful people."

Bill took out a knife and held it against Mera's throat. Her black conch shell necklace flopped in front of him. He grabbed it and tore it loose. "What is it with these damn conch shells?" he said. "If I'm going to be in trouble, I might as well enjoy myself. Now for the last time, where are Kaia and James?"

Mera started to sing, and other voices joined hers. Bill dropped the knife and turned toward her. She motioned to Grant to cover his ears. He quickly knelt on the floor and complied. He saw Bill go wide-eyed. Bill turned toward the powerboat. It had been boarded by three naked women. They sang. The man with the rifle tossed it into the sea. Another handed his keys to one of the woman. She tossed them into the ocean. The song became a compelling siren song. Grant tried to stopper his ears with his fingers but was drawn by the song to Mera. It became a compelling need for him to be with her.

Bill moved to the mooring lines and untied the powerboat. It drifted slowly away from them. Mera told Bill to jump into the ocean. He smiled at her, saluted, and dove off the port side. She waved to the woman on the other boat. They dove into the sea and transformed into orcas. The men didn't notice, but Grant did. One of the orcas pushed the powerboat away from them. Another rose under Bill and gently pushed him toward the powerboat.

Mera stopped singing and took the wheel. Within moments they were under sail. She spun the boat around. "We're going back to the marina."

"I agree. What about them?"

"They have a radio. Let them enjoy this beautiful day at sea while they wait for the Coast Guard to rescue them."

Grant snickered and then broke out in a laugh which she

shared.

"You tried to defend me," she said.

"It doesn't look like you needed it," Grant replied. "Those orcas..."

"Grant they are selkies just like me. The orca is one of our alternate forms."

"Your song..."

"James and Charles warned you. Didn't you listen?"

"Yes I did, but I didn't understand. Are you aware what that song did to me?"

She smiled and took his hand. "Grant, I really like you. I wanted you to see me as a human, not as a selkie. I hoped you'd want to stay around me. I didn't want to force you or seduce you. Now I've blown that."

He shook his head. "No, you haven't. These last few days have been the best. If you recall, I was the one who wanted to keep sailing after the Coast Guard stopped us."

"We still have a few days."

"Yes we do, at best the marina is four days away."

He picked up her necklace from the cockpit floor.

"Leave it. I'll get a new chain when we get back."

"I'll put it down below."

"Thanks, and you can put away the lifeboat."

Kaia and James were on their way to Hawaii. It was the third day, and they were no longer alone. A pod of orcas joined them and swam alongside the boat. They were joined by another pod, then a third and a fourth. The boat became escorted by orcas and later that day by spotted dolphins. Further out were humpback and other marine mammals. All were headed in their direction and changed course to match theirs when James turned the wheel.

"What's this, a royal escort?" he asked.

Before Kaia could answer, James felt a bump and heard something on the ladder. He immediately turned around and watched the Lady board the boat by the rear ladder. They locked eyes. Kaia ran over and embraced her. Nothing was said out loud. James was thankful for that. There was another bump and another selkie came up the ladder. It was followed by one bump after another. Soon there were five selkies on the boat. All wore bikinis and black conch shells that contrasted with the gold one worn by The Lady. They took up positions all over the deck and lay down in the warm sunlight.

Kaia joined James at the wheel. "They're coming to our wedding," she said. "Isn't that great!"

"Why?"

"They're family."

He looked around the boat at all the marine life that shared their course. "All of them?"

"I guess so."

"I thought we would be alone."

"Me too!" *So much for privacy.*

Several days had passed. Jake had done what he could to avoid spending time with Lana. He'd taken a couple of unplanned business trips and spent one evening with his father.

He was back in the office. The door swung open, and Lana charged in. Doria followed closely behind. "I'm sorry, Mr. Stone, she pushed past me."

"It's alright, Doria, this is my wife, Lana."

Lana turned around and glared at Doria. "Leave us."

Jake nodded to Doria. She left the room and closed the door. He watched her return to her office. Then he casually pressed the intercom button on his desk. Lana didn't notice. "Do you want to sit or stand?" he asked Lana.

She sat at the conference table. "Do you think *that girl* could bring me a coffee?"

"Lana, she's eminently qualified." He pushed Doria's resume across the table to her. Then he picked up the phone and asked an intern to bring them both a coffee. When he finished, he turned the intercom back on. Lana read the document. The coffee arrived. Lana looked up and glared when she noticed it was delivered by an intern. She set the document down. "You know I have a say in those who work closest with you."

"Yes, dear, but Dad insisted, and it's his right."

"Dad, you haven't called him Dad in years."

Five minutes with her, and I've already blown it. "If Dad decided to back out, it would bring the business down."

"I don't like her. What was her name anyhow, Dorky?"

"It's Doria, dear, and you'll have to put up with her. Ervin insisted."

"He wants to spy on us!"

"Perhaps, but I think he just wants to be comfortable the company is moving in the right direction."

"He's meddling in what's rightfully ours."

"Dear, Dad and I each own twenty-seven percent of the stock. I need his agreement to pick the board members and control the company."

"Give yourself stock options."

"Part of the loan agreement was that I'd never have more shares than him. So, if I acquire more stock by any means, I must give half of them to him."

"Then what are the slut's duties?"

"Lana, be nice. She's my Executive Assistant. She sets my appointments and makes sure I'm prepared for every meeting. In her case, she's a walking computer. Once she knows enough about this business, I'll likely have her participate in meetings and take her on business trips to customers."

"So, you want to trade me in on a younger model. I won't have it!"

"Lana, I didn't choose her, Dad did. Besides she's our age."

"I'm tired of Ervin's meddling. I wish the old coot were dead."

"That old coot is my father. I have no idea who he'll leave his shares to."

"It'll be you, of course."

"Not necessarily. I have two sisters. He could even leave some to Kaia."

"That would be devastating."

"Not necessarily, but it might change the way we do business."

The intercom blared. "You're appointment is here, Mr. Stone."

"Who is it?" Lana demanded.

"Mr. Stone it's your sister, Mera Atwater."

Jake stared at Lana. "By all means bring her up." He smiled wickedly at Lana. "You'll get to hear this first hand."

Doria opened the office door and brought Mera in. Jake noticed that Mera was neatly dressed in a blue business suit. She wore her black conch shell on a black pearl necklace. Jack touched his, hidden under his shirt. The two women in business attire contrasted sharply with Lana. He couldn't have planned it any better. Doria left, and Jake rose to greet his sister. Lana continued to sit at the table. Her eyes glared at Doria and followed her out the door. Jake hugged Mera and then took her over to Lana. "Lana, this is my oldest sister, Mera. I don't think you've met."

"Oldest sister. She doesn't look over twenty."

"Yes, well women in my family age slowly." Jake said.

"I think I was in the Orkney Islands when you married," Mera said.

"Let's get down to it," Jake said. "Repeat for me what you said on the phone."

"I had a terrible vacation, Jacob. Grant and I rented James' boat to travel to Mexico. First we were boarded by the Coast Guard and then threatened by thugs."

"Did you recognize any of the thugs?"

"Grant did. He recognized Bill, one of your guards. Grant saw him with Candice at the marina."

"Did Bill say what he wanted with you?"

"He demanded to know where Kaia and James were. We couldn't tell him because we didn't know."

Jake turned toward Lana who fidgeted in her chair. "Mera, would you leave me alone with Lana a moment. Go see Doria. The three of us can have lunch together when I'm through." She left and closed the office door behind her. "Dammit, Lana, antagonizing my sister will only make matters worse if she inherits. Bill's your problem. Take care of it!"

"I was only trying to find our daughter, dear," Lana said sweetly, but to Jake it was the cold words of a serpent.

"Get Bill under control, and leave Kaia to the police before you make enemies you can't manage."

Lana's face went cold and icy. She glared at Jake. He could see that Lana wasn't used to being treated this way by him. *Good, meet the new me.* Lana got up from the table and gave him a phony smile. Others may have missed it, but he'd had a lifetime with her. She went to the office door and turned around. "See you at home tonight."

"Sorry, I won't be there. I have a business appointment in Chicago."

"You're not taking me?"

"No, I'll take Doria. She needs to get to meet our customers."

"You'll regret this, Jake," Lana said, just before she slammed the office door.

Bill entered Lana's office and interrupted her conversation with Candice. He found Candice's eyes with his own and gave her a wicked smile. She gave him a cold glance in return.

"You failed me again," Lana said.

"So I'm supposed to control Mother Nature now. A freak wave spills me into the ocean, and you blame me."

"You threatened Mera."

"Yes I did, but she wouldn't tell me anything."

"You were excessive. She didn't know anything."

"But you told me to ...."

"Dammit Bill, she was in Jake's office this morning and told him all about you and your threats."

"How'd she know it was me?"

"Grant recognized you, idiot. He'd seen you with Candice."

"Shit."

"So be a good boy and be on your best behavior. Don't do anything rash without my express orders. Have I made myself clear?" Once again she emphasized her statement by jabbing her letter opener at her desk.

"Yes Ma'am."

"I've got several new problems that need your attention. Most important is my husband's new Executive Assistant. Find out everything about her. I want to know where she lives, where she eats, who she hangs out with, and whether she sleeps with my husband. We may need to eliminate her, and that must look like an accident. This is one you won't be able to play with before you kill. Do you understand me?"

"Yes Ma'am."

"Good. Ervin Atwater has also become a concern as have both his daughters, maybe Kaia too. We need to find out who's in his will and who will get his stock in the company when he dies. Then we need to manipulate the survivors so we end up with control of the company."

"We could create a fake will."

"He's too smart, and you've lost your touch. I'm not sure I can rely on you any longer, given all your recent failures."

This time Candice caught his eyes, and gave him a wicked smile.

Ervin was in the library, but he wasn't alone. Calvin sat beside him. "You want my thoughts about Lana," he said and set down the brandy he'd been sipping. "Lana – well she's a tough case. Her activities are criminal. She's capable of anything. I'll put a profiler on it to confirm what my gut already tells me. I suspect the whole family needs protection. With you're permission, I'll put people on that too, while we investigate her and her henchman Bill."

"What's you're plan?"

"It isn't easy. From what you've told me, your boy Jacob has dirty hands, but not as dirty as Lana's. If we close in too quickly, she will try to blackmail you and Jacob."

"That could destroy the company."

"It means we need to gather evidence that will clearly convict her. Then we'll be in control. Once she's found guilty, who will the public believe: her, or you and Jacob? Your boy will need to mend his ways."

"I already have that in the works."

"Good, the next move is Lana's. I suspect she can't conceive of failure. She's too impulsive. She'll make a mistake and we'll catch her."

Chapter 22 - Nightmare

Kaia dreamed she was resting on the deck of her sailboat in a soft breeze. James was at the wheel, and they were headed toward Hawaii. They were alone, and it was a peaceful day. Soon they would be married. She and James would be united. They already were in their hearts. Although she had put her engagement ring and necklace safely away while they sailed, she dreamed she wore them and curled up her black fluke to lie on her side.

Then, she was back in Great-Grandmother's bed on the island in her bedroom. She snuggled against James. She had been dreaming that they had sailed to Hawaii and had been married. Blackness washed through her dream. She awoke on Great-Grandmother's bed and turned toward James, but he continued to sleep. The room was bright and the sun burned down on her. She sat up. There was no bedroom. Her bed sat on a black rock. Waves washed over the rocky shore. Selkies from the painted mural rose from their rocks. As one, they turned outward toward the open sea. Something black along the horizon moved across the water toward them. It was driven forward by every wave. Soon, the sea around her island bed rolled in a shiny black film. It clung to everything and stank. Sea birds washed up in it and struggled to crawl out of the filth and onto the rocks. They were coated with oil and unable to spread their wings. Others disappeared beneath the waves or washed up dead against the rocks. Wave after wave tossed up dead fish by the thousands. They floated belly up between the rocks. A mother seal coated with oil pulled herself out of the sea and dropped her dead baby beside the bed.

Kaia screamed.

James rolled over and pulled her into his arms. "It's okay, I'm here." She opened her eyes. They were glassy. Tears ran down her cheeks and splashed against James.

"What's wrong?" he asked.

"Everything. It's terrible. A great blackness. Death, death all around me."

The Lady touched her mind. *Hush, my child, I feel it too. It's what an oil spill feels like to us of the sea.*

"What happened?" James asked

"Death of the sea." Kaia said.

"So soon?" James replied.

It happens in small stages like this, but it's death nevertheless, the Lady said.

"Is there anything I can do?" James said. Kaia rolled towards James, and he wrapped his arms protectively around her. She shook involuntarily. James ran his fingers through her hair and then gently massaged her back. Slowly, she quieted.

He leaned forward to kiss her, but she rolled away from him.

"No, it's too late," she said. "We better get dressed and get up on deck."

James gently hugged her, and then kissed her gently on the forehead. He left the berth to change into his shorts and a T-shirt in the galley. Kaia emerged a moment later. She had dressed in her shorts and her orca T-shirt. James started up the steps to the cockpit and reached down to give Kaia a hand. The Lady was at the wheel, her long black hair waving in the breeze. James stood in the doorway while Kaia walked toward her. James studied the Lady's steady hand and the way she kept watchful eyes on the sails. Sometime in the past, the Lady had been more than a competent sailor, something he didn't expect in a selkie.

It was great to have another helmsman. They didn't need to use the autopilot or be surprised at night by a sudden storm. The selkies continued to lie all over the deck, but they weren't resting. They were agitated and kept a watchful eye on the Lady and Kaia. James walked to the stern.

"Let me," James said and took over the wheel.

Relieved from duty at the helm, the Lady waved her arm, and the selkies all dove into the ocean. She walked over to Kaia, and they both embraced.

They stood side by side, and James noted how similar they both looked. But then, most selkies he'd met looked similar. Kaia broke down in tears again. They held each other a long time. When they broke apart Kaia continued to cry. "Will someone please tell me what's happened?" James said.

"Another oil spill." Kaia said.

"Where." James said.

"It doesn't matter. It has already killed some. Others will follow. The food chain will remain contaminated for years. Many will suffer and die, and for what, to keep the price of oil low. We shouldn't depend on oil. Cost shouldn't be the reason we avoid development of renewable resources."

"I'd be willing to try, but even people like your father lack sufficient resources. It's a big task."

"It takes will, but what does Dad want to do - dump toxic waste into the ocean. It only makes things worse."

"I wish he'd develop technology to prevent these spills or invest heavily in solar and wind technology."

"We can't expect businessmen to understand or care, James. For them it's all about a quick profit and big bonuses."

"Then people like us need to do something about it."

"How, James, how?"

"It must start someplace."

"Others have tried. What have they accomplished? People continue to hunt whales. Salmon are still exposed to pesticides. There are dead zones around the mouths of many rivers. Most of the ocean is overfished."

"It's just like global warming. People pretend they're unaware, or the science just can't be right. They just don't care enough to do something about it."

"They just don't feel the pain," Kaia said. "I do." She wiped the tears from her eyes. "They all will feel it when the ocean dies."

"By then it will be too late," James said.

Then what should we do, Ambassador?

"The oceans must live. If they die, the land will follow. We must fight back."

"What are you going to do, teach the whales how to attack and kill?" James said.

"If we did, we'd be responsible for a great wrong. They are innocent. Man is responsible. Man must fix it."

You're the Ambassador, lead us.

"There must be another way, something between fighting and doing nothing. I need to find it."

"Don't leave me out."

Of course not.

"What do you think we should do, James?"

"To begin - stop your father,"

"How will we do that?"

"I don't know yet, but we must start someplace."

"I could kiss you," Kaia said.

"Should I leave the two of you alone?" The Lady said.

"He's at the wheel."

"There's always the auto pilot," James said.

The Lady pushed James away from the wheel. "Go down below. You two need to talk this over."

When Doria entered Jacob's office, she carried her laptop on top of a stack of files. "Can we talk?"

"Sure, come on in and shut the door."

She set the stack on the conference table and opened her laptop. He moved to sit beside her so he could see the screen. She slid the top folder toward him.

"I see," he said. "Our newest joint venture. Is there a problem?"

"Do you really think dumping toxic waste in the ocean is a good idea?"

"The technology to encapsulate the waste is feasible."

"Who says so?"

"My scientists."

"Jake, you are really out of touch."

"Is this something personal with you?"

"Yes and no, someone went to great trouble to hide the truth."

"What do you mean?"

She set a handwritten page in front of Jake. "These are the scientists you employed three months before your overseas venture." She slid another page to him. "These are the scientists you currently employ. You will notice five of your senior scientists are missing. They were fired while the encapsulation technology was under evaluation."

"What?"

"It took some digging, but I learned they were all fired at the request of Lana."

"She doesn't have the authority."

"She seems to have control over several senior members of your staff."

"You're kidding."

"I wish I was. Lana has anyone fired who disagrees with her."

"What gives her the right?"

"She's done a great deal more than that. It's complex. I'm still sorting it out in my mind. I think a lot of managers in our company have been compromised by her."

"Damn her. I'm in charge, not her."

"Not at the moment. I took the liberty to set up an appointment with one of the fired scientists. I hope that's not too bold of me."

"No, of course not."

"I've arranged for you to meet at Ervin's house. His reputation is at stake as well."

"You'll come with me, of course."

Lana glared at Bill from the desk in her office. "Well, is the slut sleeping with my husband?" Candice had become a familiar fixture and stood behind her. Candice locked her eyes with Bill's. She smiled, but it was the smile of disdain, a gloat, a pleasure in his mistakes.

Candice, you're a bitch, he thought, I'll teach her respect with my fists. He smiled at the thought but didn't let it get the better of him. His discipline coldly took over. He turned his gaze to Lana. "No Ma'am."

"She must be doing something. It's been five days, and he still hasn't come home."

"My men report they have gone from city to city and met with customers. They didn't share a room and weren't ever alone together."

"Meeting with customers is my job, not this whore's. Well, what have you found out about her?"

"You've got my report, and I'm sure you've already heard from the Director of Personnel, since you have him in your pocket."

"She's got to go, Bill. At the very least, she's spying. At worst, she's cohabiting with my husband."

"Yes, Ma'am."

"She needs an unfortunate accident. Get her out of the way."

"Remember you can't play with her," Candice added.

"Thanks, Candice," Lana said. "You got that, Bill? I won't tolerate any more mistakes."

"Yes, Ma'am."

Before he left, he turned to Candice and gave her a sinister smile. I'll play with you, he thought, first chance I get. And the pleasure will all be mine.

She glared back at him.

When Jacob and Doria arrived at Ervin's house, there was another car in the driveway. "Herr Doctor Heinrich von Stein ist hier. Oh sorry, languages come naturally to me."

"I get the meaning. What other talents are you hiding?"

She gave him a wink and a sensual laugh.

"Let's go in," he said.

Jake got out of the car, walked to her side, opened the door, and offered her his hand. She stepped out, and Jake noticed Shelly standing by the front door. Once Doria was out of the car, he rushed up the steps. "Shelly, it's really good to see you. It's been far too long, Sis." They hugged. Doria walked up the steps and joined them. "Doria, this is my sister, Shelly. I've haven't seen her in years."

"We've met."

"Met?"

"She's been my conduit to send and receive messages. Come on, let's go in. They've got the news on." They entered the Library and heard the newscaster.

"What is it, Dad?"

"A major oil spill. Probably as bad as or worse than the one we had in the Gulf. They've already made a call for volunteers to help with the cleanup. There was a major fish kill. The beaches will be fouled. Birds are washing up on shore coated with oil."

"Kaia knows," Shelly added. "She feels the pain. We all do."

Jake turned to her. "How is she?"

"Son, we can talk about Kaia later. I've already talked with Dr. Stein. He has some pointed technical concerns you should hear about yourself."

"Ja, I don't think das container, it will hold."

"Why?"

"Der pressure and corrosion. Ve know little about either at such depths."

"So you think I shouldn't do it."

"Test das container. My concerns it will prove."

"It's a reasonable request," Ervin said, "considering the damage that might be done."

Jake turned toward Shelly. "You said Kaia was distressed by the oil spill."

"She feels it, Jacob. It tears at her mind. She cannot free herself from any pain the ocean feels."

"How can she stand it?"

"I don't know."

"Don't all selkies feel it?"

"Not to the same degree. Kaia is special. She's the ambassador. As such she feels everything the ocean feels. So does the Lady."

"Ambassador?" Jake said.

"Was ist das?"

"Sorry, Doktor Stein," Ervin said. "You've just heard some things that you must keep confidential. You were fired because you felt the proposed toxic waste disposal was questionable."

"Ja. I've been blacklisted."

"I didn't do that."

"It was Lana," Ervin said. "What will you do about it, Son?"

"You're rehired, effective immediately. I want you to test that container and report directly to me. See you in my office in the morning."

"Ja."

"Doria, make sure the paperwork is handled, and he is paid for the time he was separated from us."

"You are most kind."

"I approve, Son," Ervin said. "It's the right thing to do."

"How in the world can I undo all the other things that Lana has done?"

"One person at a time. Stay for dinner, Jacob. I'm sure you'll appreciate what Doctor Stein has to say about our science department. When he's finished, you might consider a few changes." He turned toward Doctor Stein. "I'll explain the whole story of the selkies to you since we've already piqued your curiosity. Remember, it must be confidential."

"Vie have our own legends - die Lorelei."

"They live in the river, not the ocean," Shelly said. "More siren than selkie."

"Do you know where Jake spent the night?" Bill said to

238

Lana.

"Don't tell me he's sleeping with her?"

"Well, they were under the same roof."

"Where?"

"Ervin Atwater's."

"What? And she stayed there too?"

"There's more – one of the scientists you had fired was there."

"Dammit, I've had enough of his interference. I just don't know how to do it. Bill, I need the damn will. I need it now. Either that or we need to eliminate all possible contenders except for my husband. Once he inherits, he can go too. I've worked too hard building this company to let it go."

Chapter 23 - Wedding

The private jet neared Hawaii. Charles and Cardea Cersea, Ervin, Shelly and Mera Atwater, Jacob Stone, Doria Reynolds and Grant Gregson were all aboard. For protection, Calvin was present with five of his people. David, Ervin's representative on the board, sat next to Shelly and talked about their lives. He prominently wore the black conch shell that Shelly had given him years before. Jake sat beside his father and pondered whether in taking this trip he had gone too far. He had ignored Lana for weeks. When he wasn't on the road with Doria, he stayed at his father's house. Doria frequently stayed there as well. He had to assume that Lana knew, and it must irritate her. Ervin had cautioned him against aggravating her, but, after what she had done to Kaia, how could he live with her? Did they have anything left to share? They had been married for twenty years, and he knew what she was capable of. Most of that was bad. Thank goodness Calvin and his men kept watch on Lana. They also guarded him and his father's family. Some would even be working discretely at the wedding.

Calvin had advised Jake that he played a dangerous game. His actions goaded Lana. On the negative side, she could be deadly to him. On the positive side, it could make her react in a way that could lead to her arrest. It didn't really matter to Jake. He didn't like her any longer. He couldn't stand the thought of her cold arms around him. He couldn't help the way he felt. No matter what happened, he yearned for this to be over, so he could live and swim freely again. Officially, he had a business meeting in Hawaii. That would irritate Lana because she was born in Hawaii. He didn't take her home. But Doria came along.

Jake knew his sister, Shelly, would be Mera's maid of honor. But who was Kaia's. "Does anyone know who is Kaia's maid of honor?" he asked.

Everyone looked a bit surprised at the question.

"I haven't heard," Ervin said.

"Let me ask her," Shelly said. *Kaia, who's your maid of honor going to be?*

I hadn't thought about it; you, I suppose."

I'm Mera's.

Oh. That won't work. I don't know anyone else I can trust. Who can I ask?

Shelly looked around the plane. *There's someone else here I can ask, unless you want to use one of the Lady's guards.*

Who's that.

Your father's companion, Doria.

I don't know her.

Ervin chose her for Jake's Executive Assistant.

That's good enough for me.

I'll ask her. "Doria, would you do the honor of being Kaia's maid of honor."

"Would you?" Jake said.

"It would be my honor."

With that question answered, everyone settled back in their seats. Mera leaned over and snuggled against Grant. "Soon," she said. He put his arm around her, and they talked in low whispers. Doria asked Jake what she should wear.

"Kaia doesn't have a dress yet," Ervin said. "I guess the brides, brides' maids, and grooms will all have to shop when we arrive."

"I'd like to meet Kaia," Doria said to Jake.

Charles sat in the window seat behind Ervin. "Hey look," he said, "there's a sailboat down there."

Ervin looked out his window. "Looks big enough to be Kaia's boat. There's a lot of marine life around it." He turned to the stewardess. "Ask the captain to circle around and take us lower. I'll pay him extra. I've got a feeling about that boat."

Moments later, they began to circle. By the second pass, they could see a boat surrounded by whales all swimming in the same direction. "I've never seen anything like this," Charles said.

The stewardess gaped out the window.

"Yep, that's them," Shelly said, "the royal escort." Moments later, they circled lower and saw women lounging on the deck of the boat. "My sisters."

"Sisters, royal escort?" the stewardess said out loud without thinking.

"Ask the captain to dip his wings and take us to the airport."

The plane went lower and dipped its wings. Just then, several women dove off the ship into the ocean.

"What the hell?" the stewardess said.

Charles leaned forward and whispered to Ervin. "If they're not selkie kin, you might want to buy the crew's silence."

Kaia was at the helm, and James was in the galley preparing lunch. The Lady slept on the deck with the rest of the selkies. Kaia watched a plane circle over them. When it turned a second time, she became concerned.

"James, get up here, we've got company."

He hurried to the deck.

"That plane's circling over us."

The commotion woke the Lady and the other selkies. They gathered around her. She waved them away, and they sat along the rail with their flukes over the side. The plane circled lower. They all could hear the roar of the jet engines. The selkies became worried and looked at the Lady for guidance. They weren't accustomed to the sound. Neither was the Lady. The plane flew low over them and waved its wings. Many of the selkies dove into the water and transformed into orcas. The Lady laughed. "It's your grandfather and the rest of the wedding party. Oh, by the way, I just learned this will be a double wedding."

"What?"

"Grant and Mera will be married as well."

James turned toward Kaia. "Mera's your aunt, isn't she?"

"Yes."

"Then, let me get this straight. When my best friend marries Mera, he becomes my uncle? Doesn't that seem a bit weird to you?"

"It keeps it all in the family."

The wedding took place on a rented ship in the grand salon. James and Grant dressed in a cabin while the women gathered in a suite to dress. They had worked out their outfits with the brides a few days before. James and Grant wore black tuxedos with sea blue and sea foam vests. James paced as he tried to put on his tie.

"You look nervous, old buddy," Grant said.

"Aren't you?"

"Nope."

"No butterflies in the gut?"

"None."

"I just realized that my life changes today...forever."

242

"You shouldn't have sampled the candy."

"Funny! And you spent how long on the boat with Mera?"

"I'm marrying her."

"And I'm marrying Kaia. You realize this is final, don't you."

"I hope it is."

"You know our wives will be able to read our minds. We have to behave ourselves. We can't even think someone else is pretty."

"No one else will ever be as pretty as Mera."

"Kaia's prettier."

Grant laughed. "Well, we got that straight. You know why we're getting married on a boat, don't you?"

"So we can't run away."

In a nearby suite, the women gathered to dress. At the center of attention were Kaia and Mera. Cardea Cersea watched from the sidelines. Doria and Shelly were already dressed in their sea blue and sea foam full length dresses. The selkie guards gathered around the Lady. She turned to Doria who left the group.

"Mind if I join you?" Doria said, "I'm not supposed to help. It's all because of my choice."

Cadea nodded. "What choice?"

"You don't know then."

"Know what?"

The Lady turned toward Doria and locked eyes with her.

"I can't tell you right now." Doria loosened her plain conch shell and began to rub it nervously between her fingers.

Cardea noticed her shell and that everyone else wore one. "What's with the conch shells?"

"They're a symbol of our status."

"Yours is common seashore white. There are many black ones. Mera's and Shelly's are also black, but they have strings of black pearls, very pretty. Kaia's is silver, and the one called the Lady has a yellow gold one."

"Yep – that's how you tell our status."

"So, that's why you're not with the others?"

"It was my choice, and I'm contented with it. I'm a successful business woman."

Before Cardea could ask any further questions, the women finished dressing Kaia and Mera. Kaia wore a white, full-length dress with blue fabric that wrapped around her chest at an angle. It was outlined with embroidered shells and pearls. It had a small train. Mera wore a champagne colored mermaid dress overlaid with white lace. The women who wore the black conch shells formed a circle around Kaia, Mera, Shelly and the Lady. They began to circle one way and then the other while they sang a song in an odd language with a lot of vowel sounds, much like Hawaiian. Doria smiled and swayed with them. A single tear rolled down her cheek. The sound was as ancient as the sea and pulsed like waves upon the shore. While the selkies circled and sang, the Lady opened a box and removed a silver tiara with black conch shells that matched Mera's necklace. She placed it on Mera's head and adjusted it until she was satisfied. She placed a similar one on Shelly's head. Then Mera opened another box and lifted out a silver and diamond tiara. It had a single silver conch in the middle. Mera and Shelly together placed the tiara on Kaia's head. The Lady arranged it. Shelly opened the last box and removed a yellow gold tiara. It was identical to Kaia's except it was made of yellow gold. Together, Kaia, Mera and Shelly placed it on the Lady's head.

"I never thought I'd witness this ceremony," Doria said.

Cardea noticed the tears that ran down Doria's cheek. Doria casually brushed them away. "What's wrong?"

"We all must make our choices."

"You're not married then?"

"If I do, will they honor me with a ceremony like this?"

When she said this, Cardea noticed that Doria and the Lady's eyes locked and held. The Lady handed a box to Kaia who approached Doria and Cardea. Kaia opened the box and placed a circlet of silver leaves on Doria's head. "A gift from the Lady and me."

Tears welled in Doria's eyes. "Thank you." She nodded to the Lady.

Kaia returned to the circle. Small veils were attached to her tiara and Mera's tiara.

The Lady turned to Doria when they finished. *Daughter, Cardea is part of our family now. Tell her our story.*

I've never told the story before. Do I know it?

I'll share it with you.

"Cardea, do you know what a selkie is?"

"It's an old legend."

"Not a legend and older than you think. Let me tell you from the beginning. Long, long ago, before the great ice...."

They had decided that Captain Charles Cersea would perform the wedding in the ancient sea tradition of ship captains. There hadn't been time for a rehearsal. Since he'd never performed a wedding before, he was a bit nervous. He remembered his own wedding and wondered how anxious his son was at this moment. Well, it was only their families, not a crowd, and not anything out of the ordinary. He paced outside the door to the wedding salon and waited. *Why is it that weddings seldom take place on time?* He'd been listening to the sounds from the suite where the ladies dressed. The music ceased. He realized it must be time. Most people were already seated. When he heard the door behind him open, he turned. Cordea approached. She was deep in conversation with Doria. They were followed by the brides and maids-of-honor. Another woman walked behind them. His jaw dropped when he saw her. "Oceana?" he said.

"Just the Lady of the Sea, Charles. Call me the Lady."

"It's been so long...and you look like you haven't aged a day. I see you've exchanged your silver necklace for gold."

"It's proper. The Lady of the Sea wears gold. Kaia now wears mine."

Why was she here, he wondered. Now, he had a real reason to be nervous.

"Oh by the way, Charles," the Lady said, "This will be a wedding in the ancient selkie tradition."

His face went white.

"Is everything okay?" Cardea asked him.

And I thought my son would be nervous. "It will be when this is over."

"She knows, Charles," Doria said.

"Knows what?"

"Knows about us."

"I'll give you moral support, hon," Cardea replied.

"You won't be standing in front of them."

"Relax, it's tougher on the grooms."

An usher, one of Calvin's men, walked up. He bowed slightly. "May I seat you ladies?" Charles noticed the usher couldn't keep his eyes off of the Lady. She smiled and offered him her arm.

A second usher appeared to escort Cardea. Charles followed them and went to the podium and the newly constructed arch made from shells and driftwood and decorated with yellow Hawaiian flowers. Now he understood the reason for the arch. It mixed land and sea. He crossed his fingers. Cardea noticed. He could almost hear her say - "Good luck."

Charles turned to his left and made eye contact with his son and then to the right with Grant. That was the signal. James and Grant entered from opposite sides. They took their position next to Charles. The small band took that as a signal to begin playing the bridal procession. James and Grant turned to face the entrance to the salon. The bridal procession started. Shelly and Doria, the Maids-of-Honor were first. As they entered they split, Doria moved to the right and Shelly to the left. When they got to the corner of the room, they turned to the front. Mera and Kaia followed them. Mera was escorted by Ervin in his wheelchair. Kaia walked beside Jake. When they reached the front, Ervin placed Mera's hand in Grant's and moved to the front row. Jake took James' hand and shook it. "Take care of her son; she's all I have left." James nodded. Jake joined Kaia's and James' hands then took his seat.

Charles began the ceremony, "Dearly beloved...."

James whispered, "Dad, we've written our own ceremony. You just need to make this legal."

Then the Lady interrupted his thoughts. *Charles, remember this isn't just a marriage of our offspring, it's a symbolic marriage of the land and the sea.*

The Selkie guards took up drums and flutes made from shells and bones and began to play. James recognized the melody. It was the tune played in Kaia's bedroom. Oceana got up from her seat and joined Charles at the front. "Charles, you represent the legal marriage from the viewpoint of the land, I from the sea."

The Lady continued. "The marriage ceremony we perform today hasn't been performed since the earliest of days when those of the island married those of the sea. They married each other, sea to land and land to sea, much as the kings of old were married to the land.

Kaia and Mera both reached into a basket and lifted out mussels. They handed them to their husbands-to-be. They spoke simultaneously. "Take these gifts of the sea as a symbol of my abundant and undying love."

James and Grant took flower leis made of yellow Hawaiian flowers and draped them over the necks of Kaia and Mera. "Take these gifts of the land as a symbol of my abundant and undying love."

Kaia and Mera each lifted a cup. "I give you my salt, my water, the blood of my being."

James and Grant also lifted a cup to them. "Take my wine, the blood of my soul."

Each drank from the other's cup.

"I send my mists to cover the land," Kaia and Mera said together.

"I send my rivers to nourish the sea," Grant and James said together.

"I send my waves and tides to draw you to me."

"I send my sand and stone to be shaped by you."

"The sea nurtures the land."

"The land feeds the sea."

Then together: "Land and sea. Forever joined - forever one. So long as land touches the sea and sea embraces the land, we will be one."

They exchanged rings and were finished. James looked at his dad. "You can pronounce us man and wife now."

He produced a huge smile and spoke. "I present to you, James and Kaia Cersea, and Grant and Mera Gregson."

The wedding was over, but the fun had just begun. The room was rearranged for dinner. There was a choice between chicken or salmon and eel. The married couples sat at the head table. Charles and Cordea shared a table with Jake and Doria. They were joined by Shelly, David, Ervin, and Oceana. Calvin and his people sat at another table and were joined by two of the selkie guard. The remaining selkies sat at a third table. The band sat at a small table near their instruments. Waiters served the meal. Charles noticed that the selkies received far too much attention from the waiters. Calvin was noticeably deep in conversation with the one who sat next to him.

Toasts were given. James toasted Grant and Grant toasted James. Grant was amused when James called him uncle. He thought about it. He's right, James is now my nephew. How amusing. When they were finished, Ervin turned toward Calvin and lifted a glass to him. Calvin lifted his in return, but the Selkie sitting next to him clicked her glass against his.

"What was your name before you chose," Calvin asked her.

"Mary. It's still Mary. We don't change our names."

"Mary, then. What did you do before."

"I finished high school."

"Not too long ago I would guess."

She laughed sensuously. "In 1973. I'm really more your age."

After dinner, the brides and grooms shared the wedding cakes. Shelly had arranged on-line for the cakes, so they would be ready in time. The brides' cake was three tiered. It was decorated with shells. The grooms' cake had a large anchor and rope rising out of the chocolate cake. A selkie was wrapped around the rope. Shelly had to explain to the decorators they needed to take a mermaid and change the fin to a fluke like an orca had. It turned out okay. Close, but not quite a selkie. The fluke was too big.

Charles announced, "Time for the brides and grooms to dance."

Grant stood up immediately and reached for Mera's hand. "Shall we dance?"

Kaia stood up. "Come on James." James rose and whispered, "We should have practiced."

"Don't you know how to dance?"

"Well...not really."

"It's just like sailing, James, just get into the rhythm."

"That's not the problem. What do I do with my feet?"

"Seriously, James."

He was right, he had two left feet. Grant and Mera danced circles around them.

"Did you guys practice?" James asked.

"Nope," Grant said, "this is our first dance."

"Thanks for showing me up, good buddy,"

"No problem, nephew."

They finished the dance. James looked relieved and headed back to the head table.

Next to dance were Jacob with Kaia and Ervin with Mera. For the dance, Shelly helped Ervin move from his powered wheelchair into a regular one. He didn't want to drive over anyone's toes. He wheeled out to the floor and took Mera's hands. "Don't worry Dad, I won't do anything wild."

"I don't have two left wheels. This is a party. Swing me around. And you don't have to hold on with both hands. I'll do just fine."

Jacob and Kaia moved around the floor avoiding Ervin's wild wheeling. Jacob smiled. "I'd forgotten how much Dad loved parties."

"I'm glad you're here," Kaia said.

"Me too."

"You brought Doria."

"She's my assistant, part selkie, and Dad insisted on her. Besides you needed a Maid-of-honor."

"We couldn't bring any of my old friends to a selkie wedding. It wouldn't work."

"Your life has changed. So has mine."

"Doria's attractive."

"It helps her in business."

"Okay, Dad, if you say so."

"About James. He needs dance lessons. When you inherit the company, he'll need the social skills to mingle."

"Just as soon as I can get him off our boat."

"He loves sailing?"

"I think he could spend the rest of his life doing it."

"There's more to life than sailing."

"He knows that, Dad. Don't worry; he'll be there when he needs to be."

It was time for open dance. Charles led Cordea to the floor. He was joined by David and Shelly, who were quickly becoming close. Grant nodded to James and went to the floor to join Mera. Ervin wheeled himself over to Oceana, and they were soon dancing together.

"We should have given James dance lessons," Cordea said.

"He never was interested."

"Social skills are important, Charles."

Kaia sat next to James and pointed out the dancing. "Even your dad knows how to dance."

"I didn't know he could."

"And notice, even Ervin is out there in a wheelchair."

"Easy, he doesn't have to use his feet."

"Come on, your dance lessons start now."

"Do we have to?"

"You don't want to start our first fight an hour after we married, do you?"

"But everyone's watching."

"You taught me to sail while everyone else watched. This is no different."

James knew he couldn't win this argument. This was something he had to own up to. He got up, and Kaia started to teach him. Grant and Mera danced close to them. "You'll get it, nephew."

"Cut this nephew business."

"Nope, I sort of like it."

"Don't let it change our relationship."

"You're the one who put me in the boat with her. So I married Kaia's aunt..."

"Hey, I'm giving lessons here," Kaia said.

"You're not the only one," Grant said and pointed to the selkies who had each chosen a guy and had moved to the dance floor. "It's getting crowded."

"Kaia," James said, "do selkies know how to drink?"

"Can they stand their alcohol? I don't know."

"They certainly aren't inhibited in the way they dance."

"They are dancing rather close, aren't they."

The selkies all danced. Some obviously had learned to dance before they made their choice. Others were more awkward. A few of the older selkies looked like they wanted to perform stately dances from an older era. Well, to each their own.

Jacob and Doria had been sitting and watching the others dance. Jacob played with his drink while he watched his father move from one lady to another on the dance floor. Ervin even danced with the selkies when he could. Doria reached over and touched his hand. "Nervous?"

"No...sorry. This is awkward for me. My life's all screwed up."

David and Shelly danced near them. "David's on your board, isn't he?"

"He's Dad's representative."

"I think your sister likes him."

"He seems to like her too. According to Dad, they go way back to an incident while he was in the service."

"Your family is so close to each other. I didn't have much of a family."

"I remember you and your brother. You lived down the street. I used to watch you from my yard. Whatever ever happened to him?"

"We don't talk much these days. He's married and has two young daughters. They live up in Canada."

"The daughters are selkies?"

"They'll need to choose when they are eighteen."

"This all seems so strange to me."

"It doesn't seem to bother James or Grant."

"No."

"Kaia and James seem to be made for each other."

Jake laughed. "He needs to learn to dance."

"Kaia's already changing that. She'll be good for him."

"I see that... she's always been strong willed. What about your mother? I remember her. Where is she these days?"

"I had a single mom. She didn't choose when she was supposed to. Life for her was hell until the Lady allowed her to join the others in the ocean."

"She's not here?"

"No, she went to the Orkney's. It was too far away to ask her to be here."

Jacob looked out at the dancers. Everyone seemed to be enjoying someone else's company. He took a deep drink from his scotch. "This is so awkward. I can't undo the mess I've made of my life, and I don't know how to start over."

"I understand...it's difficult, especially now that Kaia's married. You're all alone now."

She was right. He didn't want to spend the rest of his life with regrets. He reached across the table and took her hand. "Doria, would you do me the honor of giving me a dance."

She smiled. "It would be my pleasure, Jacob Atwater."

Jacob, that made sense. It was his true name, the name he used before he made a mess of his life. It was time to change the name to symbolize the change in his life. It was too late to go back to Atwater, but he could still behave as one.

By late evening, the waiters were vying with each other to dance with the selkies. Kaia continued to teach James how to dance, although they had taken a few breaks. He had improved. He stepped on her feet far less now. Was she any better when she first started to sail? She had been concentrating on her lessons to James, but one of the selkies caught her attention. The selkie dancing with Calvin started to disrobe. Others looked like they wanted to follow her lead.

Kaia broke off from James and rushed over to Oceana. "Make your guards behave."

The Lady looked across the room. "They're only being selkies." By this time James had joined Kaia. "Grandma," Kaia said, "this is a wedding, not an orgy."

"Yes, my dear, your human values." *Guards, enough, act human.* The guards froze in place and turned toward the Lady. The one who had been undressing rushed for the powder room. Calvin turned toward Kaia. He looked disappointed. "There, happy now?" Oceana said.

James looked at Oceana. "Grandmother?"

"Great-Grandmother, actually," Oceana said.

"You're Ervin's mother?"

"Yes."

"But, you don't look over forty."

Kaia took James' hand. "That's why it was dangerous for you to be alone with her when you first met. She didn't want you to fall for her."

"This is one crazy mixed up family. Any more secrets?"

"You know all our secrets," Kaia said.

"Well most of them," the Lady added. "There's still one I don't fully believe."

"What's that?" Kaia asked.

She pointed to James. "The story of his family."

"What does that have to do with this?"

"Who knows for sure, but I'm sure happy he's married to you."

Kaia blushed. "You're looking for some special Great-great-grandchildren aren't you."

"When your blood and his mingle, something very special may happen."

Chapter 24 - Swimming

The ceremony was over and they were alone at last on their sailboat. They were still anchored in the harbor, and it was their wedding night. Thank goodness the selkies had more grace than many humans. No one played pranks on them during the night.

James got up early, before dawn. Kaia reached over toward him. He smiled and kissed her forehead. She pulled him back in bed.

"Did the selkies go back to the ocean?" James asked.

"I doubt it."

"So, they're involved with the waiters and Calvin's men?"

"If Grandmother let them."

"Somehow, I don't think she'd restrain them."

"Hey, they've been out to sea for a long time. It's no different than sailors when they come back to port."

"So, we're not the only ones celebrating our marriage."

"Does that bother you?"

"Nope, how about we go topside to watch the sunrise."

"Is this some sort of ritual?"

"I guess so - it's the start of our first day as a married couple."

"I never figured you as being so romantic."

She got up, and they both slipped into casual shorts and shirts. They put on jackets because it can be quite cool just before sunrise. It wasn't completely dark. The sky to the east was cloudless and a ring of lighter colors hugged the horizon. Venus had risen and sent a bright ray of light that flickered off the waves. They sat side by side on a bench in the cockpit and watched it.

"How beautiful," Kaia said, "and symbolic. Did you plan this?"

"No, I had no idea Venus was so far above the horizon. The Morning Star - it's a beautiful way to begin our married life."

They sat on the deck and watched until the rising sun washed out the planet's reflection and its trace upon the waves.

"A new day," James said.

"Land and Sea joined for the first time since the stone age."

"A new beginning."

"For all of us."

"I wonder what Grant and Mera are doing?"

"I don't know, I think they checked into a hotel room with a Jacuzzi."

"Let's set sail for a remote shore."

"Sounds good to me."

Setting sail by now was second nature to them. By mid-afternoon they had reached a secluded beach. They anchored the boat offshore and took the inflatable to shore. They lay on the warm sand in their swimming suits and sunned themselves. James rolled over and kissed her passionately on the lips. "We're alone."

She sat up, "Not on the shore. Let's go for a swim."

"You want to do it in the water? Is this some selkie ritual I don't know about?"

"Just follow me."

They got up. James took her hand, and they ran together into the mild surf. Just before they dove into the water, he noticed two orcas swimming offshore. He broke the surface of the water beside Kaia. "Are those orcas or are those selkies?"

"Orcas, James - Aga and Siku."

"You've mentioned them before."

"They've followed us from Alaska."

"Part of our escort? Are you sure there are no other selkies around?"

"They're only orcas. Let's swim."

Is this how humans do it? Aga asked Siku. Kaia overheard but ignored it. She removed her bikini and tossed it on the shore. *Humans are so strange. Why does she keep hers covered?*

Mind your own business, Kaia replied.

James swam underwater. Kaia swam near him and transformed. She twisted around in the water and wrapped her fluke around his body. They sank deeper until James needed a breath. Then they popped up for air. "It's a shame you don't have scuba gear," she said.

"The fluke is sensual, I grant you that. Maybe I'm a bit inhibited. I'm a lucky human to be married to a selkie, but I'd rather you be human for this. Doesn't this seem a little awkward to you."

"I thought it was every sailor's fantasy," she said. But she transformed back.

"I've got an idea," James said. "Swim on your back. I'll swim on top of you." Kaia lay on her back with her head above water and propelled herself slowly forward by swishing her hands back and forth along her side.

"This would be easier with a fluke."

"No fluke, no cheating," he said.

"Oh come on."

"Try it my way first."

He swam face down using breast-stroke and moved on top of her. They were inches apart, occasionally contacting each other. Electric and erotic sensations flowed through their bodies. The closeness made them desire to grab each other, but keeping apart intensified the sensuality.

"Interesting foreplay," Kaia said. "Wow, let's switch positions."

James rolled over and swam on his back and she swam on top of him. She started to transform into her fluke and pushed herself up against him.

Siku, they do it exactly like us. Should we join them?

This is personal guys, Kaia said. *You're being rude.*

Curiosity is natural, isn't it for humans, Siku said.

Among humans, we call it pornography.

What's that?

I can't explain it.

"You don't seem to be interested," James replied.

"Let's go back to the boat."

"What's wrong?"

"I don't enjoy comments from the audience."

"The orcas?"

She nodded.

"Can't we ever be alone?"

Once again, Bill was in Lana's office to provide her an update. He told her his men had reported that Jake and Doria had gotten on a plane with most of the Atwater family. The Cerseas went with them.

"That doesn't sound like a business trip to me. Where did they all go?" Lana demanded.

"They boarded a private jet together and left California. It took some work and a few bribes. I think they filed flight plans for

Hawaii. I can't be sure. They've returned. My guys said they heard Grant and Mera were married there."

"That explains why everyone was together. Bastard, he took that slut instead of me. She didn't belong there. I did."

He smiled wickedly and licked his lips. "I can eliminate her. The question is how do I do it? What would be the most fun? Candice, do you want to help? That might make it interesting. You know what I'm capable of. I could teach you things..." He looked into Candice's eyes. She was appalled. *So, she's no killer.* He also knew Lana wouldn't hesitate. She'd pull the trigger herself and never regret it.

What does Lana see in Candice anyhow? Lana's delusional. Candice won't ever be the daughter she wants. Doesn't she see that Candice is using her? Maybe Lana will eventually figure it out, and I can play with Candice."

"Give me a viable plan," Lana said. Before he could answer Lana thought about the news Bill had brought her. "Mera's an Atwater isn't she?"

"Yes ma'am."

"Damn, more possible heirs. If I don't have a will, I'll have to eliminate all of them. I built this company, not Jake. I won't let this damn company be stolen from me by some bitch."

Several days had passed since the wedding and the aborted scene in the ocean. James and Kaia were on the way back to California in the sailboat. Kaia woke up, rolled over, and bit James on the ear. He opened his eyes, "Again?"

"Roll over and give me a hug?"

"I know where that leads."

"So lead on!"

Boom, something hit the boat and sent them sprawling. The boat suddenly heeled to one side. Kaia still had her arms wrapped around James when they rolled against the side of the boat. The boat righted itself. "We hit something!" he yelled in alarm. James jumped up and rushed stark naked up top. He popped out of the hatch and onto the deck just as Oceana appeared on the ladder at the stern. She stared at him with amusement.

"Shit." He dropped his hands to cover his package.

"Do you want your shells, honey," Kaia yelled up from

256

below.

"Why didn't you tell me Oceana was here?"

"You didn't ask. Besides this is a quite amusing picture."

"Awkward and embarrassing is the term I would use." He backed down the stairs. Once inside he turned around. Kaia walked out of the berth in her bikini. "Thanks, Princess, for making me your fool!"

"Don't mention it. Every Prince need to be humbled occasionally."

"You deserve a good spanking."

"You just try it and see where it gets you."

"What's she doing here anyhow? I thought this was our honeymoon."

"Just put something on and get up top."

"Yes, your highness," he said with a smirk. Then he swatted her buttocks as she walked up the stairs.

Kaia spoke through her teeth. "Turn-about is fair play. You just wait until she leaves."

"I'll look forward to it, but at this rate you'll end up pregnant. No wait a minute – you'll have a calf."

Kaia turned around and gave him a glare before she continued up the ladder to meet a laughing Oceana. "A lover's quarrel," Oceana asked, "Or is it some human form of foreplay? I especially like the thought of you calving."

"Grandma!"

"You're married after all, and I look forward to great-great-grandchildren."

"Great-great-grand-calves, you mean?"

They were both laughing when James joined them in the cockpit.

"Nice swim suit," Oceana said.

"I'm sorry. I hope I didn't shock you."

"Nothing I haven't seen before, besides, I had to change your diapers once or twice."

"I hope I was a good child."

"Good for a male."

"What does that mean?"

"Oh nothing." But she chuckled, and Kaia joined her. Soon they were both laughing riotously. Obviously, Oceana shared her images telepathically with Kaia.

"You were a cute baby," Kaia said. "Mischievous, but cute. I think I'll keep you anyhow."

"That's not fair. You share images and leave me out of the conversation."

"It's so tough being male," Oceana said.

James turned toward her. "What brings you here, surely it's not to check up on us, or are you pushing for a great-great-grand-calf?"

"Have you had a good honeymoon?" Oceana said.

"Past tense? I don't think I like the sound of this," James said.

"An attack has been made on our family. Bill tried to kill Doria. He failed of course. I'm very concerned. So are all the others. Kaia may not be safe this far from civilization. Too many convenient *accidents* can happen out here and never be reported."

"How did it happen?"

"Bill attacked her at her house. Calvin's guards drove him off before he could succeed. They had to let Bill escape. We need him to get to Lana."

"Are you coming with us?"

"It would take too long to swim all the way back."

"Back to Hawaii, James, we'll take a plane."

The three of them set sail for Hawaii. The plan was to store the boat there and fly to California. It was a dangerous plan because the police and Lana were looking for them. But it was necessary. It would take three or four days to get back to Hawaii, and they needed to make arrangements for the private jet to pick them up. They also needed false identities. James and Kaia looked at Oceana.

"It's about time Kaia learns how to do this," she said.

"I've only done it with you and James. I've never tried to contact Shelly. She's over a thousand miles away."

"Distance is no obstacle."

Grandma, how do I do this?

All Selkies have the ability to some degree. My offspring are especially talented. This should be simple for you.

Right, simple, just how do I do it?

You know Shelly. Think of her. See her face. Say hello.

She tried. *Hello, Shelly, are you there?*

Kaia, how's your honeymoon? Shelly replied

Grandma is here. We're back at work.

I'm still on the line, Oceana said. *See, Kaia, I knew you could do it. Call me if you need help.*

Why'd you call, Kaia?

We need Granddad's help to return to California. Can he arrange a plane? Second issue, we need false identities for us and Oceana.

I'll talk to him about it.

While Shelly talked telepathically with Kaia, Ervin and Calvin were sitting together in the Library. "I've got people on Lana and Bill. There's a third person involved, a Candice Desdemona."

"Really, I think I know who she is. That's a most interesting development. Can you put someone on her?"

"I already have, why?"

"I believe Kaia knows her. I'd like to confirm my suspicions."

"I've stepped up my protection. If Lana tried to brainwash Kaia and then have Doria killed, she's capable of almost anything. I'm not sure any of you are safe."

"Is this house secure?"

"There are five agents stationed around this house. Some are in cars for quick mobility, some are in the woods. All are armed for immediate action. Doria has managed to get eight into the company. One works in the mail room, another works as receptionist, one is a custodian and another is a secretary in the corporate office. The others have like jobs."

"What about Mera and Grant?"

"Contact Charles. I'll send him some people for the marina. What about Kaia?"

"When she gets back, put some men on her, but don't worry, you know she has her own protection."

"I understand she outdrove Bill last time."

"She has her skills and others protecting her. I'm sure you understand. When it's all over we'll continue to need your services."

"That sounds like you don't expect to be here."

"I think this is my last mission, Cal. I don't know whether I'll make it back."

Shelly entered the room. "More drinks, gentlemen?" She turned aside to Ervin. "Kaia called."

"I didn't hear the phone ring," Calvin said.

Shelly pointed to her head and Calvin rolled his eyes. "Okay then."

"Shelly, what did she have to say? Is she pregnant?" Ervin said.

"I don't know. You know it's wrong to pry, Dad. She wants a private jet to bring them home and false identities for them and Grandmother."

"Tell Kaia I'll arrange for the jet and identities. On second thought, also ask her about Candice. She may be involved with Lana and Bill. I need to know."

"Share what you learn with me, won't you?" Calvin said. Then he thought about it. "Word of mouth, please."

The plane landed at a small airport in California. Homeland security had a presence there, but it was small. Before they left Hawaii, Calvin's men had provided Kaia, James, and Oceana with false government identification cards. When they arrived in California, Grant and Mera met them. Kaia and Oceana were smartly dressed in dark skirt suits. James wore a black suit and sunglasses. He also wore an ear piece.

"Nice outfits," Grant said. "What are you, the Men in Black?"

James took out his identification. "Look and weep."

Grant examined the identification. "George Gold. Couldn't you come up with a better name?"

"You think that's bad," Kaia said. "George is more princely than my name - Sarah Gold, god - can't these guys be more creative. I can't wait to give Cal an earful."

Grant handed the identification back to James. "You guys have all the fun. I've got to get me one of these, Nephew."

That earned him a glare from James. "You've got to earn it, Uncle."

"Children," Oceana said with a sigh. "Enough bantering."

They reached Ervin's car.

"What's new?" Kaia asked.

"Doria has agents everywhere in the company," Mera said.

"Good."

"Better, Doctor Stein is back in charge of the containment vessel."

"Doctor Stein?"

"Lana had him fired because he opposed the project. Jacob rehired him. He's agreed to conduct a harmless sea test that will surely fail."

"Then we don't need to do anything drastic," James said.

"Like what?" Grant replied.

"Oh, we talked about sinking the ship or destroying the containment vessel, other militant actions. We're agents now - remember that."

"Don't let it go to your head."

"Where are we headed?" Kaia asked.

"A family meeting at Ervin's. We'll all be staying there anyhow."

Chapter 25 - Plans

After they arrived, everyone gathered in the Atwater Library to discuss the attack on Doria. Ervin had invited Calvin to the meeting. Kaia, James, Oceana, Mera, and Grant sat on chairs borrowed from the dining room. Shelly sat next to her father, as usual, to attend to his needs. Jacob and Doria stood near the bar. Calvin stood in the doorway to the bar. They all had drinks of one sort or the other.

"I hope this won't be a long night," Ervin said. "The matter is serious and involves all of us. Calvin is here to listen and provide what he and his men have learned. He will provide us what support is needed."

Calvin lifted his hand. "I'd like to hear from Doria first. My men gave me their report but I'd like you to tell us what you recall about the attack."

"Thank God your men were guarding me. I haven't been home much since I joined the firm. Bill must have scoped out the place while I was gone and waited for his opportunity. I keep the doors locked and dead-bolted, but he must have been there earlier and disabled the rear door locks. I was in the kitchen when he came in the back door and rushed me. He grabbed me before I could respond and knocked me out with chloroform, I think. When I came to, he had me gagged and bound in my bedroom. He was telling me how he was going to kill me when Calvin's men followed him in the through the back door. Bill bolted out the window and ran. There's no question in my mind - he's one sick sadist."

Doria recounted what happened casually. She was not at all deterred by the nature of his attack; rather she was appalled that a person like Bill could remain free in human society.

"Doria isn't a weak woman," Jacob added. "She didn't faint or squirm. She'd have stood up to him given the chance."

"Why do you think he tried to kill you?" Calvin asked.

"Jealousy. Bill works for Lana, and Lana thinks I'm sleeping with her husband."

"Well, are you?"

"No," she said in a casual matter of fact manner. "We're not even dating. Is it important?"

"Yes, very important. Once we put Lana in jail, Jacob will divorce her. You need to keep your relationship with Jacob professional; otherwise Lana could gain an advantage."

Jacob and Doria locked eyes. "We can do that," Jacob said.

"I don't mean to pry, but we can't have secrets here. Your reply indicates there is something between you two."

"No secrets in this family," James said.

Everyone laughed.

"I see," Calvin said.

"What secrets are kept is my decision," Kaia said.

Calvin turned toward her.

"She's right," Oceana said. "It's her decision."

Calvin turned toward Ervin. "She's your heir?" he asked.

"You know what we are, Cal. Kaia is the selkie ambassador."

Oceana nodded in agreement.

"Well, that changes things a bit." He turned toward Ervin. "I see why you want to retain my services. You've obviously planning for the future." He turned back to Kaia. "Now for our immediate situation, can we let Bill run loose, or do we turn our evidence over to the authorities? That sadist needs to be locked away from decent people."

"We need him to convict Lana," Ervin said and Kaia agreed.

"Let me explain the situation in full as well as its consequences," Calvin said. "We followed him after his failure to kill Doria. He went to a topless bar and picked up an exotic dancer. He beat her and raped her. He might have killed her. Our men couldn't just sit there. They called the police. The police arrived, but Bill escaped. We could have turned him in then, but we didn't. It eats away at all of us. It's wrong for him to be loose. Someone else could get hurt."

"Is the girl okay?" Ervin asked.

"She's in the hospital with some pretty bad injuries, but she'll make it."

"She's an innocent bystander caught in our feud," Jacob said. "We should help her. Do you know her name?"

"Elle Ann Sinder."

Kaia gasp. "Eleanor Sinder?"

"I think that's right. Do you know her?"

"Oh yes. Schoolmate and a close friend of Candice's"

"You're kidding. Bill actually beat up a friend of Candice's.

This could help us get Candice to testify. Kaia, how do you think Candice will react to her friend's plight?"

"I hate Bill. I don't know how Candice could stand the sadistic SOB."

"Okay, here's what we need to do," Ervin said. "I'm sorry; let me suggest this to you, Kaia. Someone needs to visit Elle and offer our support."

"We should pay her expenses," Jacob said. "It's not her fault we can't stop Bill right now."

"I agree," Ervin said, "someone needs to make that offer."

"I'll go," Kaia said.

"I'll go with you," Mera added. She looked at Calvin. "Two of *us* should be enough."

"I'm not comfortable with this," James said.

"You know your wife," Ervin said. "She'll do what she wants, but she'll be safe with Mera. Besides, I'll suggest a different mission that you're suited for – telling Candice about her friend."

"Wait a minute," Kaia said.

"Hush now," Ervin said. "You trust your husband, don't you?"

"She attacked him last time they were together."

"I'll go with him," Grant said. "I'll keep my nephew safe."

"If you think it would help, I can provide some very graphic photographs of Elle's injuries," Calvin said.

"That might help," James said.

"You should encourage Candice to visit Elle in the hospital," Calvin said, "but Kaia and Mera need to see Elle first."

Kaia agreed to the plan.

"All right then," Ervin said, "we'll all meet together for breakfast tomorrow morning and then go on our missions."

Arnold Black sat across a dimly lit restaurant table from Lana Stone. Lana had an attractive Asian girl with her. She created a distraction. While he looked at the girl, Lana studied Arnold Black. He had an unkempt black beard that twisted and turned in an unattractive way. He wore a captain's hat, but it was dirty and stained. Frankly, he smelled like he needed a bath, but he didn't smell of drink.

"Captain," Lana said, "you were referred to me. I know a

little of your story, enough to know you need a chance to put your life back together."

"Ma'am, my whole life has fallen apart, but I guess you know that. I fell in with the wrong sort, smuggled things I shouldn't have, and ended up a drunk with a nasty divorce."

"It was a smuggler who recommended you to me. He said you'd reached the bottom. Have you?"

"Ma'am, I've been to AA, and I've taken the pledge. It's been a month since I last had a drink. I've had to live out of my car because no one will hire me. If I'm not at the bottom, I don't know where else it could be."

"Would you be interested in the temporary position of Captain of a ship that will carry containers of toxic waste across the Pacific?"

"Ma'am, I'm desperate. I'd work for the devil himself, it he hired me."

Lana smiled. *Well, I'm not exactly the devil, but this captain is perceptive. I'll need to make sure he obeys.* "I'll give you a chance, Captain Black. Wulan will take you to the ship and see you to your quarters. Once you've had a shower, she'll take you shopping for a...more presentable uniform. I'll let you meet the crew, and you can tell me what you think."

"Ma'am, I promise you I'll stay off drink." His voice wavered and a tear rolled down his cheek. "Thanks for giving me a chance."

Putty in my hands and ready to be molded just like most men. Lana reached across the table and gently took his hand. She patted it. "You deserve it." Then she slid a piece of paper over to him. "You'll live aboard the ship. Will this do as a salary for the next three months?"

His eyes opened wide. "That's a lot of money."

"I want to make sure you take orders only from one person - me. Do you agree with that?"

"Yes, ma'am, sir."

Chapter 26 - Elle

It took some effort and a few lies, but Kaia knew Elle well enough to pretend to be her sister. It helped that Mera dressed like a nurse and pretended to be from another hospital. Kaia chucked at it. Mera was quite a chameleon - she so easily slipped into other characters. Grant must be fortunate. She was Kaia and could only be Kaia. Together they managed to get into intensive care.

"Hi, Sis," Kaia said as she entered the room. Mera quickly closed the door.

Elle looked surprised and puzzled at first, but then recognized Kaia. "At least someone cares," Elle said bitterly. "Thanks for coming Kaia. That bastard really worked me over."

"I have a stalker who could do the same to me. Might even be the same person. I'm sorry this happened to you. Is there anything I can do for you?"

"Find the bastard, tie him up, and leave me alone with him for a day or two. I don't want my revenge to be too swift."

"Elle, don't lower yourself to his level. We're better than that. The bastard will get his fate. I'm sure of that. Dad has hired a private detective firm to catch the people behind this."

"There's more than one?"

"We think you were an innocent bystander in a plot against my family. That's why we want to help."

"I thought you didn't like your family, except maybe for your grandfather. That's what you said at school."

"Dad's changed. Mom never wanted me as a daughter."

"I can understand that. My step-dad abused my mom," Elle said. "One night, Mom took a gun and blew his brains out. She's in prison. She stopped him but in the process made me an orphan. Granddad adopted me. That's how I got to go to school with you. He always wanted the best for me. Look what I've become - a stripper."

"Why didn't you go to college?" Kaia asked. "I thought you wanted to become a marine biologist?"

Elle lowered her eyes.

Mera interrupted telepathically. *She's part selkie, Kaia. She denies it, but that's what she is.*

"What stopped you?" Kaia asked.

"I got pregnant in high school, then the bastard dumped me, and I lost my baby. It made me cynical. Look at me. I look terrible. Who'd come and watch me strip now?"

"Here's what we'll do. We'll pay your hospital expenses, and we'll spare no expense for whatever plastic surgery is necessary." Kaia looked up a Mera then back to Elle. "And, we'll pay your way through college."

Elle began to cry. "You'd do that for me? I was never nice to you."

"Kindness has to start someplace, Elle."

"You're too kind."

"Maybe you can help another someday." A nurse opened the door and entered the room. Kaia looked up. "I'll ask our sister Candice to visit you, is that okay?"

James and Grant walked into the bar at the marina. It was easy to spot Candice. She was crowded at the bar by four guys. They all vied for her attention. James walked up behind her.

"How many do you need, Candi?" he asked.

She turned abruptly at the sound of his voice. They're eyes met. "Just you."

"Sorry," Grant said to the other guys, "looks like she'll be occupied for a while."

Candice got up from the barstool and turned toward James. "I don't know whether to kiss you or punch you."

He backed up. "Let's be polite," James said. "You don't want to be thrown out of here again, do you?"

Grant stepped between them. "Candi, come to the office for a minute. I've something to show you."

She smiled back. "Oh, you're good." She put her hand on Grant's chest.

Grant took her hand and moved it away. "I think you're drunk," he said.

James ignored the flirting and led the way to the office. He entered. She followed. Grant came in behind and shut the door. She turned around and looked at Grant. "You're married, and you want a three-some?"

Grant blushed and stammered.

"That's not what this is about," James said. He took out a photograph and handed it to her with his left hand. She noticed the ring.

"You've married Kaia," she said between her teeth. "I've got nothing to say to you."

She moved toward the door, but Grant grabbed her arms and turned her back toward James.

"I'll scream," she said.

"I don't think so. Do you like Bill? Let me show you what Bill did to one of your high school friends."

He held out the photographs, and she looked at them. "Who's that?"

"I agree, it's hard to tell after he worked her over. It's Elle Ann Sinder. He beat the shit out of her and might have killed her if the police hadn't interfered. So I ask you again, is Bill a friend of yours?"

Candice's face hardened, and Grant released her. "He's a bastard."

"So it is true."

"I spent one miserable night with that sadist. He only put me in cuffs and rudely assaulted me. Lana wanted me to understand what could happen to me if I ever disobeyed her. What did Elle do to deserve this?"

"Bill tried to kill Doria and failed. We believe he took his frustrations out on Elle. She was just in the wrong place at the wrong time. We have to end this, Candi, before more people get hurt. You need to decide whose side you're on. That sadist will get caught, and the trail could lead back to you."

"I've gone back to my high school name. I'm Candice now. Lana knows about Grant's wedding but not yours. She wants control of the company for herself and plans to kill all the heirs, if necessary, including you. A copy of the will might limit the damage."

"You know that's not going to happen," James said.

"At least let me know if Jake will inherit."

"I don't know, and even if I did, it might mean Lana would kill him. No, I can't do that."

She put her hand on James' arm and gripped it tightly. "You need to help me."

"No, Candice, you need to help me put Bill and Lana in jail."

She dug her nails deeper while she stared into James' eyes. Grant grabbed her hand. "Let go," he said.

She released her grip but still stared into James' eyes. "I need to talk with Elle."

"Good, I'd appreciate that."

"Do you want me to lie to Lana about you and Kaia?"

"Tell the truth and stay out of trouble yourself."

Candice smiled and thought about the gesture. James, James, you are such an innocent. That's why I love you so much. "I can't" she said. "If she thinks Kaia might inherit, she'll kill you both."

"We're willing to take that risk," James said.

"That's not enough," Candice pleaded. "For both our sakes, you must help me eliminate Bill. I don't want to end up in his hands. He'll enjoy killing me and take his time at it."

"I can probably have him arrested," James said.

"That won't work. Lana will buy him probation, and I'll be dead or worse – like Elle."

"I'm not going to put a hit on him," James said, "if that's what you're suggesting."

"I don't know what I'm suggesting. Maybe he can drop dead from a heart attack."

"Wishful thinking. Go see Elle. When you're done, don't call me. Don't call any of us. Visit Dad in his office."

"Okay, can I go now?"

"Yes."

She grabbed James and laid a passionate kiss on him. He pushed her away.

"That's for what could have been," she said and left the room.

"You're not going to tell Kaia, are you?" James said.

"James, our wives...they can read minds."

"Kaia knows Candice. She'll understand when I tell her about it."

"I'll vouch for you, nephew."

Moments later the four guys that had hung around her at the bar entered the office. They were the guards assigned to the marina to protect them.

"Thanks, guys," James said. "Good job."

Candice easily made her decision. She had her own skin to think about. She'd learn what she could from Lana. Once Bill was out of the way, she'd have her own business, and somehow, someday, she'd make James hers - no matter what it took. So, she took her new knowledge to Lana and told her what Bill did to Elle. Lana wanted to know how Candice knew.

"I'm not sure of the facts," she said. "I heard about it from Grant. I'll go see Elle and find out."

They chatted a few more minutes until Bill arrived.

"You stupid asshole," Lana said. "What did you do with that stripper? Did you have fun?" She took a revolver out of the desk drawer and fondled it. She set it on the desk in front of her. "Do I need to replace you? You failed again, and now both Doria and Ellee live to testify against you. I can't trust you to finish the job, and I've got my own skin to think about."

He didn't like the direction of this conversation. It would take him three steps to reach the desk and more time to reach over it for the gun. All she had to do would be pick it up and shoot him. She would say it was self-defense and it would be. Candice was smiling. She would obviously back up her story. Shit, he was trapped. He was dead if she wished it so.

"Ma'am we now know Doria is guarded. That wasn't my fault. I couldn't anticipate it."

"And you couldn't just stop there. You just had to attack someone else. You let your blood-lust take over. Was she guarded too?"

"No ma'am. Someone must have tipped off the police."

"Maybe the same guards followed him," Candice ventured.

Lana picked up the gun and fondled the barrel. "And you were unlucky enough to escape." She pointed the gun at him and gave him an evil grin. "I could kill you right now and have the police identify you as her attacker, even say you threatened me."

Am I dead, he thought? He looked at the way she moved the point of the gun around his body. Will she kill me with one shot or make me suffer? He knew the answer. She'd make him suffer.

Internally, Candice seethed. She didn't want Bill to die here, in front of her. If anyone killed this bastard, it had to be her. "Kaia and James are married," Candice blurted out.

"What!" Lana said. "When did that happen?"

"I don't know. James told me yesterday."

"He's back?"

"Yes. He was with Grant."

"The whole Atwater family was gathered together last night," Bill said. "I couldn't get close. There were three guards in the woods."

"They've anticipated us," Lana said. "They have some detective agency working for them. Jake is a traitor. This is war, and I don't intend to lose. Just remember both of you, Jake is mine."

And James is mine, Candice thought.

Chapter 27 - War

They had finished their assignments and were once more gathered at the Atwater estate. Together they discussed what had happened over the breakfast table. Oceana took her formal place at the head of the table. Ervin sat at the other end. Kaia sat next to James on one side and Grant next to Mera on the other. Jake and Doria sat next to Kaia, and Calvin sat on Mera's side next to Ervin. It had become their assigned spots. After serving breakfast, Shelly sat next to Ervin.

Calvin asked how our meetings with Elle and Candice worked out.

Kaia spoke first. "Mera and I were able to meet with Elle. It was worse than I thought. Bill tried to turn her into hamburger. It makes me shudder. What would he do with me if he had the chance? I'm sure he wants revenge for my escape. It will take time and money to put Elle back together. We promised to pay her expenses including a college degree. I hope that's all right, Dad."

Jacob put his arm around her. "It's the right thing to do."

"Elle is a Selkie who hasn't made the choice," Mera said.

"Which way will she choose?" Oceana asked. "I can't see her."

"You couldn't see Kaia either," Shelly said.

Oceana grinned. "True - it's been that way with every life Kaia touches. Something changes in them. I can't see them."

"Well," Mera said, "time will tell. First, Elle must be returned to health."

"If she chooses to be a selkie, she'll heal faster."

"We shouldn't push that on her too quickly," Mera said.

"I agree with Mera," Kaia said.

"Then it's settled," Oceana replied.

"What about Candice."

"She's hard to read," James said.

"I'll agree with that," Grant added before he blushed. He turned to James. "I told Mera all about it."

James groaned. "Lana fully intends to gain control of the company by eliminating all heirs. That's us. Candice asked me what was in Ervin's will to reduce the damage."

"Dad, what's in the will?" Kaia asked.

Before Ervin could reply, James chimed in. "Don't tell anyone. It's a bad idea. If by chance Lana finds out, it will allow her to focus on the heirs."

"Kaia?" Ervin asked.

"I agree with James. It's a subject I don't want to think about."

Ervin nodded and James continued. "Candice is afraid of Bill."

"I don't blame her," Kaia added. "Every woman should be."

"She wanted us to eliminate him. I told her we don't assassinate people." He looked at Calvin. "We don't, do we?"

"No," Calvin said emphatically.

"Good," James said. "When it comes to nailing Lana, I'm not sure whether Candice will be on our side or Lana's."

"There's a third alternative - a more likely one," Calvin said. "She could play both sides for her own personal gain."

"That sounds like her," Kaia added.

"Then we must find a way to make her take our side."

"Just how will we do that?"

"We'll watch her and wait for her to make a mistake." Calvin turned toward Jacob and Doria. "So far we've managed to keep the attack on Doria from the press."

"We'll continue with our next business trip as if nothing happened," Jacob said.

"Daddy," Kaia said, "remember to keep appearances professional."

"We're not going to do anything stupid," he said.

"They'll be under observation by my security one hundred percent of the time."

"Grant and I are going back to the marina," Mera said. "Grant has to return to work."

"Dad wants me to stay with Kaia. He's told the staff I'm on a honeymoon. You two can stay on my boat. Take it for a sail if you like."

"James and I will be in my bedroom pool," Kaia announced.

"All day?" Mera asked.

"What?" Kaia said. "We're married. You heard James; we're still on our honeymoon."

"Great-great-grand-Calves," Oceana said. "That's what I'm

waiting for."

"I'm driving Grandmother back to the ocean today," Shelly said.

"Just remember everybody," Ervin said, "security is watching all of us. They're discrete, but don't give them too much to talk about."

Lana finished swimming her laps and lifted herself out of the pool. Candice had been sitting in a chair watching because Lana never let her use the pool. Candice got up and handed Lana a towel and she started to dry herself. "Help me decide - how do I eliminate them and keep control of the company? Obviously, Jake would have to be last. He needs to inherit before he dies."

"Who do you think is likely to inherit?"

"Likely is not the right word," Lana said. "Damn Bill anyhow, I need a copy of the will. I hate guessing. It means I have to kill them all. All that killing will look suspicious. I can't live under that cloud. There will have to be accidents - untraceable and unfortunate accidents."

"Well, as far as I can tell, the possibilities for inheritance are: Jake, Mera, Shelly, and Kaia."

"Doria has to go before Jake gets her pregnant."

"Are you sure they're having sex?"

"Honey, a wife knows when she's being betrayed."

"Mera and Kaia could get pregnant."

"You're right. If Kaia got pregnant, had the child, and died, I could be the foster mother and control the company through the child." Lana chortled. "If she isn't pregnant, I could arrange it. Bill would enjoy that. Then I could still control the child."

All this planned murder and manipulation. Candice would have shuddered if she could, but controlled herself to avoid showing her feelings to Lana. This time she wondered what she had gotten herself into, and how would she get herself out of it. "You're so devious," she said.

Lana smiled back. "Thanks for the compliment. What about the other daughter, Shelly?"

"From what I hear she doesn't have a boyfriend or any interest in one."

"She could still inherit."

"Ervin's death determines who inherits, doesn't it?" Candice said.

"You're right, and Ervin could change his will any time. That means James and Grant could also inherit. They'll all have to go, every last one of them."

Candice fumed inside. *That does it. James is mine, not yours.* "James and Grant aren't important. It's their wives who need to go."

"Not if the will has been changed, or Mera and Kaia have made wills and will inherit from Ervin."

"What about Jake. If he dies, you get his share of the company, won't you?"

"I want control. That means twice his shares."

"So what's the plan?"

"That slut, Doria, has to go first. Any child she would have could end up owning both Jacob's and Ervin's shares. I'd be divorced, and I'd be totally cut out. I won't have it. This is my company."

"Didn't you sign a pre-nuptial agreement?"

"There wasn't a company then."

"Wouldn't you get some of it in a divorce?"

"I'm not officially part of the company. At best I'd get the house and some alimony. I've build this damn company. I want it. That slut has my husband. She needs to go. Get me my damn phone."

Candice went to the end table and returned with Lana's cell phone. Lana placed a call to the corporation. Candice only heard part of the conversation. Lana closed her phone.

"Good news, the slut's on a business trip with my husband. Go get me Bill. This time he's not going to work alone. I'll insist he take his two best men. Three against one, those are good odds. She'll die this time."

This time Candice visibly winced. *Oh God, I don't want to be alone with Bill, even for a moment.* "After I get him, do you mind if I go see Elle. She's the one Bill put in the hospital."

"Of course dear, one must always cultivate kindness and mercy."

The words sent an icy chill through Candice. *What sort of woman did she work for?*

When Candice arrived in Bill's office he dangled handcuffs. "Did you come to play?"

That sent a shudder through her. "Not today, your boss wants you - NOW! I wouldn't keep her waiting if I were you. Someone needs to be eliminated."

She saw his eyes light up at the prospect. He left and she hurried on her way. As soon as she left the house, she went to see Elle. When she signed in at the reception desk, the receptionist looked up at her. "Oh, you're another one of Elle's sisters."

She thought quickly. "We have a large family."

"Let's see" she reached down and typed something on her computer. "Kaia Cersea and a Mera Gregson visited her yesterday. You all must be married."

"All except for me. May I go see her?"

"I'll clear it with the floor nurse."

Moments later Candice was on the third floor and walking into Elle's room. She froze in the doorway. Elle lay on the bed. She looked like she had been run over by an SUV. An IV was attached to her arm. She was monitored by an array of instruments. Her head was bandaged and eyes swollen and black. Her lips were swollen and a cut along it had stitches. A nurse was checking her chart.

"Candice, how's my big sister?" Elle said then coughed and reached out with a bandaged hand to cover her mouth.

"God, what happened to you? James said you'd been attacked."

"I'm lucky to be alive. I think the bastard meant to kill me, but someone must have seen him and called the police."

"Whoever he is, he deserves to be dead." Candice studied the injuries in terror, realizing that Bill would gladly do the same to her.

"Think this is bad, you should look under the covers. There isn't much of me he hasn't ravaged."

"I can guess what that feels like. A sick bastard brutally raped me. He enjoyed it and took great pleasure in giving me pain."

"Don't you just want to kill him?"

"Slowly."

"Kaia said she had a stalker who would do the same to her. What's with these men?"

"I wonder if it's the same person," Candice said.

"Then one of us can get revenge for all of us."

"I certainly hope so." At that moment, Candice knew for a

certainty what she would do. Bill was hers. He was dead meat.

"Kaia and Mera said their family would pay for my recovery and send me to college. It goes to show there are still decent people in the world."

They are decent, Candice thought, even generous, but obstacles to overcome. She realized she was thinking too much like Lana. Candice wanted to say that even good people had a dark side, but that was inappropriate. "I guess so," she said finally.

"They said I got caught up in a plot against their family. Do you think that's possible?"

"It might be. That gives me an idea of who might have done this to you."

"Promise me you'll make him suffer."

"Elle, I give you my word, if at all possible I will make sure the bastard who did this to you dies.

It was time to plan. Just how would she do it?

Jacob and Doria sat together at dinner in an upscale restaurant. Their table was located in a quiet corner of the room. Doria sat with her back to the wall and Jacob sat beside her. They both faced the doorway.

"Dr. Stein is about ready to test the containment vessel," Jacob said.

"I understand he's filled it with some strong dye for this test."

"Yes, we can send submersibles to check its status once it's in place."

A waiter approached them. "Are you ready to place your order?"

"A minute please," Doria said and looked down at our menu.

Jacob smiled up at him. "Are they all in place?"

"Yes, sir," he said.

"Our guards?"

He nodded.

"Damn, they're good."

"Dad says they're the best."

"So anyone out there could be one of our guards?"

"Yep."

Bill and his two men met outside the restaurant. All wore

conservative suits and ties and looked like three businessmen out for the evening. No one would suspect they were armed and ready to make a hit.

"Did you see where they are seated?" he asked one of his men.

"I took a quick look inside. They're at the table in the corner under the canopy."

"Remember," Bill said, "the girl only. Do not hit Jake. He has to survive, or I'm dead."

"Yes, sir," they said.

"Don't worry about any other casualties. If you have to shoot through someone, do it."

They entered the restaurant.

"Three?" the receptionist asked.

He nodded.

"Follow me please."

They walked in. Bill touched the receptionist on the shoulder. "Any place over there?" He pointed toward the canopy.

"Let me check."

Bill continued to move toward the table where Jake and Doria sat. He began to sweat. He'd already made too many mistakes. Killing was never easy. Unexpected things always happened. Were there guards here? He paused and quickly glanced around the room. He knew any number of people could have carry permits. Anyone could be a threat to them. His men stopped when he did. Bill noticed a waiter stood between them and Doria.

One of the guards Calvin had assigned to Jake and Doria saw Bill stop and glance around the room. This could be trouble. He stood up from the table. Three others followed his lead. Jacob noticed and looked past the waiter. He recognized Bill.

When he made eye contact, Bill knew he was out of time and too far away to get a clean shot. He drew his 38 revolver. His men drew at the same time. It would be a difficult shot because the waiter partially blocked Doria, but they were out of time. Three shots were fired, almost simultaneously. Two hit the waiter in the back. One hit Doria in the shoulder. The impact spun her behind the waiter. The waiter collapsed on the floor. Jacob watched Doria fall behind the table. He stood up and pulled the table over protect both of them. *Damn you, Lana, you'll pay for this.*

Before he could join her on the floor, three more shots rang out. Two of Bill's men went down. Bill grabbed a woman from a table and shielded himself with her. He held his gun to her head and backed toward the door.

"Don't anyone move, or she dies," he said.

He looked down at his men. One had both head and chest wounds. The other was bleeding from his side. Tough luck, Bill thought.

His adrenaline was up and he felt high, in need of excitement. He backed toward the door. The lady in his arms was terrified, so perfect for his current mood. If only there was time. When he got through the door he hesitated a moment before he released her.

"Ah, we could have such fun together," he said before he pushed her away and fled to the getaway car.

Jacob reached Doria behind the table. "Are you okay?"

"Damn that hurts."

"I'm here. You're safe now."

"We got caught off guard."

"No, Lana has declared war. She didn't send one person, she sent three. She wanted to make sure."

"They didn't target you."

"She must have something special planned for me."

One of the guards flashed what appeared to be a badge. "Federal Agents," he said. "This appears to be a hit on a CEO we're guarding. Everybody please stay where you are seated. Agents Mathew and Peter, get the surviving attacker out of here for questioning. Jacob, can Doria move?"

He stood up from behind the table. "She's been hit in the shoulder, but I'm sure she can be moved.

"Out, I'll cover you. Backup is on the way."

Jacob picked her up and started to carry her.

"I can walk," Doria said.

"Don't argue. I'll carry you."

"How many cell phones are out there?" Doria said.

"Why?"

"This will make the papers. You'll be pictured carrying me. We'll be hounded until we give an interview."

Chapter 28 - Compromised

*D*oria has been shot, Oceana said telepathically to all of them. *She's on the way to the hospital. They're guarded.*

Grant and Mera spun the sailboat around and headed back toward the harbor.

Are we safe? Mera asked.

No one in the family is safe. Lana has declared war.

Shelly rushed over to Ervin. "Mera and Grant are out to sea. They're exposed."

"Tell Mera I'll have Cal reinforce the guards at the marina. I'll try to get some to them by boat to ensure their safe return. I'll call Cal while you talk to Mera."

"Doria has been shot," Ervin said to Calvin over the phone.

"My men have already reported," Calvin said. "They had to choose between protecting Jacob and Doria or letting Bill get away."

"Are they safe?"

"My men are transporting them to the hospital and will stay with them for protection. I recommend calling in more men."

"I don't care about the cost. Lana has to be stopped." He took a deep breath. "Mera and Grant are out sailing. Can you reinforce the marina and send some by boat to ensure their safe return."

"I'll get right on it."

"I'll call Charles. Do you think he and Cardea are safe?"

"Probably, but we'll keep an eye on them too."

"Thanks."

"I didn't expect this to turn into a shooting war."

"Neither did I."

"It would be easier to protect you if you were all in one place."

"It would also be easier to attack us, and it won't help us convict Lana."

"It's a risky game you play."

"Cal, we outnumber them and most of us have ways to protect ourselves."

"That didn't help Doria."

"We were blindsided. Now we are forewarned."

"You make my job difficult."

"Has it ever been easy in anything we've done together?"

"You have a point there."

Ervin said his good-bye and immediately called Charles. He let Charles know what had happened. Charles was concerned - Jacob was a brother to him. Ervin let him know Jacob and Doria were guarded. He asked if Grant could be excused from work until the crises was over. For their safety, they needed to be at the Atwater estate.

By the time he finished talking, Kaia and James had arrived in the library. Kaia's hair was still wet.

"Swimming again?" Shelly asked.

"I need to strengthen my legs."

"Right."

"I'm going to see Dad," she said.

"You've always been impulsive and overconfident," Ervin said.

"I'm the Ambassador," she said. "I'll decide."

"Mother," Ervin said.

She is the Ambassador and it is her right.

"But..."

The future takes form around her whenever she chooses.

"Good," Kaia said. "Now that we've settled that, James and I will get tickets and fly out of here as soon as possible."

Bill flew back to California in the private plane. Not once did Lana call him. That wasn't a good omen. Bill dreaded his return to Lana's office. He had to go. If he didn't show up at the designated time, Lana would place a hit on him. Dealing with Lana was easier than spending his few remaining days on the run, wondering which stranger would do him in. Then again, she might take pleasure in seeing how long he could survive. She might even bring him back and kill him herself.

He knocked on the door.

"Come in, you bastard."

He started to open the door and heard a thunk. Then he saw the knife sticking out of the door. He slowly opened the door the rest of the way. She sat at her desk with the gun pointing at him. "Retrieve it, William. If I wanted you dead, you wouldn't have made it this far."

Candice and Lana were seated at her desk. Lana had today's paper open on the desk in front of her. After he arrived, Candice smiled up at him. He realized that Candice only smiled when he was in for it.

Lana looked up from the paper. "Have you read the headlines or the article. Stone Corporation CEO attacked by unknown assailants. One killed, one captured, one escaped. They have a rather good picture of you by the way. I think I'll mount it on the wall...with my other trophies. Jacob's also carrying that slut. She's supposed to be dead! Why isn't she!"

"Ma'am, Lance is tough. He won't talk."

"I hate lose ends, Bill, you know that! You should have shot him, made sure... What do you use for brains, your dick, or do I have to do all the thinking for you?"

He needed to change the subject, and quickly. "Ma'am, my men said that James and Kaia have joined Jake and Doria. It would be easy to get three of them at one time."

"I'll think about it. You had sniper training didn't you?"

"At the rate he's going, he couldn't hit the broadside of a barn," Candice said.

That earned her a glare from Bill.

"Well, Bill?"

"Yes, Ma'am."

"You still have your sniper gun?"

"Yes, Ma'am."

"Could you position yourself across from the hospital and shoot them in the parking lot?"

"Yes, Ma'am."

"You know I could turn you over to the police."

"It would implicate you."

"Yes. I've half a mind to put you in handcuffs and let Candice turn you over to all the girls you've used and abused. I'm sure they could find interesting ways to get revenge."

"No, ma'am, PLEASE."

I don't think I want to share him, Candice thought, except maybe with Elle. She deserves revenge. I'm prepared. I've got a variety of poisons to incapacitate him to exact my revenge, maybe to kill him. Just give me the chance.

"Well, Bill. Think you can finish the job this time? No failures. And don't try to run from me. I'll make sure you're found, and my girls get the pleasure of killing you."

Pleasure, Candice thought - now there's an idea. I'll do it myself, Lana, and you won't even have to pay me.

After Bill left, Candice turned to Lana. "Do you want me to follow him to make sure he doesn't get distracted?"

"That's what happened last time he failed, wasn't it? Do it, but stay out of sight and report to me. If he disobeys again, I will turn him over to my girls."

While Candice walked out the door she knew, Lana wouldn't need to. He wouldn't live long enough to kill James.

Candice followed Bill in one of Lana's discrete surveillance cars. He briefly went home. She waited outside in her car a respectable distance away and watched through night vision binoculars. Lana's cars were all well equipped. A while later, he left the house and carried what looked like a large black case to his car. That must be the sniper rifle, she thought. She considered a call to warn James but that could be traced. Lana could find out. That was a risk she couldn't take. Well, now it was up to her to stop this bastard.

As she hoped, he didn't drive directly to the airport. Instead he drove to the seedy side of town, to a topless bar. He parked and went in. This is where Elle Ann worked, she realized. How appropriate he should spend his last few hours here. I can't wait to tell Elle Ann where and how he died. She got out of the car and walked toward the building. She had learned a few things from Lana. Being bold was one of them. Instead of entering through the bar door, she turned and went to the door the dancer's used. It was guarded of course. She explained to the guard that Elle Ann had sent her there for an audition. The guard slowly studied her voluptuous body with his eyes and smiled. "If I let you in, you'll do a private dance for me, won't you?"

Candice smiled and kissed him on the cheek. "Of course, sugar."

Once inside, she went into the dressing room and found two of Elle's friends. She showed them Elle's hospital picture and explained most of her plan. She didn't tell them he would be given poison, only something to make him horny as hell but too weak to do anything about it. They nodded in agreement. Candice took Francine, one of the dancers, to a curtain and pointed out Bill. Francine nodded. "He's a regular, and a bit rough, but generous with money."

"Honey," Candice said, "be thankful you've never been close to him. The bastard raped me in more than one way, and you saw what he did to Elle." Francine thought Candice was going to take advantage of Bill as a form of revenge and took the bottle from Candice. She boldly walked over to Bill and sat with him. Candice turned and went back to the dressing room where the other dancer helped her pick out a costume. She dressed and then waited. It took time, but then she wanted to be sure Bill was good and drunk.

Francine entered the dressing room. "He arranged for a private dance with me just like we planned."

A broad grin spread across Candice's face. "Revenge is sweet!"

"Just don't get me in trouble," Francine said.

"Don't worry," Candice said and handed Francine three hundred dollar bills. "Will this do?"

"Oh, yes, you were never here."

Candice entered the private room dressed in leather so Bill would obsess over her. Bill looked up from his chair. His eyes opened wide, wider than she had ever seen before. "I thought I bought Francine?" He looked Candice over with leering eyes. "Love the costume. I especially like the dog collar you're wearing. Did you bring the leash?"

She held it out in her hands.

"I've always had this fantasy of you anyhow. This could be interesting. Why the hell not?"

Candice locked the room and made sure the half empty bottle of whiskey sat beside Bill. She knew how the poison acted. She'd read up on it on the Internet. He should start feeling the effects soon. She put on the leash and began her strip tease. She took time to drag the leash across his cheek. She wrapped it around his neck and withdrew it slowly. He tried to grab the leash, but he was far too drunk. He followed her every movement with his eyes. She smiled back and continued her act but noticed his skin tone changing. His eyes began to glaze.

Now's the time for a lap dance, she thought as she moved onto his lap.

She kissed him on the forehead. "Too bad you don't feel this, but I'm enjoying myself. What did you say when you had me - 'the pleasure is all mine.' You've maimed my friend Elle Ann. It's my time to enjoy myself."

He tried to say something.

"Can't talk? You didn't know she was my friend?"

He made unintelligible sounds more like grunts.

"I didn't care about Kaia, but you plan to kill James, you bastard. The poison is slow but effective. You'll live maybe another thirty minutes, if you're lucky, before the paralysis stops your heart."

Bill rolled over and fell on the floor.

"Or not so lucky. Shit. Where's the pleasure in this. Lana would have told me to practice this before I tried it, but practice on whom?"

Candice began to clean the room but had to leave it to dump the remaining poisoned booze in the toilet in the ladies room. She flushed it twice. What to do with the bottle? She realized that Lana would have made her plan out every act with contingency plans. Instead, she had acted impulsively. Calm down, calm down, Candice, who would suspect this is a crime scene? Be bold, acting guilty only makes one suspicious. If I walk out into the bar, someone might remember me. I've got to dispose of it here. She tossed the bottle in the trash with the paper. It sat on top. She went back and pushed it under paper towels. Then she compulsively washed her hands. That's done. She went back to the room with some paper towels and cleaned Bill's face of all the drool. Then she cleaned the remainder of the room.

Shouldn't I feel guilty? Shouldn't I feel some kind of remorse? I've killed someone - someone who deserved killing. No - I felt good. That's sick. Am I becoming too much like Lana?

She left the room and found Francine. She slipped Francine five hundred dollars this time. She remembered what Lana said, 'be generous with money - it buys cooperation and silence'. "We've got a problem. He couldn't handle me. I was too hot for him. I hope it wasn't the aphrodisiac. He's dead."

"This could cost me my job," Francine said. She panicked."We've got to get him out of here."

Candice was cold and controlled. "My thought precisely. We'll pretend he's drunk. Don't let anyone in the room. I'll change into my clothes - then we'll just carry him to my car."

"How will we get past the guard?"

"Easy, they don't want the cops here. He'll do anything to avoid that. At worst you can promise him a dance. He's a sucker."

A couple of minutes later, they carried Bill between them to the dancer's door.

"What's this," the guard said.

"He died," Candice said. "I'm sure you'd prefer him someplace else, or should I call the police?"

"How did he ...."

"I was too hot for him. I think he had a heart attack."

His eyes darted over her entire body. "I can't wait to see you dance for me."

Two men in the parking lot turned suddenly toward them. One drew a gun and pointed it at the guard.

The guard gulped. "That's a Ruger Mark III semi-automatic, isn't it?"

"You know your guns, son. Complete with noise compensation. All your guests will hear is a little pop."

"Shit. Do you want these girls?"

"Just this one," the man with the gun said and waved his gun at Candice. He turned to Francine. "Go inside now and forget we were ever here." Francine and Candice dropped Bill on the ground. He laid there an amorphous mess. Candice stared at the gun.

He turned the gun toward the guard. "If you know what's good for you, none of this ever happened. Got it?"

The guard swallowed hard and nodded. The other man put Candice in handcuffs and took her toward a large black car. The man with the gun waved it at the guard. "You there – carry that body to the trunk."

"You're not the police," the guard said. "What is this, a hit?"

"It's best you don't know. Let's say we had some unfinished business with the deceased. This little lady, if she knows what's good for her, will help us with our little problem. That's why I recommend you to forget she was ever here."

Candice swallowed hard. Shit, if they're not the cops, who are they? What have I gotten myself into? Damn, it means I didn't get away with it. I've been caught. Now she felt guilty and a cold sweat spread over her body. She began to shake.

The guard easily picked up Bill's body and carried him to the car. The man with the gun followed close behind with the barrel pointed at the guard's head. He dropped the body into the trunk, carefully repositioned it, and then closed the trunk. He turned and looked at the revolver.

"Get back to your post and face the building until we're gone.

If you turn around, I'll kill you."

Candice sat in the back seat pondering her predicament. These guys threatened to kill the guard. Who were they? What possible way could she help them? Oh God...no, Bill was bad enough!" With that thought she began to shake involuntarily.

The guard with the gun sat down beside her. "Go," he said to the driver then turned toward Candice. "The bastard deserved to die."

"What?" Candice said.

"Thanks, you made our job a little easier. We've been following Bill for days. We had to call in the police, or he might have killed Elle Ann. He got away and our orders were to let him go, but the bastard deserved to die. No one treats a woman that way."

Candice felt a little relieved. They didn't sound like they would turn her over to the police. "Then what could you possibly want from me?"

"Your testimony against Lana so we can put her in prison for the rest of her life."

"She'll kill me."

"She'll kill you if we turn you over to the police along with his body. How did you kill him anyhow?"

"Poison."

"Amateur. Too easy to detect and trace. Okay, that means we'll need to burn the body, clean the bones, smash the skull and dump them all in the ocean then burn this car. Damn, woman, you've made this expensive and difficult."

The driver said, "I was beginning to like this car."

"Necessary losses are covered in the contract."

"Who are you guys?"

"You can call us private investigators of a very special sort. We can turn you over to the police and testify against you if you don't go along. We'd rather not, but that depends on you? Jail suicides are so easy to arrange when you have the police working for you, like Lana does."

Candice knew she was trapped. How could she get out of this? "Bill raped me. He beat up my best friend, Elle Ann and he planed to kill James."

"Were you there when she ordered Bill to kill anyone?"

"Yes."

"So you can testify that Lana conspired with Bill to commit multiple murders."

"Yes."

"Were you involved in any way with the conspiracy?"

"No. I had agreed to help James. You can ask him."

"Be assured, we will."

"I'll need protection."

"That's a given. We are going to keep you safe, very safe, even from the police. But you have to agree to help us."

What choice did she have?

Chapter 29 - Lana's Black Book

Lana smiled into her phone. "Captain Black, How are things with you?"

"Better, now that I'm eating regularly. I don't know how I can ever repay you for giving me this chance to redeem myself."

"My pleasure. How's Wulan?"

He was silent a moment. "She's been...very helpful. Thank you."

She would be. Wulan had exceptional talents. She would mold Captain Black into the Captain Lana wanted. "Are you ready to sail?"

"I thought it would be a few more weeks before we're ready."

"Captain, we've talked about this. I alone make that decision. You will deliver the containment vessel to a position I have selected in the pacific where it will be tested."

"Yes Ma'am, but I've been told the containment vessel isn't ready."

"Who do you take orders from?"

"You Ma'am."

"The containment vessel will be delivered to you tonight."

"But Jake?"

"He'll never get around to testing it. I won't waste any more time and money. It must be done. I want you underway as soon as it's secured."

"Yes, Ma'am."

"Once you are under way - do not take orders from anyone other than me."

"Understood, you're my boss."

"Tonight, then. Make sure your crew is ready."

She knew they would be. They were all hers. They'd already been given their orders. Nothing escaped her planning.

Lana leaned back in her chair and surveyed the trophies that lined all the walls of her office. Normally they brought her pleasure. Not tonight. Dammit, where is Candice? What happened to Bill? It's been three days. Bill never got on the plane, and Candice never reported back. There's only one conclusion - Bill is a runner, and he's done something to silence Candice. Bad timing - Bill, you've always been good at that. They're people I need to remove. I need it done right now, and I'll need someone to hunt you down, you bastard. My girls will have their sport. After this, I might even help them. I was beginning to like Candice. If you've hurt her....well, there were punishments for that.

She had a special book for situations like this - all those underworld people who could be useful for the right amount of money - or pleasure with her girls. She'd done business with some of them before. They'd recommended the others. In her mind, underworld people were just people, people with special skills. She used a book rather than a computer. The best encryption can eventually be broken. A small black book is easily hidden, especially when her desk had hidden compartments. She opened the top left hand drawer, lifted out some items including a cell phone and slid its false bottom back to retrieve the book.

It had been a while since she had need of it. The pages were organized by skill. She flipped through several pages until she found the right heading. Yes, she'd worked with some of these people before. It was time to call in some favors and spread around the wealth. She circled the numbers she sought and picked up the prepaid cell phone she'd just taken from the left hand drawer. She used it to place the first call - no need to leave an electronic trail. Over the next few minutes, she hired two hit men and a replacement for Bill. He went by the name Sly. No one knew his real name. He was a professional. She'd used him once before. Unwanted people just disappeared, and his guys loved her girls. This would be a match made in heaven. Sly wanted the job and would report to her first thing in the morning. One other precaution - she'd give the cell phone to Sly. That way if anything went wrong, he'd have the phone, not her.

Now what to do about Bill. There was a bounty hunter, an occasional hit man she knew of. He'd bring Bill back alive - wounded or not. He always got his man. And he always went for the big money. One more hit man was needed for the Atwater estate. No mistakes this time. She needed a sharpshooter, a real one, who understood stealth, and would wait until the job was done to get his reward. Bill obviously lacked stealth and self-control. It didn't take long for her to find just the right one in her book.

Finished, Lana slipped her book back into a hidden compartment in her desk. She spent the next hour checking up on the activities of her girls until the phone on her desk interrupted her.

"Lana, it's Frank."

"Yes. Hello Frank."

"Did you get my delivery?"

"Delivered and processed."

"Thank you. The account will be credited."

"It's good to be able to help you."

"I'll contact you when I have more."

"It's a pleasure doing business with you."

She hung up. The whole message had been coded. Companies and hospitals had problems disposing of radioactive waste, especially the more dangerous types. Like magic, Lana knew how to make it disappear - deep into the ocean depths. The first load was already in the containment vessel. The money would be transferred to her private offshore account. A girl needs some security, and Jake didn't need to know everything.

At seven-thirty in the morning, the phone at the Atwater estate began to ring. Shelly hurried out of the kitchen and picked it up. Doctor Stein was on the phone. He blurted out the message. "Die containment vessel, she is missing, ship too."

Shelly rushed back to the dining room to tell Ervin. "Get everyone up," he said. She sent a telepathic message to Mera, Kaia, and Doria. Kaia and Doria were still asleep. Mera was...occupied. Shelly apologized for the interruption and tried to wash away the strong emotions she felt while in Mera's mind. It made her think of David. Could he ever love her that way?

A few minutes later everyone had dressed and rushed downstairs. They gathered in the dining room. Kaia, Mera, James, and Grant clustered together around the breakfast table. Doria and Jacob sat next to Ervin.

"How could this have happened?" Kaia asked.

"Lana and Bill no doubt," Jacob said.

"Didn't I warn you," Doria said. "She has control over most of the company."

"Then a purge is in order."

"Not that easy," Doria said. "If I may suggest a solution, it will have to be done carefully. You need to know who are hers, who are yours, and who rides the fence. That will take time."

"I'll call the ship back," Jacob said. "That should take just a moment." He placed the call, but no one answered. He tried three more times then called his office to make sure he had the correct number. He did. "Whoever is piloting that ship is ignoring my call."

"Lana," Ervin said. "Only possible answer."

"Who's the captain?" Kaia asked.

"Arnold Black," Jacob said. "Lana hired him, but I approved it. I interviewed him. He's got a shady past, but he's trying to put his life back together. I believe him. Doria interviewed him and agreed. I think we can trust him. He's not the dangerous type that Lana usually hires."

"But he won't answer to you," Ervin said.

"Maybe he's being forced," Doria added.

"Who else is on the crew?" Kaia asked.

"I'll find out," Jacob replied.

"Let me do it," Doria added.

"Okay, you're better at this." She took out her phone and called the office.

Captain Black had left port at four o'clock in the morning. He pushed the ship, but not to maximum speed. He'd been a smuggler long enough to avoid undue attention. Better slow than caught. Rather than make an immediate run for the two hundred mile territorial limit, he headed up the coast toward Canada. Once in Canadian waters, he would turn out into the Pacific and toward Lana's designated location. His former smuggling misadventures would make him sweat until he got there. He kept his eyes on the skies and the horizon, expecting at any moment to see either aircraft or ships on an intercept course. Well, he wasn't smuggling this time, and Lana would back him up; but what about the cargo? He had misgivings that gnawed away at his stomach. This didn't look like a test. The personnel who loaded it on the ship all wore heavy protection suits. What was in the container that was so dangerous? This looked like it was more than a little toxic. He needed to get rid of it as quickly as possible.

The ships phone rang. He ignored it. It rang three more times. He continued to ignore it. Too early, it was way too early. Something was wrong. He called Lana.

"Someone's trying to call the ship," he said.

"You didn't answer, did you?"

"No ma'am."

"Good. I have word from the office that Jake called to make sure he had the number to contact the ship."

"What am I supposed to do?"

"I had one of my men disable the GPS transceiver on your ship."

Captain Black shuddered - one more way to draw undesired attention to them. She may be smart but she doesn't have smuggler instincts. Now he was sure this was no test cargo. They were carrying something toxic - highly toxic by the looks of it. Does she know the game she's playing? I've got to get rid of this cargo and then find another job. Working for her is too dangerous. I'd like to live out my natural life. Working for her could get me killed or locked up in prison for the rest of my days. This lady is worse than the legendary Dragon Lady.

Lana continued. "You can't be tracked. Unless you tell them, no one will know where you are. You're staying away from the usual shipping channels, right?"

"I'm heading toward Alaska, just as you planned."

I can't trust her, he thought. She lied to me. She's forced me to be a smuggler again. Maybe I should do the planning from here on. He turned toward his charts and wondered what other course he could take. Maybe if he hugged the shore line?

"Good. Maintain course and don't do anything to draw attention to your ship," Lana said,

Right, my gut tells me we should change course. Without the transceiver she would have no idea where we are. He hung up the phone. The mate called his attention to the weather forecast. "A strong storm is brewing."

"Change course, we'll hug the coast. We'll be north before it gets here."

Lana sat drumming her fingers on her desk. Damn, Jake found out about her deception way too early. It would still work out to her advantage. That's why she hired Captain Black - he had smuggler instincts. She just loved someone who listened to their intuition - smugglers had to have them or get caught. By the time they find the ship it will be too late. Just stick to the plan, Captain Black, and everything will work out.

She was in the middle of her thoughts when the office door opened, and Candice walked in. She had a black eye and bruises on her neck and wrists. It looked like she had been tied and beaten.

"Bill never got on the plane," Candice said.

"I already know that! Where's the bastard?"

"Dead - I did it."

"When? How?"

"It was me or him, and it damn well wasn't going to be me. He went home, picked up his gun, and found me watching him. He went berserk, dragged me out of the car by my hair and punched me in the face. He cuffed me, put me in the trunk of his car, and drove to the ocean. I think he planned to rape me and drown me in the ocean. I guess he expected me to be timid and afraid. Big mistake. He went over the cliff."

"Are you sure he's dead?"

"He's dead."

"Why were you gone for three days?"

"Some private investigators for the Atwaters caught me. They wanted Bill dead, but they threatened to turn me over to the police. I used the female skills you taught me to escape. I've been hiding from them for two days while trying to get to you."

"Well, damn! You had all the fun. My girls will be disappointed. What about his body?"

"That's the good part. They put it in the trunk of their car. If they try to implicate me, I'll testify that they killed Bill."

"Good thinking. I'll testify that I was ready to turn him over to the police because I suspected he had beaten and raped Elle Ann."

"Do you want me to stick around, or should I go home and recuperate."

"You best stay with me until you're presentable again."

There was a knock on the door. "Right on time. Have a seat, Candice."

Sly walked into Lana's office. "Good morning, Lana. It's been a while. Must be desperate for you to need my services." He turned toward Candice. "Who's the girl? Looks like someone had a good time with her. Got any more like her?"

Oh my God, Candice thought, not Bill II.

"She's not that type, but I can find you some if that's what you want."

"Okay, I'm in."

Lana slid a briefcase across the table to him. "Five hundred thousand in small bills. You get the rest when the job's done."

"Who's the target?"

"My whole damn family. I've got others working on this as well, so we'll need to co-ordinate. One problem - my husband, Jake, has to go last, after the will is read. There's a profile of all the targets in the briefcase. And every one must look like an unfortunate accident."

He gave her a big grin and winked at Candice. "Where do I start?"

"Last I heard, nearly all of them were at the Atwater estate. Location and surveillance details are enclosed. I don't think they will stay there. They'll be chasing a ship. You might want to start at the Cersea marina. I've enclosed information on it as well."

"I'll get right on it."

"Keep in touch with me on this phone. It's prepaid. I used it to call you. You understand why I'm giving it to you. Destroy it when you tell me the job's done. Then come back for the rest of your payment."

"I prefer a redhead."

"I'll find one for you."

Doria was still trying to obtain a crew manifest when the phone rang again. Shelly picked it up and spoke a few words. "Doctor Stein," she said and handed it to Jacob.

"We have an emergency," Doctor Stein said. "The dye is still in the laboratory. It was never put in the containment vessel."

"So the vessel's empty."

"I don't think she is."

"Why?"

"She weighs too much."

"Then what's in it?"

"I'm suspicious. The material was dense, so I checked. The sensors in the laboratory they indicate radioactivity, a trail from laboratory to loading dock."

"It has radioactive material!"

"The deliveries. The same occurred at the delivery dock yesterday afternoon."

"You think Lana had it loaded with radioactive material?"

"That's the probability."

"Dr. Stein. I have five operatives in the building. Contact David. He'll have them contact you. Find out who did it, and under whose orders. We need to know what's in that vessel. Is it waste or is it fissionable material being delivered to terrorists."

"Ja, Herr."

Jacob hung up. "Dad, she may be sending fissionable material to terrorists. Can you get Calvin to help?"

"I'll call."

"You mean the vessel contains radioactive material?" Kaia said.

"Likely. At any rate we have to act as if it does."

"How far could the ship have gotten?" James asked.

"Depends on when it left."

"I can find that out," Doria said and placed another call.

The Lady heard about the nuclear waste through Shelly's ears and alerted all of the Selkies worldwide. First order of business - find the ship. Second order of business - if it drops its container, note the location but keep every living thing away from it. Even the whales and dolphins were committed to the task.

Ambassador, I have committed the selkies and all sentient marine life to find that ship and keep away from the containment vessel if it's dropped.

Thank you, Grandmother.

"Finding the ship is not good enough," Ervin said. "There's little we can do if it gets outside territorial waters. We'll have to act anyhow, and that would directly involve the selkies and orcas."

"What would you have them do, attack the ship," Kaia said.

Better that, Oceana said telepathically, *than watch their slow death.*

"Then we need to get on that ship and turn it around before it gets that far," Jacob said.

"How do you expect to do that?" James asked.

"I'm going to call in a favor from an admiral I know," Ervin said.

Moments later an aide walked into Admiral Jay's office. "Sir, there's an Ervin Atwater on the line. He says he knows you, and it's a national crisis."

"I've already had two of those today. What else could

happen? At least this isn't from the Chief of Staff. Put him on."

The aide left, and Admiral Jay picked up the phone.

"Major Atwater, what's so important?"

"Retired, Sir, but still at your service. We have a ship carrying nuclear material. We don't yet know if it's waste or fissionable. It's someplace off the coast of Northern California, maybe as far north as Oregon. It does not respond to messages to return to port."

"Terrorists?"

"Of a sort. Home grown if you like."

"They're the worst sort. We can't let nuclear material fall into the wrong hands. I won't ask how it got there. You'll explain that to me later. Let me see, I have no ships in the vicinity. There is a Coast Guard vessel I could request."

"I doubt they'd stop for it."

"Then we need to board and take over the ship."

"Precisely."

"You were in Special Forces. I could assign some to this emergency. They know how to keep silent. We don't want this incident made public."

"That's why I called you, Sir."

"I can only send a few at my discretion; otherwise I must notify my superiors."

"We still think alike."

"We ought to; we were on many of the same missions."

"It shouldn't take many. I've got people searching for the ship."

"We understand each other then. I can't send resources to find the ship, only to board it."

"We'll find the ship. In a few minutes we'll know when it left and where it will likely be."

"How will you let me know?"

"You remember Captain Dickerson?"

"Yes. He was with us when you performed that miraculous rescue."

"I'll send him and two others. They will be in communication with me. We'll find the ship, but need your people to stop it."

"Why can't you come?"

"Damn legs."

"I'm feeling it too. Old age sucks."

"Can you send a chopper with your men and pick my men up at my estate. I'll send you the GPS coordinates."

"Give me an hour."

"Done."

Ervin hung up the phone and placed a call to Calvin, telling him what happened and to hurry to the estate.

"Who are the other two?" James asked.

"Why, you and Grant, of course. Who else can represent our interests?"

"We can," Mera and Kaia said simultaneously.

"You're not mechanics. We may need James' and Grant's knowledge before we're through."

"I won't sit here," Kaia said.

"Me either," Mera said.

"I'm with them," Shelly added.

"Ladies..."

"James, doesn't your father have a fast boat?"

"Yes...but..."

"Call him. Tell him what's happened. Ask him to loan it to us."

James was ready to say no when the Lady spoke to them all. *I will go too. I can coordinate the search from the boat and get us to the location.*

James threw up his hands. "Women..."

Ervin laughed. "Selkies, James, selkies."

Chapter 30 - Dangerous Cargo

The women rushed out the front door. "I'll drive," Kaia said.
"Only two will fit in your Corvette," Shelly said. "We need to take Ervin's car."

"Too slow."

"Then I'll have to follow you," Shelly said.

Jacob rushed out the door behind them. "Stop, all of you. We don't have someone at the office. I can't send Doria. She's still recovering, and I won't leave her." Kaia gave him a wry smile but he continued to talk. "Shelly, I can't order you, but you should go to David and help him and Dr. Stein sort this out. You can coordinate with Oceana."

"That makes sense," Shelly said, "and I don't mind. We all must do our part."

Mera smirked and hugged Shelly. "Sis, I know, it will be hard on you, forced to work with David. Oh my. Come on Kaia, show me what this Corvette can do."

"Remember girls," Shelly said, "It's wrong to use the selkie voice on policemen."

"Dang," Mera said.

"And remember ladies, you're married," Shelly added.

The Corvette sped off before Shelly got into Ervin's car. She dialed David. He answered. "I'm on my way," she said.

"Good, I can use your skills."

"I'm looking forward to being with you."

"Quit teasing me, this is serious."

"Until it's over....then we'll be together."

Calvin arrived moments before the Special Forces helicopter landed on the circular drive. A soldier stepped out of the chopper and strode to the door. He saluted. Calvin saluted back. "Major Atwater?"

"God, it feels good to be back in action. No, former Captain Dickerson."

"I heard you'll be joining us."

"Yes, yes, the Major's inside. Come on in."

They entered. "In the library, Cal," Ervin yelled. Jacob appeared in the parlor and waved them forward.

When they entered, they saw Ervin at his desk with a nautical map in front of him. Doria sat next to him. She was still on the phone. He'd stuck a pin at the port and had drawn a circle for the maximum distance the ship could have traveled since it left.

The soldier snapped to attention and saluted. "Major Atwater, the Admiral assigned me to you for this mission."

Ervin saluted him back. "Sorry, I can no longer stand. Are you aware of our situation?"

"Yes, sir. Terrorists have nuclear material on board a vessel and are headed out to sea. We must recover it."

Ervin looked at his name tag and smirked. "Right you are, Captain Hook."

"Yeah, it usually gets a lot of laughs. I like to think I put my hook into the bad guys. I don't plan to change my name. It'll be better when I make Major."

"Major Hook...it has a nice ring to it."

Hook looked down at the map. "That's a big area."

"We've got parties out searching all of it. No sense leaving here until we've got a better idea."

"Beg you pardon, Sir, but we can be part of the search. If you were the enemy, what course would you have taken?"

"Two possible: a direct run for the territorial limit or a run toward Canada. I doubt they'd go south. If they make international waters, the Admiral may need to send in the big ships. Secrecy will be out the window. It's up to us to stop them."

"It would be easiest for us to search north and if they went west, we'd still be closer than we are now, although we may have to land on the Coast Guard ship if we don't have enough fuel to return to base. Who goes with me?"

"Captain Dickerson will represent me. The other two are civilians, but they report to the company that owns the ship. You may need their expertise before this is over."

"You know civilians don't belong in what might become a firefight."

"There are no civilians when terrorists attack. They treat everyone as their enemy. You will need them. I insist."

Captain Hook saluted. "Yes, sir. We'll leave immediately."

Lana and Candice had been talking about Bill when her

phone rang. "Ma'am we've been following the women with our helicopter. They have taken a boat from the Cersea marina and are headed toward the northwest.

"How many are on board."

"Three."

"Good. Must be Mera, Shelly, and Kaia."

"Follow them."

"I must refuel soon."

"Can you follow them for a few minutes?"

"Yes, Ma'am."

"I'll call you right back."

She called Sly. "Where are you?"

"I'm at the marina."

"Three are on a boat that just left."

"I noticed."

"They're being followed by some of Bill's men in a chopper. I'll put them in contact with you."

"Lana, just a suggestion. They're too close and follow their every movement. Your guys need to learn some stealth."

"They'll point you in the right direction. Follow them until they turn off to refuel."

"I'll steal a boat and be on my way."

"Remember, I need to know where everyone is before you take action."

She hung up and received a call from Bill's man at the Atwater estate. "Ma'am, a military helicopter just left the Atwater estate and headed north-west."

"Who's on it?"

"Some military men, a civilian I didn't recognize, although he's been at the estate many times. The other two were James Cersea and Grant Gregson."

"That leaves Ervin, Jacob, and Doria at the house."

"Yes, ma'am."

"I'm sending a sharpshooter to you. Take orders from him as you would Bill."

"Understood."

She hung up and slammed her fist on the table. She grabbed the knife she so often threatened Bill with, and threw it at the wall. It stuck and quivered. Candice ducked. "Shit," Lana said.

"What's wrong."

"The damn military is involved."

"Are you going to tell the captain?"

"No - best he doesn't know. He'd surrender rather than fight. I own the crew. I'll contact them. They'll make sure he doesn't turn around. The cargo either goes into the sea or the ship goes down."

Then Lana smiled. "It's too good to be true. I could lose this cargo but kill off all the contenders at one time."

Candice had to turn away. She couldn't let Lana see either her smile or her concern for James. She touched her chest. She'd done her job. She wore a wire. Lana just incriminated herself, and they could all pretend that it was Lana's office that had been bugged. She would walk away free, just because she was willing to cooperate.

Shelly walked into the lobby of Stone Enterprises and was immediately recognized by the receptionist. "Miss Atwater. You're to go directly to the laboratory." She buzzed the door open.

"I know my way," Shelly said and hurried through the door.

Dr. Stein and David were in the laboratory when Shelly arrived. She winked at David. "Here's what we know for sure," David said. "The container definitely contains nuclear material - we think it's radioactive waste but we can't be sure. The people who loaded it on the ship all wore protective suits. That made it easy for us to track them down. We have one of them secured in the office. We've put some of Calvin's men hunting down the others. I can't trust company security. I'm sure most of them work for Lana rather than us. The dude we caught won't talk. He says he only takes orders from Lana."

Shelly relayed the information to Ervin and Calvin. Calvin still wasn't used to telepathy. That would take time, if it ever happened. He framed a response in his thoughts. *I hope this works.*

"Calvin says to hold the suspect for his interrogation," Shelly said. "He may help us incriminate Lana."

"If we can catch his colleagues, they may also help us. Their protests point right at Lana." David said. "They may unwittingly incriminate her."

Meanwhile, Dr. Stein was thumbing through papers and punching numbers into his laptop. He looked nervous.

"What's wrong," Shelly asked.

He looked through his notes then up at her. "Not sure. Too heavy. Too heavy for handles. Radioactive material ist zehr heavy. Lift points will fail."

"The lift points must have worked - they loaded it."

"Are you sure?"

"Let's ask our reluctant prisoner," David said. "You question him, Shelly."

"David, it's wrong to look inside his mind."

"Even if all the Pacific selkies are in danger of being irradiated?"

Let David ask, Oceana said. *Looking into his mind is not the same as controlling it. If there's a problem we need to know it.*

In the prisoner's mind, there was a problem. They had difficulty loading the container. There was a disturbing image. One of the lift points appeared to crack. Then the container smacked down hard on the deck before it was strapped in place with chains.

"There is a problem," Shelly said. "One of the lift points is cracked."

Oceana sat at the controls of the powerboat. The selkies and whales searched the whole region. "There are no reports of a ship in the southern half of our search area that matches the image I sent out. There has been a sighting of a possible ship running north near the black reef."

"Doesn't he know the selkies hang out there," Mera said.

"But it increases the risk," Kaia said.

"It's where we're going." Oceana said and pushed the throttle to maximum.

"Should we tell them?" Kaia asked.

Oceana pictured the ship in Kaia's and Mera's mind.

"Humans can't see those reference points," Kaia said. "They're underwater. Yes, the Black Reef is near, but we need coordinates."

"Then get out the charts."

James sat next to Grant in the helicopter. They sped over the ocean. It was his first time in a helicopter. It didn't move the same way an airplane did. It was disconcerting - but okay. Powered boats moved differently than sailboats. Sailboats slip through the water, powerboats pounded it. He'd survive, stomach and all.

Suddenly he heard Kaia in his mind. *James, here are the co-ordinates for the ship.*

Kaia, how do I tell them without breaking our cover.

Do you still have the earpiece you wore when we came back from Hawaii.

Good idea.

James reached into his pocket and put the earpiece in his ear. Grant grabbed his arm. "What's up buddy?"

"Just a minute, Grant. I've got a message....Yes...Yes...I've got it...Okay I'll tell them." He wrote down some numbers on a notepad and turned toward Captain Hook. "Here are the present co-ordinates of the ship."

The Captain handed them to the pilot and the chopper changed course. He turned back toward James and Grant. "Okay guys, keep your little secrets. There's no damn way in hell that earpiece works out here...unless." He looked at Calvin. "You guys aren't as civilian as you make yourselves out to be."

James reached for his fake ID but Calvin shook his head no. "We said this was a national emergency," he said. "I'm sure I can count on your discretion, Captain. When this is over, we were never here. If necessary, the Major will explain to Admiral Jay."

James and Grant managed to keep a straight face.

They headed out toward the target. Thirty minutes later, it was visible on the horizon.

James acted as if his earpiece activated again. It was Shelly this time. *There's a problem, the lift points on the container are cracked. The nuclear material was too heavy. It would be dangerous to lift the cargo.*

James turned to the Captain once again. "Bad news," he said. "The nuclear material was too heavy for the container. The lift points are cracked..."

The Captain interrupted him. "Smugglers usually drop their cargo. Shit. There's no way to negotiate." He turned toward his fellow soldiers. "Arm your weapons. We'll have to take control of the ship's deck. Keep them from dropping their cargo at all cost."

"Lana," Captain Black said into the phone, "there's a helicopter moving toward us from the coast, and radar shows a ship closing at us from the north. What should I do?"

"What would you do if you were a smuggler?"

"Dump the cargo."

"Why do you even ask?"

As soon as she hung up, the mate pointed a gun at Captain Black. "You'll take your orders from me."

"We need to slow down if we're going to drop it."

"No, we drop it on the run..."

"Do you realize how that risks the ship?"

"Do I have to kill you?"

"Okay, okay. We can't be caught with that cargo aboard."

Captain Black was forced out on the deck by the gunman. There, they met several of the crew. The mate explained they needed to dump the cargo, and the crew rushed to comply.

"Do you know what's in the container?" Captain Black asked.

"Doesn't matter."

"Don't you wonder why they wore hazard suits when they loaded it? If it's dangerous, the crew won't be protected."

"I don't give a damn. It's what I've been told to do."

"By whom?"

"Who do you think, our boss."

Captain Black looked up at the approaching helicopter. He motioned to it with his head. "Looks military to me. What are you going to do about that?"

The mate yelled down to the deck. "Kurt, Larry, Manuel, get your guns. We're about to have company."

"You can't win this fight," Captain Black said. He recalled the last time he was caught. Better lay down the guns and accept your fate. You tend to live longer that way.

The three crew members looked up at the helicopter and moved to positions where they could fire on it from cover.

"Don't you think we need some cover too," Captain Black said. "I feel kind of naked standing out on the deck."

They rushed back into the bridge.

As the helicopter moved in, they watched the crew rush around on the deck. Some moved to the container and the wench; others scrambled about with guns and took positions around the deck.

"They're armed and ready to fight," Captain Hook said. He

turned toward Calvin. "Sorry, we must observe the niceties." He reported the situation and their location to Admiral Jay.

Moments later the helicopter came close enough to hail the ship and ordered them to stand down. The request was met by gunfire from the ship.

"The rules of engagement have been met. They don't have antiaircraft missiles or they would have used them."

But, too much time had been wasted. The crew with the wench was ready to lift the container. They watched as the container rose inches above the deck then snapped loose. It fell and began to roll with the ship. The ships crew fled out of the way.

"If that container breaks," Calvin said, "radioactivity will all spread over the ship and into the ocean."

"We'll stop it," Captain Hook said. Then, he ordered the deck of the ship to be strafed.

When the shooting started, the Mate turned to look out the bridge door. That was all the distraction Captain Black needed. He had dealt with mutinous crews before. He harshly slammed the Mate's head into the wall. There was a loud crack. He grabbed the gun with one hand, and then punched him several times in the gut. The Mate collapsed. He set the gun down on the console where he could reach it, if needed. Just in case the Mate survived. He intended to surrender, not to be shot. When he joined AA, he made a commitment to do the right things. He had to honor it now or retreat to that dark place he never wanted to see again.

Something tells me I've been set up with a very dangerous cargo. Why else would the military be here? He was on the wrong side. How could he change that?

When the helicopter finished shooting, they had hit at least two of the shooters on the deck. The crew members who had been at the wench and container put their hands behind their necks in a posture of surrender. Five of the Special Forces rappelled to the deck and took up positions to defend themselves. The crew members who surrendered were taken aside and held at gunpoint by one of the Special Forces. Two others sought out the remaining gunner, and two headed for the cabin.

But, the container continued to roll back and forth on the deck as the ship rolled in the waves. It smashed into one side of the rail then rolled and smashed into the other. Each time, it dented the rail a bit more.

James and Grant felt helpless. For the first time they wished they could telepathically warn the selkies to flee the area.

"There's still at least one shooter to be concerned about," Captain Hook said. "Keep a good lookout. If he appears, shoot him. Team two, get ready to rappel to the deck and restrain that container."

Moments later, team two was on the deck. But when they tried to reach the container, shots were fired at them from the region of the wench. No one was hit, but they all fell to the deck. Two got up and ran behind the container, using it as cover while it rolled to the other side of the ship. They got beneath the wench and took positions in the operating machinery. The gunner tried to shoot again, but when he appeared, he was shot from below.

When two soldiers entered the bridge, Captain Black knelt on the floor with his hands above his head. He nodded to the console and the gun. "I was forced. The mate had a gun to my head."

Just then, the lights went off, and the ship began to coast. Emergency lighting came back on, but they were adrift.

"What the..."

"May I talk to your commander," Captain Black said. "We have an emergency. There's a big storm coming. It will drive us onto the black reef unless we immediately get the engines back on line." He pointed out the window and waved his arm. "Over there is the black reef. The storm will push us toward it."

The message was relayed, but Captain Hook was reluctant to trust Captain Black.

"The ship owners trust him," Calvin said. "We believe he is reliable. What I've heard about the crew however..."

"We need to get down there," James said, "right now."

"No," Captain Hook said.

"Grant and I are mechanics. I'm an engineer. We can work on the engines."

"Absolutely not."

"Captain, there's a storm coming. It will spread nuclear material all over the western seacoast. Untold people and wildlife will suffer..."

"Have you ever rappelled?"

"I have," Grant said. He smiled and looked at James.

"I understand the theory," James said.

"Captain," I'll take responsibility," Calvin said. "Put them down on the deck, preferably away from that careening container."

Moments later, James and Grant were ready to drop to the deck.

"Are you sure this is safe," James said.

"No problem. It comes naturally. Just like falling on the deck."

"It's the fall that scares me."

"Don't worry about the fall, just do it slowly. It's the impact that hurts."

"Great."

Grant reached the deck first, and James came down in spurts. They met Captain Black on the deck. "I understand you're mechanics," he said.

James pointed to Grant. "I'm a degreed marine engineer."

"Good, if we can't fix this I'll have good company when the ship goes down."

"My grandfather's already down there," James said. "His ship wrecked on that reef. But, we're going to get this ship out of here. Captain, did you know you were carrying radioactive material? We can't let this ship be wrecked on the reef."

"Lana lied to me," Captain Black said. "She said this was a test cargo."

"Lana uses everybody. We need to take her down. Are you on our side or hers?"

"I'll lose my job."

"You'll lose more than that if the ship goes down. If you succeed you might even be a hero."

"But I won't have a job."

"Didn't Jacob approve your hire?"

"Yes."

"If you succeed, you'll still work for him, so let's get this job done, Captain."

James turned toward the two soldiers. "Whoever sabotaged the ship could be armed. Please see us safely to the engine room and keep us guarded."

"There it is," Mera said as she pointed out the ship.

"It's drifting," Kaia said.

"And there's a bad storm coming," Oceana said.

James, what's happening?

Someone sabotaged the ship's engines. Grant and I are on the way to the engine room with Captain Black.

What about the cargo?

It's loose on deck. I doubt they'll be able to restrain it unless we get power back and can point the ship into the waves.

Do you realize where you are?

Yeah, where Granddad died.

There's a storm coming.

I don't want to end my life here.

We'll remain to rescue you if needed.

I hope we won't need it. Better clear the area.

Kaia shared her thoughts with Oceana who ordered all the wildlife that could hear, to leave the area immediately.

Aga and Siku replied that they and their pod would stay. It was their duty to protect the Daughter of the Sea.

The soldiers tried to restrain the container, but it rolled back and forth on the deck every time the ship rocked in the waves. The lift points were gone, but there were some loops left to secure the container in place on the deck. They tried to attach chains to them, but every time they got close, the container rolled to the other side. If they didn't get out of the way, they'd be crushed. It didn't matter how many people they put on it, it didn't look like the container could be restrained. The question was, how long could the rails stand the battering before they failed? Still they would continue to try until the very last minute. They didn't think of themselves as heroes. They were soldiers doing their job to protect their country.

Down below in the engine room, James felt the urgency grow in his mind. The storm was near. The black rock was near. Granddad was near. They could lose the cargo at any moment. Still, the three continued to debug the engines. By then, the soldiers had found and caught the ship's engineer. He wouldn't cooperate.

While they worked, Captain Black complained about being set up by Lana. He wanted to quit. He was through being a smuggler. He wanted an honest job. James told him to be patient. First, they had to get the ship away from the reef. Doing that was an honest man's work.

"Fuel lines," Captain Black said. "It must be the fuel lines."

"Of course," Grant said. "Whoever did this would want an escape plan."

Still, it took several minutes to locate the problem and start the engines. The power came back on. The military helicopter had to leave to refuel, but a Coast Guard vessel would intercept and accompany them until they were back at port.

"Got to rush to the bridge," Captain Black said.

"Grant and I need to leave," James said.

"Why? Who'll mind the engines?"

"We're not supposed to be here. It's a long story. It's Kaia's story, not mine to tell. The military will have to do the job."

Captain Black turned to the soldiers. "Bring that mutinous engineer in here."

Once he was present, Captain Black grabbed him by the throat. "You've got two choices: one I give you what you deserve - a very long swim; or two, you keep these engines running." He looked at the military men for approval. They didn't even wince. "Keep the engines running, and I'll ask them to look the other way when we get to shore and let you walk."

If I keep this job, Captain Black thought, I'll do the hiring. He pointed his finger at the engineer. "I need reliable people, not mutinous ones like you. And don't expect a reference from me."

"We'll leave as soon as the container is restrained," James said.

"To avoid the reef, I'll have to steer a course out to sea, directly into the storm," Captain Black said. "We have to face the storm head on. There's no way to safely reach port before it hits."

"I understand," James said. "Once you head into the waves, the cargo will be less likely to roll. The military should be able to restrain it."

Chapter 31 - Collision

Once the ship was under control, the ladies arrived in Charles' powerboat. They cruised beside the ship while the cargo was secured against the wench. Then James and Grant were lowered by the wench into the powerboat. Captain Black headed out to sea and into the storm. Oceana steered the powerboat away from the ship.

"Do you trust Captain Black?" Kaia asked.

"Yes," James said. "He seems genuinely angry with Lana. He thinks Lana just ruined his chance for a renewed career. I suspect he'd testify against her."

"Ocean dumping may cost her financially, but it isn't a crime that will land her in prison," Kaia added.

"It's leverage and will give her a bad name."

"But the company too."

"It was nuclear material," James said. "That could be considered a terrorist crime."

"You'd have to show motive. She was clearly trying to dump it."

"Still, it's leverage."

"We can take that up with Calvin when we get back home," Oceana said. "We still have to avoid the storm."

"It seems to reflect my mood," James said, "and it's a sour one. I didn't want to join my grandfather on that reef."

She turned toward him. "Then think calm, will you? Remember Circe."

"Can we make it back in time?" Kaia asked.

"It's a small boat," Grant added, "and a long way to swim. Of course, you girls don't have to worry about that."

"Relax, nothing's going to happen."

"Uh oh," Oceana said. "There's another helicopter moving toward us."

"Lana," Sly said. "We've got them. James and Grant are in the boat with the girls."

"Where are they?"

"Off the black rock reef and there's a storm coming."

"How fitting. Do it NOW."

311

"With pleasure."

She could almost see him smile.

He turned his stolen boat toward the target. There was the coming storm to consider, but the job would be done in a few minutes. He'd still have to head north and find another port.

Once she was off the phone, she placed another call to the sharpshooter. "Tonight, do it. Make sure it's Ervin and not my husband."

Grant pointed up toward the distant shore. A black helicopter flew over them and passed further out to sea. That itself was strange - flying into a storm? It would have made sense if it was a Coast Guard copter, but it wasn't. It was a solid black. So they kept an eye on it. He knew the reef was nearby.

"We stopped the dumping," Grant said.

"It's just one battle, not the war," Oceana said.

"Can't you let us enjoy one victory? It was tough enough."

"Shouldn't we go north?" Grant asked. "There must be a safe harbor we can put in until the storm is over."

Oceana turned the boat toward the north.

Grant pointed to the sky and yelled. "That helicopter, it turned when we did."

"Is it following us?" James asked.

"Looks like it," Grant said.

"That helicopter feels wrong," Mera said. "Didn't we see one like it when we headed out from the Cersea Marina?"

"Then change course towards shore," James advised.

"The black rock shoals?" Oceana said. "Are you sure you want to do that? It's your Dad's boat."

The helicopter swooped low over them and then turned back for another pass. Oceana changed course toward the shore.

"They're not friendly," Mera yelled. "It's the same feeling I had before Bill attacked Grant and me."

"How inevitably suitable," Kaia said, "Right back to where this all started."

"The helicopter's coming right at us," Grant yelled.

"What's that?" Mera said. She pointed toward the shore. A cigarette boat sped in their direction.

"Mom intends to sink us," Kaia yelled.

"We can't outrun him," Grant added.

"Then call the orcas," James said.

"Go ahead, Kaia, you can do that," Oceana said. "They will defend us."

"Call them, dammit," James yelled. "They're getting too close."

"You want us?" Siku said.

"You're here?"

"The pod is here. Others are near. You're in danger. We sense it in your mind. What do you wish of us?"

"Keep that boat away from us."

"The noisy one?"

"The little fast one."

Meanwhile, Oceana swerved one way then the other to avoid Sly who overshot them with every turn. The helicopter joined the chase. Mera looked up. "How close to shore?"

"Why?" Grant replied.

"Because they're going to shoot us,"

"Shit, that's a long way to swim."

"I'll ram their boat," Oceana said.

"That's suicide. We'll never make it to shore."

"Mera and Oceana can carry you two," Kaia said. "I can transform and swim with them."

Oceana turned toward them. "We can't fight bullets. James and Grant, get your life preservers on. Everyone will have to jump except for me."

"We can't jump at this speed," James yelled. The spray of machine gun bullets splashed beside the boat. "On second thought, I can do it."

"We'll use the inflatable to break the impact," Grant said. "Inflate it as we jump."

Within seconds, they were ready. Oceana turned the boat and aimed at the bow of the cigarette boat. They sped toward each other at high speed.

"I'll wager you that they chicken," Grant said.

"This is no time for comedy," James replied.

Grant and Mera joined hands. Kaia and James did the same. Then, with both hands, they all grabbed onto the inflatable and Grant pulled the cord. It popped open, and they sailed into the air before it impacted in the ocean. The shock of the inflatable becoming airborne tore them loose, and they plunged into the water.

As the inflatable hit the water, it was torn apart by gunfire. At the last second the cigarette boat turned away. The two boats sideswiped and overturned. The cigarette boat burst into flames. Charles' boat sank. Oceana turned into an orca and joined Siku's pod. Other selkie orcas appeared from toward the shore. The selkie guard joined the orca pod. The helicopter rushed to the site of the cigarette boat. It was in flames.

Lana's phone rang. "Sly's dead, but so is everyone on that boat."

"You're sure?"

"We shot them. Besides, there's no way they could swim to shore from here. From all the orca's milling around, there won't be anything left of them."

Lana hung up, and a broad smile spread across her face. "This is better than planned. By tonight the company will be mine."

Candice turned away. She didn't want Lana to read her face. She seethed inside. If you've killed James, for sure I'll see you in prison - if I don't kill you myself first. At that moment, she regretted she wore the wire. She knew where Lana kept her gun. If she hadn't worn the wire she'd kill her right now.

The pod surrounded Kaia and supported James and Grant. Together, they were herded toward the shore. James and Grant found the water icy cold. They knew survival in these conditions was only minutes. Oceana joined them. "That was fun," she said. "I got a little singed, but wow - the thrill."

"James needs your help," Kaia said. "Will you carry him? Grant, Mera wants you to ride her."

"Right now, in front of the whole pod?" Grant said.

"Can't you take anything seriously?" Mera said.

Moments later, the two guys each clutched the dorsal fin of an orca. The pod swam swiftly toward the black rock. Grant sat saddle style on Mera and waved his arm around like he was riding a bull. "Yippee," he yelled.

"*The noisy metal bird,*" Siku said, "*carried the bad two-legged away. The noisy boat sank. It will join the others.*"

A party was taking place at the black rock. A mixed group of twenty-four college students sat on blankets around a large bonfire drinking various forms of booze. It was a foggy evening, familiar to those expecting a storm. One member of the group stood and told the ghost story about the shipwrecked sailors. "And it is said, on a misty night like this, the ghosts return from the sea to capture those on shore and drag them into the depths..."

One of the girls screamed. Five bodies started walking out of the water. Two were in clothing that looked like rags waving in the wind. The other three were women and dressed only in seaweed that hung loosely on their bodies. "The ghosts," someone yelled and they all fled.

Oceana and Kaia helped James limp to the fire. He could barely feel his legs. Mera helped Grant who appeared to be in better shape. Kaia and James each grabbed blankets from the ground. Mera picked up a blanket and wrapped it around herself and Grant. They moved toward the fire and sat. She looked at Kaia, "Just sharing the body heat."

Kaia threw her blanket around James, and they huddled together. She was cold, but James felt icy.

"You know how to warm yourselves up quickly, don't you?" Oceana said.

"Grandma!"

"You're married. It's only a suggestion, mind you, but consider this, James and Grant are at their limits. They need all the help and support you can give them."

James shivered and held tightly to Kaia.

"Take off your wet clothes," she said.

He still shivered. "You'll have to help me."

Kaia and Mera both helped their husbands undress under the covers. While they struggled, Oceana looked around. A lone girl from the party stood near the cliffs and watched them. Oceana got up and walked toward her.

"Don't be afraid," Oceana said. "We were shipwrecked."

The girl paused. Oceana reached her. "You're almost eighteen?"

"How do you know?"

"Your mother?"

"You know her?"

"I know all my daughters. How's she doing?"

"Mom's miserable. Dad abandoned her. She can't keep a job. I don't know what she's going to do. I don't know if I can finish college."

"I'll make you an offer. Come back here on your birthday and bring your mother with you. I'll meet you here. Perhaps I can change your lives for the better."

Shelly and Oceana were still linked telepathically. She was aware of the entire incident regarding the shipwreck and survival. But she wasn't able to help. She was too far away. She couldn't be there herself, but she could do the next best thing.

"Doria, Kaia and the others are shipwrecked at the black rock. They urgently need warm clothes and transportation. Can you ask Jacob to help?"

Doria could see them through Oceana's eyes. *"We're over an hour away. How can we get there in time?"*

She saw them close to the fire. *"I'll let Jacob know."*

She turned to Jacob. "They're all shipwrecked at the black rock. They need warm clothing and transportation right away."

"If they've been in the ocean, time is important. Help me grab some blankets."

"I'm going with you."

"There isn't room. I have to bring five people back."

After twenty minutes, Grant grabbed another blanket and stood up. He walked the beach in search of additional driftwood. Kaia noticed that James continued to shiver. "I can't get warm," he said.

At that moment, Kaia realized that she could never rescue James at sea by herself. "I don't want to do this anymore," she said. She looked in James' eyes. "I could have lost you tonight."

"Anything worthwhile has its risks," he replied. "Doing nothing will only cause more pain. If we do nothing, more lives will be lost. Doing nothing means the ocean will die. I will fight even if you don't."

Kaia wrapped her arms around James. "Together then, but we must always have a pod near us."

"I'm always here to serve you mistress," Siku said.

"Do you always eavesdrop?"

"I'm just a thought away."

Unaware of the conversation, James kissed her. From underneath the blanket a black fluke appeared and flapped on the ground.

"Um, Kaia," Mera said, "Your..um...fluke's showing."

"Jealous?"

"Even Grant hasn't tried it that way."

Kaia turned bright red. "We're not. Well, we're not."

"That's not what it looks like from here."

"It was just a kiss."

"And you always flap your fluke when he kisses you."

"Siku interrupted me."

"And I thought I had your undivided attention," James said. "Do I always share your kisses with him?"

"Only when he eavesdrops on us."

Kaia suddenly felt something was wrong with Ervin. She cried out. Oceana and Mera immediately joined her cry. They knelt down and continued to wail.

James wrapped his arms tightly around Kaia, What wrong?"

"Granddad's been shot," she said.

"Doria's with him," Oceana said. "Jacob will be here soon. Time to head up the cliff.

"Douse the fire, Grant," Mera said.

Oceana's face became solemn. "I'm in his mind. I'll hang on to him until we all get home. I'll give him what comfort I can."

David and I are on the way, Shelly said. *Where's Calvin?*

The helicopter should drop him off soon, Oceana said.

"Is it safe?" James asked. "What about the shooter?"

"They caught him."

"Dad needs to be there," James said.

"We don't have a phone," Grant replied.

"No problem, Kaia said, "I'll let him know."

"Oh boy," James said, "that will be the shock of his life."

Charles sat at his desk. With Grant and James gone, he had security duty. Cardea was keeping him company. Suddenly, an image of Kaia's face appeared in his mind. *Charles, Ervin's been shot.*

The image was so vivid he didn't give it a second thought. "Cardea, Ervin's been shot. We've got to go."

Chapter 32 - The Prince

Images floated around him in a dream. They faded in and out of resolution. One moment there, then gone. He briefly saw Kaia and James as they bent over him. Kaia had tears in her eyes and clung stiffly to James. He turned when he felt a touch on his hand. It was Jacob. He tried to smile at his son. Doria put a hand on Jacob's shoulder. He blinked twice and then saw his two daughters. He knew where he was, but he was surrounded by ghosts.

Hold on, my son.

'Mother,' he thought, but it was hard to hold onto these thoughts. They drifted away from him into darkness. He pulled hard to hold himself in this place. He thought about it. 'I must be in the library.' He opened his eyes again. The room was filled with solemn looking people. Most shed tears. He was near death. He knew that. There was no question about it, and he would face it as he had faced his life. There was no room for fear. This was a battle he could not win. But whatever awaited him in the next life could wait a little longer.

He turned toward Jacob. "The sea calls," he painfully whispered. He saw it, the sea, the warm waves washing over the rocks, the cry of the gulls, sandpipers running along the surf. He walked there and waded in the surf alone within his thoughts. He briefly saw his old friend James Dylan Cersea walk along the surf toward him from the black rocks. Sedna sat on the black rock and blew him a kiss. In a moment of cognizance, he returned to the room and reached for the conch shell that hung on a silver chain around his neck. He struggled. His hands, his fingers, wouldn't obey his commands.

I will do this for you.

He was back on the beach. He looked out over the ocean. The sky was gray and held layered clouds. Orca fins swam in pods toward the shore. When they reached the surf, they transformed. His mother, Oceana, walked out of the surf surrounded by her host of guards. The sun became brilliant, almost blinding. Oceana wore the golden coronet she had worn at the wedding. All the selkies wore black shell bras and black skirts. They walked toward him.

He opened his eyes and blinked twice. Oceana was here. She

bent over him. She took his hand. He recognized the sensation of telepathy before, but now he actually saw through her eyes. He became alert. Shelly, Mera, and Kaia knelt to Oceana. In this strange vision, Oceana had a radiance about her, solemnest surrounded her splendor. Ervin looked around the room at their faces and studied them carefully. Kaia, Mera, and Shelly all wore silver conch shells. They were the princesses. James still wore the common conch shell on the rope necklace. That seemed wrong. James was much more than common.

Yes, my son.

The scene faded. An evil wind blew off the ocean, whipping up the waves, throwing spray and stones far inland. His jacket flapped wildly as the wind whipped through his layers and cut deeply into his skin. His old friend, James Dylan Cersea, stood in spray with arms open wide to greet him. Sedna rose from the rock and walked toward him. Salt spray stung his eyes, but he forced himself to look out to the sea. He could still see orca fins. "Is there a storm coming?" he said.

Ride the waves with me, son.

But they're not here, Ervin thought. I'm imagining this. Oceana took his right hand and Kaia took the other. They all surrounded Ervin and laid their hands upon him.

I'm proud of you, Son. You have done your task, and done it well.

Ervin was confused by the vision. The room no longer seemed solid. Bright lights shone in the windows and everything seemed brighter than ever. *Kaia and James.*

Their task has begun.

Jacob, my son.

His choice lies before him.

The sea?

We've done what we can, you and I. Kaia and James will take the wheel. The choice is not ours alone.

Then I have failed.

No, Son, you've succeeded better than I could have anticipated. I'm sorry I kept secrets from you.

Secrets?

Too many. You, my son, are a prince. I've always sent my best servants to wait on you. We are here with you now to honor you until the end."

Lay the conch shell by my ear so I can hear the sea.

She placed the shell next to his ear. He listened. At first he heard the sound of the sea, then beneath it something else, something indefinable at first. Below the sound of waves, he heard a faint cry for help. An almost indiscernible voice called him.

The funeral director had never witnessed a scene like this before. Six women in long black robes and wearing black shells on black pearl necklaces carried the coffin through the crowded chapel to the waiting vehicle. They were followed by the immediate family - four women and three men in a solemn procession to the vehicle. The vehicle would transport Ervin to be cremated. His ashes would be dumped at sea.

James and Kaia sailed his former boat to a point off the black rocks. It was crowded. The whole family was on board. So were Doria, David, and Calvin. They knew they had reached the appointed spot when they were met by a gathering of pods of whales of all types. They circled around the boat. They spy hopped. They breached.

"To honor him," Oceana said. Oceana held the urn and took out a small trowel. She tossed a trowel full of ashes into the water. She handed the trowel to Kaia. Kaia dug into the ashes tossed some into the sea. One after another they followed. Jacob was last and poured the rest of the ashes into the sea. This was accompanied by several pods of different whales collectively breaching. Then everything was silent. The whales disappeared.

Oceana said a brief prayer. When she finished, Oceana held out Ervin's conch shell to Jacob. "Wear it."

"I'm not worthy."

"It's not whether we're worthy or have somehow earned it. It's what we all must do. No one can escape responsibility. You are now the prince. It's your destiny."

"Can't James be the prince?"

"He has a different wave to swim."

"I can't do this."

"Look around you. You're not alone. Try to make the difference. It's the only thing any of us can do."

"You'll not let me refuse."

"I won't either," Doria said. She stood in front of him and looked into his eyes. He stared back, but his refusal softened, and he finally nodded. Oceana grinned and handed the silver conch shell necklace to Doria who placed it around Jacob's neck and fastened it.

"Kaia is my ambassador, and you are my prince," Oceana said.

"Yes, Lady," Jacob said.

Kaia walked over to her father and put her arm around him. "We all know in our hearts what is right and wrong," she said. "It's what we will do about it that will make the difference."

Chapter 33 - Warrants

Lana gloated. "Mine, all mine.""Best of all, I don't have to pay Sly."

Candice was still with her.

At that precise moment, the door flew open, and three FBI agents burst in and pointed guns at Lana and Candice. "Which one of you is Lana Stone?" one asked. Candice pointed at Lana. "Who are you?"

"Candice Desdemona."

"We don't have a warrant for you, only for Lana. But we will want to question you." He turned toward Lana. "Lana Stone, you're under arrest for criminal conspiracy in the attempted murders of Kaia Atwater Cersea, James Cersea, Mera Gregson, Grant Gregson, and an unidentified female."

"What - they're alive?"

"So you admit to conspiracy?"

"No."

"Do we need to read you your rights?"

"Shit no, I know them." Lana turned to Candice. "It's up to you then."

"Yes Ma'am. I'll keep the company going in your absence."

The FBI agents put Lana in handcuffs and led her out of the room. Once they were gone, the two private investigators entered the room. "Good job. She'll sing for you. Come on let's go to our safe house."

Much later, Lana sat in the jail cell waiting for her attorney, Gem Bailer. He arrived with another attorney. "Who's this?" she asked.

"Jake's attorney. He has some papers to present to you."

"What?"

"Jake's filing for divorce."

"I'll destroy the company first. I will tell everything."

"As your attorney, I recommend against it," Gem said. "Think about it. Confession of any sort will just add to your prison sentence. Revenge of that sort will likely cost you dearly in the divorce. There are other ways to deal with this. You won't enjoy a long stay in prison."

"What do I get?"

"He's leaving you the house and a generous alimony."

"Did he say anything about my business?"

"No, what's your business is your business."

"Good, I'll sign."

"I'll also recommend you plead guilty to a lesser charge. That might reduce your time in prison."

Epilogue

The Lady of the Sea walked out of the ocean carrying a conch shell. She carefully placed it on the black rock. She pondered the situation. Selkies and mankind are not so different. We are both part of the sea. It's our mother. The sea flows in our veins. It's pumped by our heart. It carries nutrients to our cells. Take away the wash of sea water, and we all will die. She looked back at the shell. Who would pick it up? Who would listen to the call of the sea? Who would learn? Who would care?

She turned and walked back into the surf. Waves washed over her and she was gone. The beach was empty now except for the gulls and sandpipers. The waves reared up, broke and stroked upon the shore. The sea continued to rhythmically breathe in and out - for now. Her heart pumped the cycle of life through the veins of the earth. Storm clouds cried her tears over the land and continued to wash the poisons into the sea. How long could she survive?

The conch shell sat on the black rock waiting for an answer.

About the Authors

H. E. Thomas and P. D. Garty met in a creative writing class. They were assigned to write a modern fairy tale and agreed to write on the same subject. P. D. Garty asked for permission to use one of H. E. Thomas' characters from a previous assignment. When they read each other's stories, Kaia was born. They collaborated on the story the rest of the term and then spent the summer writing the first draft. Every story goes through growth, adolescence and maturity. This story was no different. It took four years of working closely together to create the published novel.

H. E. Thomas grew up in Eastern Tennessee. She graduated from Karns High School and later from Pellissippi State Community College, as a science major. She dreams of becoming a marine biologist. Several of her poems have been published in issues of *Imaginary Gardens*. Her short stories have been published in *Shadows*, available from the Kindle store. She is a member of the Knoxville Writers' Guild.

P. D. Garty is a native of Monroe, Michigan. He graduated from Monroe High School and later from The University of Michigan. He currently resides in Eastern Tennessee. He has poems and short stories published in *Imaginary Gardens*, and recently won an award for best fiction from the magazine. He and H. E. Thomas collaborated on the writing of *Shadows*, a collection of short stories of various genres. He is a member of the Knoxville Writers' Guild and the Tennessee Mountain Writers.

Made in the USA
San Bernardino, CA
23 April 2014